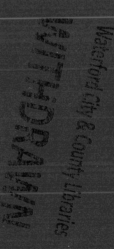

TROUBLE IS
OUR BUSINESS

TROUBLE IS OUR BUSINESS

Edited by Declan Burke

Foreword by Lee Child

NEW ISLAND

Trouble Is Our Business

First published in 2016 by
New Island Books
16 Priory Hall Office Park
Stillorgan
County Dublin
Republic of Ireland
www.newisland.ie

PRINT ISBN: 978-1-84840-563-9
EPUB ISBN: 978-1-84840-564-6
MOBI ISBN: 978-1-84840-665-3

British Library Cataloguing Data.
A CIP catalogue record for this book is available from the British Library.

Typeset by JVR Creative India
Cover design by Anna Morrison
Printed by ScandBook AB, Sweden

New Island received financial assistance from The Arts Council (*An Chomhairle Ealaíon*), 70 Merrion Square, Dublin 2, Ireland.

10 9 8 7 6 5 4 3 2 1

Contents

Foreword by Lee Child   1

Editor's Introduction by Declan Burke   4

Patrick McGinley   A Doctor in the Making?   9

Ruth Dudley Edwards   It's Good For You   21

Colin Bateman   The Gaining of Wisdom   37

Eoin McNamee   Beyond the Bar, Waiting   45

Ken Bruen   Miller's Lane   59

Paul Charles   Incident on Parkway   73

Julie Parsons   Kindness   89

John Connolly   The Evenings with Evans   101

Alan Glynn   The Copyist   119

Adrian McKinty   Fivemiletown   137

Arlene Hunt   Thicker than Water   157

Alex Barclay   Roadkill Heart   171

Gene Kerrigan   Cold Cards   177

Eoin Colfer   A Bag of Hammers   195

Declan Hughes	The Time of My Life	213
Cora Harrison	Mara's First Case	225
Brian McGilloway	What Lies Inside	237
Stuart Neville	The Catastrophist	263
Jane Casey	Green, Amber, Red	277
Niamh O'Connor	Crush	291
William Ryan	Murphy Said	303
Louise Phillips	Double	315
Sinéad Crowley	Maximum Protection	329
Liz Nugent	Cruel and Unusual	341

Foreword

by Lee Child

Generally I'm wary of national stereotypes, but experience and observation have proved a few things true: the French are great cooks; the Italians make great coffee; the English can't play tournament soccer; and the Irish are great storytellers.

Some Irish people don't like to hear that. Some say using the word 'storyteller' rather than 'novelist' demeans them by focusing on an earlier, primitive, oral tradition. I say that's a distinction without a difference. For about a hundred thousand years all storytelling was oral. Mass literacy and mass-market printing are very recent. If the history of human narrative was an hour long, then novels as we understand them are about five seconds old. The newer tradition was born of the old, and has deep roots there. Novelists are oral storytellers, at a temporal remove: not face to face and contemporaneous, but later, with the printed text acting as a crude audio recording. The two traditions are inseparable. The Irish are good at both. I can pick up an Irish novel and feel the same warm, anticipatory glow as I do when sitting in a pub and watching an Irish friend's eyes light up as he launches into a long and convoluted tale.

Why? Obviously there are reasons. They can't be based on literal DNA, because all humans share the same basic genes. I think they're based on a kind of cultural DNA. Like French cooking: it's the penultimate stage in a precious and well established ritual, that starts with daily shopping for locally grown artisanal ingredients, which by dint of stubborn tradition remain largely organic and unadulterated. Typically the cook lets the best available ingredients dictate the recipe, rather than vice versa. The actual stove-top work is one component among others, all of which collectively guarantee the quality of the result.

Same with Irish storytelling, I think. Whether writing or speaking, an Irish storyteller leans in and begins with a certain kind of aplomb that seems to come from a certain kind of confidence: he seems to assume he'll get a fair hearing. Because storytelling is a two-way street. It's a transaction. First a story is told or written; then it's heard or read; then it exists. The better it's told or written, the better it will be; but also, and crucially, the better it's heard or read, the better it will be.

The Irish are great storytellers because the Irish are great story-listeners.

Irish writers start with that knowledge. Sure, if they're boring, eventually they'll be ignored. But they'll get a fair shake first. That breeds confidence. They can relax. Nothing needs to be rushed. A little patience is permissible. The basic transaction is underwritten by cultural DNA. It's a virtuous circle.

The proof is in this collection. Trust me, these writers are saying: Give me a minute or two, or a page or two, and I'll give you a story. And what stories they are. The mutual agreement between writer and reader produces organic tales, going where they need to go, free of anxiety, free of nerves. It's a glorious, spacious, permissive ritual, and long may it last.

Lee Child
New York
2016

Editor's Introduction

I was very pleased, of course, when Dan Bolger invited me to curate a collection of crime stories for New Island. Roughly two decades on from when a number of writers – Patrick McGinley, Colin Bateman, Ruth Dudley Edwards, Eugene McEldowney, Eoin McNamee, Hugo Hamilton, Joe Joyce, Jim Lusby, Vincent Banville, Julie Parsons, John Connolly, Ken Bruen – began regularly publishing crime fiction and mystery novels, it seemed a good time to celebrate Irish crime fiction.

About five minutes after agreeing to do so, however, the doubts set in. The first had to do with who to include – or, more pertinently, who could be left out (a few omissions were unavoidable, in that some novelists simply don't write short fiction, some writers were so tied to deadlines that they were unable to contribute, and some of the earlier practitioners are no longer publishing). A collection featuring twenty writers, we felt, would suffice to provide a timeline from the 1970s to the present day, to give a sense of the progression and evolution of Irish crime writing. Naturally, we were wrong. The number of writers publishing under the Irish crime fiction banner has mushroomed dramatically, especially in the last five years, and it immediately became clear that we could not include every writer who deserved to be represented. Any collection such as this invariably gives rise to the 'But what about . . . ?' question;

it goes with the territory. Unfortunately, had we included every writer we would have liked to include, the book could easily have ballooned to twice its current size. If your favourite writer isn't to be found here, we beg your indulgence.

Another doubt revolved around whether there is actually such a beast as 'Irish crime fiction'. Some of the best-known Irish crime writers weren't born in Ireland; others have yet to set a novel in Ireland; some began by setting their stories elsewhere before choosing Ireland as a setting, while others have moved in the opposite direction. Indeed, 'Irish crime fiction' is probably a little too diverse for its own good, at least for the purpose of definition (or, as it's known in publishing, 'marketing'): it encompasses thrillers and private eye stories, urban noir, who- and why-dunnits, psychological thrillers, police procedurals set at home and abroad, cosy crime, historical mysteries, conspiracy thrillers, comedy crime capers, domestic noir, spy novels ... In other words, 'Irish crime fiction' is a very broad church, and grows broader by the year, to the point where attempting to impose a definition would be virtually meaningless. And yet here we are, with Irish authors merrily ignoring any attempt to corral them into any definition and by now firmly established as best-sellers, prize-winners and ground-breakers on the international crime fiction stage ...

Further complicating the issue (in a good way, we hope) is that the remit offered to the contributing writers was something of a blank slate – all we asked for was a short story, without specifying that it should be a crime or mystery story. Some writers responded with a traditional crime/mystery, others with stories radically different from their previous work, or offering an unexpected variation on the traditional crime/mystery story, while others sent stories that couldn't be considered crime/mystery at all. *Trouble Is Our Business*, then, isn't so much a collection of Irish crime fiction stories as it is a collection of stories by Irish crime fiction writers, which I'll cheerfully admit was something of a relief: I was dreading the idea of editing an entire collection of stories in which Inspector O'Plod tries to discover who murdered whom in the library with the shillelagh ...

Finally, a word on gender. One of the most notable trends in Irish crime fiction over the last five years or so has been the way women have come to dominate the number of debut Irish crime novels being published. Very few women feature in the first half of *Trouble Is Our Business*, but women outnumber men in the later stages of the collection (a fact reflected in the fact that the past four winners of the crime fiction gong at the Irish Book Awards have all been women). The reasons why are beyond the scope of this collection, but along with the emergence of a generation of Northern Irish crime writers engaging with 'the Troubles' or the 'post-Troubles' landscape, it's the most exciting development in the current incarnation of Irish crime writing.

Declan Burke
May 2016

Patrick McGinley

Several of Patrick McGinley's novels (e.g. *Bogmail*, *Goosefoot*, *Fox Prints*) occupy an ill-defined place somewhere on the periphery of the crime genre. *Bogmail*, first published in 1978, was nominated for an Edgar and received a special award from the Mystery Writers of America. Patrick was born in Donegal in 1937 and was educated at Galway University. He moved to London in 1962 to pursue a career in book publishing. He now lives in Kent with his wife Kathleen. His latest novel, *Bishop's Delight*, is published by New Island. His favourite detective novel is E. C. Bentley's *Trent's Last Case*. His favourite crime story is Roald Dahl's *Lamb to the Slaughter*.

A Doctor in the Making?

'Telephone engineer,' he said solemnly.

To judge by his manner he could have been a solicitor or even a doctor, though he looked too young to have qualified as either. Tall and fresh faced, he wasn't what she'd call handsome. He was what Melanie, her flatmate, liked to call 'a middling man'. She led the way into her office and pointed to her desk telephone and computer.

'No matter what number I dial, I get the same response,' she explained. '"The number you have dialled has not been recognised." I can't send or receive emails either.'

He picked up the receiver, dialled a number, and listened.

'It's probably a faulty connection,' he said as if to remind himself. He was obviously not a talker. Probably one of those men who communicate from behind an invisible screen. Melanie knew about men; she 'collected' them as you might collect butterflies. She would be interested to hear about this latest specimen of what she called 'the problematical sex'.

He opened his tool bag and rummaged through an assortment of screwdrivers, flex and electronic gadgets. He tested the connections to what he called the router. Next he opened the junction box and then the socket and terminal in what she could only describe as willed silence. Still, she watched him at work because she liked to find out for herself how things related one to the other. Now and again she asked a question, to which he replied without pausing to look at her.

The thought occurred to her that perhaps he felt shy with young women. Melanie said that some young men open up to middle-aged women more readily than they do to women of their own age, but then Melanie had her own view on everything. She said that electricians, plumbers, and boiler men in particular like to wrap themselves in mystery as if they were some sort of secular priesthood without the grandeur of robes or vestments.

'None of the connections is at fault,' he said as if delivering a hard-won diagnosis.

'So what can it be?' She felt pleased that finally he had spoken without being prompted.

'It can only be the wiring.'

He inspected every room in the flat, including both her bedroom and Melanie's, tracing the path of the wiring and examining Melanie's computer and micro-filter. Wherever he went, she followed, because she felt that she should keep an eye on him. To soothe any feeling he might have of being monitored, she began telling him all sorts of tittle-tattle about Melanie, about how she and her boyfriend were keen bridge players, for example. Melanie was so bright that her boyfriend was worried he might lose her to some clever dick from Trinity, where she worked in administration.

At eleven she gave him tea and two chocolate biscuits. When she asked if he took sugar, he said, 'No sugar, just a dash of milk.' That surprised her because Melanie claimed that all workmen took three spoons of sugar in their tea with lashings of milk. It had become obvious that he was no ordinary workman. Earlier she had spied a book protruding from the pocket of the anorak he'd draped over the back of a chair – having first asked for her permission. She concluded that he'd had a good upbringing and liked to give the impression that he was something of a gentleman.

'Sections of the wiring are old and defective,' he said. 'I'll have to replace them, I'm afraid.'

'These flats were once part of a Victorian mansion. Very likely some of the wiring may be up to eighty years old.' She felt pleased that at last she could offer an intelligent comment relating to the work in hand. She had no wish to leave him with the impression that she was yet another dumb blonde. It was now 12.30, and she was seized by an idea that gave her a sense of largesse.

'What do you do for lunch?' she asked.

'I work through my lunch hour so that I can knock off early.'

'I'll prepare a light snack for us both,' she said casually. 'That is, if you don't mind.'

Since he did not respond one way or another, she went to the kitchen and put a quiche in the oven to heat up. Half an hour later she brought him half the quiche with a glass of Chablis, thinking that perhaps he'd never had Chablis with quiche before, and that the combination would surprise him. When he thanked her and said he'd eat while he worked, she insisted that he join her at the small round table in the living room.

'I can see you're a reader,' she smiled. 'I spotted a book sticking out of your jacket pocket.'

'It's my favourite book, the story of a young man called Gregor Samsa who woke up one morning to find that during the night he had turned into a monstrous beetle.'

'Sounds positively revolting.'

'But it's true. I would even say that it is the truest story ever told. You see, it has layer upon layer of meanings, so many layers that no one reader can ever hope to exhaust its range of possibilities. I have now read it fourteen or fifteen times and I still haven't come to the end of its wealth of suggestion. At times I feel that what I need is a kind of literary potentiometer to measure its full potential.'

'You're not a professor on sabbatical, by any chance?'

'Oh, no, I haven't read enough unreadable books to qualify as a professor. I just keep reading and rereading the same handful of books over and over again.'

'So you're a specialist then, reading deeply rather than widely?'

She felt pleased that he had begun to talk. The Chablis had helped him overcome his shyness. She poured more wine and asked if he would like some coffee.

'Quiche with white wine, and now coffee! I'm living it up today!'

When she came back from the kitchen with the coffee, she found him stretched out on the sofa in his stocking feet with one arm over his eyes. It was not what she had expected. A trifle eccentric, even irregular, she thought.

'Coffee up!' she said, loud enough to rouse him.

He rubbed his eyes and looked all around in a daze. 'Well, blow me down! It must have been the wine. I never have wine at lunchtime, you see.'

He did not allow the wine to impair his dedication to his job, however. He worked steadily through the afternoon until he had renewed all of the defective wiring. Finally, around 4.30 he asked her to test her phone and computer.

'Well done!' she said, noting his delighted smile. 'What a relief to be back on the air again. I simply felt marooned without my computer and telephone. I really must get myself a smartphone. I'd like to have your name or business card in case anything goes wrong again.'

'Nick Stout,' he said.

'I love monosyllabic names because they sound so strong. Before you go, we'll enjoy what's left of the wine while you tell me the complete history of Gregor Samsa and all the potentiometers you have found in it.'

She meant it as a joke because she thought the word 'potentiometer' amusing. He was not offended, however. As he sipped the wine, he told her the story of Gregor Samsa from start to finish, and then began telling her a few of the thousand or more interpretations that might be put on it.

'It's a most original story,' she said in order to encourage him further. Melanie was always saying that she should talk to men more often and find out about their fads and fancies. She even suggested that she harboured an unconscious hatred of men, which she knew wasn't true. 'Not talking to men is one way of making yourself ill again,' Melanie had advised. When she replied that she could never think of anything interesting to say to men, Melanie claimed that if you talk to any man about himself, he will listen to you for hours on end.

'Why do you say the story is original?' Nick asked.

'Because thinking up a story about a man turning into a giant beetle takes nothing short of genius.'

'There are several stories of men turning into wolves, and gods turning into bulls and swans. That is not what makes it so original.'

'A bull is strong and a swan is beautiful – but a big, ugly beetle! It's disgusting.'

'And isn't that what makes reading it such an unforgettable experience – the horrible obscenity of the subject. Just think of the misery endured by poor Gregor, coping with life in the body of a beetle while his mind remains that of a man. And think of his sufferings as he tries to cope with his enraged father and uncomprehending family, not to mention his impossible boss. His life is hell – hell in himself and hell in his relationships with other people. Hell both inside and out.'

'How he must have longed to be back in his own familiar skin again! I suppose we all should value our bodies more,' she smiled. 'After all, they're more comfortable to live in than a beetle's repulsive frame.'

'That isn't what the story is about,' he said with a vehemence that made her take note.

She was enjoying the conversation, telling herself that for once Melanie would be proud of her. 'What do you think it's about then?' she asked.

'It's about an ordinary man with an extraordinary handicap, and how he tries to get by in an indifferent and indeed hostile world.'

She did not agree with him but she thought it best not to express dissent just yet. Instead she smiled and asked him what he himself would like to turn into, thinking that he would say a billionaire.

'I'm saving up to become a doctor. I'm a medical student, you see. In my holidays I work as a telephone engineer to get enough pocket money together for the next term.'

'I admire determined men. Dedication is the surest way to success. Just imagine all the good a truly dedicated doctor can do. My father was a surgeon, so absorbed in his work that his patients and students saw more of him than I did. When you qualify, try to lead a balanced life. Balance is the secret – no matter what you're doing.'

'Balance!' he raised his head and looked at her as if he had never really looked at her before.

'You've given me a fresh insight into the life of our friend!' he said enthusiastically. 'I do believe that between us we've hit on something. I'll read the story again in the light of your idea.'

'I've just had another idea,' she said almost conspiratorially. 'If you're not planning to go out this evening, I'll prepare a simple meal for us both and we'll talk more about the effect that living in a beetle's body must have had on poor Gregor's mind. With your interest in medicine, you must have a view on the subject.'

'After a day's work I look forward to going back to my flat, stretching out on my old horsehair sofa, and listening to music

– mainly Bach, Haydn, Mozart, and Stravinsky. All four had an impeccable sense of balance.'

'If you stay to dinner, you could listen to some Scarlatti sonatas with me. You can tell me about Stravinsky, and I'll let you in on the secret of enjoying Scarlatti as interpreted by Vladimir Horowitz.'

'It's very kind of you but I simply couldn't sit down to dinner without at least having had a shower after my day's work.'

'Nothing is impossible in this most impossible of worlds,' she assured him. 'Let me show you to the bathroom and get you a fresh towel. Sadly, I don't rise to a razor. As you may have noticed, I have no need of such male accoutrements.'

While he showered, she prepared a chicken salad with avocado, cucumber, grated carrot and radishes. She felt quite pleased with herself and with how the day had gone. Here she was doing something Melanie had never done: giving dinner to a doctor in the making, perhaps even a dedicated humanitarian with a life of good works ahead of him.

He entered the living room refreshed and smiling. He now looked quite handsome in spite of his stubble. He was no longer tongue-tied. Over dinner he asked her what she did for a living, and she told him that she was a freelance researcher.

'I work on projects for authors, journalists, professors, publishers, in fact anyone who needs a dogsbody to ferret out facts in libraries or wherever they are to be found.'

'You must be a treasure-house of abstruse information!'

She could see from his look that he was impressed. 'I enjoy the ferreting, but I spend far too much time here on my computer trawling the internet for leads – you know the drill. Ideally, I'd like a job where I could be with other people without being seen by them.'

'How come?'

'No matter where I go, I feel that people don't see me as one of themselves. They treat me differently and say things to me that they'd never say to each other. It began at boarding school. The other girls didn't like my bleached hair and whiter-than-white skin. First they called me Albino O'Leary, then AOL, and finally Whitewash. Life at a girls' school can be very cruel.'

'But your hair is lovely, so fine to look at. They were obviously jealous of your smooth good looks and so transparent skin.'

'I was different. That's the nub of it. I was another Gregor Samsa. Now you know why I am so taken with his story. I really must read it because it's the story of my life so far.'

'Please have my copy. I've read it so many times that I know it by heart.'

'I wouldn't dream of accepting your copy of such a precious book.'

'I have it in seventeen different editions, including a limited edition of five hundred copies. My copy is numbered 432. If you add those numerals together, they come to nine, a mystical number, you see. For me it's a kind of bible, a book of life that has often rescued me from despair.'

'We've only just met but I feel I know you better than anyone I've ever spoken to.'

'And I feel I know you as well as I knew my little sister Emily, who died when she was ten. She was very dear to me. I think of her every day.'

'It's so nice to be compared to a favourite sister. I envy women who have a brother to be close to. I'm an only child, you see.'

'I know the feeling. When I lost my little sister, I felt I'd lost a world. My father and mother stopped talking to each other. No one laughed or made fun anymore. I grew up in a house of silence which at times made a screaming noise inside my head. At school I found it difficult to talk to the other boys and girls. I had become another Gregor Samsa long before I knew his name. It's strange how a story written before I was born could foreshadow my life with such daemonic accuracy.'

'The world is full of Gregor Samsas, I suspect.' She gave him a sympathetic smile.

He looked as if taken aback, perhaps even angry, as if she'd said something quite outrageous. For a moment she felt afraid.

'Gregor Samsa was a very special person,' he declared, 'and only very special people can claim to know what he came through. We mustn't exaggerate the extent of our sufferings but neither must we make light of them. Like Samsa's, they are unique. There is no Samsa Society, and never will be … Oh, I do think I've talked too much. If you don't mind, I'll have a little snooze on your sofa before I leave. It's been a lovely evening for me, a visit to fairyland and a world of childhood simplicity that I didn't know still existed on this ravaged planet.'

'You look tired. You'd better lie down for a while,' she advised. 'I'll wash up and wake you at eleven.'

She, too, had enjoyed the evening, so different from anything she'd ever experienced. She had proved to herself once and for all that a man could take her ideas seriously. She found herself hoping that their paths might cross again. If not, she would still have something interesting to tell Melanie when she returned from Paris.

He woke up on her bed the following morning. They were both naked and her body felt cold in his arms. He looked for blood but there was none. Next he examined her face and arms for signs of violence. He turned her over on the bed. There were no telltale marks on her back or buttocks. It simply made no sense. Then he noticed the open drawer and her underwear strewn all over the floor. The silk scarf was still around her neck. Beneath it were the marks he had hoped never to see again.

The last thing he could recall was her promise to wake him up at eleven. In death she reminded him of Emily when she was only ten and he fourteen. She, too, had a silk scarf round her neck but he had no recollection of how she had died. His father whispered the word 'blackout' to his mother. They told the family doctor who nodded and put it down as a childhood accident.

This was different. It was 8.30 on a Saturday morning in April. He was now twenty-two, and his real life had not yet begun, as she had reminded him twice over dinner. The company van was still parked in the road outside for all to see. She had a perfect body, and she was such a lovely person, just like Emily. It was his personal tragedy, falling in love with girls he should never have loved. He would never again meet anyone like her.

What on earth was he to do?

Ruth Dudley Edwards

Ruth Dudley Edwards is an historian and journalist. The targets of her satirical crime novels include the civil service, Cambridge University, gentlemen's clubs, the House of Lords, the Anglo-Irish peace process, the Church of England and literary prizes. She won the 2010 Crime Writers' Association Non-fiction Gold Dagger for *Aftermath: The Omagh Bombings and the Families' Pursuit of Justice*, the 2008 CrimeFest Last Laugh Award for *Murdering Americans* – set in an Indiana university – and the 2013 Goldsboro Last Laugh Award for her twelfth novel, *Killing the Emperors*, a black comedy about the preposterous world of conceptual art. www.ruthdudleyedwards.com

It's Good For You

'That Deirdre Plunkett must've been a saintly woman,' said Detective Inspector Jeffrey King. 'And that's the thanks she gets for it!'

'It could have been an accident, Jeff. Couldn't it?'

'You're too soft, Mandy. I've seen people who've fallen down stairs and people who've been pushed and I'm telling you Miss Plunkett was shoved by that woman she was caring for. Why else would the two of them have fallen?'

'Maybe Miss Plunkett was helping Kate Kenna down the stairs and one of them tripped and brought the other one down. You know, like mountain climbers on a rope.'

'Maybe, but I doubt it. It doesn't fit with the way they were lying or that mark on Plunkett's face. I'll bet that loony did for her in a fit of temper. Only consolation is it did for her too.' King took another slug of coffee, banged the mug back on the coaster that said 'Save Water Drink Beer', and shook his head with despair at the frightfulness of the human race. 'Murderous bitch.' He embarked on one of those rants about modern society that Sergeant Mandy Cox was well used to. Absentmindedly nodding as words like 'entitlement' and 'ingratitude' floated by, she focused her mind on the scene in Acorn Cottage. The two women sprawled together in death on the stone slab at the bottom of the wooden staircase had been a striking contrast. Underneath, facing upwards, plump, pink-cheeked, enveloped in a scarlet kaftan and with her hair dyed orange, was the house-owner, Deirdre Plunkett. On top, facing down, was scrawny, mousey Kate Kenna, wearing a dirty pale pink polyester nightdress.

Mandy was still more squeamish about corpses than she could afford to let on, and so had been relieved that these two weren't long dead. Had the postman not seen them through the hall window when he rapped on it to get Deirdre Plunkett's attention, who knew how long they might have lain there.

'However, I'd better shut up and you'd better get a move on,' said King, one of whose saving graces was that venting his ire restored him to relative equanimity. 'We'll need more info about these women for the inquest. And since I'll lay you a tenner at 5-to-1 that the PM finds some evidence that Kenna pushed Plunkett, we'd better look for a motive other than her being mental or the human rights brigade will be after us.'

'The postman didn't seem very clear what he meant by "mental", Jeff.'

King yawned vigorously. 'We know sod all. I've got to get back to work on those stabbings, so you bugger off and get busy. And come and tell me about it when you've got something.'

'That's terrible,' said the ward sister. 'I remember Kate Kenna very well. Nice woman. Very gentle and undemanding.'

'But with mental problems?'

'No. She'd been a bit low, but so would anyone have been. Her parents had been killed in the car crash in which she broke her legs and pelvis, an operation went a bit wrong, she was in traction on and off and she got a nasty infection. So she was here for several months. Anyone would be depressed.'

'That's odd. The postman spoke of her as "mental".'

'Did he know her?'

'No. He said he'd never met her but that he'd once seen her waving at him from an upper window and Ms Plunkett told him she was recovering from a nervous breakdown. He thought Plunkett was a saint to be looking after her.'

Sister Coulson had another look at the file. 'This is a bit odd. When Kate was discharged four months ago she was thought to be well on the road to a full recovery. Her legs and pelvis had healed and she was beginning to walk normally again, the infection had cleared up, and though she was still grieving, she seemed anxious to start a new life. It says here she was offered antidepressants, but she said she was fine and turned them down.'

She shrugged. 'I don't get it, officer. And I don't get why she stayed so long with Ms Plunkett. She definitely said she was going travelling soon in France.'

'Did you know Deirdre Plunkett?'

'Just a bit. She was a patient here for a few days after she had a nasty break to her arm. That's how she met Kate and afterwards she used to visit regularly.'

'Did you talk to her much?'

'Sometimes she'd stop by to say hello, and, of course, Kate sometimes talked about her. They were both Irish so they could chat about places they knew and so on. She seemed to be a lovely person, full of life and energy and with a big personality and you couldn't but be struck by how much she wanted to help people less fortunate than herself. Kate said she talked about all the suffering in the world and how only little acts of kindness could improve things. And she was a great one for those. She'd bring little treats for Kate and chocolates for us. "They're good for you," she'd say laughingly when we said she shouldn't. And she insisted that when Kate left she should stay with her for a few days of normality and a bit of cosseting after being cooped up so long in hospital.'

'A few days?'

'Yes, that's definitely what Kate said.' Sister Coulson shrugged again. 'Maybe they got on so well they decided she'd stay for much longer.'

'Or maybe she had some kind of relapse soon after she went there and Ms Plunkett was looking after her.'

'But you'd expect her to come back to the hospital, and there's nothing about that on the file.'

'Maybe she went to Ms Plunkett's doctor.'

'Maybe. I don't think I can help any further, officer. Here are the contact details and copies of the medical records and if I find anyone who might be able to tell you more about either of the ladies, I'll let you know. But I think it's unlikely.'

'It's plain as a bloody pikestaff, Mandy. The postman was right. She must have been mental to launch herself like that at poor Miss Plunkett and kill the two of them. The pathologist was clear that Kenna head-butted her. The coroner shouldn't have any difficulty in coming up with a verdict of murder and suicide. After all, wasn't there a padlock on Kenna's door, presumably for when she was violent?'

'I just don't think it's that simple.'

'Oh really! So what was going on? S&M wrestling at the top of the stairs that went wrong? These days, you never know.'

Mandy smiled indulgently. 'No. They didn't look the types. But I don't think we can be certain that Kenna was mad and Plunkett was an unlucky victim. There are a few inconvenient facts. First, why didn't Plunkett mention Kenna's condition to her doctor? What right did she have to lock her in? Why was Kenna so much less healthy than when she left hospital? The pathologist mentioned malnutrition. And why was she dirty?'

'Here's a question for you. Why do you have to complicate everything? Can't we just leave it as it is?'

'If you really believed that, Jeff, you'd have pushed the interpretation that it was a double accident instead of wanting to nail it on Kate Kenna. It's from you I've learned the satisfaction of trying to find out what really happened rather than what's convenient to believe.'

'Flattery never fails with me, does it?' King sighed. 'You can have a couple of days and PC Jones to dig around and then I'll haul you back to something useful.'

Mandy loved working with Joe Jones, a solid, unambitious, conscientious constable who lived for his family, his church and his improbable fan-ship of Deanna Durbin, a wholesome film star who had blossomed in the 1930s and 1940s and then faded into obscurity as a good wife and mother. She had, Joe explained, the rare combination of talent, beauty and goodness. When lumbered with yet another investigation into greed or violence or degradation or just plain wickedness, he found it a great release to go home and watch her singing on YouTube, or to chat on Facebook to some of the faithful about the finer points of one of her movies about the triumph of innocence.

'You know what I want, Joe.'

'Everything I can find out about the two of them on the net and the phone.'

'That's about it. When I've harassed the IT crowd about getting into Plunkett's computer, I'm off to check out the house and the neighbours.'

The only neighbours, several hundred yards away from Acorn Cottage, knew nothing about Deirdre Plunkett except that she was big, wore bright clothes and had lived there for years. She would wave at them if she passed them in her little car, but from the beginning she'd turned down all friendly overtures by making it clear she liked to keep herself to herself. Seemed a bit odd, they said, that anyone would want to live such a solitary life, but there was no accounting for tastes. Extracting from them an address and number for the couple they'd bought the house from, she walked back to the cottage, which didn't seem initially to yield much either. Forensics had done their stuff and had cleaned up after themselves.

Apart from the room at the top of the fatal stairs, it was clean and rather characterless. The store cupboard and the wide range of cookery books in the kitchen indicated Deirdre Plunkett had been a keen cook, the sitting room suggested she enjoyed intricate embroidery and watching nature films, she was keen on books of quotations and her wardrobe had a lot of loose, bright clothes. All of which made the room that was presumably Kate Kenna's a strange contrast.

There were a few books and DVDs – all majoring in violence. If these were her choices, this woman was big on horror, particularly Clive Barker and Stephen King: as a viewer, she opted for the likes of *The Texas Chainsaw Massacre*, *Reservoir Dogs* and *Django Unchained*. Mandy looked disbelievingly at *Crash*. Wasn't it beyond weird for a woman who'd been in a fatal accident to want to watch a film about people with a sexual fetish for car crashes?

And how could Deirdre have put up with such a filthy visitor? Everywhere was dusty, and her bedclothes looked as if they hadn't been changed for months. The bathroom wasn't much better except for the bath, which looked unused. A dead insect was lying near the plughole, and Mandy turned on the cold tap to wash away the corpse, but nothing happened. There was no hot water either. The sink provided cold but not hot water.

You could hardly blame Kate for being dirty if there wasn't any water, thought Mandy, texting Joe Jones to find out if local plumbers had done or been asked to do any work at Acorn Cottage recently. Didn't seem to be any bathroom cleaner either, or even soap, and the only towel was very small. She looked in the closet for clothes and found none. The drawers were empty too, and there were no suitcases and no handbag.

Maybe Kate had lost all her belongings in the crash, thought Mandy, but she wouldn't have left hospital wearing only a nightdress. She went around the house looking for her possessions, and found nothing. A search in the tidy garage was similarly unsuccessful. She sat down in the little conservatory and tried to make sense of this, until interrupted by a cat that came through the door flap and seemed to expect her to be overjoyed by his antics with a tormented baby bird. When she reluctantly wrung the fledging's neck and dropped the tiny corpse in the bin in the kitchen, the cat was extremely indignant. It slunk off to the end of the small garden in search of more prey, which seemed to be promised by a bird table in a corner of a tiny rose garden overlooked by a tree which the cat scaled rapidly. As he crouched on a branch looking expectant, she went uneasily back into the house and looked vainly for cat food to distract him. She was out the door like a rocket a few minutes later, shouting as the cat approached bearing a new squeaking burden, an adult sparrow which proved already too injured to save. This time she placed the dead bird under one of the rose trees, which were arranged in a row, which looked odd because they were at very different stages of growth. It's the cat I should be strangling, she thought: he's going to work his way through the entire family by the weekend at the rate he's going.

Leaving the scene of his crime, she went back into the house and made phone calls.

'I've talked to the previous neighbour, Joe. He met Deirdre Plunkett about fifteen years ago when she became companion/carer to Acorn Cottage's Maggie Hayward. He said that when Maggie became ill she became reclusive, as was Deirdre after Maggie died, leaving the cottage to her.'

'What did she die of?'

'He thought pneumonia.'

'Do you want the death certificate? And anything the doctor might remember?'

'Yep. And the will. And anything useful from the solicitor.'

'Of course. Now here's what I've got that's interesting …'

She brought Joe Jones with her to back her up when she'd made her case to DI King, who took copious notes and didn't interrupt. 'OK,' he said, when she'd finished. 'You've concocted a pretty tale, but there's no proof.'

As she opened her mouth to object, he went into familiar demolition mode, banging right-hand index finger against left as he numbered his points. 'One! The doctor didn't think Margaret Hayward's death suspicious.'

'But why hadn't Plunkett called him in?'

'Because pneumonia doesn't always show. Two! It's perfectly natural that Hayward would have left the house to Plunkett. She didn't have close relatives.'

'But she did change her will, sir,' said Jones.

'Yes, but why shouldn't she have? She wasn't robbing any relatives. You tell me she'd left her money to the Distressed Gentlefolk's Aid Association, for God's sake. Seems perfectly reasonable that instead of leaving it to toffs, she'd be glad to leave it to someone who'd looked after her.'

'But the solicitor did admit to slight unease that he never saw Mrs Hayward alone to discuss her change of mind.'

'Slight unease butters no parsnips, Joe. Three! You've discovered that Plunkett felt done down when her grand-aunt left her nothing in *her* will. Happens all the time. Doesn't turn people into murderers.'

'She'd looked after her in a lonely farm in the west of Ireland for five years,' said Mandy. 'And then she leaves everything to the son in America who hardly ever came home to see her. It could sour anyone.'

'That's the sort of thing Irish peasants do, isn't it? Favouring sons and that and everyone making a big deal of it. I saw some movie where they were all killing each other over some grotty old field. One of my wife's Irish cousin's been conducting a feud over a will for the last twenty years.'

'Exactly. Plunkett had been promised a substantial legacy, and she got nothing, sir.'

King spotted that his contribution had not helped his rebuttal. 'That's just the story the gossipy old neighbour told you, Joe.'

'Isn't what's relevant is that it's what Deirdre told the gossipy neighbour?' asked Mandy.

'No, because either of them could be making it up. Now let's get on with it. Four! Joe's found a couple of old biddies that everyone's lost track of that are supposed to have been friendly with Plunkett when they met at church. So what? They're still drawing their pensions.'

'But are long gone from the addresses their banks have for them.'

'So they've moved and didn't mention it. Old ladies vanish. Happens all the time. Five! Mandy thinks Plunkett wasn't looking after Kenna properly. And the plumber she used says he hadn't been called to fix her bathroom. Bloody hell! She was inefficient. And as for those possessions, maybe she'd got rid of them until Kenna was better and they could get some more. Maybe she thought they were infected. Old people get funny ideas. What have I forgotten?'

'Kenna's money, sir?'

King knew Mandy was rebuking him when she called him 'sir'. He suddenly grinned in the disarming manner he employed when he most needed it. 'I grant you that, Mandy. Haven't come up with a way of explaining it away. I don't know why so much was being steadily drawn out on her debit card and where it went and I grant you it looks suspicious. You two can have another twenty-four hours to come up with something.'

He looked sternly at her. 'But you can forget that stuff about what might be in the rose garden. We're cops. Not fiction writers.'

Mandy had another go at the IT people, and was promised a result later in the day. She left the money-chasing to Joe and, bearing a tin of cat food, returned to Acorn Cottage to look for inspiration. There was no sign of the cat, so maybe he was an impertinent stray and the cat flap was from earlier days.

Having been back to Sister Coulson to ask more about Kate, she had been grimly unsurprised at being told she was a) fastidious and b) mostly read Victorian novels.

Unhappily, she went up the stairs to where Kate had spent her last days, surrendered to her imagination and pretended she was imprisoned. She considered escaping through the window, but it was double-glazed and appeared to have been glued shut. Besides, the drop was sheer and even at her age and with her relative fitness, she doubted if she could have reached the ground alive. She searched the bed to see if by any chance some of Kate's treasures were hidden there. All she found was a biro under the dirty pillow.

But there was no paper.

It took her only a couple of minutes to race through the books flicking through the pages until she found one with writing on the inside of the covers and wherever else there was space. Kate Kenna had – if not a black sense of humour – an instinct for the apposite. She had left her testimony in Stephen King's *Misery*, a book about someone being tortured to death by a woman who had claimed to be his saviour.

'I'm in a nightmare and can see only one way of getting out of it, which will probably prove fatal to me. I've been imprisoned for several months by someone who is trying to drive me mad or kill me, or both. Does anyone realise I'm missing? If they do, they won't have the faintest idea where I am. Having no access to a phone or the internet, I haven't been able to communicate with the outside world. I stare out the window in the hope of seeing someone pass by, but no one does except for the postman and he never looks up since the time I waved at him.

'What happened to me? Well, I was very vulnerable and Deirdre was very charming. Solicitous, sympathetic and interested. She asked me for my story, wanted to hear everything, listened intently and asked good questions. I was desperately lonely and opened up to her. I told her about my marriage in America, about the hopeless attempts to conceive, the divorce and about how I could no longer face teaching. I told her I'd always been close to my parents and would ring them every week, but had no other family except my sister whom we hadn't seen since she joined the enclosed convent. About how I'd gone back home to County Clare to lick my wounds and work on the farm and about how at that time I hadn't been ready to socialise. And how my parents and I decided to make a new start and sell the farm. And about how, after getting a good price, after their lifetime of drudgery and mine of disappointments, we were intent on enjoying ourselves for a change and were on our way to France to find a little house to rent somewhere warm before deciding where we wanted to settle. She kept saying what a good idea that had been and that at least when they died my parents were happy.'

Mandy's phone announced a text message from Jones. 'Blimey! Wait till you see what's on her computer!'

'Back to you in ten,' she replied.

'It was nice that she was Irish, and had been to my part of the country and that we could talk a bit about the scenery. And she seemed to know a bit about some writers I mentioned. I now realise that if I said a name, she went home and looked it up, which is why she'd later produce germane quotes from Jane Austen or Dickens or Yeats. In fact, she'd quote bits of poetry to me that were sometimes comforting and inspirational. She found out what kind of books I liked and gave me the odd one.

'I'd been in such a half-life for a long time, I was only just coming back to some kind of normality. I would ask her about herself, but didn't realise until later how sparing she'd been with information. There had been a period caring for a beloved cousin who'd left her some money, she had a modest pension from her job working for a world peace charity, a peaceful little cottage in the country and a rescue cat. She had a gift for play, and we had silly games about pet hates and our Room 101 terrors. Talking like that was good for me, she said. It was her favourite phrase and it seemed very positive at the time. All I can remember is that she hated beer, marmalade and beige. As I later discovered, she noted my admitted hates and fears and put them to good effect: pale pink, polyester, parsnips, lumpy porridge, liver, snails, oysters, organs, Creme Eggs, graphic violence, horror and ghost stories. Anything I didn't like, Deirdre had conscientiously stocked up on. Dirt came naturally.

'The cat! I couldn't understand in the beginning why there were no feline mealtimes, but it turned out that she believed cats should hunt for themselves. It was good for them, she said. They weren't naturally domestic animals and were happiest being allowed their feral instinct. Indeed, she would chirrup at him in a congratulatory manner when she found him playing with another mouse or baby bird. Where most of us would be revolted by the torture and would have tried to put the prey out of its misery, Deirdre rejoiced in it. That's when – only a couple of days in – I told her I'd had a lovely time but needed to move on. But it was too late. She doped me the night before I was to go and when I woke up the following morning all my clothes and possessions had gone, my books had been replaced by the kind of thing I'd run from screaming and the padlock was on the door. Since then I've lived in the nightdress she provided when I vomited all over mine. Until she thought I was no longer capable of challenging her physically, she was always armed with a knife when she came in to my bedroom bearing what she knew I'd hate but was, she said, good for me.

'What she didn't reckon on was that I wasn't a baby bird. My brain still worked even though I tried to give the impression it didn't. I did everything she told me to do, listlessly, so she'd think my spirit was broken. When she told me she'd need the PIN number for my debit card to pay for my food, I gave it to her uncomplainingly, while pretending to have a bit of difficulty remembering it. When she brought a new DVD she'd make me watch it and revel in seeing me squirming and covering my eyes. I told her I was getting awful nightmares, so she told me to watch one of them every night because it was good for my character or I'd get no food the next day.

'It certainly strengthened my character. You can become immune to violent images and I was being inspired to vengeance by the likes of the *Kill Bill* films and learning handy hints from films and those horror books on how to kill someone bigger and stronger than me. I certainly was losing strength, and I told her I was too tired to get up, but I ate the most nutritious bits of the horrible food, and secretly exercised enough to keep my limbs moving. I practised head-butting.

'I sense she's finding me more of a nuisance now than an amusement. I'm getting less and less food and I think total starvation might be the next stage. Or she might use that knife. She said something about joining the ladies in the rose garden. And she came in giggling the other day quoting something familiar she said was from a Yeats poem about how there was nothing but our own red blood that could make a right rose tree. That reminded me of what he wrote about too much suffering making a stone of the heart, which he got absolutely right. These days, my heart is made of granite.

'I doubt if I'll reach such martial heights as Uma Thurman's Five Point Palm Exploding Heart Technique, but tomorrow morning I'll be crouched by the door ready to greet Deirdre with a Glasgow kiss.

'It'll be good for her.'

Colin Bateman

Colin Bateman, from Bangor in Northern Ireland, is the author of more than thirty novels, including *Divorcing Jack*, *Mystery Man* and – most recently – *Papercuts*. He created the long-running TV series *Murphy's Law* for BBC 1 and writes extensively for the stage and screen. He was made an honorary Doctor of Letters by the University of Ulster for his services to literature and is the recipient of a Major Artist Award from the Arts Council of Northern Ireland. But on the whole he would prefer to be playing for Liverpool.

The Gaining of Wisdom

They say a leopard can't change its spots, but I suppose the jury's still out on that. We certainly all get older, but not necessarily wiser. Neither does experience equate to wisdom. Norman Wisdom never seemed to learn his lesson, he was always involved in some unfortunate calamity that was generally not of his making, but for which he should have been prepared, given the number of times he found himself in those situations. Even as a ninety-year-old he was still tripping over himself and causing hilarity, although mainly amongst Albanians. Those, however, were merely inconsequential pratfalls. What are we to make of the men of violence whose time has been and gone, and who have settled into both civil and civilian life? Is there any reason at all to suppose that their capacity for murder has somehow drained away, or will it always be there, like a lining of grease and fat lurking in their mental plumbing? I only ask because today I saw Michael McAllister, killer of three men, one of them my brother, and he was very much the picture of easy contentment, a family man out for a Saturday afternoon's shopping, and I got to thinking the big thoughts about the changing of spots and the gaining of wisdom.

It has been twenty-six years since Michael McAllister pulled the trigger, and fourteen since he was released from prison, the beneficiary of a political agreement which threw open the gates and allowed everyone to walk free, irrespective of reformation. I actually saw him that day, the last time until today in the supermarket. He was part of a group being cheered to freedom by their loyal supporters, and I had just a glimpse of a pasty face dominated by a triumphant smile, it was hardly more than a few seconds caught by a television camera, but after those long weeks of denial in court, I recognised him instantly. This afternoon it took me a while longer. In fact, the penny did not drop until the second time we spoke. The first time was in an aisle devoted to spices and condiments. There was shopping trolley congestion and a noticeable lack of *after you*'s. When someone else barged through I looked at Michael McAllister, on the other side of the aisle, without knowing it was him, and said, 'It's dog eat dog in here on a Saturday,' and he said, 'Some people,' and shook his head and smiled, and his wife made some other comment which did not even register because there was something about his voice, the shape of his mouth, the greyness of his eyes which jabbed at me. I was still trying to place him as I moved on into pasta and sauces, and it took the rattling of Sasha, my six-year-old, facing me in the trolley, to bring my attention back to the grocery list in my right hand. I lifted a jar at random and handed it to Sasha, my stacker and organiser, which satisfied him enough for me to push on around the corner and back to spices and condiments, intent on another look. At that point it wasn't much more than curiosity. The woman, presumably his wife, was now bickering with their three overweight children over a brand of ketchup, but there was no sign of him, and for some as yet unknown reason that began to panic me. I quickly moved to the next aisle, presuming he had pressed on, an advance party scouting for treasures, but he wasn't there. I wheeled along to the next, and then with increasing speed to the next, driven by something clawing at me while also aware that I was being vaguely ridiculous. Sasha whooped as I swept along to the far end of the final aisle, which eventually gave me a wide view of the checkout desks. There was no sign of him there either, but then, off to the left, at the separate counter for cigarettes and lottery tickets, I saw him; he was at the back of a short queue, his shoulders wide in a cream sports jacket, and as I closed in on him I saw that he had one hand held behind his back, his fist closed around coins which he was impatiently rattling.

I didn't crash into him, exactly; I just allowed the trolley to bump into the back of his ankles; he nevertheless swore in surprise but when he turned he did what we all do – he apologised to me. Then I said sorry to him and we had a bit of a laugh about it, and it was his smile that finally did it, that flashed me back all those painful years; I saw that he was wider, and that his hair had receded, that his teeth had been capped, but that he was nevertheless the man who had killed my brother with a bullet to the face; my brother unrecognisable to his mother; my brother with the closed coffin; with the flowers which spelled out *My Son*; this man waiting to be served on a Saturday afternoon twenty-six years after the fact and teasing my son; Michael McAllister ruffling my son's hair while I stood with the grin frozen on my face and leaning on the trolley with what must have looked like lazy abandon but which was actually necessary because the power had suddenly vanished from my legs as clarity and recollection collided; I was grinning inanely while my mind was screaming 'Get your hands off my son!' but nothing would come out, nothing could squeeze through the tombstones.

The situation was only eased by Michael McAllister being motioned forward to the counter. He gave Sasha a wink and turned away. With that, I felt a little strength returning. I lifted my son out of the trolley and walked away from it, just as I heard Michael McAllister asking for an e-cigarette. I continued on out of the store. Into the car park. I strapped Sasha in the back and sat there with my hands shaking on the steering wheel. Sasha asked what I was doing and where the shopping was and I said it would be delivered later. I started the engine, and his favourite music came on and that settled him, while I sat with my head throbbing.

I was sixteen when my brother died. He was twenty-two. We didn't get on particularly well. But he was my brother. When the trial came my dad didn't want me there, but I insisted. He was my brother. Weeks of denial, weeks of forensics, but convicted in the end. He killed my brother. Shot him in the face, and there he was, with the family my brother would never have, with the spice and condiments my brother would never use, larger than the life my brother would never lead. We've forgiven, moved on, it's all about the children, we are the world, hands across the border, sign of peace, Nobel prize, a fine example, Palestine sort yourself out, except here with the rain coming down and the killer in the condiments I could hardly breathe, fine words on a page but a horror-show up close in the flesh. It wasn't about me, what I was robbed of, it was my brother, no life, no wife, no children, no Saturday afternoon shopping. No waiting impatiently for the football results or lottery numbers, no *Strictly*, no *X*, no sweet goodnights, longer dead now that he ever was alive. My brother.

Without properly realising it, I found myself beginning to lap the car park, watching out for him, wondering what kind of car he would drive, if his thriving or spiralling life would be reflected in his choice, if his parking was testament to his nature, greedily over the white line or nonchalantly hijacking a disabled space; fourth time around, and there towards the end of the row I spotted not Michael McAllister, but one of his sons, the tallest, maybe twelve years old, pushing the trolley, and I thought that maybe that was a clue to what he was like, lazily ordering his boy to put the groceries in the car while he swanned about the rest of the shopping centre spending the money that my brother would never spend, and then it dawned on me as the boy stopped, and the boot of an estate car came up and he set about unloading, that this was my opportunity for revenge. Perfect revenge. A revenge that would haunt him the way my brother's death haunted me. The boy was his father's son, the zonkey who must have inherited at least half of his proclivity for violence; killing him would be killing the father, while still allowing him to endure long years of suffering. I would just smash into him. I would crush him. It would be an accident. Nobody would ever know, or if they found out the connection it would be dismissed as an amazing twist of fate, as karma, no blame on me, just a terrible tragedy, but still, makes you think. I glanced about me. No other cars moving, no one on foot lingering because of the rain; a quick look up at the lamp posts dotted about, no obvious signs of cameras recording; there would be signs mounted somewhere, using the car park was at your own risk, but they were never meant for this.

No second thoughts, foot on the accelerator.

The beat of the wipers.

The cascading rain.

The boy with his hoody up, unaware of doom approaching.

Twenty, 30, 40, 50 miles per hour in a shopping centre car park, zeroing in.

And Sasha said, 'Mummy?'

And I hit the brake and there was a squeal and shriek that was part tyre, part Mother, as the car skidded along the last few yards before inevitable impact – but then stopped inches, yes inches, short of the son of the man who killed my brother, shot him in the face; the son who continued to lift tins of beans and bags of frozen veg from trolley to boot, somehow impervious. I could hardly catch a breath, hunched over the steering wheel, scarcely believing that I'd stopped in time, grateful and furious that I had, and for a moment I thought that the karma had made the son deaf, that that was the punishment, that if I had hit him he would not have been aware until his life was suddenly squashed out. But then he turned, and I saw that he had earphones in; he was looking at the car, wondering why it was so close but not particularly bothered by it; and then I had the window down and was beckoning to him and his brow furrowed before he moved towards me, compromising on taking one earphone out, so that as he stood before me I could hear the beat.

'What?' he asked, bluntly.

There was no hint of recognition from earlier in his dull face. I said, 'Sorry – you, you're not anything to Michael McAllister are you?'

'Aye,' he said.

'I thought so – you're the dead spit of him.'

'That's 'cos he's my dad.'

'I knew it,' I said, 'I haven't seen him in years.'

'Well, he's inside if you want to …' and he thumbed towards the shops.

'I can't stop … sorry, the boy,' and I glanced back at Sasha, and watched as his eyes flitted to my son. 'But … is he keeping well?' The boy shrugged and said he supposed so. I said that was great, but it really wasn't. I wanted him to be stricken. 'And, and what's he up to these days, what's he working at?'

'He's still on the buses,' said the boy.

'That's good,' I said, but it still really wasn't. I wanted him to say that Michael McAllister was a humanitarian. That he worked to eradicate the Ebola virus. That he was a goodwill ambassador for the United Nations or the creator of a clockwork laptop that brought education and *Tom and Jerry* to the disadvantaged billions. That he was trying to make the world a better place because he had helped to tarnish it. I tried to imagine Michael McAllister driving a bus. Pulling up at stops, waiting for old ladies. I wondered if he berated rowdy teenagers, and if, when they talked back he ever felt the urge to go where he had gone before. But no, probably not. His act had not been one of anger, it was the result of planning, of coolness, of efficiency, for a cause that was long gone. If his violence was still there it was probably a neglected and brackish reservoir, but one that could still be dipped into given the right circumstances. I stared at his son and I could see that he was unsettled by it; he gave a little shrug and took a step back and was just turning away when I said, 'I'm so happy that he's sorted his life out.' Because it had come to me that slaughtering his son was not the way to go, that I would be unmasked and punished, I needed something entirely subtler and cancerous, and in the confused look he gave me when he turned back, I knew that I had stumbled upon it. He said, 'Wha … ?' and I said, 'You know, since he got out of prison.' And his brow furrowed and his neck flexed into something that was not far removed from a Norman Wisdom double-take. 'What're you talking about?' he asked, coming forward. I said, 'I'm sorry – maybe you didn't know.' 'Know what?' 'Your dad – he killed three men. He shot them in the face. He's a cold-blooded killer.' His mouth was open and his eyes had glazed. 'Word of advice, son,' I said, 'see next time you've a row with him, don't push him too far …' I raised two fingers and an erect thumb to the side of my head, and made an explosive sound. I raised my eyebrows, and I nodded, and then I drove on, leaving the child ashen-faced, standing in the pouring rain with some gangster rapper pouring venom in one ear, the son of the killer in the condiments whose life had just been ruined by the sister of the brother with the bullet in the face, on a Saturday afternoon, with Sasha in the back demanding to know where his *petit filous* were and why his mother was crying.

Eoin McNamee

Eoin McNamee was born in Kilkeel, County Down, in 1961. His novels are *Resurrection Man*, *The Ultras*, *The Blue Tango*, *12:23*, *Orchid Blue*, and *Blue is the Night*. The latter completed his 'Blue Trilogy' and won the 2015 Kerry Group Irish Novel of the Year. Eoin has also published *The Navigator*, *The City of Time*, *The Ring of Five* and *The Unknown Spy* for young adult readers. Under the pseudonym John Creed, he published a series of spy thrillers featuring Jack Valentine. Eoin lives in County Sligo.

Beyond the Bar, Waiting

Limekiln Road, 16th November 2014
The sand pit had been opened. A yellow excavator stood by the side of the opening, its bucket raised. An articulated Scania with a covered trailer was backed up to the opening in the ground, hydraulic rams half-extended. A fluorescent works light dangled on a jack chain from a corroded derrick. Three men rendered into silhouettes stood between the pit and the light. They stood without moving, their heads bent towards the opening at their feet, functionaries of the night.

South Down Reporter, 17th November 2014
A body has been discovered in an abandoned sandpit on the Limekiln Road. A PSNI statement said that the discovery was made in the course of unlawful dumping activity. An anonymous phone call was received at Ardmore police headquarters. The body is believed to be that of a teenage girl who absconded from the Down Residential Home in 1996. Police say foul play is not suspected. An inquest will be held in January.

Mobile phone, 17th November 2014
John Upritchard to Sergeant Michael White

JU   Was that your press release to the paper?
SW   My press release?

JU   Foul play is not suspected.

SW   It was.

JU   That's rich. No foul play.

SW   She wasn't local. Nobody knew her. And I'm the police around here. If I don't suspect foul play then there wasn't any. Unless there's something you want to tell me about?

JU   Do not mock me.

SW   You'd of thought the body would corrupt. Be ate up by the sand she was put in.

JU   The sand will hold you down there until it's good and ready to let you go.

SW   She should have run.

JU   She never had a choice.

SW   She had choices. She made her choices on her back.

JU   The lord knows the way of it. For He knoweth the birds of the air and the beasts of the land.

SW   Cut it out.

JU   I'm telling you.

SW   Let dead things be dead things.

JU   Her embrace was the embrace of the pit.

SW   Steady yourself. She'll be back in the ground soon enough.

Letter Excerpt, October 1996
Matthew Flynn to Eliza Curran

… remember I says to you about the aerdrome its beside the sea theres a sandpit full of water I let on its a lagoon with the silvery moon shining on it theres a bottle of Smirnoff there for me and you haha. You can see the lights of the ships beyond the bar waiting for the tide they're going everywhere would you believe it think of all the places we could go me and you on a foreign shore …

Mobile Phone, 5th December 2014
John Upritchard to Sergeant Michael White

JU   The Flynn boy wants to give testimony at the inquest.

SW   He's no boy now. He's a grown man. Gone to the dogs. No one will believe him.

JU   Do you want your name bandied about on the steps of the courthouse?

SW   The proceedings are closed. The Press will not be admitted.

JU   At your behest?

SW   If you say so.

JU   Will you be called a liar by a drunkard boy?

SW   I've been called worse.

JU   I am a pastor of my flock. They would not tolerate it. They would regard it as an outrage.

SW   What do you want me to do?

SW   I could interview him under caution. Where does he live?

JU   Scotland. It took him in when none else would.

SW   I'll go there. Talk to him.

Letter Excerpt, November 1996
Eliza Curran to Matthew Flynn

Darling Charles
(I gave you a posh name i hope you don't mind)
I feel like a spy from a film writing to you like this I should be using invisible ink. I never knew what that was I felt sick again this morning I seen bloody Upritchard looking at me when I was late and never ate any breakfast I don't know what to do maybe when we get away I can stop my head and think …

Interview Under Caution, Stranraer Police Station, 12th December 2014

Matthew Flynn, former Inmate of the Down Residential Home, and Sergeant White present.

SW   You were admitted to Down House at what age?

MF   Fourteen.

SW   Why?

MF   My da. My ma couldn't cope. It was only weekends though. Weekends were the worst.

SW   Go on with your story.

MF   Me and these other boys from the House were playing on the banks. The riverbanks.

SW   Behind the home?

MF   Yes.

SW   You went back to the Down? After playing.

MF   It was teatime.

SW   Tell me what you saw.

MF   There was something broke in the hall. A vase knocked over. We could hear Mr Upritchard shouting and Eliza squealing like.

SW   John Upritchard the House Supervisor?

MF   Yes.

SW   What happened then?

MF   Mr Upritchard he come out and told us to go and pick nettles on the banks. We took the nettles into the Home.

SW   Go on.

MF   We could hear all this screaming from the basement so we goes down. He had Eliza in a bath.

SW   An empty bath.

MF   Full to the brim with cold water. She was sitting with her back to us. Mr Upritchard was holding her down.

SW   What happened then?

MF   He took the nettles off us . . .

SW   Was the female inmate naked?

MF   I could just see her bare back.

SW   So you know it was her?

MF   Mr Upritchard started to whip her with the nettles on her back …

SW   You couldn't see her face but you knew it was her. I'd say it was a sight you'd seen before.

MF   What was?

SW   Her naked.

MF   She was screaming. I'm trying to tell you he was whipping the back off her with them things … she was in hysterics …

SW   Why?

MF   What?

SW   Why were they punishing her?

MF   She broke the vase.

SW   You have convictions for public nuisance, possession of a controlled substance, allowing yourself to be driven in a motor vehicle knowing it to be stolen.

MF   I'm telling you what John Upritchard done to her.

SW   You knew she was pregnant?

MF   She told me.

SW   Yours, was it?

MF   No.

SW   Are you telling me lies?

MF   No.

SW   Who would believe a word that came out of your mouth?

MF   The Inquest.

Mobile phone, 2nd January 2014
Sergeant White to John Upritchard

SW   He'll be on the 7.30 sailing, January 7th.

JU   Alright.

MSU Incident Report, 26th November 1996

Mobile Support Unit Five responded to a report of a lone female in the sandpit area of Limekiln Road. On reaching the area he observed a female, between 14 and 16 years of age. The female was approached.

Sergeant White formed the opinion that she was intoxicated. Her clothing was wet. Her speech was incoherent. She was placed in the police vehicle. Sergeant White reported that the detained girl said she had arranged to meet a young male at the sandpit. There were smears of what appeared to be blood on the restraint cage and on the windows. Sergeant White reported that the female became hysterical. When he attempted to render assistance she ran away from him. He was unable to detain her again.

CCTV Footage, Ocean Swift ferry, 7th January 2014

The footage is from the gangway from Deck B to the viewing deck on Deck C. The rusted plates groan as the ship falls into the wave troughs. MF makes his way along the gangway. Shabby, furtive. He stops facing away from the camera. You always face away from the camera. He rolls a cigarette and lights it. He opens the sea-door and goes out onto the deck. The deck is out of bounds on a stormy night but the sea-door had not been locked.

The camera on the Deck C viewing deck is ineffective. The lens is salt-caked. The camera mountings are corroded. The flare of the deck lights backlights the sea-spray and the shadow between the lights. You can see the point of his cigarette. He turns his back to the spray. He looks up. You might think he has been called but there is no sound to say that he has been called. You might think he is looking at someone. He walks out of camera range. A shadow detaches itself and follows him. Less a shadow than an elaboration of the dark.

Mobile Phone, 7th January 2015
John Upritchard to Michael Flynn

MF   Who's this?

JU   John Upritchard

(Silence)

JU   I seen your police record.

MF   White showed it to you. I thought he would of.

JU   Alcohol. Drugs. Your life isn't much. You would be better relieved of it.

MF   Says who?

JU   You let Eliza down.

MF   She was looking for me at the pit – that's right, isn't it?

JU   You said you would be there for her.

MF   How do you know that?

JU   It was wrote in a letter.

MF   What letter?

JU   A letter you sent to her.

MF   I don't believe you.

JU   I seen them all. You spoke of the ships beyond the bar.

MF   She never got it.

JU   But she went to the pit anyhow. Meet me and I'll tell you what I know.

MF   Where are you? I said where are you?

JU   I'm on the boat.

MF   What boat?

JU   The Ocean Swift.

CCTV, Ocean Swift, 7th January 2015
On the lorry deck the trucks shifted on their beds and the deck plates creaked and moaned. Shadows on the rusted gangways.

Two lorry drivers sit at a plastic table in the drivers' lounge. One of them walks to the counter for a coffee.

The aft deck camera is checked. The lifeboat station camera. The gangplank camera. The camera in the crew's quarters. The bow camera. The engine room camera. All the unpeopled spaces. It's like a submerged hulk. The domain of drowned mariners.

Mobile Phone, 8th January 2015
Sergeant White to John Upritchard

SW He's gone.
JU You don't say.
SW Jumped off the ferry they're saying.
JU May he find peace.
SW More peace than he ever got here.

Letter extract, 23rd November 1996
Eliza Curran to Matthew Flynn

I can get out the back wednesday night so Be There!!!! we'll take ship for foreign lands isn't that what they say maybe I can bring up a baby out there call Jose if its a boy or Conchita if its a girl I know you said you'd help me with that but you don't have to i can do it myself but anyway I'm not thinking so far ahead I just need to get out scram

Alright I know its only scotland but we're going to scram to it scramarama thats me sorry us

I'll only hold you back Charles go on without me isn't that what they say i don't mean it

Meet you at the pit

hold me kiss me charles you handsome devil you drive me mad with desire i am consumed …

Downside Coroners Court, 8th January 2015
Extract from interview with former Down Home Head of Services, John Upritchard, and Counsel for the state Edward James.

Mr James: How would you describe Eliza Curran, Mr
                   Upritchard?
Mr Upritchard: She was an extremely troubled young woman.
                   Her home circumstances were poor. She had
                   issues with alcohol and drug misuse.
Mr James: You retrieved a letter that she attempted to
                   send a few days before she absconded.
Mr Upritchard: I did. I retrieved it from the Mourne House
                   postbox.
Mr James: Can you summarise the letter for the court?
Mr Upritchard: The letter arranged a meeting with a discharged
                   resident on the night she disappeared.
Mr James: Matthew Flynn?
Mr Upritchard: Yes.
Mr James: Curran never received the letter?
Mr Upritchard: No. I had formed the opinion that Flynn was
                   a bad influence on her. I retained the letter
                   on file.
Mr James: But you didn't give the letter to police officers
                   when she absconded?
Mr Upritchard: That was an oversight on my part.

(*Extracts from letters were read into the court record*)

Mr James: Residents abscond all the time and generally
                   turn up after a few days, is that correct?
Mr Upritchard: That is correct.
Mr James: Thank you. Eliza Curran had made certain
                   allegations against the staff of the home and
                   you in particular, Mr Upritchard? Allegations
                   also made by the fellow resident named
                   above, Matthew Flynn?
Coroner: (*Interrupting*) Mr James, the scope of this
                   inquest is confined to the circumstances

	of the unfortunate young lady's death. In addition to that, any evidence that might be offered on this point would be hearsay since Mr Flynn is not present.
Mr James:	Thank your honour. I have concluded.
Mr Upritchard:	Your honour?
Coroner:	Yes Mr Upritchard?
Mr Upritchard:	I believe she was lost and now is found. I will pray for her.
Coroner:	I don't think there is anything to add to that at this point.

Coroner's Court, 9th January 2015

We the jury having been duly sworn and serving at the inquest into the death of the above named have determined the following facts:

Name: Eliza Curran
DOB: 16th November 1980
Date of Death: 16th January, 1996
Place of Death: Sandpit, Limekiln Road
Medical Cause of Death: Not ascertained.

South Down Reporter, 16th March 2015

A verdict of accidental death has been recorded in the case of a 28-year-old man who was reported missing off the Warrenpoint ferry last year. Matthew Flynn was last seen on the deck of the ferry before it docked in Warrenpoint. Flynn was identified on CCTV footage from onboard cameras two hours before docking.

The camera footage was viewed by the jury.

Evidence was given by the victim's GP Doctor Douglas Kerr of Stranraer. Doctor Kerr was asked if the victim had a history of suicidal ideation. Doctor Kerr replied that he had no evidence of such but that the victim had been treated for substance abuse and had been prescribed Antabuse and Valium. There was evidence of a chaotic lifestyle. Petty crime and pilferage. Suicide could not be ruled out. In the absence of corroborative evidence, the coroner directed that a verdict of accidental death by drowning be entered.

The deceased man had been due to testify in the inquest into the death of Eliza Curran, whose body was found at Cranfield earlier in the year. That inquest also returned a verdict of accidental death.

Extracted from Eliza Curran autopsy, 9th January 2015
Cadaver presents as mummified owing to high concentrates of alkali in local substrata combined with formaldehyde and other solvents present in medical waste dumped at the location of the body.

The trunk was damaged during excavations. Sand had entered the body cavities. A pregnancy in the first trimester is confirmed.

The sand maintained the body structure of the foetus to an unusual degree.

Cause of death cannot be determined.

Mobile phone, 19th March 2015
Sergeant White to John Upritchard

SW   You never did say how Flynn came to fall off the ferry.
JU   You never told me how a drunk girl got away from you the night you found her at the pit.
SW   There's something you said. At the start of this.
JU   What?
SW   Her embrace was the embrace of the pit. How did you know what her embrace was like?
JU   I am a sinner.

SW   I done you a favour then.

JU   She never escaped did she?

SW   It was like drowning a kitten. You know I don't think she wanted to be in this world at all.

JU   You could say the same about Flynn. I didn't have to lay a finger on him.

*

The sand held the skeleton of the child together. The skull plating. The bonelets of the ribcage.

*

Ships riding beyond the bar, their masthead lights against the darkness of the channel reaching up to the constellations as though you could mend with light the broken parts of the world.

*

You werent there Charles you werent there you werent there you werent there

Ken Bruen

Ken Bruen was born in Galway in 1951, where he now lives. After completing a PhD in Metaphysics he spent twenty-five years as an English teacher in Africa, Japan, Asia and South America. *The Guards*, Ken's first Jack Taylor novel, was published in 2001. Ken was a finalist for the Edgar, Barry, and Macavity Awards, and the Private Eye Writers of America presented him with the Shamus Award for the Best Novel of 2003 (for *The Guards*). Ken received the best series award in February 2007 for the Jack Taylor novels from the Crime Writers Association of America. *The Dramatist* was nominated in March 2007 for a Gumshoe Award for the Best European Crime Novel of 2006. More recently he has won the German (2010) and French (2009) crime writers' prizes.

Miller's Lane

Landing at Galway Airport I was amazed at how tiny it was. The woman beside me said:

'We couldn't land here last year because there were seagulls on the runway.'

I looked at her, see if she was kidding me?

Nope.

She seemed genuine. I asked:

'So what happened?'

'When?'

WTF.

I didn't give a fuck if she ever landed but I was kind of committed now so I tried:

'When you couldn't, you know … land?'

She acted as if that was the most inane question, near spat:

'We landed at Knock.'

Like everyone knew Knock?

I adopted that Irish response that apparently covers everything, I said:

'I see.'

I didn't.

Or care.

She turned to give me a full on look and the downturn of her mouth indicated nothing she saw was to her liking, she accused:

'You're a Yank?'

One time, that was gold in Ireland but not so much now.

But I decided to fuck with her a bit, answered:

'No.'

Left that to hover as we waited for the seatbelt sign to shut off. She was now angry, pushed:

'But you have an accent?'

I smiled, said:

'What can I say, I'm an affected cunt.'

I got a cab into the city and an earful from the driver who began:

'You're a Yank, I have a sister in Chicago.'

This was to be the norm during my killing stay. Not only did everybody in the damn country have relations in

Chicago

Jumbuck Boise

Boston

But:

'Did I know them?'

Like frigging hello?

Yeah, right.

Then he asked:

'You know the trouble with this country?'

I wanted to go:

'Yeah, mouth-shooting cabbies.'

Went with:

'Pray tell.'

And confess, a slight tone leaking over the words.

He said:

'Non-nationals.'

Checked in the mirror to see how this was being received, then tried:

'Hey, I don't mean Yanks, God forbid, but the A-Ribs, Nigerians, all those sponges, and get this …'

Waited.

I said:

'OK?'

'All of them all on medical cards.'

I nodded sagely.

Everyone should get to nod *sagely* at least once in their life. Then, as is the Irish wont, he completely abandoned this and went another road, said:

'They put a British guy in space.'

I ventured:

'Golly.'

Then the punch line:

'Proper place for them, am I right?'

Assuming, Yank – Republican.

I asked:

'Can you recommend a place to stay for two weeks?'

He could.

And did.

How I ended up in The Salthill Inn. Like a bad version of our Holiday Inns but hey, I wasn't looking for comfort, just a low profile. The receptionist, after asking if I knew his cousin in LA, informed me that they had Wi-Fi in all the rooms and get this:

'*Sky sports.*'

I said:

'I will try to contain my excitement.'

I unpacked my meagre luggage. First, a first-rate suit.

Be-spoke.

Oh yeah.

Cost a year's salary if you worked in the service industry. And fuck me, what a suit.

Hung it on a hanger and hung the hanger in the centre of the room, I had had the pockets half sewn closed to make thieving harder.

For me.

I did three passes, managed to take out a wallet almost effortlessly on two of the attempts. I was way better than that but jet lag takes its toll. Without exaggeration, I have practiced the dip and walk-over one thousand times and then some more. I could nearly do it blind.

Next, very carefully took out a faded yellowing clipping, dated:

3/1/89.

You could just about read:

'*Death of Down Syndrome girl ruled ...*'

The rest was too faded to decipher but I knew it by heart. I took out the duty-free bottle of Black Bush and poured a healthy wallop in the nearly clean glass from the bathroom.

I took a lethal slug and as it burned deep and fast I exhaled:

'Ruled *accidental.*'

Phew-oh.

I opened my laptop and looked at the exact location of Miller's Lane and felt my heart burn in my chest. Then did the Google search on:

Thomas Flynn.

Lots of laudatory shit on the man.

Man of the year.

Businessman of the decade.

Mega charity sponsor.

And photos.

Oh, lots of goddamn snaps.

With all the hotshots of the country.

An urban saint really.

I printed out his most recent photo and laid it on the table, close to the bottle of Bush.

Stepped back and then with all my might, I spat in his face.

I dressed to, if not impress, then to go unnoticed. To blend.

I knew the city pretty well from two sources.

Google maps.

Emerald / Emily / Emma.

A semi-psycho Hot Goth. I met her at an Insane Posse Event in Colorado. You can imagine the crowds but we met outside a tent selling peyote.

Yeah, that kind of vibe.

She was swigging from a bottle of Miller longneck, clocked me notice that and offered:

'Wanna suck on this, cowboy?'

Would you?

The cowboy, perhaps, because I was wearing a wicked pair of boots I stole in Houston. The kind of boots that whispered:

'Fucking A or not?'

Best asked in that semi-breathless Brit accent.

She was not conventionally pretty but something in the assembly of her features pulled you in. Her eyes had a green sheen that dazzled. If I sound smitten, I was.

Then.

We hung together for three days and she'd asked me:

'You here for the so-called music?'

I laughed, if we'd been born twenty years earlier, we'd have been hanging at a Grateful Dead happening. If we weren't *Deadheads*, were we simply *clowns*?

I answered truthfully:

'I'm working.'

Got the look, the *seriously*?

True.

Following a guy who'd embezzled his company's funds.

Those days, I did get legit work if tailing a guy is even that.

I asked her:

'And what do you do?'

Got an enigmatic smile, then:

'I lay out a new personality on the bed each night then in the morning, I slip into that and depending on who I am, I act accordingly.'

It sounded deranged, I said:

'Sounds deranged.'

She was delighted, said:

'The whole point.'

We got separated the second evening but we had a fallback, to meet at the stand dealing T-shirts if that happened. I was making my way there just as darkness was falling, feeling mellow. Saw a biker guy, big and nasty, the chains, denim, and scraggly locks. He had Emma by her hair and I heard him snarl:

'Blowjob, bitch.'

I did what you do.

I killed him.

I had learned that fast snap that does the job.

I expected her to be horrified. I asked, tentatively:

'Are you OK?'

Are you OK, Jesus.

Fuck, talk about lame.

She gave a smile of such glee, gushed:

'Show me how to do that.'

We went to New York after the concerts and did some real weird crazy shit there.

Fun though.

Then she had to return home to Ireland. I asked with complete disinterest:

'You have folks there?'

Got the look, with:

'Not for much longer.'

I understood that. My old man, after teaching me my various nefarious skills, shot himself. My mom, well, *step*-mom, a bat-shit crazy broad, lived in some half-assed commune in San Diego. You ever need stuff that is usually only available on the Dark Web, go look her up, she was the Silk Road before the internet.

So you might say, I had form.

Emma was a big help in telling me about Galway and in particular my quarry. Even asked:

'You want me to off him, Mill?'

Mill!

The obsession of my revenge occurred on Miller's Lane in Galway. And when I met Em, she was slugging from a Miller longneck.

So Miller I was.

For now.

Thomas Flynn, I knew his habits from a detailed calendar that Em had provided. So Mondays I knew he took lunch and no prisoners in the GBC. A family-cum-country restaurant off Eyre Square. He stopped in Hollands' Newsagents to get *The Irish Times*. No tabloids for this paragon of culture, though if all went to plan, he'd be tabloid fodder. Bumped him effortlessly as he came out of the shop. His fat wallet in my hand in jig time.

He crossed the street, no inkling he'd been robbed.

Be fun when this asshole asked for the cheque after he stuffed his face. I went to the mini shopping centre to meet Emma for coffee.

'What now?' she asked.

She was channelling Daisy from *Gatsby* and even managed a slight lisp which was just this side of irritating.

I said:

'Easy, I return the wallet, become the hero of his day and begin the process of ingratiating myself into all areas of his life.'

She had a slice of Danish which she was dissecting, not eating, and she whined:

'Still think we should just off the fuck.'

I leaned over and gently took the knife out of her hand, asked:

'Where's the fun in that?'

She sat back and did a neat version of the half-swoon that you find in *Gone with the Wind*, then:

'Oh Mill, the sheer rush, it's a blast, but you are not even doing this for *fun*.'

True.

I said:

'He has a daughter, Moira, about your age.'

Emma took this in, asked:

'Can I off her?'

God loves a trier.

I said:

'You need any money, Mr Flynn had a whole shitload in his wallet.'

Got a smile and:

'I need a good fuck, you got any of that?'

I prepared to go, shot:

'Very un-Daisy-like talk.'

She finished her coffee, said:

'You obviously know precious little about Daisy.'

And so dear reader:

I married him.

Ah, I'm just fucking with yah.

Wanted to let you know I know my Jane Austen.

Or that I at least knew where to purchase the *CliffsNotes*. Not sure they do those in Ireland but they are literature for dummies.

Haven't you got it yet, that I am that annoying animal:

The unreliable narrator.

If I had to describe my journey, it would most likely be:

'Grime and Punishment.'

The offices of Thomas Flynn were located on Eyre Square. Describing them, the word impressive, not to mention vulgar, sprang to mind. They screamed:

'Big bucks.'

I had on *the suit*, the one that had its very own scream:

'I'm a player.'

Oh yeah.

Went in and approached a severe-looking receptionist. She was strictly pretty, I mean she had her hair pulled so far back in a bun that it had to hurt. Her face was conventionally nice but with an edge that gave off hostility.

Dude, I can fucking do hostility in my sleep.

She didn't look up, thus establishing the gospel of:

'I'm a cunt.'

Gotcha.

I waited, doing my own version of a bollocks, humming lightly as if I had all the time in the world. It is guaranteed to test a priest and other demons.

Worked.

Her head sprang up and she snarled:

'Help you?'

Nastiness spilling all over the word.

I said:

'I very much doubt that.'

Got her attention if not her love. I added, as I literally bounced the wallet off the desk:

'I found your boss's wallet, please tell him about the warm reception you gave me for my chivalry.'

And I turned.

Was gone.

Suck on that, sister.

Took him a day to find me. His ego on the line, so I stayed under the radar to make him work for it. Was with Emma in Richardson's on Eyre Square, but a spit from Flynn's office, drinking in plain sight as it were, we were on our first Tequila Sunrise.

Why?

I guess because we could and my Yank accent ensured we didn't piss off the barman.

There was a guy in the corner, heavyset, with a boiler maker before him. He was wearing a very battered navy all-weather coat and had that look of a disillusioned smoker. The barman caught my look, said:

'That there is a former legend.'

Emma, lazily, asked:

'Legend?'

The barman shrugged, said:

'Yeah, Galway's first PI, tell you, he used to be something.'

I asked:

'Now?'

The barman looked like he might spit, said:

'Now he's a drunk.'

The door opened and in breezes Thomas Flynn, with, I kid thee not, flunkies in tow, goes:

'My saviour?'

I gave a bashful nod, came across as a blend of imbecile and gullible. I said:

'You mean me?'

Yeah, in that lame tone as Emma made puking noises. He boomed, everything about him was loud:

'You're the kid, the Yank who not only found my wallet but went to the trouble of finding my place of biz to return it.'

The legend made a sound of utter despair. We all ignored him. Flynn, I swear, grabbed me in a bear hug and with that unexpected move, was in serious danger of me snapping his fat neck. He bellowed:

'Bar keep, drinks for everybody.'

Paused. Looked across the bar, continued:

'Maybe not that loser.'

Threw a wedge of notes on the bar, still with one arm on me, said:

'I got to run but you kids stay, have fun and get this, my man here will give you my home address and you, my friend, are coming to my home for a bang-up dinner this very evening. Dress informal and hey, bring your cute little gal too.'

And he fucked off on out of there.

Em said:

'Call him a prick but I think but I think he's kind of *hot*.'

I said:

'We are out of here.'

And as we left, the legend said:

'I might be off base, as you Yanks say, but that man is a dangerous bollix.'

I had me one hell of an evening at Mansion Flynn. He sure pulled out all the stops, champagne, three-course dinner, with get this, servants. His lady of the evening, as he termed her, was named Natasha (read: hooker).

Her English was limited but when she heard my name, she giggled, tried:

'*Miller Light.*'

Like no one ever trotted out that before. But then, she wasn't employed for her scintillating chat.

The time went quickly and as I took my leave, I made a point of letting all gathered see me depart. Flynn said:

'Don't be a stranger.'

I said:

'You can bet your life on that.'

When I returned hours later, the house was in darkness, all sleeping the sleep of the little troubled. Breaking in was a piece of Irish cake. I crept up the stairs and sat in the corridor. I had the syringe with Raeford 4 in it. Emma had brought it back from one of her trips to Russia. It subdued without fully paralysing you. Flynn's age, he'd need to piss many times during the night and sure enough, round three, he staggered down the corridor, the amount of champers still in his system.

I said:

'Boo.'

Rammed the needle in his neck.

I got him in the Volkswagen (shades of Bundy?).

Nice scenic drive to Miller's Lane. Flynn in the shotgun seat, unable to talk but looking at me with eyes of bewilderment and terror. I said:

'Better buckle up there, partner.'

On Miller's Lane, it was quiet as death. I turned to Flynn, said:

'Remember the day, oh so many years ago, you knocked down the Down Syndrome child, and you put a spin on the *hit-and-run* gig.'

Paused:

'You hit and *reversed*.'

I let that hover, then said:

'Get this, my younger sister. But hey, you could give a good fuck, right?'

He managed to shake his head and I saw pleading fill his eyes. I added:

'My mother was in bits and shortly after, she emigrated to the good old USA, with her very young son.'

Pause:

'Da dah, me.'

It wasn't too hard to get him into the middle of the road, then back up, rev and hit him at close to 80 MPH.

He literally bounced, then came down hard on the road.

Did I reverse?

Did I fuck.

Paul Charles

Paul Charles was born and raised in the Northern Irish countryside. He is the author of the acclaimed Detective Inspector Christy Kennedy series, with *A Pleasure To Do Death With You* the tenth in the series. His current mystery is *St Ernan's Blues*, the third in the Inspector Starrett series, which is set in Donegal.

Incident on Parkway

Years are a bit like fivers, Kennedy thought as he walked down Parkway at the Regent's Park end of Camden Town. They are fine when you're saving them, but once you break into one, it disappears just as quickly as a taxi driver's smile. The Ulsterman believed that you had to consciously slow yourself down, take pause, every now and again, to avoid waking up some day an old man with most of your life behind you.

He wondered how that would feel. You know, to know and admit to yourself that the majority of your life was behind you. He returned his attention to the money simile. Were you more likely to break into that fiver if you had, for instance, several other similar, or even higher denomination notes, remaining in your pockets? That seemed logical and perhaps the reason for wasting your younger years when you had a lot more reserve in the bank.

But you never really knew how many more years you had left in the bank of life, did you? Kennedy surmised that was where his simile fell down. If you started your day with eighty pounds in your pocket and you spent forty-one of them, well … then you knew you'd thirty-nine left. But if, as was Kennedy's case, you had spent forty-one years of your life then, everything being equal, you could guesstimate you'd about thirty-nine years or so left. It suddenly dawned on him that he had actually slipped into the second half of his own life, and without even being aware of it. He could have maybe less than half of his life left, but, unlike the brass in his pocket, it wasn't guaranteed.

You could step out of your door tomorrow morning and walk under a bus and that certainly wasn't really something you could anticipate, was it? That or any other way your life might end. The only precaution you could take was to ensure you stepped out each and every morning in clean underwear.

Kennedy was sitting by a pavement table at the Pizza Express on Parkway. He liked to watch the world go by; there was something incredibly comforting about it. It was like freezing your own life as you watched others spend a chunk of their own.

The Ulsterman noticed a man and woman walking down Parkway. They came across as an unlikely couple. The man was thin with a completely shaven head. His black bushy eyebrows and droopy moustache offered the only contrast to his bone-coloured complexion. He had small eyes, set wide apart. Kennedy pegged the man to be in his mid-thirties. He walked on the balls of his feet and his long fawn woollen coat kept falling open, revealing a small but muscular body, clad in a tight black T-shirt and jeans. He kept gathering his coat about him, the way a woman does with her dressing gown as she goes about her early morning routine. Every few steps he would wrap the coat around him and clasp the buttonless, shapeless garment shut with one hand. Then, when he would unconsciously use that hand in a gesture, the coat would fly open again. The woman was dressed in black, loose-fitting and unfashionable clothes. She was heavily made-up and her hair was brown and unkempt.

Kennedy tried to imagine their story; how had they met? Who'd approached who and why? How did they get it together physically for the first time? Strange though it seemed, that was the thought that ran through Kennedy's mind. They walked pretty much together but whereas his stride was confident, the woman walked tentatively and hesitantly, needing to add a half-skip every now and then to keep up with the man. Kennedy wondered what that revealed about them. What was there to be learned from the way they talked to each other? He was highly animated; she looked like she was continuously trying to pick up the courage to say something. What was there to be gathered from the way they looked at each other? He looked guarded, she disappointed.

As they walked past him, Kennedy felt in his pocket for cash, he had two twenty pound notes and a few coins. He felt confident enough to order his green salad – 'To start, please.' – pizza, an American with an egg, walnuts but 'No tomato, please.' He had dined there often enough that the 'No tomato' request no longer raised eyebrows. By the time the waiter returned with knife, fork, serviette and a glass of still mineral water, Kennedy had started to focus on a couple of the regular Parkway characters. Frank, the owner of the Italian Restaurant, and Peter, the owner of Regent's Bookshop, who were both kicking their heels on the pavement and audibly discussing Manchester United's slaughtering of Highbury's finest the previous Sunday.

'We were doing OK until they started to score goals,' Frank, ever the optimist, claimed.

'Yeah, and as we are both obviously dealing in fiction, I think I'll write the next Harry Potter adventure,' Peter laughed.

At that moment, a pristine Vauxhall VX 4/90 pulled up by the pavement about three feet away from Kennedy. The single occupant of the car, a glamourous elderly lady, climbed out. From the toys scattered around the back seat of the car, Kennedy guessed she was a grandmother. He wondered if she or her husband was the original owner of the car. It was certainly a possibility; whoever owned the car was very car-proud; even the walls of the tyres had been freshly painted in a black gloss.

The green car with its white side-flashes had been polished so magnificently that Kennedy could clearly see his reflection in it.

Kennedy was then distracted by another reflection, that of the couple who had passed him a few minutes ago. They were standing in the doorway of the tile shop. Occasionally one of them would step onto the pavement, look back into the doorway and then step back in again. The woman raised her voice as she stood back from the man. 'You've never, ever, been there for me,' she hissed, her voice close to breaking, 'you're just never ever there for me.'

Kennedy was surprised because although their body language was now highly agitated they still seemed to be pretty warm to each other. Their reflections vanished from the side of the car as they moved further into the doorway of the tile shop.

Glam-gran, the driver of the Vauxhall VX 4/90, returned to her car, tut-tutting to herself as she examined the parking permit she had just purchased from the machine a few yards down Parkway. 'It's a disgrace what they charge for parking your car,' she complained to no one in particular. Everyone in general ignored her as she carefully placed the ticket on the inside of her windscreen, closed her door gently and wandered down Parkway, zipping her bright yellow driving coat and pulling the fur-lined collar up to shelter her newly permed silver hair from the wild winds of Parkway.

Kennedy wondered where all these fine old classic cars had gone. He couldn't remember seeing one since his father's back in the sixties. He remembered being proud of his dad for buying the VX 4/90 because, unlike all the other cars around Portrush at the time, it looked quite American. Well, at least like the cars he'd seen in the American movies.

The Ulsterman's waitress returned with his starter. Kennedy was about halfway through his salad, with its signature classic dressing, when Glam-gran returned to her car. She daintily removed the ticket from her windscreen and walked back up

Parkway, stopped two cars along and knocked on the window of a red Mercedes SL280. The young woman who had been getting ready to exit her car, snapped shut the safety-lock on her door. She lowered the window about six inches, carefully eyed the stranger, didn't appear threatened, wound down her window completely and smiled to Glam-gran in thanks as she accepted the part-used parking ticket. Glam-gran returned to her Vauxhall and with a contented smile, fastened the seat belt, started up the classic car and, using her wing mirror, carefully pulled out from the pavement and slowly merged with the traffic.

The Mercedes' driver positively leapt out of her car, quickly glanced up and down Parkway while locking her car door. She wore a pair of snow-white pumps and a tartan miniskirt over a pair of black skin-tight trousers. Even though spring had not long since arrived, the young lady's ensemble was topped off with a red sleeveless T-shirt. She skipped off down Parkway and, at the last possible second, diverted into the Regent's Bookshop, causing Peter and Frank to have to interrupt their conversation about the virtues of Arsenal and Harry Potter.

Kennedy's attention returned to the couple in the middle of their escalating domestic. He hated to see a man and a woman argue on the street. He felt it showed a degree of desperation on one side and a total lack of respect on the other. He thought of his relationship with local journalist ann rea. When it was sweet it was heaven, but something was just not quite right. He'd never been able to put his finger on what exactly it was that prevented them from getting to the next step. However, no matter how deep their trouble was, they'd never ever fight about it in public. They never even discussed it, let alone argued about it, in private. Was that part of the problem? Kennedy felt not. He felt that you either lived your life, or … you talked about living your life.

Sitting there on Parkway, Kennedy allowed his thoughts to follow the ann rea thread. He was philosophical about it. It no longer pained him. It just was. He hoped that they would be able to make the transition from lovers to friends. He liked being with her but he felt there was something quite wrong about continuing to be with her, in the biblical sense, when they both agreed nothing was going to become of the relationship. He was bemused about why it didn't work. In a flash of clarity, he thought of himself and ann rea in light of the man and the woman having a domestic on Parkway. Perhaps they were both dealing with a similar situation, just dealing with it differently. One couple allowed their frustrations and disappointments to brew into anger while the other couple were being civilised about their predicament. Both couples were dealing unsuccessfully with the same situation. Just because a man liked and wanted a woman, and the feeling was reciprocated, that didn't mean that it was going to work out. No matter how intelligent or tribal the couple might be, if it wasn't going to stick, you'll never be able to force it to. However, imperfect as though their current relationship might be, was it simply preferable to being alone?

A battered Land Rover pulled into the space recently vacated by the VX 4/90 and Kennedy stole another look at the reflection of the troubled couple in the new vehicle. Moustachioed-man was hopping from foot to foot, looking at the ground as the woman dressed in black glared incessantly at him. Kennedy couldn't be sure, but it looked like tears were running rivulets through her makeup. He thought anything, anything at all, even being alone and lonely, must be preferable to the frustrations that drove you to behave that way in public. He made a silent resolution concerning himself and the journalist, just as the driver of the Land Rover climbed down onto the pavement. He was dressed in grubby denim jeans and a green checked shirt. He wore industrial steel-capped boots. His curly red hair was coated in white dust. He moved slowly and cautiously, probably the result, Kennedy assessed, of a back injury. Kennedy also noticed that the builder neither locked his vehicle door, nor purchased a parking ticket. He stopped outside the tile shop and the couple involved in the domestic stepped out from the sheltered doorway to allow him access to the shop.

'I can't keep doing this,' the woman said, now clearly crying.

'Shut up,' the man screamed, showering his moustache with spittle.

Moustachioed-man was so loud that a middle-aged, over-dressed man coming out of Smart's Dry Cleaning shop across Parkway stopped in his tracks. The man looked like he was considering crossing Parkway to come to the aid of the damsel, so clearly in distress. He was holding a shrink-wrapped white shirt in his left hand. The shirt was continuously and furiously flapping in the wind. Just then the dust-covered builder exited the tile shop, awkwardly carrying a box. The couple both seemed happy to slink back into the privacy the doorway afforded them. As the illegally parked Land Rover carelessly pulled back into the Parkway traffic, the over-dressed, clean-shirt-carrying man, seemingly content the domestic had subsided, turned his back on them and walked up Parkway. As he passed Tawa Tawa, the Indian restaurant, he glanced back in the direction of the tile shop doorway. Unable to see the couple, he continued up the street, past No. 110 – by far the grandest building on Parkway.

Kennedy's musings were interrupted as his pizza arrived. The Pizza Express opened in 1965 and they had certainly spent the intervening years perfecting their main dish. Peppered up, Kennedy hungrily tucked in and was surprised as he noticed the couple leave the sanctuary of the tile shop doorway and proceed down Parkway. He couldn't tell from the couple's body language if the domestic was over; he certainly hoped so. By the time they reached the Spread Eagle she had grabbed the bald-headed, moustachioed man under the arm and pulled him affectionately into the pub.

Kennedy returned his attention to the business at hand, or mouth, eating his pizza.

The girl in the tartan miniskirt ran out of Regent's Bookshop proudly carrying the shop's famous blue carrier bag. Kennedy wondered which book or books she had purchased. In a couple of seconds, she was back at her red Merc, but before she entered the Germanic speedster, she removed the parking ticket from the inside of the windscreen and flamboyantly threw it to the pavement.

As the Merc entered the continuous flow of Parkway traffic, the driver of an ice-blue BMW had clearly been observing the girl in the tartan miniskirt's actions. At the last possible second, the BMW swerved into the space that the Land Rover had vacated a few minutes previously. The action of the BMW nearly caused a heavy-laden flat-back lorry to run into the back of the BMW. The lorry driver noisily stopped in his tracks and started aggressively honking his horn. The second the driver of the BMW got out of the car was the instant the honking stopped. The driver of the BMW was drop-dead gorgeous. Kennedy could see one of the lorry driver's chins drop onto his lap as he ogled the long-legged beauty. She, Kennedy guessed, would have been in her early twenties and her shoulder-length blonde hair was centrally parted. She wore a white, knee-length flimsy dress, a dress that left absolutely nothing to the imagination. Kennedy personally preferred a lot, if not everything, be left to the imagination. The lorry driver's aggression turned to lust as he leered from ear to ear. The blonde woman raised the middle finger of her right hand to greet him. What did he expect anyway? Kennedy thought, smiling to himself. Did the balding, unshaven lorry driver really think a beautiful young woman was going to react to such leering by climbing up into his cab and doing the wild thing with him, right there and then on Parkway?

The young blonde chose instead to turn on her heels and run up Parkway, stopping about ten yards from Kennedy and, bending over, she retrieved the discarded parking ticket from the pavement. Kennedy was happy the lorry driver had moved further down Parkway, for if he had seen what Kennedy had just seen, he was sure there would have been a major pile up on Parkway.

She returned to her BMW, smiling at Kennedy as she passed him. She placed her recently retrieved ticket on the inside of her windscreen. She walked across Parkway and entered Top Nails with its multi-coloured shop sign. Kennedy had never thought about, or considered the need for, such a dedicated establishment before.

Three minutes and the third delicious quarter of a pizza later, the young blonde BMW driver exited Top Nails and walked back across Parkway, ignoring the traffic as she closely examined her recent purchase. Luckily enough the traffic didn't ignore her vestal looks – that would have been an impossibility. She threw her purchase nonchalantly in the front passenger seat, removed the parking ticket from her windscreen and, leaving her car door wide open, walked down Parkway and stuck the ticket to the side of the ticket machine. As she returned to her car, she caught Kennedy's eye once more and smiled at him. She sat back into her driver's seat but left her feet on the Parkway pavement. Kennedy couldn't be entirely sure but he thought her next move was a calculated one. She raised her knees, her flimsy dress slid upward and she parted her legs ever so slightly, just as she swung them back into the car. She winked at him before closing the door.

Kennedy stopped mid-bite as he noticed the original bald moustachioed man and the woman dressed in black leave the Spread Eagle. This time the woman was quickest and she moved up Parkway while her soon-to-be – if her current display was anything to go by – ex-partner ran behind her, his coat billowing out behind him like Superman. Unlike Superman, he took some time to catch up with her.

'I can't believe you,' she sneered, 'just go. Just leave me alone.'

Moustachioed-man grabbed her arm and slowed her down to a walking pace. He pulled her from Kennedy's view back into their hideaway, the doorway of the tile shop.

Just then a maroon Chevy PT Cruiser pulled into the space directly in front of Kennedy. The Chevy had a weird cumbrous shape. It was badged as a Limited Edition but Kennedy felt 'Quasimodo' might have been a much better name for the vehicle.

A well-dressed woman in her early thirties was behind the steering wheel. She was sad-eyed, dressed in a blue trouser-suit and was accompanied by a well-preserved elderly gentleman. Kennedy mused on the nature of their relationship. He thought there was neither enough love, nor hate, between the couple for them to be husband and wife. Perhaps they were employer and employee? Their accents betrayed the fact that while he was American, she was from the Midlands. The man shook his legs to straighten out the creases of the dark blue trousers of his Armani suit. He walked down to the parking ticket machine, stretched his hand deep in his man-purse in search of some change. At the last moment he spied the ticket stuck to the machine. He removed it, examined it closely, checked his watch and broke into a grin, which further creased his wrinkled and weather-beaten face. He handed the ticket to his sad-eyed companion, who, surprisingly, carelessly placed it on the outside of the windscreen, before pressing the button on her remote, locking the car. They walked down Parkway together. The American reached out and caught the hand of the well-dressed woman, which he held for a few steps. She discreetly shook her hand free. He looked across to her, the hurt obvious in his eyes. She seemed uncomfortable, ignored his glare and looked instead in the direction of her travel down Parkway.

A few clues there, Kennedy figured. Being crude about it – and you could be crude about it in your thoughts, Kennedy mused, as he smiled to himself – the American provides the money and the sad-eyed lady of the Midlands provides the honey. She, in the words of the Eagles hit, knew exactly how to open doors just with a smile.

Kennedy wondered if the American suffered from avaricious tendencies and if so, was it at the expense of his romantic life. Was that perhaps why he had chosen to buy affections? While Kennedy mused further on the subject he wondered if the woman had lost a true love earlier in her life and decided from then on that she would never allow herself to be hurt again, that all men would pay. Perhaps that was all too neat and pat. But the fact that he wanted to hold her hand and the fact that she publicly shunned his open display of affection spoke volumes to those who noticed their discreet piece of theatre on Parkway.

The couple continued down Parkway. The sad-eyed lady was nearly knocked to the ground by moustachioed-man as he stumbled backwards out of the doorway of the tile shop. Kennedy imagined the man with the Ronnie on his top lip must have been standing on the edge of the step and lost his balance. The American immediately reached out to steady his companion with one hand as he pushed the offending man away with the other. The sad-eyed lady once again asserted her independence by fending for herself. Words were exchanged on the pavement between the three of them but, due to the noise of someone loudly honking their horn, Kennedy couldn't make out what exactly was said.

Kennedy turned to his left to check the origins of the noise pollution. It was none other than Glam-gran in the Vauxhall VX 4/90, who had returned to Parkway and was unrelentingly honking her horn. It appeared she was trying to catch the attention of the American gentleman. Glam-gran rolled down her window when she drew level with them.

'So this is the PA you've been screwing,' the glam-gran screamed at the top of her voice, betraying she was also an American.

'Mable, please not in public!' the elderly American gent hissed.

'If you're going to be seen out with her in public then I'm certainly at liberty to raise my voice in public.'

Moustachioed-man took the opportunity created by the new disturbance to swiftly nip back into the isolation of the doorway of the tile shop.

'I really don't need this,' the sad-eyed lady hissed, at a volume meant to be audible only to her elderly American friend. However, all activity on Parkway had ceased as everyone turned to see what the racket was about.

Glam-gran didn't disappoint her audience.

'I heard he'd bought you the Limited Edition Chevy. I have to tell you something, Missy, a limited edition you'll never be.'

The American man looked mortified and walked towards the double-parked VX 4/90.

'Mable please, let's be civil about this,' he pleaded with Glam-gran, as the sad-eyed lady, now clearly his lover, looked lost. She acted like she didn't know whether to accompany the American back up Parkway, wait where she was, or walk down Parkway – towards the heart of Camden Town – and away from the racket.

'Two domestics in one morning,' Kennedy whispered to himself. The new one, the one involving the Americans, looked like it could get messy, if only because there were three people involved and all of them were present. At least the couple secure in the entrance to the tile shop looked like they were pissed off only by each other. All seemed to be quiet on their front as Glam-gran spoke again. She seemed to be going to great trouble and potential hoarseness to ensure all of Parkway heard her.

'Civil? I'll be civil to you when you're civil to me – prancing down Parkway with your new tart!'

That seemed to be the last straw for the sad-eyed lady.

'You're welcome to him,' she shouted, as she turned on her heels and moved on down Parkway. 'I'm outta here. He … it's not worth it.'

The poor American man didn't know which way to turn. Kennedy supposed Glam-gran could be a wife (likely) or a sister (unlikely) but whatever she was, he was prepared to leave her as he chased down Parkway after his sad-eyed PA.

There was a bit more honking of the horn and Mable's next call after them was, 'A word to the wise Missy, he's got nothing as big as his wallet.'

She had a wee giggle to herself as she engaged the car and slowly moved on down Parkway. Pretty soon she was double-parked in front of Kennedy and the Limited Edition Chevy. She looked at the windscreen of the car and smiled to herself and then, when she saw Kennedy staring at her, she offered him a knowing grin as well.

'Let's see just how good the traffic wardens around this neighbourhood are,' she said, as she swiped the ticket from the windscreen of the Chevy. She hopped back in her car and drove off down Parkway. Kennedy heard her continue to berate the hapless couple with both her voice and even more honking as they all moved into the distance.

The departure of Glam-gran and company moved the couple involved in the original domestic back into the foreground again.

They were back out on the pavement. She really looked like she'd been crying as her make-up was now an absolute mess. Kennedy watched, transfixed as moustachioed-man grabbed and secured his coat around him with his left hand. He then very gently moved his free hand slowly towards her face. 'Oh, they must have made up and I missed it with all this other fuss,' Kennedy whispered under his breath.

The man continued to raise his hand. It appeared to Kennedy that all the actions were now in slow motion. He wondered why it was taking moustachioed-man so long to caress her face.

Kennedy could see the white of the man's eyes. He could not interpret the emotion contained therein. 'Something is wrong with this picture,' Kennedy said to himself, as he looked on, magnetised to the scene. The movement of the man's hand towards the woman's face seemed to be gentle and caring. However, those feelings were not reflected in the look in the man's wide-set eyes. The closer the hand advanced to the face, the more concentrated the small eyes became. At the last possible moment, the man pulled his hand back a little from the face of his fraught companion and stopped it mid-air.

He pulled his fingers back, claw-like, and shoved the heel of his hand towards her with all the force, anger and venom he could muster. As his hand connected and squashed the woman's nose deep into her face, the man was openly snarling.

Kennedy watched in disbelief as the single blow was enough to lift the woman clear off her feet and she tumbled backwards in the doorway of the tile shop. Her head hit the ancient York stones of the entrance with such a thud that Kennedy felt part of the aftershock reverberating in the ground beneath him.

Detective Inspector Christy Kennedy, acting on instinct alone, jumped to his feet. The bald, moustached head turned to Kennedy and immediately squared up to him the way a lion would if interrupted during the kill of its prey. Moustachioed-man showed absolutely no compassion or concern for the woman on the ground. In a few seconds Kennedy was at the doorway of the tile shop. A large pool of blood had already formed a dense crimson halo around the woman's head on the cold York stone beneath her.

The man froze and looked like he was deciding whether or not to take Kennedy on. He wore the look of guilt as transparent as a lion's blood-soaked jaw. In a matter of seconds the look on the man's face was transformed. Kennedy immediately recognised this transformation. It was the look of a man whose mind was running through a list of excuses for his actions. He needed to hone in on the one he knew he would have to rely on later in court.

Kennedy was aware that if he hadn't been there in person and witnessed the whole incident from only eight feet away, he too could have been fooled with, 'Well we'd been arguing and she'd a lot to drink and there was this idiot on the street shouting and hooting her horn and my friend lost her balance. I reached out to catch her as she fell, but I was too late. As she fell, my hand just grazed her face. It all occurred so fast I genuinely couldn't really tell you exactly what happened.'

Yes, a clever barrister might just use the surrounding confusion to introduce doubt, just a little doubt, but that might be just the thing to get his client off.

However, Kennedy, in the middle of his lunch, while he contemplated the big disadvantage of breaking into a fiver and how much of his life was left, witnessed it all first hand. He saw the bloodthirsty gaze of a predator in moustachioed-man's eyes. That was a look he would never forget for the rest of his life, no matter how much longer that life turned out to be.

Soon the gathering group of people had helped the Ulster detective overpower and restrain the bald-headed, moustachioed-man. As Kennedy waited for back-up from North Bridge House, he recalled vividly the look of panic on the woman's face. He had also seen that look before; it was the look of someone who knew she was being cheated out of what she now accepted was the very last fiver of her life.

Julie Parsons

After a career in RTÉ as a radio and television producer, Julie Parsons' first thriller, *Mary, Mary* was published in 1998 with critical and commercial success. It was translated into many languages and also published in the USA. She followed this up with *The Courtship Gift* (1999), *Eager to Please* (2000), *The Guilty Heart* (2003), *The Smoking Room* (2004), *The Hourglass* (2006) and *I Saw You* (2008). She has also written two radio plays, *The Sweet Scent of Cigarette Smoke* (2009) and *The Serpent Beguiled Me* (2009).

Kindness

KINDNESS: that was the quality which Gwen Gibbon admired and desired most in others. You can forget about courage, intelligence, beauty, truth-seeking, she thought, as she sat in the July sunshine on the wooden bench outside her basement flat. It was kindness that counted.

It was warm, almost hot today, so she had taken off her cardigan and let the sun fall directly on her thin, white arms. Old arms, nearly ninety-three years since they had first seen the light of day, brought forth in the big bedroom upstairs. A Sunday, so she had been told many times, her mother and father walking the East Pier, then the sudden rush of amniotic fluid, her father hailing a horse-drawn cab to take them home, and hours, hours later, her mother would stress, the baby, 'a beautiful little girl, we were so delighted,' delivered on the high iron bedstead.

That high iron bedstead, gone into a skip years ago. No one wanted it. Might be worth something now. But back in the seventies, when she had been kicked from the upstairs flat down into the basement, there was nowhere for the bedstead. Even the local junk shop turned up its nose.

Kicked out of the upstairs, the house sold and this time the new owner carved it into bedsits. Gwen had known her rights. A sitting tenant. She had faced down the man who towered over her, his sleeves rolled back as he shoved her furniture out onto the landing.

'I know my rights, I have rights,' she said as loudly as she could, although her voice was shaking, her hands trembling and she felt as if she would begin to cry.

'Rights, hmm,' and he stepped away and lifted the lid of her mother's upright piano. Picked out a few notes, then played an abbreviated version of chopsticks.

'Nice,' his fingers dawdled over the keys, and for the first time he smiled. 'OK, rights, I get it. Tell you what, how do you fancy the basement? The whole basement, front room, back room, kitchen and bathroom. All yours.'

Kindness, that's what it was. He got his lads to move her furniture. They didn't break a thing. He even got her a bed, low so the dust between the floorboards made her sneeze, but the mattress was almost new and firm which she liked. And after she'd unpacked everything and made her first cup of tea, he came to see her, sat on the sofa and produced a box of chocolates.

'All because the lady loves Milk Tray,' he said as he put them on the table.

The new tenants upstairs were noisy and often she was frightened. But he had given her his number and from time to time she went to the phone box on the corner and shoved pennies into the slot and he would come and get rid of them. And call in with the Milk Tray and an apologetic smile.

She served him Earl Grey. He liked it. He waved away the milk jug and sipped gingerly.

'Hot,' he said.

She settled in her wing-backed chair and balanced the cup on her knee.

There was silence in the small, damp room. Almost companionable. Almost, but not quite.

He shifted, his feet square on the cold floor. 'The chocolates,' he said.

'Very nice,' she smiled.

'One good turn and all that,' he sipped again.

She waited.

'The box, when you've finished the chocolates. Don't put it in the bin. Leave it under the bench outside. Tonight.'

'Yes?'

'Then tomorrow bring it in. I'll call later and collect it. OK?' He took another sip and stood. He winked. One good turn.

She remembered him for his kindness. He hadn't told her not to, but she didn't look in the box. She put it out, and brought it in again. It was heavier. She didn't want to know. It was a routine, like going to the shops to buy bread and milk, sweeping the floor, making her bed, polishing her mother's silver.

And then he stopped coming to her door. She saw something on the news. A body found in a field out by the airport. A few days later the picture on the front of *The Irish Times*. He was identified. Sean Butler. Not the name she knew. He'd been shot in the back of the head. Drugs, the report said. She felt a momentary pang. She opened the box. Ten-pound notes, neatly bound with elastic bands. She counted them. One hundred. One good turn and all that. She put them under the nearly new mattress.

The house was sold again and again and again. The tenants got worse. The owners were no better. They showed her no kindness. For that she turned to the ladies in the church. They were no better either. They felt sorry for her, that was all. Poor Gwen. No husband, no home, worst of all no money. She knew they gossiped behind her back. Told and retold the story of her father's fall from grace. Caught embezzling from the insurance company where he had worked for years. Hanged himself. Left behind his wife and Gwen and her younger brother. They had never owned the house, just rented the first two floors. And Gwen was unlucky in love. William, her fiancée, was killed in the Second World War. And her brother too. So she and her mother worked away as best they could. Her mother gave music lessons; Gwen taught French in the local Church of Ireland secondary school and had a few private pupils, evenings and weekends. They got by. Just about.

And after her mother died there was just Gwen. Alone, but not lonely. She had her ghosts to keep her company. Talking to myself, I must stop, she thought. Although to be honest she knew no one noticed. Invisible, that's what she was.

She sat on her wooden bench and watched the world go by. There were girls upstairs now, in the room where her mother had taught the piano. The sounds drifting down to the basement were no longer scales, finger exercises, Chopin études. Gwen lay in bed and listened. She folded her arms tightly across her small, frail body. She had loved William and they had made love, once. Just before he went overseas. She still remembered the fuzz of fair hair on his thighs.

Cars drove to the house, night after night. Sometimes the men and girls didn't make it up the stairs to the front door. In the morning Gwen would find her small garden littered. She put on rubber gloves to pick up the detritus.

'Sorry, love, you shouldn't have to do that.' The girl pushed open the gate. 'That's awful, you poor thing. I'm sorry.' And she bent down and delicately, her turned-up nose wrinkling, gathered together the remnants of the night. She lifted the bin lid and dropped them in. 'Yuck,' she said.

Kindness, that's what it was. The girl was a Londoner. She came over for weekends. She had a little boy back home looked after by her mother. She sat on Gwen's sofa, and drank tea. There was a strong smell of lavender from the soap Gwen had given her to wash her hands. It was quiet today in the basement. The grandfather clock ticked slowly.

'You've nice stuff,' the girl looked around.

Gwen nodded.

'Reminds me of my gran, she has nice stuff too.'

'Yes?'

'When I go back I'll tell her about you. She's in a home now, so I always try and have something interesting for her when I call in.' The girl smiled. 'Better than presents. She's not interested in stuff any longer.'

Gwen didn't reply. The silence was almost companionable. The girl put down her cup and sighed.

'Rugby weekend. It's going to be mad.' Above they could hear the sound of the radio and the tread of feet.

'Sorry,' the girl shrugged, 'can't be nice for you down here.' She moved towards the door. 'But I tell you what. I'll make sure there's none of that mess in your garden. OK?'

A lady of easy virtue, that's what Gwen's mother would have called her. Others used less genteel terms. Gwen sat on her bench and watched. There was a gang of teenage boys who lounged on the green in front of the houses. She watched what they did when the girl, Cathy, as she was called, or Tiger as the sticker in the phone box identified her, approached. Hands to their crotches, thrusting movements of their pelvises, whoops and wolf whistles. And the names: slag, slut, cunt, bitch.

'Don't mind them, I don't,' Cathy sank down on the bench beside Gwen. She pulled a small parcel from her bag. 'My gran sent this to you. Look.'

Gwen looked. Inside was a folded piece of white linen. She opened up the handkerchief. The letter G was embroidered in one corner and a delicate border of forget-me-nots trailed around the edges. Pretty against the snowy white.

'There,' Cathy leaned forward and tucked it into the sleeve of Gwen's blouse, 'now, you won't lose it.' Gwen smelt baby shampoo from her bright blonde hair. Cathy got to her feet.

'Better go, don't want to keep them waiting.'

It wasn't the scream which woke Gwen. She hadn't been able to sleep. She'd listened to the intermittent thumps she could hear on the floor upstairs. They reminded her of the sounds that the body of a mouse makes as a cat throws it around, flinging it in the air, watching it drop, then grabbing it again. A soft, but heavy thump, not quite a thud. The scream came later. Then the bang as the front door slammed. Gwen got out of bed. She heard a car start, then stop, the engine stuttering. She shoved on her slippers. Outside her breath condensed in the cold night air. The car started again. It moved slowly away. She saw the licence plate. She remembered the number. She could hear a commotion upstairs. The women stood in a semicircle, Cathy on the floor, her face a bloody mess, blood congealing between her legs.

Gwen knelt. Baby shampoo, the scent from the girl's matted hair. She pulled the handkerchief from her dressing gown sleeve. She gently wiped the girl's face.

'There, there, there.'

The house upstairs was quiet for months. But there were other noises in the square now. The screech of saws, the banging of jackhammers, the dull rumble of rubble, dumped in metal skips. And the chatter of children, playing on the green. The foul-mouthed boys had gone; now it was little ones with footballs and skipping ropes and au pairs who lolled on tartan rugs with picnic baskets.

Gwen liked the skipping.

All in together girls,
This fine weather girls,
When is your birthday
Please run out.

She had spent many happy hours as a child skipping on the green. There were lots of little girls then. She remembered in particular Jean and Cecily Hall. Their father's name was Richard. He had worked in the drapers' shop in the town until

9th July, 1921, when his body was found under a hedge, a couple of miles away. The local IRA had killed him. He was a Protestant, a Unionist, an informer, so they said. No one spoke of it. A casualty of the War of Independence. And when the Halls' mother died too, the girls disappeared. An orphanage, it was whispered. Disgrace. A life of domestic servitude.

Gwen sat on her bench and watched the world go by. Now the cars were bigger. The women were more beautiful, the men more handsome. Their teeth gleamed, their hair shone, their smiles flashed. But there was no kindness. They didn't speak to her. They didn't stop their children kicking their footballs into her garden, or dropping their ice cream wrappers outside her gate. And the new owner of the house was a woman, red in tooth and claw, her lipstick scarlet, her nail polish vermilion and a handbag that clanked as she moved.

'Out,' she said, 'I want you out. I've plans for this place.'

'Rights,' Gwen held herself as tall as she could, 'what about my rights?'

The woman smiled, a red grimace. 'Don't bother trying that on. You'd be better off out of here. A nursing home, that's where you should be.'

Kindness in short supply.

It was summer, hot this year. She sat on her bench, closed her eyes and leaned back. She had grown a few sweet pea from seed. Planted them in a yogurt pot, nursed them as they sprouted. Carefully transplanted them into a bigger pot and encouraged them to twine up the front railings. They were flowering now, dark red and purple, their scent coming in waves of sweetness. Until the football, kicked with ferocity, arrived at speed, bounced off the top of the railings, crashing down onto the plants, destroying their fragile stems, the flowers crushed.

She knelt, tried to resuscitate them. Tears came, and a shadow fell over her.

'Little fucker, gobshite.'

She looked up. The man was tall and thin, his hair dark brown, cut short.

He held out his hand. 'Here.' His palm was dry. He grasped her arm. His touch was gentle. He guided her to the bench.

'Sit.'

She pulled the little hanky from her sleeve. The stain, a brown smear from Cathy's blood, was still visible. She wiped her eyes.

He moved out of sight. She could hear him shouting at the boys on the green.

'This one, he wants to say something.' They stood at her gate, the tall thin man, and a pudgy boy, his face flushed.

'Go on,' the man gave him a push.

The boy looked at the ground. His feet scraped the footpath.

'Sorry, sorry about your plants,' his voice was barely audible.

'And you won't, what won't you?' She could sense, rather than see, the young man's grip on the boy's neck.

'Do it again. I won't do it again.'

They sat, the young man and the old woman side by side. She could smell his sweat. It wasn't a bad smell. So long, she thought, since she'd smelled a man's body. It made her feel, just for a moment, young. He asked her name. He told her he was Martin. His eyes were green, flecked with gold. His accent was what they now call 'inner city', but his tone was gentle and kind. They sat in silence. It was just about companionable.

'I'll be back later,' he stood, 'and if any of those,' he paused, looking for the right word, 'little,' he paused again, 'give you grief, I'll sort them.'

He came back in the early evening when it was still warm but the sun was beginning to angle below the trees. This time he wasn't alone. The man with him was red haired and small. He didn't look at Gwen. He cleared his throat, noisily, and spat on the footpath. Martin cuffed him across the back of his head with one hand. The other was holding a large bunch of sweet pea. He thrust it towards her.

'Oh, how wonderful,' she dropped her face into the flowers. The scent rose in the evening air. It enveloped them all. 'How kind.'

Martin smiled. 'I thought you'd like them.' He turned to the red-haired man. 'You ignorant bollocks, say sorry to the nice lady.'

She watched them walk across the green until they disappeared behind the trees. She was moved by his kindness. She sat outside until lights began to show in the windows. The world was a strange and wonderful place, she thought. You never knew what each day would bring.

The sweet pea lasted well in one of her mother's cut-glass vases. Martin came and went. He brought her presents. A punnet of strawberries, luscious and flavoursome, unlike the usual supermarket fare; more sweet pea; a box of chocolates, not Milk Tray. These were handmade, dark and filled with honey and almonds. And a tiny bit of flattery, a generous comment about her appearance, leaning close, so again she could smell him.

The summer got hotter. The threat of eviction seemed to have gone. The lady with the noisy handbag was nowhere to be seen. Gwen began to sleep better. Perhaps after all, she could enjoy the few years she had left.

From time to time she received an invitation to drink sherry with the retired judge who lived across the green. Gwen had known his family since she was a child. They had been poor; his grandmother had cleaned for others. But her son, the judge's father, had become a national hero. He was a member of the local IRA during the War of Independence. Gwen's people had called him a gunman. The family had flourished in the new Ireland. Gone up in the world, as Gwen's mother would have said.

Gwen accepted the invitations. She knew they weren't motivated by kindness. The sherry was poured to impress.

The house was designed to overawe. But invitations were few and far between so she drank the sherry, allowed herself to be patronised.

Word of the judge's death, murder in fact, swirled around the green like leaves stripped from the trees by an equinoctial gale. He'd been shot in the back of the head. No one was sure of the motive. Perhaps it was criminals he'd put away during his time on the bench. More young men came to sit beside Gwen, policemen this time. Asking questions, looking for answers.

'You've a good memory,' one of them said. 'Because of you we caught the man who killed the girl upstairs. You remembered the licence plate number, didn't you?'

They showed her photographs. There were five on the page.

'Take your time,' the policeman said. He leaned close. He smelt of aftershave.

She took her time. Five male faces. Two she recognised. The red-haired man who'd hawked and spat at her gate. And his friend, Martin, thin face, short brown hair, wide smile.

Kindness, she valued it above all other qualities. It wasn't flashy or showy. It wasn't asked for. It was generous and humble. Martin had shown her kindness. He had wanted nothing in return. She weighed it up, what she knew and what she didn't know.

She let her hand dawdle across the faces, then shook her head.

'Oh well,' the policeman grimaced. He got to his feet. 'You'll let me know if?'

If, a big word. If her father had been honest. If he hadn't taken his own life. If Richard Hall hadn't been a unionist. If her fiancé hadn't been brave. If she'd had her own home. If she didn't value kindness more than any other quality.

But she did.

John Connolly

John Connolly is the author of two collections of supernatural stories, and more than twenty novels, including the Charlie Parker mysteries and *The Book of Lost Things*, as well as two series for young adults in the form of the Samuel Johnson novels and The Chronicles of the Invaders (with Jennifer Ridyard). He divides his time between his native Dublin and Maine.

The Evenings with Evans

What is grief? Grief is the suit that fitted once and now no longer does, the jacket billowing, the waistband gaping. Grief is the house that went from too big to just right, and then became too big again. Grief is the thing that feeds upon itself. Grief is the hunger and the fuel.

Grief is a fox.

They died on December 23rd, although not all at the same time. His wife died first – instantly – when the car left the road. His daughter was still alive when the first people staggered down the steep bank to offer help, and one of them held her hand as the life left her. For that much, he was grateful. His son passed away later that evening in the hospital, with his father beside him. He lived long enough to tell the story of what happened: a fox on the road, an instinctive twist of the wheel to avoid it, and then –

Nothing, or next-to-nothing. Just a house with too many rooms, and too many fields surrounding it, and a man lost at the heart of it, like a rat in a maze, as grief reduced him to a repository of memories.

He did not have the energy to sell up – and anyway, where would he have gone? Wherever he went, he would bring his grief with him, and at least here he found a kind of comfort, if such thin gruel could be termed sustenance. The house still bore traces of his wife and children, although there was more of his daughter than his son in the rooms, for Simon had been living in Berlin for two years before the accident, helping to clean up after the Nazis. That Christmas was also likely to have been Caroline's last in permanent residence: she planned to study medicine in Edinburgh, to her mother's combined pride and dismay, as that city seemed so far away.

Gone. All gone.

Each day he would walk his estate, always with a shotgun hanging broken over one arm. He was looking for the fox. His son had described it to him before he died. It bore a distinctive white mark on its right side, he said. Simon thought that it might have been caused by barbed wire. So he would find the fox, and he would kill it, because had it not existed, his family would still be with him.

But the fox refused to appear before him and accept its fate. He glimpsed others, but not the one that he sought. Nevertheless, each day he filled a pocket of his jacket with shells, and stalked the woods and fields with the gun over his right arm.

It was the closest thing to hope he had left.

Mrs Hoggart, who had been engaged as a housekeeper by his wife, continued to come by every day except Sunday, although on Saturdays she worked only until noon. He liked to think that she needed the work more than he needed her, but privately he knew better. She represented his only regular point of contact with the world beyond his walls. If she were to vanish, he would lapse into almost total silence. Mrs Hoggart, too, advised him on the steps necessary to maintain the estate, and took care of the employment and payment of the craftsmen and temporary workers required to prevent it from lapsing further into decay. The house was not large, not by the standards of some, but it was still big enough to be called 'The Manse' by everyone in the village, and old enough to swallow as much money as might be fed to it. And money he had: the City had been good to him, and his investments had flourished, and would continue to do so, now that the war had ended. Keeping an eye on his wealth was what passed for work these days.

On the first anniversary of their deaths, something broke inside him. He could not have said why, or pointed to what might have changed. He simply felt the crack in his being widen, and grief, as though envious of what few powers of speech he retained, seized his tongue, and stilled it.

And each day he roamed his lands, seeking the fox, while each night he wept.

The Manse boasted a very distinctive wine cellar, one of the reasons why he and his wife had acquired the property. Parts of the cellar dated back to Norman times, with carvings on the walls and pillars suggesting that it might, at one point in its past, have functioned as a place of worship or contemplation. Many of the bottles came from the tenure of the previous owner, and had been included in the sale, while others were acquired in the years before the death of his family. Since then, he had neither added to nor depleted its stock. He did not entertain, and now rarely imbibed alcohol at all beyond an occasional restorative whisky or brandy to keep out the cold. He was afraid that, if he began drinking seriously, he might never stop. The door to the wine cellar remained closed for the most part, and even Mrs Hoggart rarely ventured down there for long, content simply on occasional forays to keep the worst of the cobwebs at bay.

So it was that one evening, after Mrs Hoggart had departed for the night, a pie left in the oven for him to consume when he saw fit, he was surprised to see the cellar door standing open, and what appeared to be candlelight flickering in its depths. The cellar was wired for electricity, so there was no cause for anyone to be lighting candles. It could only have been the work of Mrs Hoggart, although he could not imagine why she should have chosen to set a light. He checked the switch, but the cellar remained dark: a blown bulb, perhaps, which might explain the presence of the candle. Odd, though, that Mrs Hoggart had not mentioned it to him, or replaced the bulb herself instead of leaving a candle burning. Perhaps she had just forgotten, even if this would have been so out of character for her as to suggest some form of possession.

He took the winding stone staircase down to the cellar. There, in the centre of the floor, facing the lines of shelves that blended gently into the shadows, a table had been placed, and beside it a chair. Both were familiar to him, as they formed part of the furnishings that had come with the house. They were made of oak so dark as to be almost black, the legs of the table decorated with carved curls of ivy, the arms of the chair worn smooth by centuries of use, and a great curved back that enveloped the occupant in way that was strangely comforting. When last he had paid any attention to the pieces they had been heaped in old boxes, but both were now unburdened. On the table stood a bottle of red wine, a glass, a decanter, a corkscrew, and a single, flickering candle in a pewter candlestick.

He picked up the bottle. It was a fine Bordeaux: a 1929 Château Beychevelle. The dust had been gently blown from it, not wiped, and on the glass was visible the mark of the hand that had taken it from its perch on the shelves. He looked closely at it, and thought that the fingers seemed large and wide. Mrs Hoggart had hands like a bird: strong, but small and thin. It struck him, rather uneasily, that it might not have been she who removed the bottle and set it on the table. But if not Mrs Hoggart, then who?

Suddenly, the cellar seemed threatening to him.

He listened, but could hear no sound beyond that of his own breathing and the sputtering of the candle. He lifted the candlestick from the table and held the light before him, as though by doing so he might ward off whatever might be lurking in the dark. He moved forward – one step, then two, slowly forcing back the shadows – and yet each step he took he created darkness behind him, and the light was not quite strong enough to penetrate as far as the walls to either side of him, and so he felt himself suspended in a fragile cocoon of illumination, one that would not save him in the event of an attack.

Slowly, and not without unsettling himself profoundly, he confirmed that he was the only occupant of the cellar, and finally found himself back at the table, staring at the wine bottle and the clean glass and decanter beside it. He found the niche from which the bottle had been removed, and returned it to its previous position. Then, taking the candle with him, he climbed the stairs back to the landing, and closed the door behind him. Only then did he blow out the flame.

The next morning, he questioned Mrs Hoggart about the bottle and the candle, but she professed complete ignorance, and informed him that it had been at least a week since her last visit to the cellar. He thought that she gave him a peculiar look when she had finished speaking, and he could not entirely blame her. She had little idea of what he might get up to when she left him, and probably suspected him of indulging in the odd tipple of an evening – not that she would have blamed him for it, not in the slightest. Her concerns about him might have been confirmed by the fact that the electric lights in the cellar now appeared to be working perfectly even though he had not managed to get around to replacing the bulb.

And so there they left the matter, each puzzled by the other. But that evening, when Mrs Hoggart, as usual, departed for home, he checked the cellar: the lights were working, the table was empty, and the wine bottles remained undisturbed. He ate his meal – a stuffed capon with potatoes – and later put a record on the gramophone while he read in the library, but he experienced difficulty in concentrating on the words before him. At last, he set the book aside, and walked to the hall.

The cellar door was open, and he caught the flickering of a candle from below.

He kept his shotgun in a locked cabinet by the boot room. He went to it now, retrieved and loaded the weapon, then waited until he was at the top of the stairs before locking the gun, the click of it echoing against the stone walls.

'You hear that?' he said. 'That's the sound of a London best, and you'd damned well better believe that I'll use it if you don't show yourself!'

But no reply came from the cellar.

His mouth was dry. The shotgun wavered in his hands. He was dreadfully afraid. Still, he set the stock against his shoulder, and took the stairs carefully until he reached the cellar. There, as before, stood a bottle of wine – the Bordeaux once again – and a decanter, a glass, a corkscrew and a candle in a different candleholder, one that was unfamiliar to him but clearly old. One further detail had changed: the wine bottle was now empty, and the decanter was full, the cork lying beside it.

'I'm warning you,' he said, scanning the cellar, his eyes following the twin barrels of the gun. 'Come out, or you'll be sorry for it.'

But nobody appeared, and the depths of the cellar remained heavy with shadow. He could either hold a candle or the shotgun, but not both, so a second search of the cellar was beyond him. He stepped to the very edge of the candle's reach, squinting into the dark, half expecting a pale hand to reach out in an effort to grab the weapon.

'Who are you?' he asked, and he did not like the tone of his own voice. It betrayed his fear, although he could not have said which he dreaded more: the continuing silence, or a possible reply to his question. In the end, he was granted only the former.

A secret passage, he thought; somewhere in the cellar had to be a false wall, unsuspected and undiscovered, and an unknown person was using it to play a nasty game. In the morning he would call Crichton & Sons, the local builders, and together they would conduct a thorough test of the cellar floor and walls. In the meantime, he would keep the door locked, so that no intruder could penetrate further into the house.

He backed away from the darkness, retreating toward the stairs. He glanced at the table in passing, and froze. The wine glass had been empty when he first came down. He was certain that was the case.

But the bell of the glass was full now.

He stared around him. No one could have managed to get behind him while he had the cellar under his gun, and he would have heard any footsteps on the stone floor, yet the wine glass had somehow been filled while his back was turned.

'No,' he said. It was a denial of all of it: the intruder, the filling of the glass, the invitation – for clearly an invitation it was – to drink. He would not do it, and he would linger here no longer. He left the candle burning, and kept his back to the wall as he made his way up the stairs, his finger poised, the pressure great enough to fire a shot in an instant if he detected even the hint of an approach. When he reached the hall he slammed the door behind him. The key hung from a hook on the wall nearby: a big iron beast, more ornamental than anything else, but now pressed into service once again. It stuck in the lock, and seemed reluctant to turn. He moaned, certain that at any moment he would feel pressure on the door from the other side, and see the handle begin to twist. Then, miraculously, the key turned, and the door locked.

He was safe.

He stepped back, taking up the shotgun once again. He waited, but all was still and quiet.

That night, he made up a bed for himself in the library. He kept the shotgun beside him, and the key beneath the cushion of the couch on which he lay. He did not sleep, although he dozed a little. Each time his eyes closed, though, it seemed to him that he jerked awake almost immediately, his ears alert for the sound of some unseen presence testing the cellar door. Only when dawn came did he finally rest, and was woken some hours later by the arrival of Mrs Hoggart. If she was surprised to find him sleeping on the couch, she chose not to share it, and he was grateful that he had been given enough time to hide the shotgun from her sight. She made breakfast while he performed his ablutions, but before he ate he called Crichton & Sons, and old Albert Crichton, the paterfamilias of the company, agreed to come round sometime after 1 p.m. to take a look at the cellar, drawn to the Manse under the pretence of searching for a possible point of entry for a rat or some other rodent.

When at last Albert and his son did arrive, he opened the cellar door and led the way down the stairs. Once again, the table was empty. The candle and candlestick were gone. The decanter – one of three – was back in the sideboard, with no sign that it had ever been used. All of the glasses were present and correct. As for the bottle, the untasted wine had been poured back inside, its cork restored, and it now stood on the sideboard. This detail was perhaps the most surprising to him of all. His nocturnal visitor appeared reluctant to waste a good bottle of wine. The temperature in the cellar would keep it cool, and so it would be drinkable for a little while longer.

If it hadn't all been so disturbing, it might almost have been amusing.

The Crichtons could find no hole or other flaw in the cellar floor or walls, and appeared highly perturbed when he asked them to check for some concealed door, as though wondering how a rat might use one even if it existed. The Crichton family had been working on the Manse for generations, and Albert himself had helped his own father with remedial work on the cellar decades earlier. Albert's opinion was that the walls and floor were sound, and any kind of priest hole or passage would have been discovered long ago. Nevertheless, the new owner's money was good, and work was work, so he agreed to return with two men the next day and begin a thorough examination of the cellar.

When Crichton and his son left, Mrs Hoggart departed with them, accepting a lift in the cab of their lorry, and he could only imagine the conversation they would be having about him as they returned to the village. He was half of a mind to stay at the village inn for the night, but that would only increase any gossip that might begin to flow from whatever tales the Crichtons might tell, Mrs Hoggart being – he hoped – slightly more discreet.

Just as he was about to eat his evening meal – shin of beef – he felt compelled to check the cellar door, and found it locked. The key was in his jacket pocket, the weight of it threatening to tear the material, but he did not want to leave it anywhere he could not see or feel it.

He had just stepped into the dining room, plate in hand, when he heard the unmistakable sound of the cellar door opening. He put the plate on the table, picked up the shotgun, and went to the hall. As before, he could see the stairs winding down, and detected the distant flicker of candlelight. On this occasion though, a kind of rage infected his fear. He had tired of the game.

'Damn you,' he said, and he repeated the words over and over as he stamped down the stairs. 'Damn you, damn you, damn you …'

The bottle of Bordeaux stood opened and decanted on the table, a fresh candle had been set in the candleholder, and the same darkness occupied the depths of the cellar, but the atmosphere had changed. He could not have said why, but he was acutely aware of a presence in the shadows, one that he felt was watching him closely and curiously. Strangest of all – and for the first time since this peculiar ritual had begun – he felt his rage ebb, and his fear faded along with it. He was now certain that he was not alone in the cellar, but whatever regarded him wished him no harm. Neither, though, did it want to be seen, or not clearly: he thought that he caught movement in the dark, a hint of grey and white against black, but when he moved closer it retreated from him, although it did not vanish entirely.

'Who are you?' he asked. 'What are you?'

The presence did not answer.

'What do you want?'

Yet that, at least, seemed clear: it wanted him to drink.

Almost resignedly, he lowered the shotgun.

'Fine, then,' he said, 'if I must.'

He placed the weapon against the wall, and a thought struck him. He didn't want to drink the wine without food – in fact, he had a distinct feeling that the Bordeaux might have been re-opened with the shin of beef in mind – so he returned to the dining room, retrieved his dinner, and, after only a moment's hesitation, descended back to the cellar. He took the seat that had been prepared for him before pouring himself a glass from the decanter. His hand was heavy, and he filled the glass slightly higher than was advisable. From the darkness came an audible intake of breath, a kind of sniff of mild disapproval.

'Sorry,' he said, and then wondered to whom – or what – he was apologising.

He sniffed the wine, and took a sip, swilling it in his mouth to release the flavours. It was wonderful. He had forgotten how good a glass of wine could taste.

He ate and drank slowly, occasionally staring awkwardly into the dark from his chair, and the presence stared back at him. Oddly, it took on a greater definition when he did not look directly at it. If he tried to pick it out of the gloom, it might have been mistaken for a trick of the light caused by the movement of the candle's flame. But if he looked aside, in the direction of the racks or the cellar walls, it assumed a degree of clarity. A man, he thought: big, and dressed in the manner of a household servant. Hints of black and grey. A bow tie.

The glass was empty. He poured himself another. A peace settled over him. He should get a dog, he decided. He and his wife hadn't wanted another after the last one died. It was just too hard to say farewell, and anyway, with Simon gone and Caroline about to leave, there didn't seem to be much point. They had talked about traveling more once the children were settled, and –

He realised, quite gradually, that he was speaking aloud.

He stopped talking, and put the glass down. Emotions that had been kept constrained for too long suddenly threatened to overwhelm him.

'Enough,' he said.

He stood, abandoning the shotgun, and went up the stairs, not caring that he had turned his back on whatever waited in the darkness. He just wanted to be gone from the cellar. As he closed the door behind him, the candle was extinguished. He might once have attributed it to his own actions, or the draft from the door, except now he knew better.

The entity in the cellar, he thought, preferred the dark.

The next day, he retrieved the shotgun – the lights working once more, the cellar somehow different in daylight hours – and tramped his fields and forests with a new urgency, as though by hunting he could forget the events of the previous night. He wanted that fox. He was certain that it was not dead.

Had it been removed from the world, he would surely have felt its absence.

But the fox, as always, eluded him.

That night, the cellar door opened, but he did not go down, and in time the candle was blown out. The second night, the same.

On the third, he returned.

The bottle – a Châteauneuf-du-Pape from Saint Préfert, one of the first such wines bottled in the previous decade – stood unopened, but the glass, the decanter, and the candle were all in place. He experienced a moment of disappointment at the sight of the uncorked bottle until he recovered himself and saw reflected in its intact nature the decision of someone who cared for wine, of one who, after two nights without the appearance of the awaited guest, did not wish to waste a good bottle by decanting it and then watch it go undrunk. He turned his head to the left, taking in the racks, then allowed his gaze to shift to the right. In the shadows, the shape of a man hovered. He could almost see his face, and the grey hair above it.

He opened the bottle, checked the cork, then decanted the wine. He waited a while before carefully filling the glass to the correct level. He sniffed, tasted, and – satisfied – took his seat.

'It's very good,' he said.

If this was madness, he felt, then it was a fine madness.

He thought that the shape in the dark shifted slightly, as though it had just given a small bow of acknowledgement.

He leaned forward in his chair, cupping the glass in his hands, warming the wine.

He opened his mouth, and began to speak.

'The first time I saw her, she was wearing a blue dress ...'

Later, he barely remembered stumbling up the stairs. The house was in darkness, but he was not afraid. He ignored the couch, and the shotgun, and made his way to his own bed. His throat hurt, but he could not recall weeping.

He slept, and when he woke his sorrow had eased.

And so it went on, evening after evening: a bottle waiting for him, a glass, a candle, and somewhere in the darkness of the cellar, movement.

A presence, listening.

'Simon was always a quiet child ...'

'I thought that Caroline might have become a painter ...'

'My wife once had a new variety of rose named after me as a birthday gift ...'

He even found a possible identity for his confessor, buried deep in the records of the house and those who had served in it over the years. No first name, no hint as to his origins, just a surname: Evans, who had supervised the transformation of the cellar into a suitable repository for wine, and built up the original collection back in the early part of the nineteenth century. When he asked Mrs Hoggart about him, she claimed to know nothing. She made enquiries in the village, but no one could recall an Evans.

'Not from around here, whoever he was,' Mrs Hoggart told him. 'Someone would have known him otherwise.'

It took him three days to speak the name aloud in the cellar, and when he did so he detected a change in the emanations from the entity, a kind of closing of the distance between them, and he thought that he could somehow see the man more clearly, although still only if he did not look at him directly.

One week after he began speaking to Evans, sharing his memories, he was walking in the woods, the shotgun over his arm, when he came across the fox. He knew it from the markings on its side. A female, he thought: he could see its teats.

It was standing in the path before him, perhaps a dozen feet away at most. The shotgun was loaded. He brought the barrel up and closed the break. The click was loud, and he saw the animal's ears move in response to it, but it did not flee from him. Instead it remained where it was, as though to say *Here I am. You have sought me for so long, and I am tired of hiding from you. Do what you will. Do what you must.*

He levelled the gun at the fox, and put his finger to the trigger. He felt it give beneath the weight. Slowly, slowly …

He closed his eyes. When he opened them again, the fox had changed position. It was now sitting on its rear haunches, regarding him closely.

He lowered the shotgun, opened the break, and let the shells fall to the ground. Perhaps he had always known that it would end this way. If he were to kill the animal, what would he have left?

The fox rose, and moved away. He watched it vanish into the undergrowth, and then it was lost to him.

He never saw the creature again.

Weeks went by. Each evening he went to the cellar, but often he did not drink, and sometimes he did not even talk. But always Evans was waiting, and if he wished to speak, then Evans would listen.

The pains began to intensify about two months after he had seen the fox. He had been enduring them for a year, but had chosen to ignore them until they started to come between him and his sleep. The doctors spoke of tumours that had spread through his system, and admitted that surgery would be of little benefit at this stage. He would be helped with his pain, and they would do their best to make the end as comfortable as possible.

But death is not comfortable, and he suffered.

A team of nurses cared for him in his final weeks, and during that time he managed one last visit to the cellar. A nurse helped him down the stairs, and then left him alone, as requested. A bottle stood on the table, and a glass, but the candle had not been lit.

Evans, being careful with company in the house.

He lit the candle himself with a match. The shadows retreated. At the very periphery of the illumination, he picked out the toes of a pair of polished shoes, and a servant's livery, and a face hovering above it all like a waning moon.

He poured himself a glass of wine. It was a 1928 Château Mouton Rothschild, a jewel of the cellar, but he could only manage a few mouthfuls. It seemed a shame to waste it, he thought: he replaced the cork, and determined to give it to the nurse to take home with her when she left the next morning.

'I came to say thank you, Evans,' he said, 'and I came to say goodbye. These evenings with you have meant a great deal to me. They have helped me in ways that I cannot even begin to explain. I shall miss our times together.'

He put the glass down. He felt a strange sense of disappointment that, even now, when they were about to be parted, Evans would not permit himself to be seen. The feeling passed. He had no right to be disappointed with Evans, no right at all.

He stood. He called for the nurse, and heard her footsteps on the stairs. He wondered if she had been listening. No matter.

'Farewell, Evans,' he said.

He blew out the candle, and Evans was gone.

Three days later, shortly before midnight, he lay on his deathbed and dreamed. He was on the forest path, and he saw the fox. When the animal moved into the undergrowth, he followed it.

He slept, and he died.

*

Darkness visible through a gap in the curtains. Starlight and moonlight. Sounds, voices. His gown hanging on the door.

He rose from his bed, and put on the gown. The room smelled of fresh pine and wood smoke. He opened the bedroom door and walked to the landing. The stairs stretched down to the hall, where a woman was adjusting the position of a Christmas ribbon around a mirror.

She looked up at him.

'You're awake.'

'Yes.'

'We've been waiting for you, the children and I.'

He started to cry. He could not stop himself.

'Oh,' she said. 'Oh, oh.'

She took him in her arms, and held him until he was ready to show his face.

'Where are they?' he asked.

'Walking in the woods, but they won't be long. Dinner will be ready soon, so you'll have to hurry up and get dressed. Why don't you choose a bottle of champagne for us to share? After all, it is Christmas. And,' she added, 'I think there is someone you might like to meet.'

The cellar door stood open. A candle flickered.

He descended.

A bottle stood on the table: Krug, 1928, one of the greatest vintages. Beside it was a tray with four champagne flutes.

A man emerged from the shadows, both strange and familiar.

'Hello, Evans.'

'Hello, sir. I took the liberty of chilling the Krug.'

'I see that. A very good choice.'

'And I've set aside a bottle or two of Claret to go with the goose.'

'I expect that will be just fine.'

He looked at the Krug.

'Why don't you open that now, and perhaps pour a glass for both of us?'

'Most kind, sir.'

He watched as Evans uncorked the champagne, the candlelight illuminating the spectral cloud of the vapour. Evans poured, they toasted, and they drank.

'All is well,' he said.

'Yes, sir. All is well.'

And the evenings with Evans stretch on forever.

Alan Glynn

Alan Glynn was born in 1960. His first novel, *The Dark Fields*, was published in 2002. It was later filmed, and re-issued, as *Limitless*. *Winterland* was published in 2009 and was followed in 2011 by *Bloodland*, which won the Bord Gáis Energy Irish Crime Novel of the Year Award and was also nominated for an Edgar. The third in his 'globalisation noir' trilogy, *Graveland*, came out in 2013. His latest novel, *Paradime*, was published by Faber in 2016. He lives in Dublin with his wife and two sons.

The Copyist

This isn't going to work.

That was my first thought.

How *could* it?

As I stood there in the Oval Office, no more than two or three feet away from the president, it struck me that the project was more than likely doomed, and not because of any problem with the technology involved – I'd never questioned that – it was because of how heavily the whole thing depended on *me*.

I was Darrell Limbic, recent recruit to the Fugit Program and erstwhile gazzu practioner. *He* was John F. Kennedy.

How did I ever think I could pull this off?

But there was no turning back. Not now. The overlap was only a matter of seconds. I blinked – literally – and he was gone.

There'd been a look in his eyes. I barely registered it when he was in front of me, but it lingered now as an after-image. What I saw was shock, bewilderment, then a flicker of fear.

I wonder what he saw in my eyes.

After a moment, I glanced around. Everything here was familiar to me – the Resolute desk, the tall drapes, the green rug, the naval paintings. Somewhere in the background, I could hear muffled voices and the clacking of a typewriter. I knew that the high strangeness of all this wouldn't hit me until I came face to face with a flesh-and-blood person from 1963, or until I went outside into the clean, open air of a long-gone Kodachrome Washington DC, with its Lincoln Continentals and Buick Rivieras, its cherry blossoms and early Brutalist office complexes. Nothing, no amount of training, could prepare me for that.

Nevertheless, I *was* trained and despite my initial misgivings I knew deep down that the advantage in this situation was going to be mine. If I lapsed in some way, or failed to convince, the burden would be on them to rationalise it. In the absence of an alternative, what choice would they have?

I turned, leaned back against the desk, and gazed down at the rug, savouring these last moments of stillness. Then I heard a door opening over to my right. I drew in a deep breath and looked up. 'Bobby.'

'I think we got the son of a bitch, Jack.'

Robert Kennedy walked towards me, holding up a sheaf of papers. Another figure appeared behind him. I think it was Kenny O'Donnell, though I wasn't certain, because I was too focused on Bobby, on those familiar features, amplified a thousand times now by their sudden vividness, their immediacy.

I'd been told not to stare, so I glanced down at his shoes and folded my arms. Caution was needed here. Location coordinates were pinpoint accurate, but the timeline was a little fluid. I could guess who and what Bobby was referring to. I just couldn't be sure how far along the timeline we were. 'So, tell me,' I said. 'What have you got?'

'OK, look,' he said, handing the papers to the other man, 'Ellen Rometsch aside, I think it's airtight.' He joined me at the desk, leaning back against it and folding his own arms. 'Don Reynolds is going to sing like a goddamned canary. There's the cash for the TFX contract, the ad buys, even the Magnavox stereo set for Lady Bird.'

'He's going before the Committee?'

'Yeah. Plus, I've got a guy over at *Life* working on a big exposé. That should kick it all off. It'll be Baker, Baker, Baker, then boom, Lyndon takes it in the ass.'

I knew where I was now. It was the end of October and this was Bobby's elaborate plan to get LBJ off the ticket in '64. I glanced sideways and saw the intensity in his face, hatred and loyalty radiating from his pores. I almost felt sorry for him.

'I don't know, Bobby.'

'What? You're worried about Rometsch? Don't be. Hoover's all over it. He knows that a German call girl with links to Baker wouldn't look good for Lyndon. So believe me, she won't be showing up again any time soon.'

That wasn't what I'd meant, but I let it go. Anyway, I needed more time to orient myself, to pass a mirror or two, to hear myself pronounce certain words – maybe even to relieve a headache in the traditional Kennedy manner – before getting down to the *real* business at hand.

Unsurprisingly, my schedule was hectic. Within ten minutes I was sitting down with Dean Rusk and General Maxwell Taylor. Then I was off to lunch at the Bolivian embassy, followed by a meeting with a select group of congressmen on civil rights legislation. Later, I had a swim in the White House pool, and after that an unscheduled – apparently – assignation in the residence with Mary Pinchot Meyer. I'd read up on the relationship, and was aware of its significance, but to be honest there hadn't been any practical training in this department, so when she came on to me I got scared and told her (I can't actually believe I did this) that I had a *headache*. It was humiliating and the feeling lasted into the following morning, but I used the energy from it to deal with the Bobby situation.

'You want me to *resign*? What the fuck, Jack?' He shook his head in disbelief. 'Are you *drunk*?'

'No, I'm being . . . pragmatic.'

This wasn't easy . . . how to tell Bobby that *he* was the problem, and that everyone who hated him, who feared him – the unions, the mob, the Cubans, the CIA, Lyndon, especially Lyndon – had all more or less concluded that the best way to get rid of him was to get rid of *me* . . .

So, nip the Bobby situation in the bud, do it now, and everyone calms down.

This was something I'd spent three years preparing for in a national security facility in New Jersey. I'd undergone reconstructive surgery and cosmetic gene therapy. I'd uploaded a suite of Jack-specific medical conditions that were programmed to self-neutralise within a month. I'd worked extensively with voice and movement coaches. I'd done a wide-ranging study of relevant primary sources. My objective, my *mission*, was simply to get beyond November, and then the real Jack Kennedy, fully debriefed and nano-augmented, would be returned from the year 2053 to continue on his illustrious career trajectory.

I would be returned as well, to the facility in New Jersey, and to what would most likely be a hero's welcome. JFK had said we'd travel to the moon within a decade. Little did he know that within less than a century we'd be travelling through time. Granted, the Fugit Program was still in its infancy, and I was something of a pioneer, but there was no question – based on how *this* part was going – that the technology worked.

I looked down at Bobby now. He was still struggling with my suggestion that he resign.

'Jesus Christ, Jack . . . what the hell is going on?'

If only he knew.

'Look, Bobby . . .'

I'd have to tell him something, but it certainly wouldn't be that I had travelled ninety years back in time, and that his brother – assuming it'd *all* gone to plan – had travelled forward in my place.

(ii)

He stands still, eyes closed, waiting for this hallucination to end. He thinks it might be the medication he's on, the ever-expanding cocktail of drugs he needs on a daily basis now just to function – cortisone, procaine, phenobarbital, penicillin, steroids, antihistamines, to say nothing of Max Jacobson's indispensable amphetamine injections, or –

Or . . .

And this might be the most germane: that LSD he took recently with Mary Pinchot Meyer, eight steely-blue hours, liquid and luminous, of personal unspooling. So is it any wonder that his brain is scrambled? That he's seeing things? Seeing his own double in front of him, right there in the Oval, and then seeing, well . . . *nothing* . . . except for what appeared – in the millisecond before he closed his eyes – to be a dusty, brick wall? Holding his fists in a tight grip now, and with twinges of pain shooting down his back, he waits another few seconds. Bobby is due in any minute with Kenny O'Donnell. Then he has a sit-down with Dean Rusk and Max Taylor. After that, there's lunch at the Bolivian embassy. He needs to pull himself together here.

But there's something odd. With his eyes closed, the aural landscape is different, it's hollow, there's no sound of Mrs Lincoln clacking away in the background on her Royal electric.

He opens his eyes and is hit with an immediate shockwave of incomprehension. Because this is not the Oval Office. And that *is* a dusty, brick wall in front of him . . .

The gable end, it seems, of a –

He looks up.

Is it a warehouse? Or a . . . a factory?

Jesus H. Christ. Where is he? And how did this happen? He turns quickly, taking in his surroundings. He's outdoors, but in some kind of alleyway, where the ground is rough and muddy.

He takes a couple of steps forward, but his shoes squelch in the mud. He looks down at them. They're *dirty* now. Jesus. And –

This has just hit him.

There's a very strange smell. In the air. A heavy stench.

He looks up and around.

No hallucination can be *this* real. He must have blacked out in the Oval and then somehow wandered off, in a trance, and found his way *here* – wherever here is. But what about Mrs Lincoln, his staff, the security guys? He hasn't been properly alone or unmonitored like this in years, literally, so this whole thing is … impossible.

Unless.

Did Khrushchev really do it? Was there was a nuclear strike? The silly bastard didn't like his speech in June, the test-ban proposal?

He takes a few more steps forward, knowing in his heart that this isn't what the fallout from a nuclear explosion would look like.

'*BOBBY.*'

He's desperate now, terrified.

'Kenny? *Hello*? *IS ANYONE HERE?*'

He makes his way to the other end of the alley, which opens on to a wide thoroughfare, but it has to be a movie set or something, because all the buildings he can see are old, and grimy, single-storey units most of them. Scanning the row opposite, he registers the words 'saloon' and 'dry goods'. Then he sees why this isn't a movie set. The source of the stench, ten yards or so to his left, is a huge, rotting carcass, probably of a horse. It's just abandoned there on the side of the street.

Oh God, please make this stop.

Taking a deep breath, he turns in the other direction. The whole place seems deserted. But then he spots two men coming out of a building. He walks towards them. 'Hello? *Hello*?'

When the two men turn and see him, they flinch in what he can only interpret as shock or disbelief. And this is precisely what *he* feels the closer he gets to *them*. They're both short and gnarled-looking, with leathery skin, and beards. They're also both wearing dirty overcoats and stovepipe hats.

There is a moment of silence as each side studies the other.

'Gentlemen,' he then says, smiling deliberately, 'can you help me out here?'

'Good Lord,' one of the men says, almost recoiling. 'Look at them teeth.'

'And that suit of clothes,' the other man says. 'I ain't never seen anything like it. You must be one of them New York banker fellas, are you? Set off this panic everyone's talking about?'

'A regular Jay Cooke we got here.'

They both laugh.

He looks at them, his heart pounding. 'What . . . you mean the *panic of '73?*'

'Yeah,' one of the men says. 'That's prolly what they'll be calling it all right.'

'I mean, you have to figure,' the other man says, a smirk growing on his face, 'seeing as how this *is* 1873 and all.'

They both laugh again.

He glances around – at the desolate street, up at the glowering sky – and the absurdity of everything, the lucid, nightmarish quality of it all, becomes close to unbearable.

'So, mister, if you're not the Commodore, or Jim Fisk, or any of *that* gang, just who the hell are you?'

He turns back to face the two small men. 'Who am I? Why, I'm the . . .'

But suddenly even this strikes him as absurd.

'Yeah?'

'I'm . . .' He swallows. 'I'm ... my name is John Kennedy.'

(iii)

Shafting Bobby like that was hard, but it had the desired effect. Johnson didn't know what to think, which I guess was a new and uncomfortable position for him to be in. McGeorge Bundy and Bob McNamara were completely blindsided, and J. Edgar's reaction, I felt, was a mixture of petulence and paranoia. As for what Allen Dulles, Jimmy Hoffa and Carlos Marcello thought, I could only imagine. In any case, when I announced a few days later that I was cancelling the trip to Dallas, no one even questioned it – at least not openly. The entire Washington establishment (not to mention the criminal underworld) was now in a sort of holding pattern. None of them knew what my next move would be, but it looked as if they were prepared to wait and find out.

Which is what I wanted.

A little breathing space.

Because at the end of November (or early December at the latest), I'd be gone, *he'd* be back, and the next move wouldn't be my concern. I wasn't really qualified for the big stuff anyway, for policy questions or power intrigues. I could sustain the look and the voice for hours at a time, playing Bobby off against Jackie, say, or Dave Power off against Pierre Salinger, and I had a massive data load to draw from, but having to interact with other heads of state or to make actual decisions? That was nerve-racking. I was also conscious of an accumulating air of perplexity in the White House, one that thickened occasionally into undeniable suspicion. But then my chronic back pain, or symptoms of some other condition I had – matters well-known to members of the inner circle – would come to the fore and obliterate whatever concerns people might be having … concerns about either, I *guess*, my identity or my sanity. I learned to play these symptoms to my advantage, however, by ramping them up or toning them down, according to the circumstances.

And, eventually, in this way ... November 22 came and went.

It was strange to see the front pages of the *Washington Post* and *The New York Times* that weekend, and over the following days, taken up as they were with such relatively pedestrian issues as tax cuts and the foreign aid programme. Nevertheless, I breathed a sigh of relief. It was now a matter of running down the clock, and I kept busy, subtly directing my time and attention to the mundane, the uncontroversial. Jackie and her sister vacationed in Italy and Bobby went on an extended sulk down in Palm Beach. To the confusion of my secret service detail, I abstained from any clandestine assignations and spent a good deal of time instead with Ben Bradlee, gossiping about various congressmen and Washington insiders.

The whole experience, up to that point, had been like a dream, and I was expecting it to end like one, too – suddenly, unexpectedly. I'd be alone in the Oval one moment, and *he'd* be there the next, in front of me. We'd barely have enough time to share a grin of recognition.

But ...

I don't know exactly when I felt the first chill of doubt, but it must have been in the early days of December. It had been over a month and I was starting to get antsy, distracted. I'd look around, and think, it could be any second now.

And then, it *should* be any second now.

And then ... why hasn't it happened yet?

When my various symptoms disappeared – overnight, and to the astonishment of my doctors – I had to wrestle with a rising sense of panic. Of course, it was a relief not to feel sick anymore, or be in pain, but it was also more than a little awkward. The level of scrutiny I was subjected to, already pretty intense, went into overdrive.

When another couple of weeks passed – with Jackie home, and Lyndon showboating it in front of the Senate Rules Committee, and Khruschev on the phone nearly every other day – I was soon overwhelmed. The real Kennedy should have been back by now, the enhanced model, reinvigorated and fully equipped to take on the next four years. So what was the delay? Was there some technical hitch? How much longer would *I* have to wait?

My mental state soon became a cause of concern for those around me. Jackie stopped waving her affair with Gianni Agnelli in my face and Bobby started talking to me again. There was also pressure from various quarters to get started in earnest on the re-election campaign.

By the time January 1, 1964, rolled around, I was facing into the abyss. What if it had all gone wrong? What if I was stuck here?

(iv)

As a Kennedy, he prides himself on his stamina and vigor, on his capacity for physical endurance. But if the current situation drags on much longer – if he has no access to his pills, say, or if he misses his shots – he's pretty sure that sooner or later the pain will kill him. For the moment, this is as extreme a test of his *mental* endurance as he has ever experienced.

He leaves the 'town', which the two small gentlemen told him was in New Jersey, and walks a random mile into undeveloped, increasingly rugged countryside. As a result, he quickly discounts the idea that this might be a movie set he has stumbled across or some kind of Civil War (*post*-Civil War) re-enactment, because … well, it already extends over much too wide an area.

And besides, in any case . . . *how*?

The test here – the real challenge – is to keep functioning, to hold it together in the face of the illogical, the irrational, the impossible. If there's an alternative, it's to lie down on the ground, curl up into a foetal ball and start crying.

But that's not going to happen.

Because what would the old man do? What would Joe Jr do?

He trudges on and before long encounters a portly gentleman and his daughter, who give him a ride in their horse-drawn carriage. They ask him questions and seem by turns intrigued and alarmed by his answers. He finds *them* unutterably strange. A glance at their clothes, at their general demeanour, and you might think they were from central casting, but there are depths of realism here that confound him. There is the gentleman's wheeze, for example, his jowliness, and the girl's pale skin, her striking green eyes, her beguiling voice (he definitely *would*) – but at the same time he is repelled, almost to the point of gagging, by a dense whiff they're giving off, of body odour, or bad breath, or both. Nevertheless, he forces out as much charm as he can muster, because – he decides – he needs these people. As long as he is interacting with them, he doesn't have to think.

Later, that night, lying on a cot in a second-floor room of their timber-framed house in Bergen County, he does something he hasn't done in years, at least not sincerely – he prays. If the fabric of reality can be so casually riven, he speculates, then perhaps there is a God. And this is a test of some kind. But he doesn't *know*. Maybe it's that his brain was severely damaged by that LSD he took. Or maybe he's just dreaming. But if he goes asleep now, as it seems he might, will he dream *then*? And where will he be when he wakes up?

Or . . .

An option he can't believe he's even considering. Maybe this really *is* 1873.

He goes asleep on the cot, and when he wakes up, he's still there. He's also hungry, and in pain. For breakfast, they give him cornbread and some cold stew. For his sore back they give him a dose of Dr Abernathy's Soothing Cordial, which contains laudanum. He flirts relentlessly with the daughter, but a combination of the old man's watchful eye and some pushback from the laudanum keeps him out of trouble.

After a few days with these good people, however, he decides to move on. Just across the river lies the island of Manhattan, and two hundred miles north of that again is the city of Boston. He can't help wondering if it would be possible to make his way up there at some point – and, who knows, maybe locate his grandfather.

P. J. Kennedy.

Who would now be a boy of, what . . . fifteen?

That'd be something.

With the portly gentleman's indulgent blessing, as well as an old overcoat, a few dollars, a bottle of Dr Abernathy's Cordial, and a couple of addresses – not to mention a longing glance from the daughter – he sets off on his own to catch the ferry to New York from the waterfront in Jersey City.

(v)

As the weeks and months passed, I tried my best to fake it. I sat at the cabinet table, went to summit meetings, made speeches. I was photographed with the Beatles in the Rose Garden and attended the launch of *Gemini 1*. I even managed to seduce the odd society hostess. But the whole time I was dying inside. Nothing I did felt authentic, and never once did I see a light in anyone's eye – that Kennedy effect I'd read so much about. What I seemed to be presiding over was not only the routinisation but the very dismantling of his charisma. Articles ran week after week that asked the same question: WHAT HAPPENED TO JFK?

Ultimately, in November, Barry Goldwater took the White House and I was consigned to the garbage pail of history, a lightweight one-term president who barely had an impact at all. If I got any credit, it was for my role in the missile crisis – but that, of course, wasn't *me*.

I retreated to Hyannis Port and pretended I was writing a book. Mostly what I did was drink, and eat – and, at a push, when they'd let me, poke the local talent. What choice did I have? Even if they somehow managed, at this stage, to return me to 2053, it would be too late. The damage was done. I'd be vilified, or ridiculed, or worse.

One of the hardest parts in all of this for me was the tedium. Memories of who I really was were fading, and any new memories were compromised. As a result, I struggled to care, and eventually my behavior grew reckless. It could never be said, I suppose, that I was careful about preserving my presidential legacy and pretty much everything I did from that point on ended up being fodder for the tabloids. I got drunk and threw up at Governor Richard Nixon's funeral in '67, for example. The following summer, Jackie and I went through a messy and very public divorce. In '75, I was arrested for attempting to smuggle a kilo of cocaine into Italy (you can see photos of a fifty-eight-year-old me, heavyset and bearded, being escorted by *carabinieri* from Rome's Fiumicino Airport). Two years after that, on some sort of redemptive road to recovery, I married Farrah Fawcett in a Buddhist ceremony in Havana. And one of my final acts as a 'politician' – before the inevitable veil of long-term and debilitating illness came down – was to endorse Warren Beatty's nomination at the 1984 Democratic National Convention . . .

(vi)

It has the novelty of being a real job, the first paid employment he's ever had. Unless you count being president. But that was more paid *for*, and never felt like proper work. This does, copying documents at a high desk – mortgages, title deeds, bonds – and doing it all day long, just so he can afford to pay for his board and lodging, for clothes and books, *and* for a steady supply of Soothing Cordial (stronger, local versions of which are called McIvor's Elixir of Opium, White's Paregoric, or, simply, Poison). These make life somewhat bearable and as he sits there, back arched, scratching out line after line of dense text on sheets of foolscap paper, he has time to think, to dream.

By using a combination of moxie and natural charm, he has managed to get this far. But by using the cache of what amounts to insider knowledge embedded in his memory – that expensive education he suffered through – surely he can get a whole lot further. OK, the Panic of 1873 (as he recalls) did usher in a six-year-long depression, so the timing isn't great, but when it comes to railroads and oil, to electricity – to the *telephone*, for Christ's sake – couldn't he somehow get in on the ground floor? Steal a march on everyone? On P. J., who's still a whole five years off getting into the goddamned saloon business up in Boston? Steal a march even – a *big* one, since he hasn't been born yet – on the old man?

He just needs to figure out which stocks to buy . . . and with *what*.

This will take time. He doesn't earn a great deal, and while his various laudanum concoctions aren't expensive, he needs several of them every day now, so there isn't much left over for investing and speculation. Another possibility would be to take a crack at Tammany Hall (currently in a fever of moral probity, post Tweed), but at the moment that doesn't seem very practical. This is a very different Democratic Party from the one he knows, and although he has already forged certain strategic relationships, his own 'ring', so to speak, is extremely narrow.

At night, a Colt revolver in his pocket, he walks the streets in a sort of reverie, passing tenements, mansions, warehouses, whorehouses, slaughterhouses. In his head, he pictures being the president, *remembers* it, the Oval, the speeches, the steady stream of girls, all clean, all fragrant. He remembers the titanic struggles, as well, with the spidery network of bureaucrats and spies and generals and bankers.

Did that stuff really happen?

At the office one day, three men in greatcoats and top hats come in. They shake hands with his employer and proceed to hold a private confab not far from his high desk. As they speak, he continues copying, and assiduously so, but he listens, too, and before long has understood what it is they're talking about: a proposed alliance between the Pennsylvania, New York Central and Erie railroads on the one hand, and a handful of oil refining companies, most notably Standard Oil, on the other. He works out pretty quickly that in terms of its ramifications, this is arguably one of the biggest business manoeuvres in history. And holy shit, of *course* – that's John D. Rockefeller. Right there. The small, intense one with the beady eyes.

The chief conspirator.

'Who's that?' one of the other men asks suspiciously, pointing in the direction of the high desk.

'That's Kennedy,' his employer says. 'Fastest scrivener I ever had.'

'Kennedy?' Rockefeller says quietly, and grunts. 'I didn't know Catholics could *write*.'

They all share a laugh.

Outside, a while later, blood boiling, he follows the three men along the street. He withdraws his Colt and calls out Rockefeller's name. When the small man turns, he shoots him square between the eyes.

Dropping the revolver, he then flees the scene.

Afterwards, accounts of what happened differ wildly. According to the *Tribune*, the killer – who will never be caught – was a transient. *The Times* and the *Herald* dig a little deeper, calling John Kennedy a 'disaffected copyist' and a 'deluded soul who believed he was the president'. But the *Sun* claims to know even more. This was a carefully orchestrated plot, they say, an attempt by larger forces to halt the gallop of America's new industrial economy.

It takes him a few weeks to reach Boston. Along the way, everything deteriorates – his clothes become tattered, he gets a fever and can't stop shivering, his back eventually feels as if it has fractured, and perhaps it has. But when he arrives at the edge of Haymarket Square, he gazes around in wonder. Scanning the crowd, he looks for a familiar face . . . familiar features, at any rate. They *have* to be here.

Out of the blue, three young rowdies rush past and one of them knocks him over. As he's falling – and it's into the path of an oncoming horse-drawn delivery cart – he catches a flash of something in the kid's face. It's unmistakable. But is it the eyes? The cheekbones? The jawline? As he hits the ground, smiling one last time, he's pretty sure it's the jawline.

Adrian McKinty

Adrian McKinty was born and grew up in Carrickfergus, Northern Ireland. He has written ten crime novels, mostly set in and around Belfast during the Troubles.

Fivemiletown

I got to know her first as the girl who had never had a birthday.

'What do you mean she's never had a birthday?'

'Oh, she's never had one,' Rachel replied absently, staring out the Subaru's side window.

'I don't understand how she's never had a birthday. Was she born on a leap year or something?'

Rachel put down her iPad and frowned. 'What are you talking about? Of course she's had a birthday. Everyone's had a birthday. We're throwing her a surprise birthday party. She's never had a birthday *party*.'

'Oh.'

I finally put a face to this mysterious birthday-less girl at school the next week. It was raining and I was sheltering under an umbrella trying to decipher the latest mildly threatening communication from Brian's lawyers when Rachel came running across the playground.

'Mum . . . Mum . . . Mum!'

I looked up and she was standing next to a very pale, very pretty dark-haired girl.

'Oh, hello,' I said.

'Mum, this is Anna, can you give her a lift home? She has to walk miles and it's raining,' Rachel said.

'No problem,' I replied, turning off the phone. 'Where do you live, Anna?'

'It's not too far from here,' she said so softly I could barely hear her. Her accent was clearly Irish though.

'Get in.'

'I can walk it. It's OK.'

'Get in.'

She sat in the back seat and I got a good look at her in the rear-view mirror. Pretty yes, but a fragility about her too. Something about the vulnerability of those green eyes. And in a year or two she was going to break a lot of hearts.

We drove to the address which was a block of flats in Hackney. Windows were broken on the ground floor and what once had been the building's car park was filled with rubbish from overturned bins. There were no cars in the lot and there didn't seem to be any lights on anywhere in the complex.

'This is the right address?'

'Yup!' Anna said.

'Where do you live?'

'Upstairs.'

'Should we . . . should I walk you up?'

She thought about it for a moment. 'If you like. I'd lock the car, though.'

We walked through a broken front door and along a corridor strewn with old chip papers, beer cans and kids clothes. I could hear a TV blaring upstairs and the sound of children playing.

'Wow, this is cool. Is this a squat?' Rachel asked, much to my embarrassment.

Anna shook her head. 'Everyone thinks that, but it's actually not. We pay rent,' she said cheerfully.

We climbed a concrete staircase strewn with more clothes and a few toys. Anna's place was a two-bedroom flat at the end of the corridor. The door was open and we went inside together. Anna introduced us to her family. Her father, Rob, was about forty, a handsome, bearded Irishman who walked with a stick. He was surrounded by eight or possibly nine kids aged from three to sixteen. The flat smelled mildewy and stale but the kids were clothed and reasonably clean. I introduced Rachel and myself.

'Thanks for leaving Anna off,' Rob said.

'Oh no problem, it was raining,' I explained.

'Nice place, huh?'

'Well . . .'

'This is what the council puts us up in. Can you believe it? My wife pregnant too. All our allowance going to pay the rent on this bloody tip. Bloody Labour are as bad as the bloody Tories,' he said in a fast Irish accent that I had trouble following.

'How long have you been here?'

'We came to London just after Easter. Thought it would be better for the kids. Ha! It's worse.'

'Where did you come from?'

'Fivemiletown.'

I wanted to ask where that was but Rachel was tugging surreptitiously at my dress.

'Well, uhm, look we have to go. It was nice meeting you, Rob,' I said.

'Nice meeting you too. Thanks for giving Anna the lift. She's the apple of my eye this one,' Rob said, fluffing Anna's hair.

'Bye,' I said and hustled us out of there.

Rachel was relieved when we were back in the car. 'God. Pikey central. Now I understand why she cuts her own hair and why she never had a birthday party. Wait till I tell everyone.'

'Uhm, maybe you shouldn't tell everyone, Rachel. I think Anna might not like that.'

Rachel nodded. 'Oh? Yeah. You're probably right.'

The next time I saw Anna it was a week later in the playground as school was starting. She had a purple bruise under her left eye.

'My God, what happened to you?'

'Oh that? Can you still see that? Mum put concealer on it but I told her it wasn't going to work.'

'What happened?'

'Nothing. I fell down the stairs. No lights. I suppose everyone is going to ask about it school now.'

'Are . . . are you sure everything's OK, Anna?'

Her dark green eyes flashed. 'Jesus Christ! You're as nosey as the bloody social workers!' she said and stormed across the playground.

That afternoon I picked Rachel up at 3.30 and she wasn't pleased to see me. 'Anna said you were asking her all sorts of questions about her eye?'

'How about "*Hello, how are you mum? How was your day?*"'

'Hello mum. How was your day? Why were you hassling Anna on her way to school?'

'I just asked her about her bruise.'

'Yeah, well don't. She's sensitive about it. One of the teachers already reported it to the school social worker and they called the Old Bill. And the cops went and questioned her dad. OK?'

'I didn't know that.'

'Well now you do! It was nothing to do with her dad. Her dad's on disability. She got in a fight with her little brother, Jeremy. He's autistic, OK? He hit her when she was trying to calm him down.'

'She told me she fell down the stairs.'

'Well, that's the true story. Her little brother clocked her. Not her dad or her mum. Bad timing too for all the party photographs.'

'What party photographs?'

'Do you listen to anything I tell you? It's Anna's surprise birthday tonight. Carol, Judy's mum, is throwing it. Anna thinks she's going for an ordinary sleepover but it's really her surprise party!'

Later that night I drove Rachel to Carol's house. Carol and I had never got on. She had always liked Brian and I think she found me dull in comparison.

We rang the bell and when Carol opened it Rachel ran inside.

Carol smiled. 'Good to see you again, Kate. It's been a while,' she said.

'Yes, I've been . . . busy. Well, this is a nice thing you're doing,' I said.

She nodded. 'That poor girl. She needs something in her life. Have you seen where she lives?'

'I have actually.'

'She does all the cooking, all the shopping. They work her fingers to the bone,' Carol said.

'Rachel says the father's on disability.'

'The pub and the bookies are his disability. And the mother. Pregnant with her eighth child! She must be fifty. Typical. Cameron and I have been trying for number two for four years now. Every clinic in north London. That Rob must have magic sperm. Drunken Irish magic sperm.'

'Did you see Anna's eye? Do you think he hit her?'

'I don't know. Have you talked to him? He's an old charmer. Used to be an artist he says. Con artist more like. But he dotes on Anna.'

Carol looked me up and down. 'So how are you holding up? I don't think we've talked since your, uh, separation.'

'Oh, you know.'

'I hear you've got a new job. Is it back in the hospital?'

'No . . . I've been out of that line of work for ten years. It's just a little café in Camden, just something to occupy my time.'

A hint of a smirk crossed her features before she caught it and forced it away again.

'That's good,' she said. 'You have to keep busy. Idle hands make for the devil's work, eh? Anyway, I have a party to organise. I won't keep you.'

Anna had her first sleepover at our house the week after that and it was a pleasure to have her. Not only did she make the dinner but she insisted on doing the washing-up too, chatting to us the whole time. She talked about her life, which had been a peripatetic one through the west of Ireland and Scotland. She'd had a dog. A pony. Her father had worked in a bar and on the oil rigs and he had done paintings.

'What sort of paintings?' I asked.

'Oil paintings. Sold some of them in the galleries out there. Could have made a lot of money if he'd embraced the gypsy side. That pikey stuff sells, me ma says.'

'I'm not sure you should use that word, it might be a bit offensive to some people.'

'Yeah, I know, but you can't stop me mum. You should hear her going on about the Chinese.'

'I've never been to west of the Ireland. Is it very beautiful?' I asked.

'Oh yes. Especially at night. Camping. You should see the stars. Me dad knows all their names.'

'So why did you come to London if it was so great out there?' Rachel asked.

'Dad lost his brickie job about three years ago and then we lost the house. We lived in a caravan for a long time in Fivemiletown. Then we drove to Manchester and dad worked there for a bit but he got the sack there too.'

'How come he got the sack?' Rachel asked.

Anna mimed drinking a pint and said, 'Glug, glug, glug.'

'Before he lost his job they must have had a birthday party for you,' Rachel said suspiciously.

Anna shook her head. 'No, Joseph was born ten months after me, two months premature and he was always so sick, it was one emergency after another and then the twins came. I suppose I wasn't a priority.'

We had dessert and watched *The Voice* on TV and I put the girls to bed.

In the morning I found Anna tinkering with the piano in what we thought was going to be the nursery for the new baby. The new baby that never came. The boy that Brian had always wanted.

'Do you play?' I asked her.

'I used to.'

'Go on. I'll bet you haven't forgotten.'

She played 'Chopsticks' and 'Twinkle, Twinkle, Little Star'.

'That was great!' I said.

'I *used* to be good. I really was.'

She was so lovely sitting there but when she moved the long, ragged home-cut fringe out of her eyes I could still see the trace of the bruise.

'Anna, you'd tell me if they were hitting you, wouldn't you?'

She bit her lip. 'I know what you think, but me dad didn't do that. That was an accident with Jeremy. Sometimes he's a bit out of control, but he's OK,' she said, and started playing 'Heart and Soul'.

Anna started sleeping over once a week after that. Rachel and her became BFFs and when Anna was over Rachel's behaviour was much better. Things were looking up in other ways too. Brian got a new job as Head of Pulmonary Surgery at the Royal Free Hospital and with the new job came a big raise. Suddenly his lawyers became a lot more accommodating about both maintenance and custody arrangements. And I was enjoying working in the café, getting to know the regulars, coming out of my shell a little.

When Anna came over I gave her piano lessons and I taught her chess too. She picked it all up so quickly. I bought her art supplies which she said she would take home to her father.

It went on like this for months. Those were the good days. One time when Anna had left her bag in the car and I had run across the playground to give it to her, she hugged me and with no trace of irony said, 'Thank you, mummy.'

A pleasant September became a cold, rainy October. When I was leaving the girls off one morning, Miss Lorenz, their homeroom teacher, took me to one side to thank me for what I was doing for Anna.

'I've seen a real change in her. Her reading and writing has improved and she's in the top maths group. She says you've been teaching her piano . . .'

'Well, a bit.'

'Of course, she's never once handed in a homework on time. Not that I'm surprised by that. I've seen where they live.'

'Why can't they get somewhere better? The mother's pregnant, surely the—'

'They've been kicked out of three places already in the brief time they've been in London. Three places. Never paid rent in any of them.'

'I didn't know that. The father told me the rent ate up all their money.'

'Ha! Drink and drugs eat up all their money.'

'Drugs?'

'Big time. The mother's on methadone, I heard.'

'But she's pregnant.'

'I know. And social services know and they're not doing anything.'

'That's awful! Poor Anna.'

'She's a tough cookie. Did you know that before they found the place they're in now they spent two nights sleeping under tarpaulins on Hampstead Heath?'

'Oh my God.'

'It's not as if they don't get heaps of benefit money. God knows where it all goes.'

I didn't see Rachel for a few days after that because her dad had her for the weekend; but when I did see her after school on the next Monday she was with Anna and they were both bursting with excitement.

'Mum! Mum! Mum, guess what we did? Guess! Go on,' Rachel said, her face glowing.

'What?'

'Dad and Lucy took us to Paris!'

'Paris? For the weekend? Without telling me?'

'We wanted to tell you but your phone just went to messages.'

I was furious but I didn't want to lose it. 'How did you end up going, Anna?'

'Brian saw me hanging out with Rachel after school and he asked me what I was doing over the weekend and I said nothing and he asked if I wanted to come with him and Lucy to Paris. And I called my dad and he said it was fine.'

Anna's grin was lighting up the whole car. It was probably the most fun she had ever had in her life. An escape from the fighting and the drugs and the filth.

She didn't stay with us the next week but the week after her father called me out of the blue.

'Hi, listen, Rob here, Anna's dad, my wife Mary's in the hospital for the delivery and I'm trying to farm out the kids. You couldn't take Anna for a bit, could you?'

'Of course! I'll take her and some of the younger ones too if you want,' I replied immediately.

'Nah, nah, the younger ones are easier to get rid of. I've got, Beth, my ex, here in the city and she's baby crazy you know? She'll take the younger ones. Good for them to be with their stepbrothers and sisters. But Anna . . . you know how it is. Too much like her mum, she just rubs Beth the wrong way . . .'

Anna came that night. She insisted on making us a spaghetti dinner and of course it was fantastic.

'I didn't know you had stepbrothers and sisters. How many do you have?' I asked after dinner.

She shook her head ruefully. 'I don't even know all their names! Dad was married twice before. Here and in Ireland. With Jennifer he had nine kids and with Beth four.'

Rachel was goggle-eyed. 'So all together you have about twenty brothers and sisters!'

Anna nodded. 'About that. Never see them all though. The wives don't exactly get on.'

'That's a lot of birthdays for your dad to remember,' I said.

'Or to forget,' Anna muttered.

'I don't have a single brother or sister!' Rachel said, looking at me accusingly.

'I'm sure Lucy will help fix that,' I just about resisted saying.

After Mary's baby was born, Anna just started staying with us. I bought her clothes and shoes and a One Direction duvet for her bed. She put on a little weight and lost the deathly tubercular pallor from her cheeks. The room with the piano in it became Anna's room.

Then one night I heard the front doorbell. I opened it to Rob, who immediately apologised about the hour and for not phoning. It was time, he said, for Anna to come back to the flat – the other kids missed her and her mum couldn't cope without her.

We went into Anna's bedroom and I woke her up. 'Anna, your dad's here,' I said gently.

'What does he want?'

'It's time to go back home, honey,' he said.

She shook her head sleepily. 'I want to stay here.'

I looked at the floor. Embarrassed. Hopeful.

'Be that as it may, it's time to go,' Rob insisted.

'I'm not going to go!' Anna said desperately.

'Put your clothes on! It's time to bloody go!' he barked and glared at me. I could smell the booze on him now. Anna was looking at me with panic in her eyes.

'If you're not going to get dressed, you'll come like this!' he said and took her wrist.

'Don't touch her like that!' I said.

'Who do you think you are!' he said and tugged her across the floor.

'Stop that!' I said.

Rob made a fist and shook it in my face. 'One more fucking word out of you, bitch, and you'll get what's fucking coming.'

I shrank away from him, terrified. He wasn't a big man, like Brian, but I knew he was capable of knocking my lights out given half a chance.

The next two minutes were a horror show: me crying, Rachel crying, Anna screaming.

Then Anna had given up the fight and limply accompanied her father outside without further protest.

When they had gone Rachel handed me the phone.

'What's this for?'

'Call the police, mum!'

'I don't think I can. It's a father taking his daughter.'

'God you're useless! I'll call them, then!'

She dialled 999 and when they eventually arrived from Stoke Newington police station I told them the whole story. They were both female officers and seemed sympathetic but said that this sounded like a case for social work, not them.

'Will you at least check on her to see if she's OK?' I asked.

They took her address and called me after midnight. 'Everything seems fine. We talked to the father and he said she was asleep.'

'But did you see her?'

'We didn't see her but the flat was quiet.'

'You need to check on her.'

'We did check on her, madam. Everything's fine. Goodnight.'

A sleepless, terrible night.

At five Rachel climbed into bed with me.

We hatched a plan. We would go to Anna's building and wait for her to come out. We would offer her a lift, talk to her, see if she was alright. We parked outside her place and waited there until after nine o'clock. Anna, however, didn't come out at all. She didn't go to school that day or the next. But I was excited to see her on the third day as I was leaving Rachel off.

I waved to her across the playground. 'Anna! Anna!'

She turned her head and walked straight past me.

'Anna!'

She just kept on walking.

I went back to the car, baffled, hurt. It wasn't my turn to pick Rachel up after school that day but I was determined to go there anyway to talk to Anna.

I waited outside her classroom and at 3.30 she was one of the first ones out.

'Is everything all right?' I asked.

'Get away from me!' she snapped.

'Anna, what have I done?'

'You know what you've done.'

'What?'

'You called the police on us!' she snarled.

'I thought it was for the best, I …'

'We trusted you but you're just like all the others, aren't you?'

'Anna please, don't say that, you're breaking my heart. I—'

'Piss off, lady. You've caused enough problems.'

She pushed me away and I stumbled backwards and almost fell. I leaned against a tree to catch my breath while Anna marched across the playground.

'Hello, stranger.'

I turned. Of course it was Brian. He was tanned, thinner, even his hair looked thicker. I quickly wiped the tears from my cheeks.

'I haven't seen you in ages. How are you holding up?' he asked.

'Oh, I'm fine. Never better.'

He looked at me. 'Is anything wrong?'

'No! No, God no, everything's great.'

'You know this is my day with Rachel, don't you? And I've got her for the weekend, haven't I?'

'Yes, yes. I was just seeing one of her teachers. Well, look, I have to go, it was nice seeing you. Rachel says you're doing great. Paris and all that. Sounds like lots of fun.'

'Yes.'

'Good, well . . . anyway . . . must go.'

I ran to the car and drove home.

I felt sick. My head was spinning. I spent most of the weekend in bed, finally pulling myself together for the Monday school run. Fortunately, I didn't see Anna on the Monday and only briefly on Tuesday.

On Wednesday we both saw her waiting at the bus stop near the school.

'Don't pick up Anna, please!' Rachel hissed.

'Why?'

'She's been a real cow to me all week. To everyone, actually, but mostly me. She's so evil. She says the most terrible things about you too.'

'What?'

'That you're always looking at her in a creepy way.'

'I was worried about her.'

'She told all the boys all these private things I told her.'

'What things?'

'It doesn't matter. Just don't stop!'

We drove home. It was raining hard. What happened next was totally unexpected.

A banging at the front door.

I checked the clock: 2.15 a.m.

Rachel was still asleep in the other room.

I grabbed a rolling pin from the kitchen and went to the door.

'Who is it?'

'It's me,' Anna said.

When I opened the door she fell into my arms.

'Oh my God, are you OK?' I asked.

'I can't take it there anymore, please say I can stay here,' she said between sobs.

I drew her a bath and heated up soup and when she was dry and had eaten I asked her to tell me all about it.

'Mum and dad fighting. All the noise! I just want to stay here forever, can I do that?'

'I don't know. I don't know what the law is but you can certainly stay here tonight and we'll sort it out tomorrow.'

We were at breakfast the next morning when the police and social workers showed up. The social workers took a hysterical Anna away with them. A grim-faced policewoman gave me a formal caution about letting Anna stay here against the wishes of her parents.

'You wouldn't want to be accused of kidnapping her,' the WPC said.

'But that's ridiculous!' I replied indignantly.

'It's not ridiculous. The girl's mother has complained to us that you have an unhealthy interest in her daughter.'

'You must be joking!'

The WPC lowered her voice. 'Look, it's best you stay away from that family. They're capable of saying or doing anything. They've got a record as long as your arm in Ireland and over here. And that girl isn't entirely innocent either.'

'I—'

'You don't want to get on their bad side, trust me. They'll put the law on you, they've done it before.'

School started again the next week and this time I wasn't surprised when Anna gave me the cold shoulder in the playground or when she was cruel to Rachel.

I paid heed to the policewoman and gave her a wide berth.

The pain of seeing her gradually lessened but it didn't fully go away.

Several months later we were driving down Graham Road when I noticed a wrecking ball swinging into the building where Anna and her family had been living. 'Isn't that Anna's old place?' I asked, surprised.

Rachel looked up from her iPad. 'I think it is.'

'Where do you think the family went?'

'Oh they moved back to Ireland a couple of weeks ago. Some place called Fivemiletown.'

I was too shocked to say anything more but when I got home I looked up Fivemiletown on Google. A grim-looking country place in Northern Ireland. The next day I went to see her homeroom teacher, Miss Lorenz, who confirmed everything.

'I knew it was coming. They owed money all over London. Gambling debts, rent, and most importantly, with their various dealers. I knew one day we'd never see them again.'

'But the new baby, all those kids, the autistic boy? Social services has to do something.'

'Social services is relieved as hell. It's someone else's problem now.'

'Have you seen that awful little town she's going to?'

'It's not so bad. There's a decent local library. I made sure she knew about the library. She's a good reader.'

I nodded sadly.

December came and Brian wanted to take Rachel to the Bahamas for Christmas with Lucy. It would mean me spending Christmas alone but I didn't want her to miss an opportunity like that so I said it was fine.

We shopped for swimwear and 'dresses for fancy restaurants'.

She left on December 19th. Brian picked her up in a new Mercedes. A silver one.

I didn't see much point in getting a tree or buying myself presents.

I called my mum in Cornwall and asked if she wanted to spend Christmas with me or vice versa. But that was only so that I could say I had done my due diligence because I knew her new husband, Jack, wasn't very sociable. She declined my offer and did not reciprocate.

Christmas Eve was a ridiculous parade of clichés: a bottle of Shiraz, a Meg Ryan weepy, Ben and Jerry's ice cream.

Later: a 10mg Valium, a 10mg Temazepam . . .

Blackout sleep.

No phone messages but a text on my phone.

From Anna.

I opened it immediately:

Please come! I hate it here. I'll go with you anywhere. We're living in caravans with my uncle. It's awful here. I hate it! Help me! No police. Please can you come!!!!!!!!!!

I didn't know what to think but I knew I had to act. I texted her back straightaway:

Can you be at the Fivemiletown Library tonight at 7PM?

There was a long delay before she replied:

Yes.

I called a taxi and on the taxi ride to Heathrow I booked a flight to Belfast.

Nearly empty plane. Touchdown. Nearly empty airport.

I rented a Toyota Land Cruiser and drove west.

A bleak rainy landscape of low hills and boggy fields. I drove along what they called the M1 and then the A1 through Augher, Clogher and finally Fivemiletown.

Google maps took me right to the library.

I parked.

Waited.

Waited.

7.00 p.m. 7.15. 7.22.

An old Land Rover Defender pulled up next to me.

A woman and two men go out. I fumbled to turn the ignition but I wasn't quick enough. They opened my door and one of them pulled me out by the hair. The men held my arms behind my back and dragged me to the woman. I knew it was Anna's mother, Mary. She was tall and rangy and powerful. She didn't seem like a junkie at all.

'Do you know who I am?' Mary asked.

I nodded.

'Stay away from my family you fucking crazy bitch,' Mary snarled.

'Anna said she was in trouble.'

'Anna's not in trouble.'

'She's around fighting and drugs.'

'Bollocks! There's no drugs. We're just poor is all. That's our fucking crime.'

'But Anna—'

'Anna plays a lot of games with a lot of people. But she's just a child. You're an adult. Next time you pull something like this we're calling the peelers. Do you understand?'

I nodded. She grabbed me by the hair and tugged hard.

'Now get out of here! We never want to fucking see you again. And consider yourself lucky. If you'd been a man and tried to do this, my brothers would have beat the living shite out of you.'

I was terrified. My whole body was trembling.

As I was getting back in the car I suddenly saw Anna on the other side of the street under the library overhang. She was wearing a backpack, as if she really had wanted to go, but I couldn't read the expression on her face.

I turned on the car headlamps and when Anna saw me looking at her she raised the middle finger of her right hand.

She was smiling. Her mother walked over to her and put her arm around her.

I turned on the ignition and Anna mouthed something I couldn't catch, and laughed.

But then as I edged the Toyota out of the car park and Anna pulled up her hoodie, I saw that her smile had vanished and I caught a glimpse of something else. Sadness? Guilt? It was there for just a moment and then it was gone.

I missed the midnight flight so I slept on the seats at the gate and caught the first plane to London in the morning.

Rachel came back from Bahamas later that day.

She began to tell me about her holiday but stopped herself and asked me how my Christmas had been.

'Quiet,' I said.

'Our trip was amazing, let me tell you everything . . .'

We watched TV and when she went to bed I checked my email.

No messages from Ireland.

I knew there would never be messages from Ireland. Not anymore.

I closed the laptop, went to Anna's room and lay down on her bed next to the piano.

I climbed under the One Direction duvet and wept.

Arlene Hunt

Arlene Hunt published her first novel, *Vicious Circle*, in 2004. Her second novel, *False Intentions* (2005), introduced John and Sarah of the private eye team 'QuicK Investigations'. In all, Arlene has published eight novels, the most recent being *The Outsider*.

Thicker than Water

My sister's nose is bleeding all over the tiles of my kitchen floor, a steady drip as if regulated by a metronome. Every so often she gives a big sniff and the blood stops for a few seconds before continuing again.

'Hold your head back.'

I rip kitchen towels from the holder and pass them to her. She mashes them against her nose to stem the flow, squeezing red swollen eyes shut as she does so. Her fingernails are chewed to the quick, the skin around them raw and painful looking. There are bruises around her neck, new and old. Watching her tilt her head backwards, I lean against the worktop, light a cigarette and drag on it deeply. I will never stop smoking, not while I have the likes of Stacy as family.

'The prick,' she says, her voice muffled through her fingers. 'He swore … I thought it would be different this time.'

I am supposed to reply to this, but I don't. We both know it's a lie and the past is not something we can scrub away. There is nothing *different* about the latest piece of shit she hooked up with apart from his name; the names are always different. If someone gave Stacy a compass with 'Decent Guy' at south and 'Wanker' at north, my sister would veer north every time. No one can explain it, least of all her: some people are just wired that way, I suppose.

Yeah, that's right: we'll blame wiring, we'll blame social conditioning, we'll blame being poor, our dead mother, our drunken father, society, whatever … under no circumstances are we to blame Stacy and her uncontrollable urge to mate with fuckheads.

'I can't go back there tonight, Lil.' She shakes her head, bottom lip wobbling uncontrollably. 'Can we stay with you for a while?'

'No,' I reply in my head.

'Yes,' I say out loud. This is very inconvenient. But it's not for her that I say yes; it's for my ten-year-old nephew sitting in the next room, minding his baby sister. His eyes are older than they should be, his pinched face a carapace of anger and resignation: he needs a port in the storm that is his life. He needs me to say yes.

So I do.

Stacy nods her gratitude, but she's not grateful, not really: people like my sister are never truly grateful for anything. She came here because she knew I'd take her in, it's expected that I will provide shelter for her and her brood. Duty binds us; she knows this: blood is thicker than water, my old lad used to always say when he'd had a skinful. Cheap talk, since his blood is watered down to bitter piss by this stage.

'I'll make up a bed in the spare room.'

'Do you have anything to drink?'

'There's some cans in the fridge.'

'Have you nothing stronger?'

'No.'

I leave the kitchen and step out into the hall. Behind me I hear the sound of the chair being scraped back, the fridge door opening and closing. My sister's sigh of disappointment on seeing two cans of beer sitting in the door of the fridge.

Neither of them is mine, my friend Jim left them here months ago, after watching a game of football on the telly.

The baby is asleep on her back on my sofa, looking like a puffy starfish in her all-in-one jumpsuit. Bobby has hemmed her in with cushions from the other chairs so she can't roll off and hurt herself. He sits on the floor beneath her, knees drawn up to his chin, his eyes on the television screen.

I go to him, kneel down to his level.

'How're you doing?'

'I'm OK.'

I brush his pale red hair back off his forehead. It's too long and hangs in his eyes. His eyes are hazel, like his father's; his skin pale, resistant to tan. There are bruises fading along his jawline too. I touch them with my fingertips and feel something in my chest when he moves his head automatically away.

'You're going to stay here tonight, with me.'

'She didn't bring any food for Katie. I told her, but she didn't bring any. Katie will be hungry when she wakes up.'

'I'll nip across the road to Susan, she's bound to have some spare.'

'I told her we hadn't got any. She wouldn't listen.'

'Don't worry about that now. I'll get some from Susan.' I glance at the television. 'What are you watching?'

'*The Fast and the Furious*.'

'Is it good?'

'I've seen it before.'

I leave him and go back to the kitchen. Stacy has already finished one can and started on the other; the air is thick with smoke, so I open a window.

'You don't have any formula?'

'No, fuck.'

'I'm going across the road to Susan's, I'll be back in a minute.'

I might as well be talking to the kettle. She's staring at her phone.

'Bastard hasn't even called.'

Her right leg is jittering up and down. I want to say something to her, I want to tell her to put the fucking phone down and go see is her son alright, but the way she is now I know that this will do more damage than good, so I swallow my words whole, grab my jacket from a peg in the hall and leave my house – my quiet, tidy house – and run across the street to Susan's.

Susan fills the kettle and presses down the switch as I lower myself carefully onto one of her rickety kitchen chairs. She's an artist of sorts; her house is crammed with mismatched things she carts home from skips and junk shops, determined to fix.

She never fixes them.

'That one has some neck, so she has,' Susan says, fuming.

'Mm.'

'After all that mess the last time, you'd think she'd cop the fuck on.'

I take my cigarettes from my jacket, and light one for both of us, glad of the distraction. I don't want to talk about the last time … or the time before that. Susan takes the cigarette and clatters around, opening and closing press doors, looking for spare bottles. Her own baby has long outgrown bottle-feeding, but Susan is a hoarder. I knew she'd have a spare, and I was right.

'You don't need this shite,' she says, hauling things from the depths: salad spinners, toastie makers, old plastic trays from takeaways, washed and stacked, ready for use, not that they ever will be. 'You've enough on your plate, Lil.'

She is referring to my not-so-recent breakdown: we don't mention it of course, there's no need. We both know how bad it was.

'She's got no one else.'

'What about your old lad?'

'He won't have her in the house.'

'And whose fault is that?'

This is a simple truth. Our father's heart is broken over Stacy and part of me, a deep, vile part of me thinks it serves him right. He loves her more than me, and she repays this by stealing from him every chance she gets. The last time she stole the money he'd been saving to get the heating fixed, nearly three hundred euros. Oh, she denied it to the last, but who else knew where he kept his few quid stashed, who else had a key? Well, I did. Stacy said that, throwing my name into the suspect pool as readily as she could. My father told me this when I loaned him the funds to cover what she had taken.

'What kind of a young wan steals from her own blood?' he cried, rheumy eyes brimming with tears. 'After all I did for her!'

All he did for her? That was gas; the demented old gomb really believes he helped Stacy reach adulthood as a fully functioning human being. I didn't say anything to comfort him. I left the money on his greasy kitchen table and walked home.

'Ah!' Susan says brightly. 'Here they are, how many do you need?'

'One will do.'

She carries two to the sink and pours water from the now boiled kettle into both and rinses them out. Smoke from the cigarette clamped between her teeth coils up into her hair as she works. It's a pleasure to watch Susan work. Small-framed, light on her toes like you'd expect a dancer to be; her dark hair is cut short – she says it's easier to manage that way. It curls at the nape of her neck. I love those curls. I love her so much it scares me a little.

'She's a rip, and you're too easy on her.'

I sigh, but I'm not really in disagreement.

'What can I do, she's my sister.'

Susan tosses her head to this. What else is there to be said? She puts the bottles onto the draining board and turns to me.

'Where's yer man, the Nordie guy?'

'No idea.'

'What about Bobby's dad?'

I laugh. 'That bridge is long burnt.'

'He was all right.'

'He's an alcoholic.'

'Never hit her though.'

'No.'

'She should have stayed with him. Least she'd have a roof over her head and that young fella a father.'

I can't argue with her logic, though it depresses me and makes me feel like I should defend Stacy. Bobby's father is twenty years my sister's senior. She was still in school when he knocked her up. It's not as cut-and-dried as Susan likes to make out.

Mind you, with Stacy, nothing ever is.

I refuse an offer of tea and take the bottles and the formula back across the road to my house. As soon as I open the door I sense something is wrong.

The kitchen is empty. I put the bottles and the formula down on the worktop and backtrack to the living room. Bobby and the baby are exactly where I last saw them.

'Where's your Mammy?'

'She went out.'

'Where?'

He shrugged, eyes still fixed on the television.

'Did she say when she'd be back?'

'No.'

I digest this.

'Put on a light, you'll ruin your eyes.'

When the film is over, I put the children to bed in my room and doze on the sofa, waiting for Stacy to return. The next morning, I make two phone calls, feed the baby and take her and Bobby over to my father's house in the next estate.

Even though it's early he opens the door on my knock, looking wary. He once told me I have a Garda's knock. It was not a compliment.

'Hey,' I say.

'Well.'

I follow him into the house, down the hall to the small old-fashioned kitchen. It's warm, the money I loaned him – and will never see again – was well spent.

'You're not in work today,' he says.

'Jim's going to open the shop for me.'

I sit and begin to remove the baby's jacket, hat and gloves. Dad's dog, Muffin, ambles up on stiff legs to sniff and I push her away with my knee. Bobby slinks onto the chair opposite, sullen and pale. I wonder if he slept much the night before. It's hard to know with him.

Dad makes tea, pours three cups. He puts so much sugar in Bobby's the spoon could surely stand up in it, but I say nothing.

'Grand day out there, thank God. Although the forecast says it's going to rain.'

'Dad, have you talked to Stacy?'

'No.' He glances towards Bobby, who is slurping his tea. 'I haven't. Have you lost her?'

'She was at mine last night, she went out but she didn't come back.'

'I see.'

'Can you watch these two for me?'

'Now?'

I say nothing until he looks me in the eye. You know where I'm going, my eyes say. I suppose I do, his reply. These kids are our blood, my eyes tell him. I suppose they are, his eyes say: but there is little conviction in them and I'm reminded again what a useless article he is.

It starts to rain, driven horizontal by a rising wind, so I take a shortcut across the green. There used to be bushes along here, some protection at least, but the council removed them two years back. Now the path is strewn with shattered glass, the grass full of scorch marks and dog shit. I walk with my head down, fast, but not too fast. There are eyes on me, of course there are, but I'm not worried about them, not in the grey morning light.

It's different story at night.

I take a left off the green, walk along a street, take a right; another left and I'm in the cul-de-sac. My heart beats faster the closer I get to Stacy's house.

Her front door has been kicked in and pulled shut.

I push it open with my fingertips and call out.

'Stacy?'

There is no reply and the house feels empty. I step across the threshold into the tiny hallway, crammed with shoes, a buggy, unopened mail.

'Stace?'

The living room is empty, signs of a disturbance, broken glass, an overturned coffee table. Down the hall the kitchen is a mess; the sink is full of unwashed plates; the table covered in takeaway wrappers and empty cans. One of the kitchen chairs is missing.

Odd.

Upstairs, both bedrooms are empty, as is the bathroom. I notice a bloodstained towel in the bath, blood spatter in the sink.

Shit.

Halfway back down the stairs I become aware of someone standing in the hall below.

I stop, adrenaline coursing through my veins.

'Hello?'

With relief, I recognise the voice and descend the rest of the way. It's Stacy's neighbour from the house on the right-hand side.

'Hey Barry.'

'I thought you were Stacy.' He shakes his head. 'There was murder here yesterday, screaming and shouting. I called the Guards, but they never came.'

I shrug, no surprise there.

He runs his fingers over the busted lock, his expression grim. 'Bastard.'

Succinct, and correct; the latest one is a complete bastard. On the Richter scale of bastards, he's sitting pretty at Level 9. Everybody knows this, even Stacy. He has never made a secret of it.

'Are the little ones okay?'

'They're at Dad's house.'

He nods, looks as if he's going to say something, changes his mind.

'What about the door?'

'I'll call someone.'

'I've got a bit of wood back at the house.' He frowns, picturing the task. 'It won't be secure, mind, but it'll stop anyone from walking in off the street.'

I thank this man, this gentle, kind-hearted man. Stacy hates him and calls him names behind his back.

Raining proper now, hard, no longer slanted. At the bottom of the cul-de-sac, I stop and think about where to try next.

I spend the rest of the day tracking my sister across the city. Nobody has heard from her, nobody knows where she is. Her friends are useless, unconcerned, suspicious of me, even through most of them have known me my entire life.

I call Jim at the shop and apologise for leaving him in the lurch. It sounds busy in the background, but he is kind and tells me not to worry about a thing. He asks if I have located Stacy and I say no, not yet. He tells me not to worry.

I lie and tell him I won't.

I call Dad: he sounds tired and harassed. He wonders when I will be coming back for the kids, that he has plans of his own.

He does not ask if I have located Stacy and I feel angry and scared at the same time.

After I hang up, I stand against a wall and chew my lip. It is after three and getting dark. I'm cold and I realise I haven't eaten a thing all day. I think about the missing chair as I smoke a cigarette, my last one, and make a decision to head back to Stacy's house.

The bus across town is crowded and smelly, reeking of damp material, BO, stale cigarette smoke. The windows are fogged up, making it hard to see where to get off. I miss my stop and walk back.

It's not far.

What to do, though? The prick is married; there are kids, a wife.

Luckily for me there's a small park across the street from his house. I sit on a swing and stare at his empty drive. The lights are on inside the house and I see movement from time to time. I wonder about them, his family, his blood, going on about their day-to-day lives.

The rain stops, starts again, stops, starts again. Turning up the collar of my jacket, I try not to shiver. It's hard to know if it's from the cold or not.

A little after seven his car pulls up outside the house.

I watch him get out, willing my legs to work. Dread and fear are making my muscles rebel.

Blood, she's your blood.

Almost without thinking I hop off the swing, jog to the railing and call his name.

He doesn't hear me the first time, but he does the second, craning his fat Shar Pei neck this way and that to pinpoint the direction.

His eyes land on me.

For a moment I think he will simply ignore me and go inside. I don't have a plan for that.

Decision made, he crosses the road in short brutish strides. That's how he walks, like a fat cockerel, puffed out, arms held out from his body like he's carrying an invisible sheep under each one. From memory I know his eyes are palest blue, the only thing about him that is not ugly.

'What the fuck're you doing here?'

He enters the park and shoves me backwards, deeper into the shadows of the playground. I stumble, but remain upright. The darkness suits me.

'I was waiting for Stacy.'

'Me and that crazy hoor are done.' He grabs the back of my head in one hand and jabs a finger in my face. 'You come near this house again I'll fucking bury you. That hoor threatened my fucking family and if—'

'She can't threaten anyone now. She's dead.'

He freezes. I can see he's felt the blade against his gut. It's razor-sharp, I know, I sharpen it regularly.

'Listen—'

'I was waiting for her back at her house. I thought I'd clean up a bit, be nice for her and the kids to come back home to a clean house. I wondered about the chair.'

He tries to grab my hand, but I am too fast. I've played this scenario out more than once, and I've practiced, oh how I've practiced.

The knife slices through his skin like a hot knife through butter.

His eyes go wide. Now it's my turn to hold his head with my free hand.

'I found her where you left her. You wedged the chair under the door, she couldn't get out.'

'Ah, Jesus Christ —'

Blood, shockingly hot, spills over my hands as I drive the knife in deep.

It's strange how easy it is to slice through the stomach; people always go for the chest, which strikes me as daft, all that bone, you can break a blade that way. But the stomach is different: you might hit the liver, or the kidney, the pancreas; those suckers bleed like you wouldn't believe.

If you get really lucky you might hit the abdominal aorta.

I don't believe in luck.

I believe in blood.

Alex Barclay

Alex Barclay is the author of eight crime novels, and a fantasy novel for children. Her most recent novel, *Killing Ways*, is the latest in a series featuring the Colorado-based FBI Special Agent Ren Bryce. Alex's *Blood Runs Cold* won the Ireland AM Crime Fiction Award at the Irish Book Awards in 2009.

Roadkill Heart

A roadkill heart is a terrible thing. Soaked in liquor, it sings. And in dead-of-night bars, lonely ladies dance. As my throat burns from my favourite brand, I hold the kiss of life, when I can barely stand.

I find the exit. I think of the second incarnation of my heart as I make my way across. I may be walking steady, but I'm staggered by the loss. Connie Adams, my sandy beauty, whose tanned feet I picture on my dashboard, her white cotton dress hitched up around her thighs. She is laughing, always laughing.

When I was drunk, I let her love me deeply. In a rolling blur of neon nights, she could push her kind words into the holes of my heart. By morning, the words were gone.

On the back porch of the bar, I pause to smell the wet air. I strike a match and light a cigarette. I hold the match until the flame dies. I think of my mother, powered by passion; every time her heart was lit by the fire of another man's intent, her eyes shone in the fresh flames. And that's what she did – follow the flames until they burned her house down, leaving me ashen in the smoking embers as she walked away with the last someone new. My first heart, bright and red and brilliant – loved fiercely by the faithful part of hers – lasted six years.

I get in the car and drive. The rain is dangerous tonight. The wipers are frenzied. I remember them: all the journeys. Lights off, down empty country roads, then towns and cities, and shafts from streetlights slicing across me. Low in back seats, I let them pulse against my closed eyelids. High, so high, in passenger seats, I watched them spark through my reflection in the side window. From the driver's seat, they're a fireworks display and I'm tunnelling through in a dark cloud. Speeding from my killings, reeling from them. But to watch me, I am still.

Five miles behind me, the heavens flood the extraordinary chest wound of Reverend Garrison Clay. He lies on a manicured lawn, fat white belly to the moon, pale blue pyjama pants slowly turning translucent, taking his shape. Clay was a monster, that I know. But I hurt flies too.

It is all joyless. But I'm fucking good.

Lonnie Eades was a fly. And my first kill. I was told he would be hunting in the woods, and where he might be at 11 a.m. I was too dumb to ask how anyone could possibly know that, but smart enough to get there early to wait. I heard no gunshots, no sense that anyone was hunting anything. Eades arrived. No rifle. He was a blond, lanky, leaning kid, no more than nineteen years old. I remember every inch of him. He was dressed in battered camo gear two sizes too big, and he was vibrating inside it. Even his hair seemed to be shaking, his eyeballs seemed to sweat. It was like all around him a gallows was being constructed, faint, like in a cartoon, and he was just standing there, pulling the hood down over his head. I couldn't figure it out. It was only afterwards I learned that he was there to kill me. This was a game.

I already loved Connie by then, loved her with the kind of love most people don't ever know. It was like she robbed the breath from my soul. We were good for who we were, driven by our fears, borne of different losses, crashing together at that bar. I kissed life into her. And she into me.

'I love that wilderness, that crippled mute, whatever else you call that beautiful heart,' I told her one night.

'Yours,' she said.

I let her go, and found a woman who needed me. After all, a woman who loves you can, nevertheless, abandon you. But a woman who needs you will stay.

There are sirens now, blue lights.

The centre line of the road has become two, and the strands are moving like jump ropes. I stare until they converge, blink, find my place on the right side. They cross again. In the schoolyard the girls used to chant, and I would walk by, contained in my quick-start anger to join the scattered boys. And the girls behind us with one voice.

"Had a little sports car, two-forty-eight, took it round the corner and slammed on the brakes, bumped into a lady, bumped into a man, bumped into a policeman, man oh man."

And the slap of the rope.

I try to clench my fists.

The night before Connie Adams left, I sat on my back porch under a hunter's moon, writing my wedding vows on a beer mat. The next night, I looked up at where she used to sit on the swing, her bare feet arched, pointing at the stars, that white dress of hers, her raggedy hair trailing in the dirt. The lightest girl I knew, skyward. And the heavy weight of her absence.

I'm cold. I'm wet.

My head rolls to one side. I meet the dead eyes of the Reverend Garrison Clay, a quarter of his head blown away. The rain is soaking into me now. My beer mat vows, confetti, falling around me. My gaze moves a little lower. I see my right arm, my hand, palm up, the rain pooling a little before it runs down onto the blacktop.

I pull my head front and centre. The extraordinary chest wound is mine.

These are my thoughts: it was my mother's savage heart that beat inside me the night I met Connie Adams. And hers was its reflection, the very worst I could face. Because no good can come of following flames.

Roads and kills. Roads and kills.

Connie Adams is standing over me. Connie Clay now. She falls by my side. She takes my hand and cries into it. She's more than beautiful, suddenly older. I'll add this face to the others I remember of hers.

I think I'm smiling. I hope I am. Connie Adams, I will only ever wish you miles of happy road. And love beyond this open heart you hold.

Gene Kerrigan

Gene Kerrigan is a veteran Dublin journalist who writes on politics. He has had nine non-fiction books published, and four novels. In 2012, *The Rage* won the UK Crime Writers Association award for crime novel of the year.

Cold Cards

There's a chill coming off the cards, even as they fly low across the green, Tony Finnegan dealing clockwise around the table. Before you touch them you know that when you pick the cards up and hold them close, your fingers separating them so their values appear one by one, they'll break your heart.

And when the cards are like that, there's nothing you can do about it. Just play the odds, fold or bet small, tap out as soon as it's decent.

It's superstition, the cold card thing, and Richie Crown knew that. It's like believing in fairies. It's like swallowing all that water-into-wine shit. Weak-minded notions, for people who need a crutch.

But, still.

Superstition or not, he knew in his bones it was real – sometimes, the cards are stone cold for you.

The occasional bad evening, that's not a problem. That's winning and losing, you take what's coming. But when you return week after week and the bad run carries on like it's the way things were always meant to be, that's the worst kind of suck. Like some higher force is playing with your life.

Statistically, there's no reason why a tasty hand can't pop up in the middle of a bad run. But when that happens, Richie Crown knew, almost always it's a teaser, keeping you on the hook. You think this is where the cards are warming up, the elation makes you careless, a couple of hands further on that hollow feeling is back, eating away at your gut.

What kept him going was the knowledge that nothing is forever. The longest lucky streak comes to an end, and the dreariest cold streak, too. Then things get back to normal. Good hands, bad hands, hands that mightn't work out but they're worth a shot. Times the cards get so hot you feel you own the night. Richie remembered times like that, and he knew there would be more, as long as he stayed in the game.

Watching the cards fly from Tony's hands, Richie sipped at his C.C. and said a silent prayer to the God he didn't believe in.

Four Tuesdays on the trot, including this one – each evening, the cold cards offering nothing but more pain. It made the occasional bluff irresistible. Never works. Knowing Richie was playing against a bad run, the other players could smell the sham. And there's no pity at the table.

Richie Crown picked up his cards, cupped them in both hands, level with his chin, his right thumb teasing them apart. First card's the three of diamonds, second the jack of clubs, third's the seven of hearts, and this is shit, this really is a hand of blanks. Inside, he was imploring God to make another jack of the fourth card, make a game of it, maybe even give him something useful in the fifth card, making two pairs or even trips. Playing a hand like that on top of his bad streak, the others would read it as a bluff, so they'd play along and he'd reel in a decent piece of change.

His thumb eased open the cards a little more and revealed the eight of spades. God was offline again tonight. The fifth card was the two of clubs.

Every deal restored the hope, even this far into the bad streak, when the chill was bone deep. And every new hand was a kick in the gut from a stone cold boot.

Directly across from Richie, Joe Campbell was a grinder, working the odds, taking a small win and making a small loss, ramping things up maybe once a night and occasionally hauling in a rake of chips. To Richie's left, Tommy O'Rourke was a happy amateur. He didn't raise a lot, often folded, called occasionally and mostly lost small. It was like his losses were the price of admission to a weekly game. Any night he went home with ten cents more than he started with was a cause for celebration. Tony Finnegan, too, played for the enjoyment. The other two, Joshua Barrett and Paudie Griffin, were the serious players, along with Richie Crown.

The game was eight months on the go, give or take, always at Joshua's house off Griffith Avenue, always on Tuesday nights. All of them lived within a stroll of Joshua's place, except Richie Crown and Tony Finnegan. Compared with the kind of money that crossed the tables at some of the games in Dublin, this was just a neighbourly get-together. But it was a bad poker year for Richie Crown, even before these past few weeks.

He folded, as Tommy pushed a couple of chips into the centre of the table.

It was a little after midnight when Richie tapped out.

'We gonna be much longer?' Tony Finnegan asked.

Joshua grunted. 'You got a woman simmering somewhere?'

'Sometimes I give Richie a lift – he's on my way.'

Tony was the one man at the table who didn't drink during a game.

'You're OK, I'm fine,' Richie said, 'taxis pass the end of the road.'

'Too cold for hanging around street corners.'

'Four-five hands more?' Joshua asked. Tommy, Joshua and Paudie indicated that was about right. Tony looked up at Richie. 'What's the hurry?'

He was looking Richie in the eye and Richie nodded and poured himself another C.C. and sat some feet away, sipping, head back, eyes focused on nothing in particular, the murmurs of the poker players just a background buzz.

Behind the wheel of his car, Tony Finnegan said, 'You're down – what? Three grand, four?'

'I'm OK,' Richie said, though it was a lot more than four grand. Way back, when the poker got serious, Richie worked out the most he could lose without seriously fucking his life was six. He was always well inside that limit until – three-four months back – he got himself into a game in Rathmines. It was a high-stakes effort, with a couple of young business types, a solicitor and a TCD academic. Richie felt like it was time to step up, to test himself. He coasted for a few games, then took a hammering one evening on three major hands over a period of forty minutes. He got out of that scene a couple of weeks later, by which time he was down almost twelve grand. On top of previous losses, he was looking into a seventeen grand hole.

He'd been slowly repairing his finances since then, until the cards turned ice cold for him and stayed that way.

'You're hurting, right though?'

'I've been better.'

They were coming up to the roundabout at Ashfield Castle Shopping Centre and Tony Finnegan swung round, turned left into the McDonald's drive-thru lane and just before the squawk box he took a right and parked where the car couldn't be seen from the road.

'Someone's looking to hire. A once-off,' he said. 'You free?'

'Depends.'

'It pays well.'

In Tony Finnegan's day job he managed a shop that rented out tools and machinery – sanders, diggers, generators, shit like that. Then there was the other work.

When he was younger Tony was a sidekick of Georgie Reid. That ended when Reid threw one of his famous wobblers and

Tony woke up in an ambulance on the way to the Mater. He cut his ties to Reid and wasn't around when some other associates of the headbanger had him put down.

Since then, being a trusted kind of person, Tony had offers from several of the major operators in Dublin. He did enough to make a good living and maintain the goodwill due an experienced neutral.

'Anyone I know?'

'Roly Blount. Works for Frank Tucker.'

'Never met Tucker. What I hear, I don't believe I'd ever want to.'

'Tomorrow afternoon. That's why Roly asked me. Fella supposed to do the job suddenly can't make it, family shit. Roly needs someone in a hurry.'

'You're doing it?'

'I like working with Roly, but I'm down for an angiogram at the Mater.'

'You got chest trouble?'

'Fella I got, puts me through the wringer twice a year. Either he's being as careful as he ought to be or he's running up the meter. Either way, the missus says fuck it, you're taking no chances. So, I mentioned your name to Roly. He said to ask you.'

'What's the job?'

'Just driving.'

'Who? Where?'

'I know nothing – except he needs someone reliable in a hurry. Bonus for short notice.' Tony paused a beat, then he said, 'What Roly says – kind of job it is, it needs a steady hand, someone won't get spooked.'

'Ah, shit.'

'Yeah. It won't be shoplifting.'

'He say a number?'

'He said it's top rate.'

'Fuck. Serious shit, right?'

'Yeah.'

They sat a minute in silence, then Tony said, 'I gave him three-four names, people I rate – yours was top of the list. Roly recognised the name, said you're a good guy.'

'He said I'm a good guy?'

'Solid, is what he said.'

They both knew that meant if something went wrong Richie could be relied on to know that his best interests lay with keeping his mouth shut.

A thing like this, it could take a big enough bite out of Richie's debts to take him back to the bright side. Beyond that, do a good job for someone like Roly, someone like his boss Frank Tucker, they know you're dependable, maybe it turns regular. That kind of work, a man could soon pay off a mortgage.

What went against it – when someone like Roly and Frank hire at top rates it's a serious job and the risk and the possible comebacks will be on the same scale.

'Solid?'

'Yeah.'

'What you think?'

'You know the up and the down.'

'Yeah.'

'He's a tidy worker, Roly. No loose ends. I wasn't down for this cardiac shit, I'd jump at it. Other hand, the bigger the job – you know, like they say – the value of your investment can go down as well as up.'

After a while Richie said, 'OK, thing like this, no telling where it might lead, right?'

Tony took out his phone and sent a text message. Half a minute later he got a reply. It said, *IOU.*

Richie Crown said, 'Ask them where've I got to be, and what time.'

Coming from the McDonalds, three young men were making a big deal out of strolling home. Their high-pitched voices suggested they'd spent the evening on the jar. Each carried a bag of cholesterol and nothing any of them was saying could possibly be funny enough to justify the loudness of their laughter.

Tony Finnegan tapped out a number. He got out of the car, walked a few yards and stopped, the phone to his ear. The three young men glanced at him as they passed. One of them said something and the other two got loud and high-pitched again.

When he got back into the car Tony was taking the sim out of the phone.

'Be at home, tomorrow afternoon. Three o'clock, you get a text, telling you the make and number of a car, where it's parked, not far from your apartment. Doors unlocked, key on the floor under the driver's seat. Fifteen minutes later, you're turning into Danieli Road, fella will flag you down. He's not there, you turn left at the end of Danieli, up to the roundabout, back down to Danieli and try again. Keep doing that until the guy's there. You take him where he wants to go, then take him wherever else he wants to be taken. OK?'

Richie Crown nodded. 'I don't do anything, just drive?'

'That's all.'

'What do I do with the car?'

'That'll be taken care of.'

Richie knew he wasn't going to get an answer, but there was no way he couldn't ask. 'What's he gonna do?'

'None of our business, yours or mine. Few days later, you get an envelope in your letterbox.'

Twenty yards in front of the car, one of the three kids from McDonalds, without breaking pace, kicked out, his foot connecting with the side mirror of a parked Honda Civic. As the three walked on, the raucous conversation uninterrupted, the mirror hung limply down the side of the passenger door.

'Thanks for putting my name out there,' Richie Crown said.

'Do you a favour, do Roly a favour, it can't hurt.'

'All the same, thanks.'

'Take it easy, tomorrow. Nothing to worry about, just play it cool and everyone comes out ahead.'

Richie nodded. 'Taxi work.'

'Yeah.'

Ten minutes later, Tony dropped Richie on the corner of Ardlea Road.

'Good luck,' Tony said.

'Hope the heart thing works out,' Richie said.

It was there when he woke. A day like any other, but it was as if he was seeing it through a filter that changed everything. Getting up, stepping into the shower, waiting in the kitchen for the kettle to boil, the humdrum stuff tick-tocking by, same as always but different.

First time that happened was one evening about ten years back, he was early twenties, on a rooftop in Camden Street, two heavies coming after him. They were security thugs, came into an office just as Richie was taking a cashbox out of the bottom drawer of a filing cabinet. When they told him, hey scumbag, don't even fucking think of resisting, he put up his hands and said please, look, no problem, don't hit me, please. They relaxed. On the stairs he took one of them by the back of the head, slammed his face against a wall and reared back as the other one reached for his arm, turned, was halfway up a flight of stairs before they sorted themselves out.

When he got to the roof there was no obvious route to safety and after half a minute the thugs appeared, one of them his nose bloody. They'd now taken out extendable batons and they were brandishing them like they were soldiering for Darth Vader, waving their fucking lightsabres.

By the time Richie made it to the side of the roof he knew the choice was jumping or taking a serious beating, followed by a stretch in the Joy.

The gap to the next roof was maybe six foot. A safe enough jump across a narrow laneway, if it wasn't for the sixty-foot drop.

That was the instant in which he first felt the filter drop and everything getting sharper, more intense, knowing that he was into something that would decide how the rest of his life went – or if there was a rest of his life. What he had to do was well within his limits, but if something went wrong the consequences could be drastic.

It was fear, but it was more than that – it was a thrill, an anticipation, a relief at a decision made, the turning of a high stakes card, a higher stage of life.

He took a short run and made the jump, then he turned and stood there on the other side, smiling at the stormtroopers. They could easily make the jump same as him, but the stakes weren't the same for them.

So, they waved their lightsabres some more and one of them shouted he'd remember Richie's face.

He'd had that buzz in the run up to every serious job since, that sharper thing that kicked in when the pressure was on. Like before long he was going to step out onto a high, tight wire. It was with him this morning, that buzz, even as he opened the door and Greta appeared with the twins.

His sister worked mornings at a hairdressers in Ashfield. This time of morning, she'd normally be leaving the kids into St Finbar's.

Fucking school. Part of the ceiling collapsed in the prefab classroom, dumped a shitload of rain on the desks – lucky it didn't happen when the kids were there. It would take a few days to fix it and Greta couldn't take that time off at short notice. Richie had no problem looking after Conor and Liam until Greta got off at lunchtime. They were lively little buggers, they made him laugh.

Now, they were running into the apartment, heading for the DVD shelf. Conor got there first and was flicking through the movies, delivering his judgements – *cool, shit, shit, cool, mad* . . .

As he kissed Greta goodbye, part of Richie was detached behind that filter, wondering what she'd do with the boys tomorrow morning if he wasn't around to take them.

While the boys watched a DVD, Richie sat at the kitchen table and used his laptop to do a couple of invoices, then a few emails to potential customers pricing house-painting jobs. He'd already moved a scheduled job back to next week, to take care of the boys. Five of his guys were on three separate paint jobs and there were four more jobs pending and one that Richie knew would be cancelled – a time-wasting cheapskate who'd end up painting his own living room and living with the shitty consequences.

Work had been scarce for the first couple of years of the recession, when people were focused on paying off debts. Then, it eased – less movement in the housing market meant more people were staying where they were and spending money on improvements to their properties. If Richie hadn't had a poker habit draining his income he'd be well set up by now.

He found himself wondering what would happen to the business if things went bad this afternoon, if any of the lads working for him would have the brains to keep the little outfit going. He decided at least three of them would be well able for it.

One way or another, by teatime it would be over. He'd have earned an exceptional piece of money, or he'd be waiting for his solicitor to arrive at a cop shop. Or worse.

'Anyone for biscuits?'

Both their hands went up as Conor and Liam turned their backs on the old Stallone movie they'd seen half a dozen times.

Driving a dark brown Hyundai Accent, Richie Crown turned from the Malahide Road into Danieli Road and immediately spotted a man walking slowly towards him on the right-hand pavement. The man was wearing a flat cap, heavy-framed glasses, a bulky dark blue anorak and black cargo pants. Small guy, bulky upper body, like he took care of himself.

Whoever chose the car went for anonymity over performance. It wouldn't outrun anyone chasing it, but it would blend into the background of just about any neighbourhood.

By the time Richie was halfway down Danieli Road the man in the cap was crossing to the passenger side of the street. He made a gesture, halfway between a wave and a thumbs up, then he stood on the pavement and waited.

'We're taking the M50,' he said, when he settled into the back of the car.

His voice was light, calm. Northern accent. Like Richie, he was wearing thin latex gloves.

'Southbound on the M50,' he said.

Richie said 'Fine,' and they didn't speak again until the man gave directions just before they came off the M50 at the Lucan exit.

'Take Monument Road through Cullybawn, and left when you get to the end of that.'

'Far from here?' Richie said. 'Where we're heading?'

The man didn't reply. He gave directions when needed and about ten minutes after they came out of Cullybawn the man said, 'Pull in up here, just past the lamppost.'

He got out of the car without saying another word. Hands in his anorak pockets, he strolled up the street. After about fifty yards he came to a corner house, a Strain-type two-storey redbrick semi. He opened the gate and halfway up the path he took a key out of his pocket and used it to open the front door.

Could be this was where whatever was to happen would happen, but maybe not. Could be where the man was collecting something to bring somewhere else. Could even be this was where he lived. Richie Crown reckoned there was no point trying to figure it out, he'd know soon enough.

After ten minutes, he wondered if he'd missed something. Was he supposed to sit here? Waiting? What if the guy was gone an hour, two hours?

Is this it, or do I take him somewhere else when he comes back?

Fucking shithead has to be Mr Mystery. Can't just say come back in an hour. Can't just fucking say wait for me, I'll be here ten minutes, half an hour, whatever.

Has to make a big fucking deal of it.

Christ.

It was nerves, that's all it was, Richie Crown knew.

Shortly before he left his apartment, an hour after Greta came back from work, after Richie said goodbye to the kids, it was like something that had been simmering somewhere underneath came to the boil and Richie realised he was leaning on the kitchen counter, the knuckles of his left fist pushing hard against his mouth. He stared at the chrome handle of a cabinet door like he might see something written there that explained it all.

Solid.

Roly Blount said Richie was solid.

Richie wasn't sure that made sense.

Don't be stupid. Thinking yourself into a fix.

His ex, Rosita, said that about him all the time – he couldn't take things for what they were, had to imagine the worst, picture how that would be, how he'd deal with it.

Still.

What if.

This year, for instance, the kind of thing Richie did – there was a jewellery thing that mostly involved standing next to a couple of staff members who shivered as Richie stared them down from inside a balaclava. Then he helped to recover a large debt from a celebrity chef who lost a fortune fitting out a restaurant that closed before it opened.

Other stuff, same kind of thing. On top of his income from the painting business, it leveraged him into the fairly comfortable bracket. But it wasn't the kind of work that Roly Blount could be expected to notice.

Other hand, Roly Blount knew a lot of people. He heard all kinds of things.

What if, though.

What if they needed a disposable driver? What if they got somebody in for some heavy work, this guy, they brought him down from the North. Let's say he's someone who takes no chances.

Like Roly Blount.

He's a tidy worker, Roly. No loose ends.

They bring in this Northern guy.

They tell Tony Finnegan he's sitting this one out, he should find someone who can do the driving, someone solid, but no one they'll miss if the guy from the North decides it's safest to toss him away when the job's done.

Jesus, no, that's freaky thinking.

You cool out everyone who might be a problem, you create more ifs and buts than you started with. And the odds on something going tits up go through the roof.

No one takes that step unless they have to.

No, it is what it is.

And this is a taxi job.

Waiting's part of—

The Northern guy came out of the house, down the path to the front gate. He took his time, walking towards the car at the same gentle pace he'd approached the house.

Yeah.

It is what it is.

Nerves, that's all.

Thinking yourself into a fix.

There's no what if. No nothing. It is what it is.

Richie started the engine.

Soon as he closed the car door, the Northern guy said, 'Second right, third left – then halfway down, I'll give you the word.'

Richie moved them off and the man in the back said, 'Take it easy, no rush.'

Second right took them onto a long, straight road, third left was a cul-de-sac.

'Here.'

Getting out of the car, moving fast, the Northern guy said, 'Leave the doors open.'

As he spoke, two men were emerging from a parked Renault on the other side of the street, one of them carrying a satchel.

Richie followed the Northern guy away from the car.

The men from the Renault were leaning into the Hyundai as Richie followed the Northern guy into a zig-zag laneway that led out of the cul-de-sac and into the next street up.

The Northern guy got into the back of a red Toyota. Richie took the wheel. There was a key in the ignition.

When Richie Crown was on his way back from the gents in the Blue Parrot his phone rang and Greta told him she wouldn't need him to look after the boys tomorrow, she got a text from the school and the ceiling had been fixed. She invited Richie and his girlfriend over for something to eat next week.

Richie sat back at his place at the counter. He said, well, maybe in a couple weeks – it isn't really at that stage with Carol, yet, which wasn't really true.

He swallowed the last of his drink and said, listen, I'll call you tomorrow. Richie was looking up at the television at the end of the bar. The nine o'clock news was on and a security correspondent was standing in front of the house the Northern guy went to that afternoon.

Richie gave Novak a nod and gestured toward the screen and Novak found the remote and brought up the sound.

'... Gardaí say the shooting most likely occurred some hours ago. The body was discovered in the late afternoon when a relative – believed to be the man's nephew – paid a visit to the house. Gardaí believe the victim must have known his killer, as there was no evidence of a break-in. They say the car believed to have been used by the killer was found burnt-out some distance away. The victim, who recently moved to this house from the nearby housing estate of Cullybawn, has been identified locally as Frank Tucker, leader of a well-known West Dublin crime gang. Mr Tucker's brother was killed in a fight some years ago. Since then, the Tucker gang has expanded out of West Dublin and has for some time had a strong foothold on the Northside. Gardaí fear that this may lead to a tit-for-tat feud, if the Tucker gang carry out reprisals against whoever is responsible for this latest gangland murder.'

Novak was standing across the counter from Richie Crown. 'These guys, they play the game, they pay the consequences.'

'Tough game,' Richie said.

'You going to start licking the bottom of that glass?'

Richie smiled. 'Do me again.'

'My wife Jane, she says this place could do with a lick of paint. What she calls it is dowdy. "Your pub is dowdy as fuck," she tells me. What you think?'

'I like it as it is, but that's a civilian opinion. As a professional, you need to spruce it up a little.'

'A lick of paint, then. A small lick. A reasonably priced lick, that's what I think.'

'Let me work it out, drop in tomorrow, give you a price?'

'I'm here all day.'

Novak got him another Canadian Club.

What it felt like now was when he made the jump, on that rooftop on Camden Street, and he was standing on the other side of the laneway, looking back at the security thugs. Job done, risk taken and bested, everything back to normal, but he'd made another kind of jump, way past where he'd been.

Friday morning, he came out of the shower, filled the kettle and noticed a large envelope on the floor just inside the front door of the apartment.

The banknotes inside were in shallow layers and totalled enough to put Richie within striking distance of solvency.

Saturday was Carol's birthday. Richie had already made the bookings for a weekend in London, and they were in a mini-cab travelling in from Heathrow before ten o'clock Saturday morning. Carol was a theatre fan, so that night they went to see a play about a hangman who owned a pub. Richie had never been to a play and he found it a bit shouty at first, then he realised it was a long time since he'd laughed so much. Sunday they spent on tourist shit and they were back in Dublin by lunchtime on Monday.

Tuesday evening, Joe Campbell sent word he'd be a little late for the poker game, so the others poured drinks and waited.

Richie Crown took Tony Finnegan aside.

'The what-you-call-it, the heart thing, how'd that go?'

Tony shook his head. After a moment of silence, he said, 'Lying there, tube in one arm, tube coming out the other arm, fuck knows what's going through me, and they tell me the arteries in my heart – it's like someone's been pumping them full of shit. Anyway, month or so from now, they're opening me up.'

'Shit.'

'You?'

'Same as always.'

'What I hear, that thing went well?'

Richie shrugged. 'It went.'

Tony nodded. 'Roly's pleased with how it all worked out.'

'You've seen him?'

'He'll be in touch.'

Richie wasn't sure what to say and just then Joe Campbell arrived with a complaint about his fucking father and his fucking stepmother and how they needed a full-time fucking referee, sorry about holding things up.

Tony Finnegan began dealing. Richie Crown reached out to pick up his cards.

Eoin Colfer

Eoin Colfer is the author of the internationally bestselling Artemis Fowl books. Other titles include *The Wish List*, *The Supernaturalist* and the Legends series for younger readers. Eoin's books have won numerous awards including The British Children's Book of the Year, The Irish Book Awards Children's Book of the Year and The German Children's Book of the Year. The BBC made a hit series based on his book *Half Moon Investigations*. In 2009, Eoin was commissioned by Douglas Adams' estate to write *And Another Thing*, the concluding episode of the Hitchhiker's Guide to the Galaxy series, which became a worldwide bestseller. Eoin also writes crime novels featuring Irish bouncer Daniel McEvoy. The third and final book in his WARP sci-fi series was released in the summer of 2015. Eoin's latest work is the award-winning picture book *Imaginary Fred*, a collaboration with acclaimed Belfast artist Oliver Jeffers. Eoin has just finished a two-year run as Ireland's children's laureate.

A Bag of Hammers

My name is Louis deLacey and let me make it clear from the outset that I am no adventurer. The physical has never been my area. My father, a gifted whittler, snooker player and set-dancer bequeathed none of these talents to me. Instead I inherited my mother's quiet creativity, her fondness for digestive biscuits dunked in brandy and her attraction to men.

I am a crime writer by profession and my personality is suited to such a solitary occupation. I am prone to long silences, drifting off while a story takes shape in my mind. Prone, too, to irascibility when the details elude me, and outright foul temper when my plot line all too often reveals itself a near carbon copy of a favourite book. I am forty-five years of age, pot-bellied, churlish, physically weak and cowardly, I would imagine, though I avoid any situation which would require courage. My humour is mean-spirited and my greatest joy in life is poring over the critical lambasting of my peers in the nationals.

I live alone in the Irish town of Lock, named for the large lake or *loch* that once rippled where the Irish Premier Bank now squats, a hideous monstrosity of sandstone and marble.

My abode is quite the swanky townhouse, upon which I plonked down the deposit in a celebratory splurge five years ago when *Alone He Hunts* made a brief appearance on *The New York Times* bestseller list. Like a reluctant swimmer, it dipped a toe at number nine then ran screaming towards the twenties. As the title suggests, I write in the noir subgenre, though in interviews I refer to it as classic suspense. As a genre, it is certainly among the most popular forms of literary fiction, but I find it unchallenging and have so far managed to rehash my single story of a *murderous psychopath in a small town* fifteen times. Small town mummy's boys, small town cuckolds, small town black widows. Currently, I am in the early stages of a book featuring a mechanic who is falling for the charms of a glamorous heiress. The heiress is evil, inevitably, and the small town is in America, naturally, because you give the people what they want.

My books, though cultishly popular in the US, Germany and Finland, have not troubled any charts or shortlists in Ireland and so I live an anonymous life in Lock. People who register my existence at all have a fuzzy idea that I am a writer of some sort, but certainly not Google-worthy.

The main reason for this is that my own name does not adorn the spines of my efforts. I employ a pseudonym which makes me sound me sound a little more exotic at my agent's suggestion. I remember that lunch date well.

Anything to sell a book, Mike had said, checking his teeth in the blade of a fish knife. *You'd be amazed, Lou, how well a strong name looks on the shelf. You have to give good spine.*

How about Lance McHard-On? I had suggested drily. *Why not go the whole hog?*

Mike had rolled the name around in his head for a while.

Is it hyphenated? he asked finally.

I replied that I had always assumed it would be.

Then no, declared Mike. *Hyphens make the reader feel inferior.*

So that was that. Staid old Louis deLacey became Lance McArdon, and I have to admit it looks better on the cover.

Lance McArdon. Grandmaster of Noir.

Raymond Chandler was the master, Mike had explained. *So you have to be the grandmaster.*

I doubt that Raymond Chandler would lose any sleep had he not already gone down for the big one.

There is little else to know about me. I wear varifocal spectacles and favour brown clothing. My one affectation is a linen cap which I sport because I feel that writing entitles one to a little flamboyance. Oh, and as I may have alluded to, I am as queer as a bag of hammers. I have never met anyone who can decipher the *bag of hammers* reference but somehow the imagery is striking enough to circumvent the need for logic or meaning. It was a saying of my father's, who would smack my larger than average head outside mass every Sunday and ruefully inform members of the congregation that his son was *as queer as a bag of hammers,* as though my gayness was somehow his cross to bear. I would not have been surprised had he taken up a collection.

I remember the day he had his first heart attack. It was just after I pointed out that Jesus and the Twelve Apostles hiking off into the desert together had more than a whiff of the homoerotic about it. Father's hearing aid only caught five syllables – *Jesus whiff homo* – but they were enough to set his ventricles a-spasming. I suppose I do feel some regret over that, but I have to dig deep to find it.

Today I am at Sugar Land, Texas, which is home to an unusual concentration of Lance McArdon fans. So much so that it has become something of a tradition for my publishers to grudgingly pony up a business class ticket and book the event room in Crime Always Pays, a strip mall bookstore which has hosted my launches for a decade or more. On this occasion I am releasing my latest murder fest: *Alone He Mounts,* the story of a solitary philatelist in a small American town who excises small patches of his victims' tattoos to preserve in his murder album. Reviews have been sterling, if I do say so myself.

Detective Rad Kraven at his brutal best, said *The Sugar Land Executive,* which is a free magazine they dump in bus stop wire baskets.

And yes, my detective's name is Rad, not Rod.

Rad, short for Radical, because his father was a hippy ne'er-do-much, in reaction to whom Rad decided to spend his life enforcing rules. Rad is a big believer in open carry, and his catch phrase is *Fuckin' A*, which believe it or not is now plastered on a range of leisurewear.

The good thing about Rad's catchphrase is that it is the perfect message to inscribe on my reader's flap, i.e., *To Dolph, from Lance Mc Fuckin' A.* A terse message which keeps the line skipping along. However, the bad thing about the catchphrase is that it has become something of a millstone around my literary neck. I am not exactly the embodiment of Rad Kraven's philosophy, shall we say. I am a little more on the demure side. I enjoy a light opera and a snipe of Prosecco of an evening. Either of which would have Rad foaming at the moustache.

I feel there is more in me, writing-wise, I could aspire to a genuine literary crime novel with a little character development and story arc, and yet I do not *step away from the fuckin' cash,* as Rad once roared at Eddie Zeno, a small-time pimp from Dallas who had just slashed some John who'd fingered his wedge, to use the vernacular. My agent is eager that I maintain the Lance McArdon facade and I am eager that I maintain the facade of my beloved townhouse, not to mention my triannual holiday to exotic sun-spots, and so Lance lives on.

Of course, I am Lance and Lance is Louis but there are distinguishing features. For example, Lance sports a rhinestoned shirt and leather vest. Lance tugs frequently on his carefully applied moustache, and Lance's timbre is half an octave below mine own.

It often occurs to me that father would be so proud, and I laugh bitterly even when alone.

Fuckin' A.

And strangely, hiding behind the facade of misanthropy, I give very good Lance. Louis deLacey swears and grunts with the best of them. The ladies love him, even though he will never love them in that way. And the bookstore Crime Always Pays is the epicentre of Lance love. After the signing and obligatory hour spent chugging brews with the superfans, there is a delightful masseur called Bekandra back in the Hilton spa who could knead the kinks out of a suit of armour and nearly makes the entire trip worthwhile. We have a yearly appointment, Bekandra and I, and I swear she rubs the Fuckin' A right out of my bones.

But pre-Bekandra, I must abide. I must dwell in the shell of craggy old Lance McArdon and sign the hardbacks and be grateful there are customers to sign for. My minder today is an English major whose candy-pink lip gloss belies her foul mouth.

'Fuckin' A, Mr McArdon,' she says, sliding a book under my pen on the signing table. 'Am I right?'

'Fuckin' A, Shelley,' I tell her without fail, never flagging in my enthusiasm. To be honest with myself, I cannot help but enjoy these sessions. The fans hang on my every word and wait meekly for the stroke of my pen, and all it takes for me to make their day is a moment of eye contact and perhaps a shared profanity. A small price to pay for a life of security.

And who among us does not love to be loved? Even if it is for what we are not.

Also, it has been a good day. Rad Kraven goes from strength to strength. Hanging from the balcony they were, lapping it up. I half expected the locals to draw their openly displayed pistols and blast holes in the ceiling. Such unbridled enthusiasm.

'Fuckin' A,' burbles an elderly lady, her copy of *Alone He Mounts* balanced on the anodized bars of her walker, and throws in: 'From my cold dead hand, right, Mr M?'

Feeling a complete coward and charlatan I issue a hearty *fuckin' A* and dash off my pseudo-signature.

'From your mouth to God's ear,' says Shelley solemnly, handing the old lady her book and suddenly whatever gloss this occasion did possess feels cheap and tarnished and I long for Bekandra's fold-out table and strong fingers. And perhaps a Hendricks with a slice of cucumber.

At last there is one more customer to go. A hang-back, and these are always the most worrying kind of fan. People who hang back often want more than a generic signature. They crave a connection of some kind. Perhaps they have trucked in their entire collection of McArdons or perhaps they have an anecdote to relate. It is potentially that dreaded Annie Wilkes moment.

Shelley beckons the young man forward. His clothes are noir dark, his deep-set eyes are downcast beneath the peak of a baseball cap and there is a bag slung over one shoulder.

A bag. Hell and damnation. These bags can be bottomless.

'Mr McArdon,' says the young man, pulling a tattered copy of *Alone He Grunts*, the tale of a rural hermit who suffers from porcusthropy, and believing he is transformed into a hog by night, spends the full moon goring his victims. 'I'm your biggest fan.'

No. Surely not.

'That's great, kid,' I bluster in my practised mid-American accent. 'Whose name should I put on this old stinker?'

The young man is visibly rattled and I see his hands jerk. 'Whose name? Your name, of course. And it ain't no stinker, that's a goddamn classic.'

It is my turn to be rattled that he could really have so misunderstood my fake bogus self-deprecation.

'I'm just kidding, kid. *Grunts* is one of my favourites. And you bet my name is going on there. I thought you know I could dedicate it to you.'

The young man actually raps his own forehead. 'Yeah, yeah. Dedicate. Stupid. I'm so stupid sometimes.' There is pure anguish on his face and I know what he's thinking: that he's blown the big moment with his hero. If only he knew that his *hero*, All-American Lance McArdon, is actually little old Irish Louis deLacey who is wearing lifts in his Cuban heels, a fake moustache and believes in strict gun control.

Still, I give the young man a break.

'Don't sweat it, pal. I spent my life being stupid. You learn from your mistakes and then you get where you gotta be, that's what brought me here today.'

The young man acts like he can't believe what he's hearing. As though these are pearls of wisdom plopping from my moustachioed lips and not TV morning show platitudes.

'Yeah,' he says. 'Yeah. I knew you'd get it, Mr McArdon. I knew you'd get *me*. I musta read *Alone He Grunts* like a thousand times. There's more to this book than grunts, lemme tell you that. I heard what you were saying.'

This is all news to me. I can categorically state that there is no hidden subtext in *Alone He Grunts*, unless my subconscious is responsible for it. And it must be said my subconscious is a sneakier bastard than most.

'I could see you were a sharp one,' I say. 'You've got that look.'

Shelley has two roles in the signing queue: she moves it along and she plays the bad guy.

'What's your name, sir?' she asks the young man, taking the book from his hand. 'Mr McArdon has had a long afternoon.'

'Jonah Sweetlord,' says the young man, wincing as he reveals his second name, waiting for the insult, but in this area at least, I am a professional. And people who live in glass houses, as the saying goes.

'Sweetlord,' I say, heroically resisting the impulse to sing a snatch of a one-time Beatle's big hit at him. 'That would look fantastic on the cover of a book. A real writer's name.'

And no sooner are the words out of my mouth and I see the reaction on Jonah's face than I realise what a monumental rookie mistake I have just made.

'As a matter of fact,' says Jonah, jumping all over the segue I have gifted him. 'I am a writer. Trying to be at least.' And he reaches into his bag and I am not exaggerating when I say that I would only be minorly more alarmed if he reached for a gun on his belt, for I know only too well where this is going.

'I've been working on something,' he says pulling out a sheaf of pages. 'I thought maybe you could take a look. It's called *Solitary Prey*. About this guy living in a small town ...'

Here is where I traditionally make a pained face and let whichever Shelley is at my elbow swoop in and be the bad guy. My pained face is to convey to young Jonah Sweetlord that nothing would give me more pleasure than to spend a week or so dissecting his manuscript and making copious notes in the margins but this mean old bookseller simply will not allow it because they have a store policy against this sort of thing.

Unfortunately, the Shelley who is at my elbow is no longer at my elbow for she has disappeared, possibly to fetch a box of shop stock for signing, leaving me to be my own bad guy. This is intolerable. Shelley should be perfectly aware that the hang-backs hang back in precisely the hope that the flapper will think that surely to God the writer can handle one single person on their own.

What to say?

Jonah Sweetlord is frozen with his sheaf half aloft, awaiting permission to plonk it down like a winning hand.

'Fuckin' A,' I say to buy myself a second.

Sweetlord is nervously confused and he half-smiles, teeth glistening.

'That's great, man,' I continue. 'That you've finished the book. Finishing, that's the thing.'

Sweetlord takes this as a half-yes. 'Yeah. It was tough, you know. Well *you* know, of all people. Not that it's like 'specially difficult for you, I ain't saying that. So, you'll take a look. I know you're busy but I can wait. Lance McArdon looking at my book. Holy shit, sir.'

It's no use. I can't pussyfoot around this. It's bad enough that I write this bilge myself without having to read other people's freshman attempts.

'Mr Sweetlord. Jonah. I'd love to take this on, kid. I would. But I can't for legal reasons. My agent would murder me. I take one look at this and suddenly you're suing the shit outta me for stealing your ideas. Not you, personally. You don't have that look at all. But some guys. Happens all the time. What you need to do is go the proper route. Get yourself a stamped addressed envelope and start blanket-bombing agents. That's the way to go. I wish I could help you some more. I really do, buddy.'

Sweetlord is on the road to devastation, but to his credit he gives it one more try.

'If you could just take a look. A skim. Any words of encouragement from Lance McArdon. The man of men, you know. It would mean the world. Fuckin' A, right? Rad Kraven, right?'

He is desperate to hang onto the moment and God help me that look in his eyes reminds me of myself before the first contract came in. When I was writing two treatments a week, praying for a nibble from any publisher, however boutique, and I am a hand's breadth away from taking what is in all likelihood a sheaf of atrocious, derivative bollocks when Shelley arrives back from the stock room and goes straight to DEFCON 4.

'No, no, no, Jonah. You know store policy. No bothering the authors with your stories.'

Sweetlord is committed now, and ploughs on. 'Come on, Shelley. This is Lance McArdon. He's my guy. My guru. Just read one page, Lance … Mr McArdon. One page, then you can burn the lot if it doesn't grab you by the throat. It's two minutes of your time.'

Come on, Shelley, I broadcast at the bookseller. *Extricate me from this nightmare.*

Shelley shows me exactly why she's the event manager. She gives Jonah Sweetlord the full Peter Pan stance and cocks her head.

'Jonah, come on now. This is gosh darn puckey of the horsey variety. Do you get what I'm shovelling?'

I am impressed. Perhaps this afternoon has gifted me an unexpected boon. This Shelley person is going directly into my next book.

Sweetlord is deflated suddenly. 'Yeah, Shelley. I get it. No bothering the authors. No exceptions.'

Shelley wags a stern and stiff finger. 'You should know better, sonny. This is my livelihood right here and you are interfering with it. Do you think I could get the real big-shots like John Connolly or Harlan Coben to come in here if you won't even leave Lance McArdon be?'

I let that go. Fair comment, I suppose.

But, you know. Hmmm, all the same.

But Jonah Sweetlord backs off immediately. And more than that, his assault collapses utterly and he folds in on himself, drawing his manuscript into the cavity of his chest and retreating from the signing area softly, without another word, ducking down under the brim of his baseball cap. It is a spooky kind of exit and maybe I should have paid more attention but I am happy to have the burden of any expectation lifted. Normal service resumed, as they say.

Shelley unpacks the box of stock and flaps them on the table.

'I surely do apologise for Jonah, sir,' she says. 'He gets a little eager, but there's no harm in him.'

'Fuckin' A,' I say automatically, though it makes little sense in this context, which in fairness is usually the case.

'We'll have you out of here in no time flat,' Shelley assures me, brushing her boob reassuringly against my shoulder, God bless her optimism. ''Cause this gal here is the best flapper in Texas.'

Shelley is not wrong and in five minutes flat I am five hundred feet away in my air-conditioned room in the Mercado Hotel.

Once my door has clicked behind me, I am safe to be myself once more. The entire room is my closet, so to speak. Not that Louis deLacey is in the closet you understand, but for the moment Lance McArdon most certainly is. Not aggressively so, but more of a neutral stance on the whole gay issue. I buy my conscience off by imagining the day when I shall pen my memoirs and rip off my McArdon moustache during a particularly hetero-testical festival and read the most ribald chapter. Not that my own ribaldry is anything to write home or indeed anywhere else about. There have been a few men. I say a few, but a couple would be more accurate. And neither turned out to be love.

But I did have my chance.

A boy from my choir. Can you believe that? You couldn't make it up.

Picture the scene. The 1980s in Dublin. Two young men on a spring afternoon lounging by the riverside and sharing the last ember of a cigarette after Saturday practice, for God's sake. The grass springy between our thighs, shirts unbuttoned to the waist. And Gordon says to me, 'You sing good.'

And for him I am prepared to ignore the syntax.

'You too, Gord,' I tell him.

'It's like you believe in Jesus, or something like that.'

This is a stretch, but I am not about to argue as I have been dreaming of a moment like this for months.

'Jesus is OK,' I say, which is sacrilege coming from a tenor.

Gordon has more compliments up his sleeve. 'I like your hair too. How you do it. Swooshy, or whatever the word is.'

Backcombed is the word, but we are on the brink of something here.

'You know Connie?' I ask him. 'From the Pres. She does it for me.'

'I am going to see her,' Gordon resolves.

'You should,' I say, jumping onto the compliment bandwagon. 'She could do a lot with you. Your hair is so thick and shiny. You're worth it, you know.'

A little joke there, to pop the tension bubble, and it seems to work, for after I scald my lips on the next-to-last pull I rest my hand on a flat rock and am busy admiring my delicate fingers and the smoke curling between them when Gordon reaches for the cigarette and rests his fingers on mine, leaving them there while we both hold our breath.

It was a good moment. Not as good as I had imagined but nothing so far in my life has lived up to my imagination. But good enough that I want to stay like this forever, but instead I feel the spectre of my father's gaze upon me and I blurt: 'What the hell are you doing, Gordon?'

And of course he snatches his hand away and the hurt in his eyes is indescribable. 'Nothing. I thought ...'

'You thought you'd feel me up?'

Gordon turns from me as though we are in bed. 'We were talking about hair.'

The lightning rejoinder has always been my curse so I say: 'It's the eighties, Gordo. Men can talk about hair. You're a goddamn fag. Queer as a bag of hammers.'

And that pretty much did it for lovely Gordon and myself. We never spoke in any meaningful way again. There was no particular fallout other than that. No one self-harmed or anything, but I do feel that Gordon was my chance and I blew that one in a major and irrevocable fashion.

So here I sit in my hotel room, a little weepy all of a sudden. Indulging my own beautiful sorrow, my upper lip a little raw from the moustache, pulling the folds of my kimono tight to my throat when there is a delicate knock on the door and I actually say aloud: 'Oh, sweet, Bekandra. You, at least, knead me.'

Funny and maudlin, not easy to pull off.

I give the room a quick squint to ensure that there is nothing unseemly lying about, and then fling open the door, on the point of repeating my statement of only a moment ago, when I see not Bekandra before me but Jonah Sweetlord with a face like thunder.

'You know,' he says. 'You know you could have at least …'

Then he sees a knobbly kneed, kimonoed man quailing before him and the anger drains to his boots.

'Hey, I thought … Never mind, sir. I wasn't expecting a man wearing …'

Unrecognised out of my McArdon rig-out. It can be useful sometimes.

'Real Japanese silk,' I say, for some ludicrous reason, feeling the need to share this information.

Jonah nods, just being polite. 'Real silk, huh?'

And then I break into character and say, 'Fuckin' A.'

Jonah Sweetlord puts his cowboy boot in the doorway.

He forces his way into the room. It isn't difficult for the man to do. It's not as though I can resist him. Well, perhaps I could try if I had an iota of experience in that area. I do a good verbal spar, but not an actual spar. It's comical really: I backpedal into a Queen Anne chair upholstered in Paul Smith, I believe, and suddenly I am in a crime story. Being virtually held hostage.

'Oh, for heaven's sake,' I say, more peeved than scared if I'm honest. 'How did you find me?'

'I followed you,' says Sweetlord. 'It's two blocks away, man. And what … is that a dress? Is Lance McArdon wearing a dress?'

I feel a ridiculous urge to justify myself. 'It's a kimono, Jonah. Legitimate loungewear for a man. Not that I can't wear what I wish.'

Sweetlord paces. 'Two minutes. That's all I wanted. You know, you start people off on a career path. You inspire them, and all the time you don't give a shit.'

'I do care,' I protest. 'But I have a life and everyone's writing a book. You have no idea.'

'I don't believe it,' says Jonah, shaking his head. 'You're some kind of homo. Lance McArdon. I loved that guy. And not like *you* love guys.'

This is preposterous, even for Texas. 'Now listen, Jonah,' I say. 'I may be gay but that's no excuse …'

But he's having none of it. 'No, *you* listen. How could you do this? Pretending all this time. You have fans all over the world. A liar, that's what you are. Pretending to be a role model.'

This is ridiculous, although I can't help thinking of those stories a person hears. Crazed fans and so forth.

Still.

'Jonah. This is ridiculous. You can't barge in here. You don't own me.'

Sweetlord begs to disagree. 'I do own you. I got a sack of books to prove it.'

The boy makes a good point. Perhaps I could look at his manuscript.

'I spend my hard-earned dollars on a fag. A goddamn fag,' Jonah's tirade rolls on but it doesn't sound right coming out of his mouth. Forced, I would say.

I stand and touch his arm. 'Mr Sweetlord. Jonah. Calm down.'

He jerks as though electrified and I see pain in his eyes that has nothing much to do with me.

'What?' he says. 'Are you gonna feel me up now, Lance? You wanna go on a date now?'

And bingo, suddenly I'm looking in a mirror of glassy river water. Ain't psychology grand, for I see that same fear of discovery in him that I still harbour in a hidden corner of myself, and so I take an almighty risk and pull Jonah close for a hug, fully expecting a knee in the testicles with the power of the Bible behind it, and for a moment I feel his leg jitter, and tense my groin for all the good that will do, then Jonah Sweetwater's entire body spasms and I am holding him up almost, and as his arms wrap around me I know I have hit the nail on the head.

We stand like that, cowboy and geisha, for a long moment. It feels like a minute but it's probably no more than forty-five seconds, which is still an uncomfortably long hug between strangers even if one of them is having a life-changing moment.

Jonah lets me go and mopes his way out the door without another word and I sigh a long sigh and collapse into Paul Smith's arms wondering why the hell Bekandra is late and also wondering whether Jonah Sweetlord will be OK.

I don't need to wonder long for the doorbell rings and I check the fisheye to see the man himself shamefaced at my door.

'I should apologise to you, sir?' he says, when I open the door having not learned my lesson.

'Yes, indeed and you should,' I say, throwing in the extra conjunction in the Irish fashion.

'Well then, I guess I'm sorry,' he says, eyes still on his stitched boots. 'Can you tell me, sir, what should I do? Tell my folks?'

'Maybe your mother first,' I advise. 'Test the waters as it were.'

And then, I literally do not believe it, he holds out the manuscript.

'I know we got off on the wrong foot,' he says, finally lifting his eyes. 'But I spent two years on this.'

'One page,' I say, plucking the top sheet from the sheaf. 'And I am very direct. I have been known to reduce writers to tears.'

Sweetlord has no choice but to accept that deal. 'I see now,' he says. 'You make it up, the stories. So you can be whatever you want to be.'

'That's the idea,' I say. 'Some of our best-loved male crime writers aren't even males. A lot of them aren't even writers.'

I close the door on the poor boy because a man must hold onto the power in any situation, and I watch through the fisheye as Sweetlord considers knocking again and then makes his way down the corridor, and I breathe a sigh of relief. A man can only be expected to endure so much drama in an afternoon, especially when I had myself psyched for a distressing massage.

But. Even so. Jonah's predicament has touched me, and so I read his page, which is garbage of the worst type. Honestly, where is his sense of awareness? How can he present this in public? Sweetlord uses the verb *undulate* five times in one page. On the first page. And of course the main character's entire family is brutally murdered by a serial killer who leaves Bible-related messages.

In the name of the sweet baby Jesus. What is the point of even talking to these people?

Anyhoo. Still no sign of Bekandra and so I open the lid of my own laptop and study the title of my own latest effort: *Alone He Pines*, which features a murderous lumberjack.

The title. That's all I have so far, though I don't anticipate a problem filling the pages.

No problem but certainly no challenge.

'My Sweetlord,' I say. 'Jonah, Jonah, Jonah.'

Then I delete my title and type in:

A Bag of Hammers: A Fairy Story by Louis deLacey.

It looks well. People might read it.

They might.

And so I delete *A Bag of Hammers* and retype my original Pine title.

I am such a coward. So dependent on creature comforts that I cannot even be myself.

Then the bell rings.

'Bekandra!' I exclaim, clapping my hands. 'At least you knead me.'

Hooray.

Declan Hughes

Declan Hughes is the author of the Ed Loy series. His first novel, *The Wrong Kind of Blood*, won the Shamus Award for Best First Novel and the *Le Point* magazine prize for best European crime novel. His work has been nominated for the Edgar, Macavity, CWA New Blood, Theakstons and Irish Book Awards. His other novels are *The Colour of Blood*, *The Dying Breed*, *All The Dead Voices*, *City of Lost Girls* and *All The Things You Are*. Declan co-founded Dublin's Rough Magic Theatre Company. His plays include *I Can't Get Started*, *Digging For Fire*, *New Morning*, *Twenty Grand*, *Shiver* and *The Last Summer*.

The Time of My Life

This is a story about the time of my life. It's about the apartment no one knew was there, behind a rusted steel door with no lock and no bell and no address plate. There always had to be someone at home in order to get in and there was and mostly his name was Jeff (I know, right? 'Jeff'). In all the time I knew him, Jeff never left the apartment, apart from to snip the lock on a bike and pull it inside the building.

Outside the door was a lamppost and then there was nothing to the east for a mile only the disused warehouse with its bricked-up windows and doors running right to the canal bank. To the west, a vacant lot overgrown with brambles and Buddleia and strewn with dogshit and broken glass and the sagging girders and joists of whatever building stood there once. After that, the crossroads, with a Spar and an internet café and a chipper and a pub. People who came from the east tended to lock their bikes to the lamppost outside our door, and Jeff tended to steal them. And when I lived there, I stole them too.

Only I hadn't been living there for a while. But then I broke up with my girlfriend, or she broke up with me. She … I … does it really matter? Something happened between us, cheating or lying, or something stopped happening, kindness, almost certainly, and she noticed first and acted on it, and there I was, on the street with all my stuff in two bags and an unfortunate expression on my face. I walked and I walked. I had to stop and sit in a park for a while so I could stop crying. I stopped crying, and I made some calls, and I started walking again.

Without quite knowing where I was going (except I totally knew where I was going) I found myself approaching the rusted steel door and the lamppost with the bicycle locked to it. I made a call and waited and the door opened and a blond head emerged, looked west, looked east, looked at me.

'Dude,' Jeff said.

'Dude,' I said.

'Karen, man. It was coming, right? *Man.*'

'Man.'

'So. You wanna crash here for a while?'

I looked at Jeff, skinny, six-two, streaky blond hair in dreads, black military shirt hanging open, black cargo shorts, tan feet bare, alert blue eyes glittering in the moment.

'It was coming?'

Jeff ran his face through a sequence of expressions: *Everyone knew; feel for you man; we've all been there.*

Had Jeff been there? He never seemed to get entangled. There were always women and they always left.

I blinked back some more tears. I seemed to have an inexhaustible supply. Loneliness and wounded pride vied with humiliation and fear. And I did need somewhere to stay.

'If it's OK. Until I get sorted.'

'I'd like the company,' Jeff said, standing aside so that I could enter.

'Just a second,' he said as I made for the stairs. He went out on the street, turned his back to the traffic, pulled a fearsome-looking bolt cutter from his shorts pocket, snipped the chain that was locking the bike to the post, rolled it into the hallway and slammed the door. Under the stairs, the bike joined three others; two were shabby affairs that had known better days; one was a red-framed Trek bike I had seen somewhere before. Ali the Bike Guy called once a fortnight, paid twenty for the crocks, more for the fancier models.

Upstairs was a vast warehouse space that Jeff had animated over the years. There were Victorian hatstands and Chinese screens and burgundy plush curtains on free-standing rails and Persian and Afghan rugs that helped break up the sprawl; there were chaise longues and red leather Art Deco armchairs and two semi-circular aubergine couches that formed the centre of the room, with occasional side-tables in smoked glass. There were scarves draped over lamps and pictures leaning against walls and piles of books and manuscripts spilled across every flat surface.

Jeff's dad did something in Dubai. 'Too much money,' Jeff used to say when he'd fail an exam and suffer no adverse consequences. 'Way too much money,' he said when he dropped out after third year. He found this place then, bought the freehold for a pittance and spent his time decking it out to look like whatever it looked like, a 1920s' bordello, or Keith Richards' hotel room.

Dust and damp and the sweet tang of wine and dope and Thai food hung in the air, along with another, woody, musky scent that flooded my brain with full audio screenshots of tangled limbs and swollen mouths and red-and-black underwear and long lazy afternoon fucking.

Jeff sank onto one of the aubergine couches and gestured to a Moroccan water bong seething on a side table. I shook my head.

'Got to make some drop-offs later,' I said.

Jeff took a long hit and laid his head back on the couch, nodding at me as if all was, if not understood, easily explained.

'What did you mean by "it was coming"?' I said.

'Drop-offs,' Jeff said. 'Because you're not at Karen's any more. You'll have to call them?'

'I have called them. What did you mean by—'

'Jennifer Moran, man,' Jeff said.

'What's that supposed to mean?' I said.

Jeff laughed and gave me an ironic salute and took another hit on the bong. There was music playing low, something trip-hoppy with crackling samples and spacy loops and a lot of repetition. It felt like some metallic reptile was hauling itself slowly around the room. I reached out for the pipe.

'Maybe I'll just, ah …' I said.

The hot metallic smoke crimped the back of my throat and set my head reeling. I took another hit and held on to the edge of the couch, sweat on my upper lip, nausea coursing down my spine; it crested in a little pile between my bowel and my prostate and began to spray its delirious reflux right back at me.

'Fuck,' I said.

'Fuck yeah,' Jeff said. 'Dude said no when he meant fuck yeah.'

'This is the shit.'

'That it is.'

'So. Who … what did you hear?'

'Jennifer Moran? You and her in the Bailey.'

'I don't go in the Bailey. I never go to the Bailey. The fucking Bailey, man? No way.'

'Okay then, Bruxelles. Bloom's. Bartley Dunne's. Somewhere that begins with B, I don't fucking know, that place where all the culchie politicians go. Buswell's.'

'It *was* Buswell's. On the basis that no one we know would be seen dead there.'

'Ah but. Our friends in business and law, since they graduated, all be hanging round there with wannabe politicians and lobbyists, giving it the way of the world and in this town and shit. And one of them saw you and La Moran, said you had your tongue in her mouth and your hand up her skirt. Or maybe it was the other way round. Said why didn't you get a room.'

'We did get a room. We very got a room.'

'Which is exactly why your bullshit is so full of fucking bullshit,' said a female voice. Karen, and her musky scent, sandalwood and sex, appearing from behind a free-standing screen, dressed, as ever, head to toe in black: Doc Marten shoes, lacy tights, A-line mini, boxy jacket, red flower in her black boy hair.

'Weeping, and oh me, and poor little lost boy. Like we were, what? Some vanilla couple that held hands in lectures and volunteered for the Green Party.'

Karen, oh, Karen. Black boy hair spilt across creamy tan, lightly freckled brow, black pupils dilated to fuck in deep brown eyes, flashing with, not rage, satirical amusement. Flashed on those eyes rolling back as I thrust into her, her nails scraping down my back, gripping my ass, driving me deeper. She sat beside Jeff, dragged a crooked finger across his cheek, perched a laced leg over his bare leg. Jeff had the grace to affect embarrassment, laughed a Jeff laugh.

'Game playing. Is all it is, Mark man.'

I looked from one to the other.

'Game playing? What kind of game is this?' I said.

'You should know,' Karen began. Jeff decoupled himself, stood up, tossed a cease-and-desist towards Karen with his long, elegant arm, took a thinking walk around the brass spittoons, the free-standing mantelpieces, the whatnots crammed with bibelots, antiques by Salvador Dalí, holding the moment between outstretched arms.

'Jennifer Moran, dude.'

'Yeah, and? Is Karen fucking you? Is that why we're all here?'

'This is not about who's fucking who, man.'

I blinked hard, shook my head like a dog, trying to throw off the effects of the skunk. Karen was cutting lines with a credit card on a pewter serving dish and methodically snorting them through a fifty-euro note.

Who's fucking who? I have fucked each of you, many times, was the thought I couldn't extract from my head. Stoned out of my twist with Jeff, the hash smoke hanging like mist in the folds of the drapes, red and burgundy and aubergine tones dancing like flames. The first night, I dreamed of Jeff, the planes of his bony face, the blue eyes, the stupid, cold beauty of him, dreamed of his cock deep in my ass, then woke on the sofa, underwear damp and glistening with come stains, Jeff noticing and laughing. The next night – we were mostly smoking back then, smoking and making plans we couldn't execute because we were smoking – I rocked forward from my sofa to his on my knees and ran my hands up the inside of his shorts. He looked down at me like it was the best joke anyone had ever made.

'Mark, man. Are you sure?'

'Strangely, yes,' I said. I unbuttoned him, traced a finger along his perineum and up between his balls and oh, his cock sprang stiff into my mouth. The salt taste, the pleasing hardness on my tongue, against the inside of my cheek, the roof of my mouth, the comforting ache in my throat, the hot rush of come like a salve, like a bracer.

'*That* was a surprise,' Jeff said, softly, smiling, reaching for me.

'You don't have to, just *because* ...' I said.

'Oh but I do, man. Reciprocation. What makes us human in the end.'

We did ... all the things that night. And for the rest of the summer, we did all the things whenever we could. We still had girlfriends, and we saw them when we saw them, and when we didn't, we saw each other. Then I moved out, moved in with Karen. Didn't give it a second thought. We weren't 'gay.' At least, I wasn't. At least at least, I never found another man I wanted to have sex with, I can't speak for Jeff. All it was was, something that happened.

And now. Now. The sex was one thing. The main thing, usually. But not in this instance.

'Jennifer Moran's brother. Anto. Is trying. To. Fuck. Me. Up,' Jeff said, breaking the statement into units of unleavened, non-ironic reality.

I looked at him as if I didn't know what he was talking about.

'Clients you were handling for me. Accountants and solicitors, hush puppies too scared to come up *here*, you were able to put them at ease with your, what, your suburban charm, your lower-middle register, your rugby club glottals. You've passed them over to Anto. And now he wants more.'

'I didn't pass anyone to Anto. I've just called them—'

Jeff waved his phone at me.

'Stephen Nolan. John O'Connor. Eamonn Doyle. You'd fall asleep in the middle of their names, they're so respectable. I called them today, after Karen let me know what had happened—'

'Because that was the first you'd heard about it.'

'I called them, half a dozen others, hyphenate consultants all, and they all sang the same tune: Anto Moran was seeing to their narcotics needs, thank you very much; no need for any alternatives. They're not scared of him anymore.'

That was why none of them had returned my calls. Oh Jennifer, you worked me over good.

'Dude is called the Cyclist now, in the *Sunday World* and shit. Can you believe that? Pathetic ... fucking ... narcissism. The *Cyclist*. 'Cause he wears the Lycra gear all the fucking time.'

That's where I had seen the Trek bike before. I scrolled through my numbers, weighed my options.

'I need you to get those clients back, Mark, man,' Jeff said.

'Off Anto Moran? How would I do that, man?'

'I don't know. But if you don't ... well, I know people with nicknames too, man. Can't afford to seem weak like that. Amigo.'

'Is that a threat?'

Jeff looked at me then, eyes cut with … what was it? Looked like menace, smelt like fear. Fuck you, amigo. I sent a text message to the number I had found.

'I'll still need somewhere else to crash,' I said. 'If you and Karen …'

'I'm not staying here,' Karen said, sniffing and wiping her nose and running her tongue around her teeth, her eyes two black glistening holes. 'Anyway, you and Jeff. Before we met. For an entire summer. He told me, Mark. How come you never?'

'Didn't seem the right moment.'

'Which moment?'

'Any of them.'

Karen looked at Jeff, then at me.

'It makes sense of it all now,' she said.

'Of what all?'

'You and Jeff. Jeff and me.'

'Jeff and you. Since when?'

'This is hardly the point of the exercise,' Jeff said.

'Since the beginning. Since we got together. Jeff paid attention. I was flattered.'

'Both of us? Since the beginning?'

'Why not? Two gorgeous boys. Any girl would. We so should have all got a room.'

I tried to feel something, failed. All of a sudden, I wanted to be anywhere but here, living any life but this.

'You told Jeff about all this?' I said to Karen. 'Why? Because you were jealous of Jennifer?'

Karen laughed.

'Jealous of Jennifer? I don't think so. I was actually concerned that you couldn't see she was using you, she was a pawn in her brother's game. And she was costing you money.'

'Costing Jeff money.'

Karen turned a sniff into a shrug.

'As it turns out, costing us all money.'

There was a loud crashing on the door downstairs. It was down to me, what would happen next.

'That's Ali, for the bikes,' Jeff said, flashing me a '*don't sweat it, amigo*' smile. 'Play nice now, you two.'

I could have stopped him, or warned him. Please remember that about me. I always do. When Jeff left the room, I followed as far as the steel door that led out to the stairwell and I didn't call down to stop him or warn him. Instead, I pulled the door shut and locked it.

'What are you doing? Open the door, Mark.'

'It's not safe,' I said.

'I don't feel safe here with you,' Karen said, and came at me with a brass implement, a poker maybe. 'Open the fucking door!'

The poker halted its motion, suspended in the air before my face, as Jeff's voice turned from declaration to protest, from pleading to screaming, as stamping and crashing rang up the stairwell and in under the locked door.

I put a finger to my lips and we waited in silence, barely daring to breathe, as the sounds of violence prevailed, and the sounds of Jeff subsided.

'What the fuck?' Karen said in a hoarse whisper.

'Anto Moran's red Trek bike was stolen.'

'Did Jeff steal it?'

'One very like it.'

'And you gave him up?'

'In what fucking version of reality was I supposed to get Anto Moran to give him those clients back?'

Steps crashed up the stairs then, and feet and fists pounded against the door. Karen came into my arms and made sounds against my neck, sniffs and sobs. I held her tight, held on until the pounding stopped, and the steps crashed downstairs, and there was silence, and voices, and laughter, and the sounds of the street outside. We pulled apart and looked at each other.

'Fuck, Mark. He could be dead.'

'And if I hadn't locked that door, so could we.'

I'd like to tell you that I didn't have sex with Karen before we rang for an ambulance. Frankly, I'd like to tell you none of this at all. But I had stopped having the correct feelings. All I had left was a sore throat and a hard cock. Afterwards, we walked away and rang the ambulance and watched until it arrived. Still I felt nothing, except maybe relief. I wanted Karen and Jeff and all the drugs and all the sex and all the crazy to be over. I wanted to be someone else.

And of course, now, I am. I am someone with a name and a family and a life so boring you'd fall asleep in the middle of it.

Jeff is still Jeff, with a limp and an eye-patch the only signs that in his past, Something Happened. He gave a TED talk in Montreal last year about … fuck, I don't know. What are any of them about? Technology and smart environmental choices and world hunger and sustainable development. Caring About Things. Way Too Much Money. We never spoke again.

Karen teaches in a university and Cares About Things on Facebook: Monsanto and Fracking and Rescue Dogs and Mindfulness and Gender and the Patriarchy. We see each other across crowded rooms. We pretend we don't.

Me, I don't care about anything. Not the way I used to. I used it all up, cried it all away. I did all the things, and now I don't do any of them anymore. I wish I did though. I wish I was back there, in the mire of it. The only time I felt, however briefly, alive. The best worst time. The time of my life.

Cora Harrison

Cora Harrison was born and educated in Cork, went to England and worked there as a teacher and head teacher, moving back to Ireland when she retired. Researching the history of her home in County Clare led to the Drumshee books, tracing a small farm's evolution from Iron Age fort to twentieth century cottage. She published twenty-seven books for children with Irish publishers and then began on the sixteenth century Mara series, fourteen Brehon law mysteries set in the Burren, County Clare, published by Macmillan, and by Severn House, who are now publishing the Reverend Mother series about Cork city in the early 1920s. Macmillan also published four of her novels for young adults and Piccadilly Press published six mysteries for children set in Victorian London. www.coraharrison.com

Mara's First Case

Brehon or Early Irish Law
An Seanchas Mór
(The Great Ancient Tradition)
There are two fines that have to be paid by anyone who commits a murder:

1. A fixed fine of forty-two *séts*, twenty-one ounces of silver, or twenty-one milch cows.
2. A fine based on the victim's honour price (*lóg n-enech* – the price of his face).

In the case of *duinethaide*, a secret and unacknowledged killing, then the first fine is doubled and becomes eight-four *séts*, forty-two ounces of silver, or forty-two milch cows.

'It's funny how you never forget your first case, especially when it was a murder,' said Mara to her grandson. 'Mind you, I think it was the strangest and most puzzling case I have ever dealt with.'

'What made you suddenly remember it?' asked Domhnall.

'Coming down this hill in Glenisheen, I suppose. It was a day just like today, sun sparkling on the sea, orchids and primroses everywhere, stone pavements more silver than grey.

There used to be a little thatched alehouse, just over there, built against the cliff edge, at the side of the road. It's been gone and forgotten about for years and years, but today I've just noticed the outline of the stones, just behind that clump of purple orchids and that reminded me.'

On that April day over thirty years ago when Mara, the twenty-one-year-old newly appointed Brehon, had been riding down that road, elated and excited at the thought that she was now responsible for law and order in the kingdom of the Burren, the orchids had been even more profuse. She slowed her horse to admire them as they rose, pink and purple ruffles between spears of pale green, from the cracks between the stone slabs. And at that moment the door of the alehouse was flung open and the innkeeper came rushing out.

'Fetch the Brehon,' he shouted. 'There's a man dead in here. He must have been murdered! The physician says that he's been poisoned.'

Mara did not hesitate. 'I am the Brehon now, Barra,' she said proudly. He was a nice man, this innkeeper. Unlike many of his occupation, he had never taken to drinking his own wares, but spent most of his time carving cups and platters from pieces of wood from wayside hedges. Despite his distress, he beamed at her now.

'Wouldn't your father have been proud,' he said as she swung herself from the horse's back, tied its reins to a willow tree and went straight into the alehouse followed by the wolfhound.

It was very dark in there, dark and smelling of ale, and of the clusters of yarrow, mint and wormwood that hung from the beams of the low ceiling. The alehouse was almost empty, just three men beside one of the tables and a dim form on the floor at their feet. Malachy, the physician, knelt at its side and she walked towards him with a steady step. There was piece of parchment on the table that she recognised. It was a co-ploughing agreement in her father's handwriting, written many years ago, dark with the smoke from the peat fire, marked here and there with splashes of ale, blots of ink and large, unsteady crosses. April was the time of year when the co-ploughing agreements were made, and these were normally solemnised in an ale house. It was, in fact, the only form of contract, under Brehon law, where drunkenness could not be held to invalidate the pact as farmers traditionally agreed on the terms over cups of ale.

Malachy had glanced up briefly when she came in and then, impatiently, at the door behind her, as though looking for someone else. The fire flared suddenly and now Mara could see the corpse, his eyes wide open and staring.

The other men, too, looked towards the door. It was time, thought Mara, to stamp her authority on the proceedings.

'Was anyone else present except you four when this man fell dead, Barra?'

'No,' said the landlord, and then, hastily, 'No, Brehon.'

'Wait up there, all of you, please.' She indicated a place beside the door. They went and perched on the barrels.

Despite the glow from the sods of peat, it was quite dark where she and Malachy stood. The small alehouse had no windows, just a door and the oil lamp was not lit.

'Poisoned: deadly nightshade,' said Malachy quietly. He picked up one of the wooden cups, a pale cup with a small bird carved on it. 'This is his one. Smell it.'

Mara smelled, mainly ale she thought, and then caught the faint bitterness beneath the familiar odour. One by one she picked up and smelled the other three wooden cups – all slightly different; none had that distinctive smell. She beckoned to the landlord.

'Have you had anyone else in here this morning, Barra?'

'Not a soul, nor a sinner,' he said.

'And how many drinks did the men have?'

'Just the one.' Barra was a red-haired man with a white skin, but he had gone even paler with agitation. 'I poured all four from the same pitcher and these other three men are as right as rain. Nothing I put in it! Look, here's the pitcher, still some ale in it.' He reached up and unhooked another oddly shaped wooden cup with a large handle from the first of the pegs above him, tipped in some ale and drank it defiantly.

'That's right, that's what happened.' The other three voices chimed in and tentatively the three customers approached.

'We all drank our first cupful,' said Faol. 'Not one of us touched his drink.' His voice and narrow face were aggressive and challenging, and the wolfhound moved a step forward towards her mistress.

'And then, just when I was ready for a second, Seán started choking.' Aeden clasped his own throat dramatically.

'We could see that he was purple-like and he wasn't breathing. We didn't do a thing to him.' Darragh's bull-like face, with its wide-apart eyes and low forehead, had a threatening air, and Mara stared at him coolly before turning to Barra.

'Who went for the physician?'

'There was a lad driving a donkey up the road, Brehon, so I told him to jump on its back and to ride as fast as he could. I thought Seán had a fit. It was only when the physician came that he said the man had been poisoned.' Barra looked distressed, and the other three exchanged glances from beneath their eyebrows.

'Well, I'll call in the house and make arrangements for his son to collect the body.' Malachy went towards the door.

'Peadar's not there, doctor, he's gone up Boolona to bring the sheep and their lambs down to the valley. Aoife, my daughter, you know, was telling me last night when she came to give me a hand with cleaning. She'll be there, though, with the little boy,' said Barra.

'I'll be off, then,' said Malachy. 'Could I have a word outside, Brehon?'

Mara followed him out of the dark room. Barra, she thought, should renew the limewash on his walls. It must be years since he had painted the stone and the dingy surfaces were covered with scrawled jokes, poems and sketches done in charcoal.

'You've got a problem on your hands, Mara,' said Malachy abruptly as he pulled the door shut. 'I'd send for Fergus, if I were you. This is a nasty business.'

'Why?' asked Mara. Fergus MacClancy had looked after the legal business of the Burren, as well as that of Corcomroe since the death of her father, but now she was Brehon. He had spoken very highly of her to the king and she was not about to let him down by quailing before her first big case.

'I'd say that they were all in it, all three of them,' said Malachy. 'They'll bear witness that none of them put the poison in Seán's drink and you won't shift them. The man was the most unpopular fellow in the parish. Have you seen all those drawings and satires on those walls in there? He did most of them. Not a word of truth in them most people would say, but you'll get others to whisper that there's no smoke without fire. There was a bad fist fight last week when he scrawled up a poem about Aeden paying court to another man's wife and then he has one about Faol stealing sheep – drawing and all, and he drew one of Darragh with his own face and the body of a bull and a cow, well, I won't sully your ears with the verse he wrote …'

Mara thought about this. 'And the poison?'

'Deadly nightshade grows everywhere on the Burren, you'll find it among the clumps of hazel. Not hard to make.'

'What about the son? What about Peadar? Could he have come down from the mountain?'

Malachy shook his head. 'That's a big job getting all those creatures down safely and he's just got the three boys with him, and none of them a day over fifteen. He couldn't leave them to look after the sheep from the four farms. Peadar's fond of his father, too, that's the funny thing. Fond of him and proud of him, thought he was very clever. And to give Seán his due, all the profits of that small farm went to Peadar and his wife. Seán built himself a little house on the land when Peadar married. He had no interest in farming, was happy if he had the price of his ale and he didn't drink too much of that, either. His pleasure in life was in writing these satirical poems. He seemed to enjoy being hated. I'd leave it alone, Mara. Send for Fergus.'

And then Malachy climbed on his horse and went off to break the news of her father-in-law's death to Aoife and Mara went back into the alehouse. She settled down to spend half an hour reconstructing the scene, questioning all four men. Each was adamant that none had moved from the table; that their cups were filled one after the other by Barra, starting with Faol's cup, next the dead man's and then moving around the table to the three others. They had toasted a good harvest and then all drank at the same moment.

Aeden had a long shepherd's crook. Could he have secreted some powder in the large split in its handle? But wouldn't Barra have noticed that? The three men apparently drank simultaneously as he stood there with the pitcher in his hand. Faol had a stoppered horn filled with a garlic mixture for a sick cow. Mara sniffed it dubiously, but could not discern that bitter smell that still permeated the cup of the dead man. The floor was of roughly levelled stone, but reasonably clean. Mara ran a finger over it. Despite the lack of rain for the last week it was slightly damp at one spot, just beneath where Darragh's mantle hung, but she could make nothing of that. Malachy was probably right: the case was unsolvable, but something stubborn in her refused to give up. There was, she noticed, a slight hole in the thatch above the table. Could the dead man's son have come down from the mountain and dropped a pellet of poison into his father's drink? Almost impossible, she thought. And what would be the motive? Malachy, who knew the family well, felt that there was none. She left the four men, unfastened her horse and rode slowly down to the small farm at Aillwee, closing the gate carefully behind her as she could see a small, bright-haired boy running energetically around, waving a stick.

'Don't worry about the wolfhound, Aoife,' she called. 'Saoirse is used to my own little girl. Come over, Seánín, no, put down that stick. Now come and stroke the big dog. Don't be afraid,' said Mara, neatly extracting a stone from the child's mouth.

'Bless him, he's afraid of nothing,' said Aoife. The dog's face was level with the little boy's and a pink tongue was licking some of the mud from his cheeks while he gave her a big kiss on her furry head. Aoife beamed proudly.

'You've heard the news?' queried Mara.

'Yes, I have, to be sure. Poor misfortunate man,' said his daughter-in-law. She sounded mildly regretful, but not distressed. 'I can't believe that anyone would have killed him. Sure, he had no real harm in him, just mischievous, like that fellow there,' she added with a fond glance at her son who had picked up his stick again and was now chasing the hens. 'What poisoned him? The doctor didn't say.'

'It was deadly nightshade,' explained Mara.

'Deadly nightshade,' said Aoife. 'That's that stuff ...' And then she stopped and said in a low voice, 'Oh, my God, so that's what he was doing.'

'Who?'

'It was Darragh. Those old berries. It's just come back to me. I saw him in that hazel wood over there. Sliced the whole clump of them off with his knife,' said Aoife. 'What will Peadar say? His own father. And a neighbour to do that to him! I dread to tell him.'

'Let me do it,' said Mara, seizing the opportunity. Above their head came faintly the noise of a few score sheep coming down the mountain. 'I'll leave my horse here with you. Saoirse and I will climb up and meet him.' It should, she thought, be easy to get Malachy to inspect Darragh's knife for traces of poison. But perhaps the woman was trying to shield her husband. There was something glib about the way that those words came out. She thought about it as she climbed.

By the time Mara met with the herders, the sheep had stopped to drink. It had been a wet winter and the Glenisheen spring well had spilled out, filling a hollow in the limestone pavement.

'I'd love a dog like that,' said Darragh's son, looking enviously at Saoirse as she greeted the sheep dogs. It had been a happy chance that she had brought the wolfhound as the three boys answered her questions about their day in an absent-minded fashion, being occupied with admiring and measuring the height of the enormous dog. By the time Mara turned to Peadar, she was satisfied that there was no possibility that he could have gone down the mountain to the wayside alehouse at any stage during the morning.

'I'm afraid I have some bad news for you, Peadar,' she said, drawing him away from the three boys. 'Your wife and little Seánín are well, but I'm sorry to say that something has happened to your father.'

Malachy, she thought, as she explained what had happened to the weeping man, was right. Peadar had been fond and proud of his sarcastic old father. His grief was genuine. He had, she thought, neither motive nor opportunity. So who could possibly have killed the old man? And why?

When they left her, Mara sat on a limestone slab, one arm around Saoirse's neck, absentmindedly staring at a clump of mountain avens which had miraculously escaped the tramping feet of the sheep. Something about the bright gold stamens and the pale, innocent faces of the little flowers reminded her of Seánín and she began to understand.

Hurriedly she got to her feet and went back down to Aillwee by a narrow, precipitous path, hastily planning as she went.

'Aoife,' she called urgently as she came through the gate. 'What has Seánín got hold of? That's not deadly nightshade, is it?'

'Oh, my God,' screamed Aoife. Her eyes went immediately to a spot of disturbed soil next to the shed. In a second she was at her son's side. 'That pig must have dug them up!' She scraped frantically at her son's mouth. As usual he had put something in his mouth, but she only extracted a few cloves of garlic that Seánín had pulled up from a newly planted row. And then she stopped, her face turning white as Mara said quietly.

'So it *was* you who killed him with the deadly nightshade.'

'I didn't ... How could I? I wasn't near him.'

'I think that you killed him by pasting the powder into Seán's cup the night before. They all have their own cups, don't they? Barra carves them from bits and pieces of wood. There are no two alike. And Seán's is alder wood, as white as milk. You knew that the four men would be drinking there to sign the co-ploughing contract, so you pasted the powder into his cup the night before.'

'What would I do a thing like that for? What harm had the man ever done to us? Don't say it was for the farm. He had handed it over to Peadar when we were married. He had no interest in it.' Aoife's voice was scornful. She was beginning to recover, but her face was very pale.

'I think that you did it for the fine,' said Mara. 'Everyone knows about the fine for a murder. For a secret and unlawful killing of the dead man's son, Peadar, would get forty-two milch cows. That would have been a fortune for you both and a great inheritance for your son.' Something in the woman's face alarmed her. There was a look of desperation, a look of a trapped animal as Aoife looked around the farmyard, her gaze pausing on the stone building where the bull bellowed behind a stout wooden gate. She snatched up her child, almost threw him into the cottage, slammed the door, ignoring his cries and then moved towards the bull.

'Saoirse!' called Mara and made rapidly for the gate. Saoirse advanced towards Aoife, standing directly in the woman's path, lips curled over a fearsome set of teeth, fierce low growls coming from her. Aoife stopped. Mara went through the gate, then called to Saoirse, who cleared it with a flying leap. With an effort Mara steadied her voice as she mounted her horse.

'Judgement day at ten o'clock next Monday, Aoife,' she said. 'I will pass sentence then. I'll leave you to tell the truth tonight to your husband.'

The Brehons of the kingdom of the Burren held their law court in a large field that contained the ancient dolmen of Poulnabrone. The field and the surrounding walls were covered with people when Mara arrived. In the intervening days she had sent her farm manager around to arrange for an announcement at every church, smithy and mill as the regulations, according to Brehon law, stipulated.

Mara placed her scroll on the flat surface of the dolmen and advanced. Her father had taught her, when she was a small child, how to project her voice to the back of the crowd and she thought of him as she greeted the people of the Burren. She cast one glance at the white face and shaking form of Aoife, but hardened her heart. Justice had to be done, had to be seen to be done.

'A man has been unlawfully killed in our kingdom,' she began and told the story of the death of Seán. Then, in dead silence, Aoife stumbled through her admission of guilt and her repentance. Mara stepped forward again.

'The fine of forty-two milch cows is due to be paid by the guilty person to the son of the dead man,' she said. 'But as a woman's husband is responsible for her debts, in this case there will be no fine.' Aoife, she thought, would suffer for years for this crime. Neighbours regarded her with horror and even her own husband stood apart from her. She raised a hand to silence the murmurs. Something else needed to be said.

'The ancient laws of our country,' she said, 'were ratified anew by St Patrick. Three bishops, three kings and three doctors of knowledge approved the *Senchus Mór* and laid down the principle that loss, injury and death should be compensated, and not avenged with savagery and death. I have sworn before the king to uphold these laws and now I swear to you that as long as life and competence remain to me, I will administer them to keep the peace and to heal loss. And I am resolved that never again will those laws be mocked in this kingdom. So help me God.'

Mara paused in her story to her grandson, and smiled a little to think back at her own very earnest self, thirty years ago. 'And, do you know, Domhnall,' she said, 'when I said that, the whole crowd – almost every person in the Burren was there – they all cried out: "Amen".'

Brian McGilloway

Brian McGilloway was born in Derry, Northern Ireland in 1974 and is the author of eight novels. The first novel in his DS Lucy Black series, *The New York Times* and UK No. 1 Bestseller *Little Girl Lost*, won the University of Ulster's McCrea Literary Award in 2011 while his DI Benedict Devlin series of novels have been shortlisted for a CWA Dagger, an Irish Book Award and the Theakstons Old Peculier Crime Novel of the Year. In addition, Brian's screenplay, *Little Emperors*, won BBC Northern Ireland's Tony Doyle Award in 2014. His ninth novel, again featuring Lucy Black, will be published in early 2017. Brian currently teaches English in Strabane, where he lives with his wife, daughter and three sons.

What Lies Inside

I hear the clunk of the lock, the grind of the handle, the grating of the hinges, as the door swings inward. It is 8 a.m. Another Tuesday.

The screw comes in bearing a tray, glances around the cell, smirks when he sees the porno lying open from last night.

'Rise and shine, sunshine,' he says.

I stretch and twist my neck. 'I still need another pillow,' I say. 'The doctor told me, on account of my neck. I can't take tablets, so I need to have two pillows. This is the fifth time I've asked.'

The screw smiles. 'Make it a sixth and you'll have no pillows at all. This isn't the Ritz. Breakfast is served.'

He drops the tray on top of my desk, then is gone.

I move across and pick it up: a thick grey stodgy porridge; powered orange juice that's been over-diluted; a cold slice of toast, cut diagonally, all hard angles and crumbled crust and a smear of butter.

In the corner, on the TV, some idiot jabbers away to the camera, bouncing up and down on a sofa like a grateful puppy. I don't want to listen to him but then, I don't want to listen to the noises in the silence either; the groans and shouts from the cells, the ringing of bells continues through each night. On the rare occasions they do stop, my room fills with the humming of the heating pipes and the sounds, in my head, of my own thoughts, my memories of that other, dreadful, silence.

I'm surprised when I see my name on the visitation lists that get pinned up that morning. For a second I think it might be my mother, changed her mind after eighteen months. The last time I saw her was in the hospital. She'd stood at the end of my bed without a word, without discernible emotion, just staring at me. I think I know now what she was doing: trying to feel something when she looked at me that would make her recognise me as her child.

But, in the end, she'd turned and walked out, closing the door quietly behind her. It would have been better if she'd flipped: screamed, spat on me, slapped me, told me the wrong one died. Her silence was the worst part of the whole thing, like I'd broken something inside her that would never work again. So I didn't judge her not visiting. I'd not have allowed myself to think about her but that seeing my name on the visitation list prompted it.

Instead, my sister, Maggie, sits, straight backed, watching as I lope into the room, take my place on the opposite side of the table, one of a dozen clad in grey tracksuits, slouching opposite their loved ones. The new fish – the recent arrivals – are easy to spot. Some of them are in tears, clinging to their parents in the hope that if they hold on hard enough, they'll not slip out the exit gate in forty-five minutes' time and leave them here. Some of the other newbies don't care; this is not a new experience for them, just their latest seat on the carousel.

'Alright,' I say, sitting.

Maggie nods, regards me coolly, her head slightly angled so that she's not looking at me full on.

'You've lost weight,' she observes,

I nod. 'The food's shit.'

She nods but doesn't sympathise, doesn't even feign annoyance on my behalf.

'How's mum?'

'How do you think?' she replies curtly. Not even a beat for thought.

'You look good,' I say, for something to fill the silence. It's untrue. She's aged ten years in the two since I last saw her. Her hair is grey now and thinning. She's had to draw on her eyebrows, I reckon, and there's the edge of a scar just visible on her neckline.

'Marty's coming here,' she says apropos nothing.

I nod. 'To visit?' Marty is my nephew, though he's only six years younger than me.

'To do twelve months,' Maggie says.

'What?' I straighten up. Marty was sixteen, the last time I saw him. He'd just finished his GCSEs and was planning his A-level choices. He was a pimply wee shit, thin faced, narrow featured, but with these big almond eyes that he'd got from Maggie. The rest of him was from his father, a weaselly-looking bastard who'd screwed Maggie and then pissed off back to England.

'What did he do?' I'm careful not to sound like I'm gloating, deriving any pleasure from this. In truth, I'm not. I wouldn't wish this on anyone and my memory of Marty was that he was alright.

'Joyriding. He was stoned when they pulled him over,' she says, levelly, staring at me, daring me to pass comment. When I don't, she continues, 'I wanted to know what … what he can expect inside.'

I don't tell her; she doesn't really want to know, even if she thinks she does. 'How did mum take it?'

'Marty or me coming here today?'

'Marty.'

'She said it was your fault,' Maggie says, then lowers her gaze to the table, as if to show she doesn't share her opinion, that it embarrasses her a little.

We sit like that, in silence. I know now why Maggie is here. I could wait it out, make her ask, be a prick, but what's the point? 'I'll look after him,' I say. 'He'll be OK.'

She nods and I see tears slip from her eyes. She smiles, briefly, without humour, as if acknowledging the fact that I've spared her being in my debt by offering before she had to ask. With that she stands and leaves without looking back.

I first see Marty on the Tuesday morning. I'd asked around, asked to be told when he arrived. I'd had to pass one of the screws a pack of ciggies to find out the wing he'd be in. It was a waste for in the end he'd been assigned a cell three doors up from mine; our surnames are different and no one had made the connection between us.

He smiles when he sees me, shaking hands like an adult, self-conscious, his grip firm, his other hand cradling my elbow.

'Uncle Darragh,' he says. 'Alright.'

I nod. 'What the fuck, wee man?'

He raises one shoulder. 'Cops nabbed me. I was in a stolen motor.'

'Why?'

'We were having a blowout after the exams. Thought it would be *craic*. I was driving and I'd taken something. They done me for the lot.'

'How're you finding it?'

'It's better here than the other place. They had me there while they processed me; it was a nightmare.'

I remember my first days in the other place too, when I was on remand. It *had* been a nightmare. I'd been coming down, forced to go cold turkey. They put me in a room with some

Polish fucker with no English and tattoos all over him. We had a slop bucket at the bottom of the bed. They locked us in twenty-three hours a day. You had to press this bell if you needed to use the toilet, but the fuckers would deliberately leave you sitting for two hours before they'd come to let you out. I'd the runs my first few weeks so every time I had to shit, I had to squat in front of this Pole, hovering over this bucket. The fucker just sat on his bed, like a statue, cigarette in his mouth, watching me doing it through squinted eyes and a haze of grey smoke. Those first few days, the shit was running out of me; exploding against the sides of the bucket, the wind ripping from me. He'd just sit and watch, never comment. When I was done, my arse red sore from wiping, he'd take one big deep breath, hold in the smell of the smoke and our sweat and my shite, like it was the freshest thing he'd ever smelt.

In the end, I stopped going. They had to give me suppositories eventually, because I doubled over with the pain, started bleeding from my back end. I asked them to move me too, but they said no. There were no other cells. I'd be moved when they sentenced me, I was told. I'd four months in that place.

'Here's better,' I agree.

He cries the first two nights and he's grand after that. For the next eleven months, my sister visits him every week. She never asks to see me during any of that time.

He's on day 333. I head out to the yard at nine once the doors are opened. A group of cons wander across to the library, some clutching piles of DVDs they've borrowed and re-watched for the fortieth time and are now leaving back. Some others carry their books, heading to the Education wing. Further down the roadway, the first of the fluffies are arriving: the civilians who come in here to work with us. I recognise the English teacher, a heavy-set guy who waddles as he walks. He has his hands in his pockets, moves with the nervous shuffle of someone who isn't at ease here. Why should he be? He uses his swipe card at the gate, presses his palm against the hand-reader, then tucks his card away again, glancing furtively around lest anyone is watching where he puts it. He catches my eye and raises his chin in acknowledgment; he recognises my face but can't place where, I think. Then I realise how stupid that sounds; where else would it be but here?

Marty is standing outside the tiling block when I get down. He shifts from foot to foot, as if to keep warm, but the sun is already cresting the roof of the unit and the temperature is past ten degrees. It'll be a scorcher before the day's out.

'Did you watch *Dexter* last night?

I nod. 'I was up until two to finish it.'

'The last episode's shit, isn't it? The CGI is crap.'

Marty sucks at the butt of a rollie, twisted between his thumb and forefinger.

I raise my shoulder in a half shrug. 'S'alright.'

Marty snuffs his nose against the back of his hand, flicks the butt into a quick flash of embers against the unit wall. He dances lightly on his toes.

'What's up with you?'

'Nothing. I got good news is all.'

'What good news?'

'Balmoral.'

Balmoral is the wing they place you in before you leave. Marty is on his last month. If he gets into Balmoral, they'll allow him home every second weekend before he gets out for good.

'I'm delighted for you,' I say. And I mean it.

'I see Big Mick's back inside,' Marty says, glancing over to where Big Mick Duffy is holding court outside the Education block.

'What happened him?'

'He did a chemists.'

'How did they catch him?'

'He'd no mask on.'

I laugh. 'The fucking muppet.'

Marty jogs on the spot, turning his head quickly from side to side like a boxer limbering up for a fight.

'He's only in for three months. He's packed himself up, he says. Zoly.'

Marty glances at me, gauging my reaction. I've stayed clean since I came inside and I've tried to keep him clean too. But I can see what he's thinking; he wants to celebrate his good news and Big Mick's arrived at just the right time.

'Stay the fuck away from it, Marty,' I said. 'You've only got four weeks left.'

He nods. 'I know, I know,' he said, without sincerity. 'It's me ma's birthday today. Me in here. I'm going to tile the fucking kitchen for her when I get out,' he adds, nodding at the unit, thinking I'd not noticed he'd changed the topic. 'If this fluffy fucker would hurry up,' he adds.

I don't mind waiting outside. The air's warm and alive with the buzzing of insects. Once indoors, we'll be practising, tiling sheets of wood then breaking the tiles off again and doing it over tomorrow, always the same wood, always the same tiles, always the same fucking mistakes.

'Stay clear of Big Mick, Marty,' I say again. 'He's a using bastard.'

'Ah, he's not the worst,' Marty says. 'He's gas craic.'

Big Mick did his first stretch for possession and intent to supply. The thing was, he realised very quickly that inside he could make ten times what he could outside, what with a captive audience and boredom levels going through the roof. And it was easy, too. Everyone wanted downers, something to take the edge off the waiting and the walls and the thoughts ballooning out of all proportion inside your fucking skull. He worked out that if he could get himself sent inside once a year for a few months, he could stock up before he came and make a fortune. On one of his previous visits, he'd brought hash to the court with him. He'd gone to the toilet just before his case was heard, stuffed blocks no bigger than OXO cubes up his arse, shuffled back into court, like he was shitting himself, pleaded guilty to save himself any undue time wasting, and then shat it all back out a day or two later after a few feeds. That first time, he'd offered me some.

'Dope that was up your hole?' I said. 'No thanks.'

'It's always been up someone's hole,' he said. 'At least you know mine.'

'I'm good,' I said.

'Marty told me about what happened you, outside. I can get you whatever you want. Pills?'

I shook my head, glared at Marty. It was the only time I was angry with him; he was the only one who knew the whole story, about why I was inside. About Dad.

Big Mick knew better than to come near me after that. But Marty had liked him the first time they'd met and I was pretty sure Mick had sold him something then. The last thing I wanted was him getting caught with something now.

Halfway through the morning, Marty asks the fluffy if he can get out for a slash and a smoke. I watch him heading out the door, cutting across the yard to the Education block, one eye on his watch. There are no toilets over there.

I ask can I grab a smoke too and head out, picking up my pace.

'Marty? The fluffy wants you back in a moment. He needs you to leave something up to the cell block for him.'

I can tell Marty's caught between wanting to see Big Mick and wanting to keep his nose clean in case he fucks up Balmoral.

'Can you not do it?

I shrug. 'He wants you.'

Marty rolls his eyes, muttering a curse under his breath then heads back in.

I continue on, around the back of Education to where the library unit is housed. Two prefabs sit on cinder blocks next to the library to be used as classrooms. They're the only part of the area not well covered by cameras, partly because they put them up as a temporary measure when the library block was being stripped of asbestos a few years back and apparently they never intended for them to still be here.

It's where Big Mick holds court on his arrival days when the drugs are literally hot from his arse. There are normally a few hangers-on standing with him, sharing a smoke and a joke and hoping that sticking him for ten minutes might earn them a discount.

Sure enough, when I round the block, Big Mick is standing, his neck stretched up, his face turned towards the strengthening sun. Two new arrivals are standing with him and I guess he's using them as security. The fact that no one has noticed the three of them missing from wherever they're meant to be suggests someone with a bit of authority is turning a blind eye to Big Mick's activities. Why wouldn't they, I reason. Stoned prisoners are much more compliant, sleeping all day; the screws would want us *all* stoned if they had any sense.

'What's up, Mick?' I say.

He stares at me, then past me, looking for Marty. I know I've only got a minute before the tiling instructor realises I'm up to something.

'Where's Marty?'

'About that,' I say. 'He's on his way out, Mick. I don't want him taking anything. You hear me?'

'That's between me and him,' Mick laughs, his hand shifting to the gap at the buttons of his shirt, one finger exploring for his belly button. He glances at the two newbies, who straighten up, meaning to be threatening. Three against one isn't great odds and I know I'll not win, but I reckon I don't have to. All I need to do is enough to have the screws come across or, better still, to leave Big Mick in solitary or the infirmary. I take a check of the two again. The one to his left has tats on his left arm that were done inside; the one to the right is on his first stretch. He'll want to prove himself; he'll strike first.

'Not anymore, Mick,' I say. 'I'm asking nicely. No drugs. We clear?'

Mick smiles. 'You're doing time for crashing a car, Darragh. Your hard-man act doesn't scare me.'

As I expected, the one to the right shifts forward now. He's got the measure of me, he thinks.

'Don't push your luck, mate,' he says.

I ignore him, move closer to Mick instead, telling him something I've told no one, not even the hospital pysch who dealt with me. 'I tried to put my Da's heart back inside his ribcage with my bare hands, Mick. I felt it going cold after I wrapped the two of us around a tree, because I was off my face. Do you think I give a fuck about you and your goons?'

Mick glances past me now, uneasy. The guy to his right fancies his chances and he's moving forward fast. 'Right, fu—'

The jab to his throat cuts off his air, kills the words dead. He gags, doubling over as if winded. I bring my knee up hard to his face, pushing down with my hands, feel his nose break against my kneecap. He straightens, gripping his nose now and I punch him once, swiftly, to the side of the head. It's enough to bring him down. He hits the ground hard, the wind coming from him with an 'ummph'.

His mate moves in now and clocks me. He's aiming for the head but clips my shoulder instead. As I move past him, I pull the plastic sealant remover that I've lifted from tiling class from my pocket and aim it square at Mick's throat. My aim's off, but it's no matter. I hold it near the tip but it still shatters as it strikes his left shoulder.

He roars, louder than he meant, loud enough to alert the screws. His two cronies are on me, kicking and punching for all they're worth, but it makes no difference now; Mick's been so loud that someone is bound to come.

I curl on myself, take the kicks, keep my head shrouded in my hands and wait. Mick's joining in too, but his kicks lack the venom of the other two.

Finally, through the caul of my hands, I see the steel-toe-capped boots approaching, hear the shouts of the screws. The three have done some damage but not as much as I've done on them; Big Mick will be in solitary when he starts shitting out his produce. Let him explain that one.

One of them – the left one, I'm guessing – gets in a final boot before the screws reach us. It's the last thing I remember.

Twenty minutes later and I see Petey Haines, the orderly who cleans the medical block. He's a sleekit character, all hunched up and sanctimonious. He'd been promoted to medical after the old orderly finished his stretch for sex offences. It was a measure of how hard-to-like Petey was that most people preferred his predecessor even though he was a short-eyes. I'd heard Petey had started a peer support group for other cons, but my guess was that it probably had a membership of one.

I'm lying on a bed in the infirmary wing. Haines is standing looking at me. He's playing with this tennis ball, flattening it between his palms then letting it pop back into shape again. The rhythmic slurp and pock is irritating me, but he continues regardless. He should be in lockdown by now, with the rest of the inmates, but they must have made him stay to keep watch until the doctor arrives back from lunch, locking the two of us together in here.

'The Cooler King,' I joke, trying to gesture towards the ball, but the reference is lost on him and my lips are too dry to start whistling the tune.

'You look like shit,' Petey says. I groan and throw up all over the floor, the vomit splattering on his shoes.

'Fuck's sake, not again,' he mutters and I pass out again.

The doc gives me a once-over, shining a light in my eyes, pressing at the wound on my head. My face feels tugged slightly to the left and I touch it with my fingers. The doc slaps my hand away. 'You'll tear the stitches,' he says. 'You look like shit.'

'You should see the other guys,' I joke.

'They're all in solitary,' Haines comments.

'You're headed there, too,' the doc says. 'We'll keep you under observation for the night. You're in here until lockdown is finished.'

I lie and doze. The doc has given me paracetamol which I'm loath to take but the pounding in my head finally convinces me I should.

Just after two, when the doors should be opening, the emergency siren begins squealing across the compound. Something has happened which has forced them to lock down again. The doc is getting annoyed because he can't go anywhere until this stops. Some days, these things have gone on for ten hours.

Just then his phone starts ringing. He answers it, his expression drawn. 'Which cell? . . . I'm locked in here at the moment; you need to send someone down.' He grabs his bag and heads to the door.

He waits a moment until we hear the clunk of the lock and the door is opened. The doc sets off at a sprint while the screw who unlocked the door stands sentry in his place.

'What's going on?' Haines asks.

The screw regards him, coldly a moment, then turns his attention outside. After a few moments, I hear the growing wail of an ambulance on the road outside; the medical block abuts the external wall and you can hear the traffic passing if the room is quiet. Absurdly, I think that it's come for me. Instead, its pulsing echoes back off the high wall surrounding us as the vehicle enters the compound and roars past our unit and up towards the cell block.

It is almost an hour later before one of the other screws comes in and stares at me where I lie.

'Marty's hanged himself,' he says simply. 'He's dead. Sorry.'

Maggie comes again. It is one month since Marty died. I've expected her, known it was coming, dreaded it.

She sits opposite, looking at me, her mouth a tight white line like mum's the day she saw me in the hospital bed, wished me dead and my father alive again.

'I'm sorry, Maggie,' I mumble, the words shockingly inadequate.

Maggie glares at me. 'Do you know what happened to him?'

'I know he hanged himself, just.'

Those almond eyes fill. 'Why weren't you there?'

'He was in his cell, over the lunch lockdown. Besides, I was in medical—'

'You should have been there!' she snaps, the tears escaping her eyes now. She wipes them away with a curt rub of her sleeve.

I nod, understanding her anger. There is no point in protesting. 'I'm sorry for your loss, Maggie,' I repeat. 'I did my best.'

I make to stand up, but she grabs my hands quickly, forcing me to sit again.

'I need your ... I need to know. Did you see him before he ... ?'

I nod. 'Before lunch. I was with him in class that morning.'

'How was he?'

I think back to him, bouncing on the balls of his feet, excited.

'He was good. Happy.'

Maggie nods eagerly. 'They're saying he was depressed. Depressed? Marty? Said that he was struggling, unhappy, in with a mentor or someone, every whip-around talking about how he wanted to die,' she says, the words tumbling out as if they'd been hiding inside her, waiting for someone who would sit opposite her, hold her hand, listen to what she had reserved in the darkest corners of her heart. 'He'd only weeks left. He'd applied for transfer to Balmoral. They'd approved him,' she said, as if pleading with me to believe her.

'I know. He told me the day he ... He was hoping to get moved within the week, once they had space in the wing,' I say.

'He wasn't depressed,' she whispers, quickly. 'I've asked for toxicology reports, but the governor said it was an open-and-shut case. Prisoners do that – kill themselves. I said about him being released but they said that's more common. Someone so institutionalised, they don't know how to cope with the thought of freedom.'

I nod.

'He'd done eleven months,' she says. 'That's hardly enough to be institutionalised.'

'Eleven weeks could be enough,' I say. 'Eleven days, depending. Habit is a deadener.'

'I think he was murdered,' she says, simply. She sits back, pulls her hands from mine, which have lain unresponsive to her touch throughout. This was what she'd come to say, what she'd been building to.

'He was alone in his cell, Maggie,' I say.

'I know he hanged himself,' she says. 'I'm not stupid. Was he using in here?' she added.

I look to the table, the scores in the walnut finish veneer, the edging strip peeling off and sellotaped back into place. I pick at it, peel a piece away, balling it between my finger and thumb.

'Was he on something?' she repeats.

I shrug. 'I tried to keep him clean,' I say.

'That means he was.'

'I didn't say that.'

'You didn't say he wasn't either.'

'What difference would it make?'

'Then whoever sold it to him would be to blame,' she says. 'Because without taking whatever he took, Marty'd still be alive. I thought you of all people would understand that.'

I sit back, regard her more coolly now. The almond eyes have narrowed. I think she's going to apologise for a moment, but her jaw sets and she sits back too, waiting for my response.

'He was going to meet a supplier the morning he died. I went ahead, gave the guy a kicking. He got put away in solitary. There's no way he sold anything to Marty.'

'Someone did.'

I shrugged. 'I don't—'

'You said you'd watch over him,' she says, leaning sharply forward.

'I tried my best,' I say, holding my hands up, yielding to her anger.

'That's the story of your life!'

I can see the screw on watch reacting now, heading towards us. I raise a placatory hand. 'They're going to throw you out, Maggie.'

Maggie stands, turns to the screw, rubs viciously at her eyes. She casts me a final look.

'Mum sent a message. She said she hopes you never see outside of this place again. She said it was a pity you didn't die instead of Marty.'

I don't believe her for a second. My mother had the chance to say that herself once before and didn't, so I don't see her saying it now. But I'm pretty sure she thinks it, has thought it every day since the cops landed at her door with the double news of how her husband had died and her son was his killer.

'I did my best, Maggie,' I repeat.

'All you had to do was watch my boy,' she says, crying. 'All you had …' the words splutter into tears, dissolve in her throat. The screw is at her now, his hand on her elbow, guiding her out.

'I'll ask about,' I call to her retreating back, suddenly desperate to have her turn around, to look at me. 'I swear, I'll ask about.'

I complain about headaches all afternoon through tiling. The fluffy, who I vaguely remember introducing himself as Jason on his first day, doesn't want to listen to me complaining and phones down to medical. He gets a message back to send me down.

Haines is picking about in the flowerbeds outside the unit, pulling out the weeds. He raises his head in a brief salute as I pass.

The doc runs through the usual torch-in-the-eyes routine. He prods at the healed cuts, teases the skin apart where the stitches had been to check for signs of infection, but it's mostly healed up now.

'A bit of scarring,' he says. 'I've seen worse. The headaches are to be expected.'

I nod, accept the two paracetamol he offers me without hesitation.

'The guy who hanged himself,' I say. 'You were there?'

He looks at me quizzically, then nods with recognition. 'That's a bit ghoulish.'

'It was the last day I was here. You went up to his cell, right?'

He frowns a little as he looks at me, but doesn't answer.

'You *were* there; I remember you leaving. Did you notice any drugs in his cell?'

The doc smiles coldly, shaking his head in disbelief. 'Take your pills and get back to your class.'

I stand up, trying not to be threatening and to be so simultaneously. 'I'm not just asking out of curiosity.'

'Yes you are,' he says. 'We're done.'

'He was my nephew,' I explain. 'His mother says no one has told her exactly what happened to him.'

'He hanged himself,' the doc says. 'There's no mystery.'

'You know what I mean. If there was something else involved.'

The doc straightens himself, drawing himself up to my height. 'I'm not comfortable with this—'

'Marty was looking to buy some stuff that morning. It's why I got into the fight in the first place, to try to stop him. I left his supplier in solitary. But my sister thinks he took something anyway and flipped. He was waiting on a transfer to Balmoral; he was on his way out.'

'I can't talk about this,' the doc says suddenly. 'You need to leave.'

'I'm not asking you to break any confidence, doc,' I say. 'I just want to know if Marty had taken something. That's all.'

He stares at me a moment, as if trying to gauge the sincerity of my question.

'I don't know,' he says with a half laugh. 'I'd say they probably did tox on him. The results will be available at the inquest.'

'Anything,' I ask. 'Please. She's in pieces. She just wants to know if he was out of it. Between us, I think she'd prefer that he was, that it'd be easier than believing he was thinking straight and he still did it.'

'Either way he's dead,' the doc says, but he stoops a little, leafs through the sheets on the desk, closes my folder.

I say nothing, wait for him to decide.

'I'm sorry,' he says. 'I didn't mean that to sound harsh.'

Still, I wait in silence, waiting for him to talk.

He eventually does. 'There were empty packets of Black Mamba lying on the floor,' he says. 'I hope your headache clears.'

Big Mick's lying on his bed when I go into his cell, two days out of solitary. He's been having a wank even though the door's open, not caring who sees him.

'What the fuck do you want?' He makes no effort to conceal himself.

I move quickly, kick him once, hard, with the sole of my foot on the soft roundness of his stomach. It winds him and he spills to the floor, his bottoms dropping below his hips. He tugs at them.

'I warned you,' I say. 'I told you not to sell to him.'

'Who? Marty? I didn't fucking sell to him,' he says. 'I was in solitary thanks to you.'

'He had Black Mamba in his cell—' I say, but Mick cuts me off, his hand held up to silence me.

'I don't sell Mamba,' he says, standing now, pulling up his bottoms, straightening his T-shirt.

'I don't believe you,' I say.

'I don't give a fuck,' he says, standing almost a head taller than me, any advantage I had now well lost. 'I was in isolation, thanks to you. How would I have sold to him?'

I shrug. 'You have your ways.'

Mick laughs. 'You're giving me too much credit.'

'Where else would he have got it?'

'You're kidding, right? The place is fucking coming down with the stuff. People fucking tennis balls full of pills over the walls, fluffies bringing stuff in in their lunch boxes. Last year someone I know up above had a drone drop stuff into the yard for him.'

'You must know who's selling then.'

He lumbers towards me. 'Why the fuck would I tell you? I had to flush everything I brought in with me down the shitter in isolation or risk the screws catching me with it. You cost me five grand easy.'

'I'm sure you've re-upped.'

He allows himself a brief smile. His tongue flicks against his upper lip. 'That's not your business. You owe me five K.'

'Help me out and I'll do us both a favour,' I say.

'What favour?'

'I'll take out one of your competitors,' I say. 'Whoever sold to Marty.'

Big Mick chews at his lips, holding my stare, as if considering my proposition. He doesn't want to be seen as a tout, but is clearly tempted by the prospect of removing some of the competition inside.

'There's only so many places he could have gone here, let's face it. He had to be back in his cell by noon. Marty was in that tiling class with you. Start there.'

'I need a name, Mick,' I say, aiming for threatening, coming off as desperate.

Mick looks at me, then past me to where the screws are visible out on the corridor. He laughs, loudly, without humour. 'Fuck you, Darragh,' he says.

'If I find out it was you sold to him, I'll be looking for you,' I say.

'You know where to find me,' he says.

The tiling instructor, Jason, arrives twenty minutes late again the next day.

'Sorry, lads,' he says, opening up and letting us in. 'Car trouble.'

I wait until everyone has settled into their work. One of the lads from my wing has been breaking up the cut off tiles and started making a mosaic of Jimi Hendrix. While the rest are over watching Hendrix take shape, I approach the workbench. Jason's made himself a mug of tea, a metal spoon sitting next to it that he lifted from the staff tearoom in Education. The rest of us make do with plastic ones.

'How's you today?' he asks, clearly not remembering my name.

'Good, yeah,' I say. 'Listen, do you remember Marty?'

'Was that your mate? The one who ... who died?'

I nod.

'I was sorry to hear about that. Nice lad.'

'Do you remember that morning, he was here?'

He nods. 'Vaguely. He went out to the jacks and you sent him back in saying I needed him or something.'

'That's right. Did he stay in here for the rest of the class or did he go back out again?'

'He stayed here,' he says. 'Why?'

I move a little closer, my fingers spidering across the work bench towards where the spoon sits, still damp from his tea.

'Why?' he repeats.

'He was my nephew,' I explain. 'I never saw him again after I sent him back here. I was wondering how he was, is all. Maybe if he was showing signs of what he was thinking of doing.'

Jason looks as me, quizzically. For a moment, I think he's doubting the veracity of my claim that Marty was family, but then he shakes his head. 'He was with you, sure. When you went down to the infirmary.'

My hand closes on the spoon but his comment stops me. 'What?'

'Yeah. We heard the shouting and whistling and everyone went outside to see what had happened. One of the officers came round the back of Education with you, holding you up, helping you walk down. Marty ran across and took the other side of you. He took you down to the infirmary. He must have stayed with you until lockdown because I never saw him again.'

'He was in the infirmary?'

Jason nods. 'Do you not remember?'

For a second I think that maybe I do, but I can't be sure it's not a false memory I've just made because he told me Marty had been there. All I remember is Petey Haines and the slurp and pock of the torn tennis ball as he squeezed and released it between his hands, the gash along its circumference like a smile. Marty is not there in that memory.

I shake my head. 'Thanks,' I say, and move back to the board I've been tiling.

I wait until 11.45. We'll be finishing up soon and I know all the staff will be heading out before lockdown. 'I need to leave a form over in Education,' I say. Jason nods then starts inspecting the other cons' work.

Big Mick is where I expect him to be, his two goons standing with him. Neither of them needed stitches, I note. They straighten as soon as I appear around the corner, move in closer to him.

'All right, Darragh?' Big Mick says.

'I know who sold to him,' I say and make a mad rush for the three of them, swinging for Mick, missing, barely connecting with the guy to the left.

Mick steps back from me, allows the other two to beat the lining out of me. I don't bother fighting back; there's no point.

'That's enough,' Mick snaps and they stop. He stands over me, regarding me coolly. I can feel my eye swelling already, my ribs aching as I breath. He could have let them work at me for another while and he wants me to know it.

'You're a smart bastard, too,' he says, with something approximating admiration. Then he spits on the ground and steps over me.

I hear him, rounding the Education block, shouting for help. 'Oi! Some fucker's had a beating,' he shouts.

By the time I get down to the infirmary, it's just coming noon and the doc's gone for lunch. I can tell the screw's pissed because he should be on break now too. He locks us in the waiting room, me and Petey Haines once again, until the doc gets recalled. I see his silhouette through the window where he stands out in the sunshine, chatting with some of the other Guards.

'Another kicking? You're a tube,' Haines says. 'And don't puke on my floor again.'

I nod, try to sit up. My lip is burst and I can taste blood in my mouth, like old pennies.

'What the fuck? Going after fat boy and his gang?'

'I thought he sold to Marty the day he died,' I say. 'I knew Marty was going to see him, so I picked a fight. Got him put into isolation before Marty could get to him.'

Haines watches me. He doesn't react.

'You knew that?'

'Marty told me that day,' he says carefully. 'He was raging at you.'

'No Cooler King today?' I ask.

'What?' he asks, genuinely confused by the change in direction.

'The last day you were squeezing a ball and letting it get back into shape. I was wondering how you did it, cause there's fuck all to you. Then I remembered, there was a slit in the ball.'

Haines nods. 'It was burst when I found it in the yard.'

'What had been inside it?' I ask, sitting up.

Another quizzical look. 'Air.'

'I've been a muppet,' I say. 'You swanning around down here, everyone trusting you, working in the only block against the external wall. It must be easy getting stuff fucked over.'

'You're full of shit, Darragh,' Haines says.

'The peer support groups. Was that where you sold? I'd not known Marty attended them, but then his mother told me he'd been seeing a mentor. The only mentor I can think of is you.'

'Whatever you think,' he mutters, but it lacks conviction.

'I figured Marty must have made it to Big Mick the day he died,' I say, trying to stand. I'm feeling woozy, the blows to the head making me sluggish. 'But I was wrong. The only person he would have seen between class and his cell was you.'

I see Haines glance to the locked door. Behind him I can see the prison officer's head bob about, hear the raucous laughter of a shared dirty joke.

'And?' He's tensed, waiting to see where I go with this, his casual disinterest gone now.

'And someone sold him something. Something that fucked with his head. Something that made him hang himself in the same week they were going to move him to Balmoral. There was Black Mamba in his cell. Is that what you're selling?'

'You've taken too many knocks to your own head,' Haines says, standing now himself. He's smaller than me, narrower. He'll be quicker, but speed won't help him.

'Did you know that I got five years for killing my own father?' I say, suddenly. 'I was stoned, fucking prick that I was, driving him back from a night out. He wanted to get a taxi and I insisted I'd pick him up. I killed my own da and they gave me *five* fucking years.'

'It's harsh, man,' Haines says, but I know he doesn't mean it.

'Harsh like fuck!' I snap. 'They should have given me life; that's what I'll be doing anyway, in here or outside.'

'I don't know—' he starts, but I cut him short.

In one fluid movement, I have the teaspoon out of my pocket. The tapered end of the handle is just pointed enough that with the force of my swing, it lodges in his neck. I grip his head with one hand, covering his mouth and yank the spoon forward with the other till the artery tears and the first pump of blood horsetails onto the ceiling and wall.

I can see the terror in his eyes, terror I've seen before. That time I tried to reason with my father: lied and told him it would be OK, even as his pupils dilated and the light left them. I don't lie now, not to Haines. I look into his eyes, return their stare, their deadness, and wait until I feel him slump.

Then I let him drop to the floor and I go back to the bed where I had been lying. I take out a smoke and light it up. Outside I can hear the Guard shouting to the doc, who must be approaching the block, something about his missing a round of golf, not knowing what he's coming back for, what lies inside.

I hear the clunk of the lock, the grind of the handle, the grating of the hinges, as the door swings inward.

Stuart Neville

Stuart Neville's debut novel, *The Twelve* (published in the USA as *The Ghosts of Belfast*), won the Mystery/Thriller category of the *Los Angeles Times* Book Prize, and was picked as one of the top crime novels of 2009 by both *The New York Times* and the *LA Times*. He has been shortlisted for various awards, including the Barry, Macavity, Dilys awards, as well as the Irish Book Awards Crime Novel of the Year. He has since published three critically acclaimed sequels, *Collusion*, *Stolen Souls* and *The Final Silence*. His first four novels were each longlisted for the Theakstons Old Peculier Crime Novel of the Year. *Ratlines* was shortlisted for the CWA Ian Fleming Steel Dagger. *Those We Left Behind* was shortlisted for the Irish Crime Novel of the year. His current offering is *So Say the Fallen*.

The Catastrophist

Tom Shields sat quiet in the passenger seat, watching the fields roll past the window. Morning rain made tracks along the glass, water chasing water. Reminded Shields that he was thirsty. There hadn't been time for so much as a cup of tea before they left the house.

Gerry Fegan drove the Ford Granada. Shields could have driven himself, but Paul McGinty had insisted Fegan do it, seeing as Shields didn't have a licence. Neither did Fegan, Shields might have argued, but there were certain men you didn't argue with. Just accepted their word, even when you knew they were wrong.

The knock on the door had come late last night, waking Nuala. She had cursed as she reached for her cigarettes, an overflowing ashtray on the bedside locker beside the bottle of Buckfast, a few mouthfuls left at the bottom. She had lit the cigarette and swallowed the last of the wine.

Shields stepped around the empty crib on the way to the window. Five months and she still wouldn't let him take it away. As if Ruairi would somehow reappear there, returned from wherever he'd been. As if he'd never been inside a white box and covered with earth.

They had fought before they went to bed, both of them drunk. Over something so stupid he could barely remember what it was. All he could remember was losing his temper, and unwilling to hit her, he had hit himself, again and again, until his head went light.

He and Nuala had endured the worst tragedy that could befall a person, they had survived it, yet he lost control of himself over something so trivial that it was now lost in the fog. Clearly, it hadn't seemed trivial at the time. It had seemed terrible enough to make him ball his right hand into a fist and strike his own jaw.

Shields looked down to the street below, saw Paul McGinty and Gerry Fegan waiting beside the Granada.

Downstairs, in the kitchen, McGinty laid it out for him. Fegan would be back in the morning, 6 a.m., to bring Shields down to the border. A young lad had been killed, not one of their own, in a barn in County Monaghan. The barn belonged to Bull O'Kane, and a punishment beating had gone too far.

Now the lad's family were threatening to kick up a stink. They knew they risked getting the same treatment as their son, but still they wouldn't quiet down. They wouldn't go to the cops, they weren't that stupid, but they were agitating around the border village, in church, in the pub, in the GAA club. The locals were getting riled, questioning the Bull's authority.

Time to sort it out, McGinty had said. Head down there, figure out what had happened, straighten everything out. Fegan would be the muscle, Shields the mouthpiece.

Shields didn't like Fegan. Mid-twenties, tall and thin and quiet, a hardness to him that didn't need bluster to back it up. Fegan might have been fifteen years Shields' junior, but there was no question who was really in charge here. There were only three men in the world that had ever truly frightened Shields. One had been his father, ten years in his grave now. The other two were Gerry Fegan and Bull O'Kane, and not long from now, Shields would have to be in a room with both of them.

'Christ,' he whispered.

Fegan turned his gaze away from the road for a moment, then back again. He said nothing. Fegan hardly ever said anything.

They had planned a route this morning while Nuala slept upstairs. A Collins road atlas laid out on the kitchen table. A contact in the RUC had supplied a list of police and army checkpoints, and Fegan and Shields had mapped a way around them.

'Not long now,' Fegan said as the road markings changed.

They had quietly, secretly crossed the border. Soon Fegan steered onto a single-track lane, the car rocking and rattling over the rough surface. After five minutes they came to a single-storey cottage, a few outbuildings surrounding it. A Land Rover stood in the yard, its tyres and doors caked in mud.

'Was it here?' Shields asked as the car slowed in front of the house.

'Yeah,' Fegan said, pointing. 'That big shed.'

Fegan applied the handbrake, shut off the engine.

The front door of the cottage opened, and Bull O'Kane stepped through, his bulk taking up almost all its frame. A flat cap pulled down low and tight on his head to keep the rain off, an overcoat buttoned to the neck. Two men that Shields didn't recognise followed him out of the cottage.

Shields opened the passenger door and climbed out, but he stayed there, one foot inside, the car between him and the Bull. Pushing fifty, Shields reckoned, but the Bull had always seemed older than that. The way powerful men do.

Fegan got out of the Granada, pulling his collar up to keep a little of the rain from his thin neck. Cold rain, hard drops like nails. The kind of January day when it feels like the sun forgot to rise.

'Gerry,' the Bull said, his voice deep and soft. 'Tom.'

Shields returned the greeting with a nod.

'Sorry to hear about the child,' the Bull said.

'Yeah,' Shields said.

'You know these two?'

Shields shook his head.

The Bull pointed at one, then the other. 'Barry McGowan, Fintan Hart. If you ever need to know what a pair of arseholes looks like, just think of these boys.'

The men each turned their gaze away, their jaws tight.

The Bull leaned his head in the direction of the same shed Fegan had pointed to a few moments before. A squat structure made from sheets of corrugated iron.

'This way,' he said.

The Bull and his two men trudged off towards the outbuildings, Fegan behind them. Shields waited before he followed. He never liked to have a man at his back when he entered a strange place.

The shed's door creaked and groaned as the Bull opened it. He reached inside and a single bulb blinked on, a warm orange glow. A heat lamp like farmers used to keep the freeze out of their barns.

The Bull stood back, extended his long arm, indicated that Fegan and Shields should step through. Fegan did so. Shields said, 'After you.'

Shields entered last, felt the heat of the lamp on the top of his head. He smelled animal shit. Fat raindrops clanged on the metal roof. Points of light leaked through holes in the walls. Steam rose from their wet shoulders.

One dark stain on the concrete floor.

'This is where you did the young fella?' Shields asked.

The Bull looked to his two colleagues. McGowan and Hart both looked at their feet.

Hart said, 'Yeah.'

'It shouldn't have happened,' the Bull said. 'But it can't be helped now.'

'What had the young fella done?' Shields asked.

Hart let the air out of his lungs and looked at McGowan.

The Bull's huge right hand lashed out, the palm slamming into the back of Hart's head. Hart's feet left the floor, and he fell face first, his hands and elbows saving him. As he tried to rise, the Bull kicked him in the arse, sending him sprawling again.

'You see this man?' the Bull said, pointing at Shields. 'This man has put more boys in the ground than anyone I know. When he asks a question, you fucking answer it.'

Hart got to his feet, went to McGowan's side, rubbing his grazed palms.

'There was a fight in the pub,' Hart said.

'You and the young fella,' Shields said.

Hart exchanged another glance with McGowan. 'The both of us.'

'Let me guess,' Shields said. 'Did the young fella get the better of you?'

They didn't answer. They didn't have to.

'So you decided to teach him a lesson.' Shields spoke to the Bull. 'Did they OK it with you?'

'They were supposed to just have his knees,' the Bull said.

'He kept fighting,' Hart said. 'If he'd just took his punishment, he'd have been—'

'Stop talking,' Shields said.

Hart shut his mouth, an audible click as his teeth came together.

'Let me get this straight, then. This young fella beat the two of you in a fair fight, so you thought you'd have his knees. He wouldn't just lie down and take it, so you stoved his head in.'

McGowan spoke now. 'It wasn't like that.'

'No? That's what it sounded like to me. Which one of you actually did it?'

McGowan pointed at Hart, took a step away.

Hart's eyes widened as his gaze flitted from face to face. 'It was the both of us. We both did it.'

Shields turned to Fegan.

Fegan shrugged and said, 'Up to you.'

Shields nodded towards Hart.

Fegan reached behind his back, pulled a small semiautomatic pistol from his waistband. He racked the slide to chamber a round, thumbed the safety, and aimed it at Hart's forehead.

'On your knees,' Fegan said.

Hart's face went slack. McGowan began to shake.

'I said, get on your knees. Both of you.'

Hart lowered himself to the floor, his eyes welling. 'No, no, don't, I swear to God, I'm sorry, I didn't mean it.'

McGowan backed away as Fegan approached, the pistol still trained on Hart's head.

'You too,' Fegan said.

McGowan did as he was told. A dark stain appeared on his crotch, spread down his thighs.

'Hang on,' the Bull said. 'I didn't agree to this.'

'I was told to come down here and sort this mess out,' Shields said. 'That's what I'm doing.'

The Bull stepped between Fegan and Shields. 'You don't do my boys without my say-so.'

'It's not your decision to make,' Shields said. 'Get out of the way.'

'Watch who you're talking to,' the Bull said, glaring. 'You don't come onto my land and tell me what to do. Not if you ever want to leave it again.'

'McGinty gave me authority to fix this any way I see fit. Your boys killed a young fella because they got their arses kicked in a bar fight. The people round here need to know that kind of shit isn't tolerated.'

'The people round here need to know who's in charge,' the Bull said, stabbing a meaty finger at his own chest, his voice rising. 'Me. I'm in charge. And we stand by our own men, no matter what.'

'I've been given a job to do,' Shields said.

'I don't give a fuck about your job. Gerry, you shoot this boy, you'll have to shoot me too. If you don't, you and Tom will never make it back across the border.'

Fegan didn't move, didn't flinch, kept his finger on the trigger.

Gerry Fegan wasn't afraid of anyone. But Shields was. He kept it hidden, kept his face blank, his voice even and calm.

'We have a problem, then.'

'Looks like it,' the Bull said.

'What do we do about it?'

The tip of the Bull's tongue appeared between his lips, wet them. 'How's the wife coping? It's hard, losing a baby.'

'That's none of your business,' Shields said.

'Maybe not, but you might want to think about how she'll take losing a husband.'

Shields said nothing.

'There's a phone box in the village,' the Bull said. 'Let's go.'

Shields sat in the Granada's passenger seat, watching the Bull through the glass of the phone box. Fegan sat on the car's bonnet, watching McGowan and Hart as they waited in the Land Rover.

The phone box stood at the middle of the village's single street, opposite a pub. The same pub where the fight had broken out. Shields imagined it: the raised voices, the calls for calm, we've all had a drink, just leave it. Then the explosion of violence, the fists swinging, glass shattering.

A hundred yards along the street, beyond the last buildings, the border lay. The village in the North, a whole other country visible from where Shields sat. He'd joined up, sworn the oath, to fight for that border to be scrubbed out. Almost twenty years ago. Thousands dead, but the border survived. Not a single rotten thing that Shields had ever done had made his world any better. That thought kept him awake at night.

The Bull pushed the phone box door open and stepped out, let it swing closed behind him. Shields got out of the car, didn't meet the Bull's stare as he went to the box. He entered, felt the air inside thicken around him. It smelled of piss. A scattering of coins lay on top of the small shelf. The phone's handset dangled by its cable. Shields lifted it, brought it to his ear.

'Well?' he said.

'We've reached a compromise,' Paul McGinty said.

Shields swore beneath his breath. 'What sort of compromise?'

'Five grand to the parents,' McGinty said. 'The Bull's going to put that up himself.'

'Five grand,' Shields echoed, the box giving his voice a hollow resonance.

'It's a decent chunk,' McGinty said. 'The government will probably give them a payout too, so they're doing all right out of it.'

'They lost their son, for Christ's sake.'

'McGowan and Hart,' McGinty said. 'Take their knees. You can do it yourself, if it makes you feel better. Use Gerry's gun.'

Shields felt his anger rise. He swallowed it, breathed in through his nose, out through his mouth.

'That young fella beat them in a fight,' he said, 'so they took him out to a barn and beat him to death. You think a few quid and visit to the hospital is a fair price for that?'

McGinty sighed, a distorted rush of air against the mouthpiece.

'You know what you are, Tom? You're a catastrophist. Anything goes wrong, you think it's the worst thing ever. Even with everything you and Nuala suffered over the last few months, you still haven't learned to keep perspective. You have to learn to let some things go. Not everything is a catastrophe, you know? So, some young culchie messes with the wrong boys, gets what's coming to him. And you know what? The world's going to keep turning.'

'Not for his parents.'

'There you go again. A catastrophe. It doesn't have to be like that. Just give the parents the cash, then sort McGowan and Hart out. Then it'll all be over, you can go home to your wife, and life goes on.'

'It's not right,' Shields said.

'I never said it was,' McGinty said. 'I've made my decision. Just do what I've told you.'

Shields hung up and said, 'Fuck.'

He set the fat envelope on the kitchen table.

The mother's eyes streamed, a constant flow of tears. The father looked defeated, like all the life had been sucked out of him. Her fingers were stained nicotine yellow. He smelled of whiskey. They all sat around the table, the two brothers and three sisters in the other room. Fegan waited outside in the car.

Silence. A deeper quiet than Shields had known since his own child's wake.

'His name was Kevin,' the mother said. 'Kevin Doherty.'

'I'm sorry,' Shields said.

'Kevin was a good boy,' the mother said. 'He didn't deserve it. He was just home from university for the holidays. He was over in England. He took the chance to get out, make a decent life for himself. He never wanted anything to do with your lot.'

'I'm sorry,' Shields said again, his voice not even a whisper.

'Them two wouldn't leave him alone that night, kept at him, why wouldn't he join up. Why did he run off to England? Did he think he was better than them?'

Shields went to speak, but she raised her hand like she was his mother, ready to slap him across the head. He reflexively ducked, as if he was a child, as if this was his mother's kitchen and he had done some terrible mischief for which chastisement would surely come.

'Don't you dare say sorry to me again,' she said, venom on her tongue. 'They picked the fight because they didn't like him, because he was different. And you know what? He *was* better than them. Better than that bastard Bull O'Kane. Better than you. And they couldn't stand it, so they killed him.'

Shields cleared his throat and said, 'McGowan and Hart will be punished for what they did. I'll see to it myself.'

The father paled further, his shoulders slumped, folding in on himself.

'Punishment,' the mother said. 'You'll break their knees, maybe shoot them in the leg. And they'll go on living while my boy's lying up in Belfast waiting for someone to cut open what's left of him.'

For a moment, Shields considered telling her about the baby. He knew what it felt like to lose a child. But your child wasn't murdered, she'd say. And he would have no answer for that. He would have to turn his face away.

Shields pushed the fat envelope across the table to her. She looked at it as if it were some foul thing. Then she reached for the envelope, lifted the flap, looked inside.

'How much?' she asked.

'Five thousand,' Shields said. 'It'll cover the funeral, and you'll have enough left to maybe take a holiday, or whatever you—'

She threw the envelope. The weight of it smacked against Shields' cheek. It burst. Tens, twenties, fifties, they all scattered and fluttered to the floor.

The mother stood and said, 'Get out of my house.'

The father slipped from his chair, got down on the floor, gathered up loose bills.

'Leave it,' she said.

Shields went to say sorry one more time, but her fierce stare carried a warning. He got to his feet, left the kitchen, walked along the hall and out through the front door.

Fegan looked up as he approached the Granada. Shields opened the passenger door and lowered himself inside.

'OK?' Fegan asked.

'Just drive,' Shields said.

They waited in the barn. McGowan and Hart in the centre, under the glare of the heat lamp. The Bull with a shotgun slung across his forearm. Four more men, two of them armed with AK-47s. Hart stood silent while McGowan trembled and whimpered.

Shields let Fegan enter ahead of him, then followed. He smelled the men, the odour of their sweat cutting through the lingering animal scents.

McGowan burst into tears, snot dripping over his lips.

'Christ almighty,' the Bull said. 'Pull yourself together, boy, you're getting off lightly.'

McGowan wiped his cheeks and mouth on his sleeve, leaving a trail of mucus on the fabric.

'We ready?' Shields asked.

'Aye,' the Bull said. 'Let's get it over with.'

He stood back, let Shields come close to the two men.

Shields took the pistol from Fegan's outstretched hand. A Walther PPK, now that he saw it up close. Compact and light in his grasp. Shields checked the chamber; the cartridge was still in there. He thumbed the safety off.

'It's a small-calibre pistol,' he said to the two men. '.22 rounds. They won't do too much damage. Now lie down.'

McGowan and Hart hesitated, looked to the Bull.

'No getting out of it, lads,' the Bull said. 'Do what you're told and we'll get you to hospital when it's done.'

They both lowered themselves to the concrete floor, lay on their backs. The two unarmed men hunkered down and grabbed their ankles, held the legs steady.

Shields stood over them and thought of the fat envelope hitting his face, the money scattering. He thought of the mother and her vicious tongue, the pain scorched onto her face. The father and his narrow shoulders unable to bear it.

'The Bull's right,' he said. 'You're getting off lightly.'

Shields aimed the muzzle at Hart's left knee, put his finger on the trigger. He imagined the small hole appearing, the gasp and the scream that would follow.

He saw money flutter. Saw a boy boarding a boat to England, maybe a plane. A life ahead of him, away from all this.

He thought of his own son, Ruairi, dead and gone. He thought of how the baby cried. How the noise had been the worst thing in the world, drilling into his head every night until he couldn't think. How he had just wanted him to be quiet.

He hadn't meant it.

Honest to God, he didn't mean for it to happen. But the noise, the constant crying, crying, crying.

The baby weighed almost nothing. Like shaking a doll. Stiff for a moment, then loose like a handful of rags.

Then no more crying.

Shields blinked, cleared his head.

'The young fella's name was Kevin Doherty,' he said, 'and you killed him for no good reason.'

Before anyone could stop him, he moved his aim to the centre of Hart's chest. Pulled the trigger twice. Saw Hart's eyes widen in the fraction of a second it took to shift his aim to McGowan.

McGowan's tongue went to the back of his front teeth as if making an N sound, as if he were going to scream No, don't, don't kill me. But he never got the chance.

A ringing in Shields' ears, a billow of smoke in the air above the two dead and dying men.

He tossed the pistol away. It clattered across the concrete, into the shadows.

The two men who held McGowan's and Hart's ankles let go and stood. The other two raised the AK-47s and aimed them at Shields.

'Jesus, Tom, I wish you hadn't done that,' Bull O'Kane said.

'I had to,' Shields said.

The Bull let the air out of his lungs, shook his head. He turned his attention to Fegan, who lingered by the door.

Fegan stood with his weight on both feet, his hands out from his sides.

'Go on home, Gerry,' the Bull said. 'I'll deal with this.'

Fegan met Shields' gaze. Shields knew then that Fegan would fight for him if he asked it. But he would not.

'Yeah, go home, Gerry. It'll be fine.'

Fegan stared for a moment longer, then turned to the door.

'Gerry,' Shields called after him.

Fegan stopped in the doorway, looked back into the shed.

'Tell Nuala I love her,' Shields said. 'Tell her I'm sorry.'

Fegan nodded and pulled the door closed behind him.

Shields got to his knees, closed his eyes, and waited for the world to end.

Jane Casey

Born and raised in Dublin, Jane Casey published her first novel, *The Missing*, in 2010. She also published the first in her Maeve Kerrigan series, *The Burning*, in that year. In all, Jane has published six novels in that series, most of which were shortlisted for the Irish Book Awards; *After the Fire* won the Ireland AM Best Crime Novel award in 2015. Jane has also published a number of titles for young adults, the most recent being *Hide and Seek* (2015).

Green, Amber, Red

Caroline chewed her thumbnail and watched her husband. He was standing by the deep farmhouse sink, staring out the window at the night. She hadn't really looked at Fergus for a while, now that she came to think of it, not since Saoirse landed in their lives.

It was because of wanting Saoirse that they had moved all the way out beyond the safe little suburbs of Cork to the middle of absolutely nowhere. The house had been a farmhouse once, and had a straggle of outbuildings full of petrified shit from animals long since dead. There was a loose-stoned roofless cottage by the gate: the original house, abandoned 150 years before and not a moment too soon. Every time the wind blew, a handful of slates slipped off the roof of the big house. The gutters leaked. The septic tank was suspect. But it was what they wanted, even the heavy dark furniture that came with the property, that belonged to the previous owner who had died in the bed where they now slept. They had a new mattress, of course, but thinking of it made Caroline shiver sometimes, when Fergus was snoring beside her and the shadows seemed to move across the old flecked mirror on the dressing table. The house creaked and groaned in the middle of the night, like a living thing. It smelled strange, like hot, dusty metal. Like blood.

Fergus said it was her imagination.

'It's very big for a couple of newlyweds,' the estate agent had commented. And Caroline had smiled at her, and at Fergus, who was eyeing it with all the doubt he'd learned from his building experience.

'We'll fill it.'

She had imagined they would turn it into the house of her dreams.

The trouble with dreams, of course, was that sometimes they didn't turn out just as you'd intended. Caroline suppressed a little sigh. Better not to think about it.

Caroline was very good at not thinking about things.

Now she thought about Fergus. His jeans were hanging lower than usual, a strip of pale skin visible between the waistband and his T-shirt. His feet were bare, the soles black with dirt. The state of the floor. It needed a good scrubbing. Caroline rubbed her forehead, trying to rub away the guilt. The house was her responsibility. Since Saoirse had come she'd neglected everything.

A good wife would scrub the floor. A good wife would put her arms around his waist and speak softly to him until he turned to kiss her.

Caroline stayed exactly where she was.

'I just think we should have paid the extra.'

'Not this again.'

There was an edge to Fergus's voice that should have been a warning, an edge that Caroline acknowledged. She couldn't seem to hold the words in. It was like running her finger along a razor blade: stupid and dangerous, but somehow satisfying as the blood bloomed on her skin.

'It would be easier if we could see her. Instead of just listening.'

'I looked at the reviews, OK? They were unreliable and overpriced.'

'But if we could see her, we'd know what she was doing.'
Caroline chewed her nail again. 'You know what she's like. She's
an escape artist.'

'She can't get out of her room.'

'You'd think. But you weren't the one who found her halfway
down the stairs yesterday.'

It had given Caroline the fright of her life when she found
her there. Crawling down step after step, as if she was entitled
to roam around the house whenever she wanted. And how
she'd cried when Caroline took her back to her room. There
had been no comforting her.

Wilful, that was the word. Caroline had been proud of her
for it.

Fergus was the one who'd been angry.

And he was still angry. 'That was your fault. Imagine if she
was able to walk, Caz. Imagine if she'd got outside.'

'I turned my back for five minutes. Five. It's all right for you,
being out all day. I'm the one stuck here with her.'

'Remind me, wasn't that exactly what you wanted? Wasn't
that why you had to have her? So you could spend every hour
of every day with her?'

Caroline didn't like his tone, but she didn't want to provoke
him either.

The monitor sat in the middle of the table. It was small,
white, simple. A row of lights ran across the top, shading from
green to amber to red. The louder the screaming, the more
lights displayed, so even if the sound was off – which it was – it
told them what was going on upstairs. Caroline watched the
lights flicker back to green for a second every time Saoirse took
a breath. Green. Amber. Amber. Red, red, red. She was sobbing
her heart out, poor darling. Caroline reached out and pressed
the volume button. Instantly, the sound of screaming filled
the room. Fergus flinched. Caroline leaned forward, trying to
analyse the sound.

'She's getting tired.'

'Turn it *off.*'

'We should listen.'

'Why?'

'Because she might need us.' Caroline glared at him. 'You can't just pretend she's not up there.'

'That's exactly what I'm doing. I don't want to think about it. I think it's cruel.'

'We agreed that this was the right course of action.' She muted the monitor again.

'You suggested it.'

'I suggested lots of things and you didn't want to try any of them.' Caroline couldn't hold back the flash of anger but she regretted it. *Don't give him the chance to turn this into a fight.* 'We made a deal. This is the best way. It's the most effective, the least demanding—'

'Could you stop, please?' The muscles flickered in his forearms as he dug his fingers into the countertop. Caroline really didn't want to make him angry. He might take it out on her.

Or he might take it out on Saoirse.

Caroline felt her throat close up at the very thought, as if he was squeezing those calloused builder's hands around her neck instead of just imagining it.

Because she knew what he was thinking. She knew him better than he knew himself. She knew his weak points. She knew the triggers for his temper. She knew what to say to make his hands ball into fists, to turn his eyes black with rage, to unleash the violence within him. She'd had to learn. She'd taken the bruises. The bloodied nose. The split lip. The cracked ribs. The arm he'd broken the night she spat in his face.

It had taken a long time to train him not to lash out. To show him that he couldn't break her physically, that every time he tried, she became a little bit stronger. Every time he begged her to forgive her, she made it harder for him. He had to earn her love and her trust again. He had to prove himself. He had to see himself in all his violence and rage, and know that it made him less of a man when he lost control.

She knew how to taunt him. How to diminish him. How to break him into a million tiny shards of malice.

And she knew how to build him up. She knew how to wrap him in a cloud of love and caring, so he was devoted to her and only her. When he woke up screaming in the night, she was by his side. When he wept in her arms, she was his comfort. When she let him touch her, he knew it was a privilege. He couldn't live without her.

He was everything she'd ever wanted, Caroline thought. Without him, there would have been no Saoirse. And Saoirse was the most important thing in her world.

The lights on the monitor were red for so long that Caroline started to worry that it was broken. She pressed the mute button again and caught a split second of the noise Saoirse was making: an unimaginable noise, an *unbearable* one.

'How long do you think she can keep it up?'

Fergus shook his head. He was still staring out across the fields.

'We'll need ear plugs if she doesn't give up soon. I'll never sleep through that.'

He didn't answer her.

Talk to me.

She didn't like it when he was silent. Silence was dangerous.

She stood, the chair scraping on the floor so he knew she was moving towards him. It was better not to surprise him, she'd found.

'What are you looking at?' She ran her hands down his arms to his wrists. 'It's dark out there.'

'Nothing.'

'Are you looking at yourself?' She let the amusement into her voice. 'Can't say I blame you.'

'Stop.'

'You're such a ride.' She stretched up to nuzzle his neck, his ear, flicking the lobe with her tongue. 'I'm so lucky.'

'Caroline.'

'I've been missing you.' It was the truth. She had wanted Saoirse – she had never wanted anything as much as Saoirse – but she hadn't realised how much it would change things. Change *her*. She wasn't the person she'd been before.

A desperate wail from upstairs cut through the air in the kitchen and Caroline hid a smile against Fergus's broad shoulder.

'It's a good thing we don't have any neighbours.'

That was deliberate. They were surrounded by farmland – good rich green land grazed by solid, dark-eyed cattle. The fields were enclosed with high hedges, the narrow boreens lined with spreading trees that dripped rain on Caroline when she was out walking. She went out two or three times a day, to feel the air on her face and let the rain run through her hair, and she never saw another person. It felt safe, to Caroline. She was tired of other people. Their stares.

Their judgement.

The way you had to watch what you said.

The way you had to hide the marks on your skin, in case some busybody called the Guards.

The way no one would listen to her when she tried to tell them she was fine, that she loved Fergus and he loved her.

They wanted to climb inside her head. They wanted to hollow her out and wear her skin.

They wanted to stop her from living the life she chose for herself.

As if she had fallen into her marriage without knowing exactly what it entailed. As if she hadn't walked into it with her eyes open. As if she hadn't known what Fergus was the second she saw him on Patrick Street, watching the girls walk by. As if he had the ability to hide his heart from her.

She knew his *soul*.

And people had the insolence to tell her she could do better.

Caroline bared her teeth and let them graze the nape of his neck.

'I can't, Caz.' He sounded exhausted. 'Not now.'

'I just want you to hold me.' She made him turn around so she could nestle against him, small and vulnerable. It was his thing, he'd admitted: it was her doll-like prettiness that appealed to him. She looked younger than she was – certainly younger than she *felt*. And she was delicate. He could circle her wrists between his thumb and little finger. He could break her neck without blinking.

Intrusive thoughts. She chided herself for it, snapping the imaginary rubber band she could always feel on her wrist. She couldn't help that her mind sought out what was violent and dark. It had been a genuine surprise to her when the therapist explained that most people didn't look at a picture of a soft, fluffy rabbit and imagine how terrible it would feel to press out its eyes.

'Would you not think of stroking it?' he had asked her, almost pleading, and even at nine years old she'd known she should agree. But it wasn't a choice. Thinking the unthinkable. Staring into the darkness.

It was no wonder she was drawn to Fergus. He burned so bright. She needed that light; she could bear the heat even if it charred her flesh and split her bones one day.

And Saoirse would bind them together forever.

She was the best thing either of them had ever done.

'Is she still crying?' Caroline murmured.

'Can't you hear her?'

'All I can hear is your heart.' It was true. Her head was pressed against his chest. The sound always soothed her.

A sigh hissed out of him, stirring her hair. 'Caz, it doesn't feel right.'

She leaned back so she could see his face: his eyes, averted from hers. His mouth, narrow and bitter and afraid. She kissed the corner of it. 'You pretend to be such a tough guy, don't you? Am I the only one who knows what you really are?'

'God, I hope so.' He said it with feeling and the tension eased for a minute, the two of them closer than ever. Then Fergus started again with the same old argument, a disjointed waltz in a minor key.

'We shouldn't be doing this. We should never have done it.'

'How can you even say that? Don't you care about Saoirse?'

'Saoirse.' He looked away again, not saying what he thought: that Saoirse was a stupid name. He'd said it once. He'd said it a hundred times. She'd had to talk him round. Of course he wasn't convinced, not really, but she'd got her way. And he was wrong; Saoirse was a beautiful name, an Irish name, a long syllable followed by a short one. *Seer-sha.* It meant freedom. What could be more perfect?

Now she pressed her hands against his cheeks, looking up at him, forcing him to look at her. His stubble grazed her palms.

'This was what I wanted. What we both wanted.'

'If I'd known—' He stopped and bit his lip. She could fill in the end herself.

If I'd known what it would be like. If I'd known I wouldn't be able to rest. If I'd known I'd be worried all the time. If I'd known she would take up all our time. Our energy. Our joy.

If I'd known you would put her first all the time, and my needs would be forgotten, I'd never have let you have her.

It was very unfair of him to think that way, Caroline felt. She did her best. She'd given him what he wanted when he asked. She'd been smiling and kind, dutiful and loving, even if she'd been stretched a little too thin.

She had kept them apart, from the start.

It was partly that she didn't trust him, and partly that she wanted to be Saoirse's favourite. And it had worked. Saoirse turned to her for comfort, when she was hurt. Saoirse wanted her when she was afraid. Caroline lived for those moments. When Fergus came home it was time for Saoirse's light to be turned out, for Caroline to settle her to sleep. In the morning, Caroline was up first, keeping him away from her door. He saw her at the weekend. He played with her while Caroline watched; he played the games that she suggested.

Never alone.

Never for a second.

Oh God, the fear of what he might do if he was alone with her. If he lost his temper.

If he lost patience with Saoirse altogether.

Caroline's fingers tightened on Fergus's arms so that he made a small noise of protest; she hadn't even realised she was holding him.

'You know what it said on the internet. This is a long process. It can take days and days, but it's worth it,' she whispered. 'It's a kindness in the long run. This crying – it's a sign that it's working. Tomorrow she won't cry as much. She'll know we're not coming. She'll learn there's no point in all of this noise. One day, she won't cry at all. She'll just drift off, peaceful as an angel. Keep that in your mind.'

'You don't think it's cruel. Leaving her like that.'

'I read up on it and I believe it's the best thing we can do.' She held his gaze for a long moment, then went on tiptoe to kiss him. He held back for a second and she felt a jolt of fear: what if it didn't work this time? What if she'd pushed him too far?

Then his mouth softened, his lips parting for her tongue. The passion was still there, not far below the surface. His hands were on her, pulling at her clothes, grabby and desperate.

A little shiver of disgust raced over Caroline's skin – no, she couldn't – and she pushed him away.

'Not now.'

He was breathing heavily, his eyes blank with desire. She reached down and squeezed him hard.

'Stop.'

'*Bitch.*' He lifted his hand and she showed him her face, offering it to him for the heady moment while he fought with himself. His fist eased open, the fingers straightening – a slap?

No. He had control of himself now.

Or rather, she had control of him.

'Why don't you go and watch a DVD? Turn it up so you can't hear her anymore.'

'What if something happens?'

'I'll be listening.' She shrugged. 'I don't mind it as much as you do.'

'Why doesn't that surprise me?'

And what did *that* mean, she wondered, watching him leave the room. He lifted the bottle of whiskey off the dresser as he went, as if she wouldn't notice it was gone. Well, let him drink through it if he needed to. She was there to stop him if the liquor went to his head.

Hopefully he would drink until he passed out, and Saoirse would sleep, and she could get some rest herself. Her nerves were in tatters.

Caroline made herself a cup of tea and sat at the table, watching the lights on the monitor. Green, green, amber, red. Green, green, amber. Amber. Amber. Red, but briefly – the merest flicker. Caroline might have missed it if she hadn't been watching so closely.

She was definitely getting tired. Caroline allowed herself a small smile. It would work.

It had to work.

As she sipped her tea, Caroline started to feel more like herself. Refreshed. Restored. As if she could cope with anything. She turned up the sound on the monitor, keeping it very quiet so Fergus wouldn't hear over the noise of the TV. A low grizzle made it vibrate, a sound of pure desolation. Her throat had to be raw, Caroline thought, after all that screaming.

God love her, she would be thirsty.

Maybe it wasn't that she didn't want to cry anymore. Maybe it was that she *couldn't*.

Caroline looked across at the sink.

Fergus would disapprove.

Fergus would *really* disapprove.

He didn't have to know.

The trouble with Fergus was that he liked to know the rules, and then he insisted on keeping to them. She was more of an easy-going person. She'd learned to take life as it came. Being able to change your mind was a valuable skill, her therapist had told her. She could picture his face now, bearded and kind.

Caroline stood up, silently this time, and drifted to a cupboard. She found a plastic cup with a lid and a cartoon rabbit on the side. It was a second's work to fill it with water.

Actually, it had been a different therapist who said it. The court-appointed one. Caroline frowned.

She hadn't liked that therapist.

The door was open to the sitting room but Fergus had his back to her. He was absorbed in the action on screen, even though he'd seen it a hundred times. Caroline had too. She knew to wait for the gun battle to start before attempting the stairs. They were alive with creaks, the old wood shrieking when she stepped on it.

Up at the top of the stairs, the crying died away. Saoirse had heard her. Brave, brave girl, Caroline thought, standing in the dark, listening to the smothered sobbing as Saoirse waited for her.

Help me.

Rescue me.

Love me.

Caroline almost danced down the hallway, feeling for the key around her neck. She flicked on the hall light and had the door open in a second.

'I'm here.'

Her hands were gripping the bars, her face red and swollen, streaked with tears. She was angry, obviously, but there was hope there too, and something Caroline thought of as love. She couldn't do anything but sob.

'Poor darling,' Caroline cooed. 'Are you thirsty? Do you want a drink?'

A nod.

Caroline picked up the tongs and nipped the cup between them, staying well back as she pushed it through the bars. They had learned that the hard way – a couple of nasty incidents. A near miss or two. They'd got better at handling her, and she'd learned not to fight and they'd muddled through together.

Saoirse waited until she had the cup, until she'd drunk half of it in shuddering, sobbing relief, before she tried to speak. It was the usual nonsense but Caroline listened with an indulgent smile.

'Please. You can't do this. You have to let me go. I won't tell anyone what you've done. I'll tell them I was in an accident.'

'Of course you will.'

'Please. Please. You can't leave me here with no food. No water.'

'I've just given you water.' Caroline gave a little laugh. 'Greedy girl.'

Saoirse shook the cage but Fergus had made it well and it didn't rattle at all. It wasn't quite big enough for her, Caroline thought. It couldn't be comfortable. But there was nothing she could do about that now. They wouldn't take her out of it again. She'd promised Fergus.

When Caroline was bored, she held up her hand. 'I'm going to bed. If I hear you screaming again, I'll take your tongue.'

'That wouldn't stop me screaming.'

'No. But it would be fun.' Caroline closed the door on her and made sure it was locked; you couldn't take chances with a girl like Saoirse. She still had spirit, after everything they'd done.

Caroline turned and stifled a scream of her own. Fergus was leaning against the wall, his arms folded. She hadn't heard him; he must have come up the stairs like a ghost.

'What are you doing?'

'She needed a drink.'

A look of genuine pain flitted over his handsome face. 'You said it would take longer if we gave her water.'

'Yes, I did.' She moved towards him, trying to look guilty. 'I suppose I'm just not ready for her to go yet.'

'Caroline.'

'Just a little longer.' She brushed his cheek with her lips. His skin felt cold. 'For me.'

'It's *torture*.'

Caroline put her face against Fergus's, her mouth close to his ear, so when she spoke her breath would tickle him. 'I know.'

The weariness in his eyes when she leaned back – oh, it made it all so much sweeter. It was everything she had ever wanted, everything she had ever *needed*.

And once Saoirse was gone, they could talk about having another one.

She had the name picked out already.

Niamh O'Connor

Niamh O'Connor has a degree in English, and a master's degree in journalism. She worked as a crime editor in the *Sunday World* before returning to college to study for a master's degree in screenwriting from the National Film School. She has written four crime novels and three non-fiction bestsellers.

Crush

I wake the way I always do – with a heart-slamming start, saying 'Adam'.

'I'm OK, Mum,' he murmurs, somewhere between sleep and wake.

Reaching across I touch his sandy hair, the exact same shade as John's. Five years old, this little boy has been through more than most people ten times his age. He's got his dad's 'don't fuss' tone too, even in his sleep. Adam's twin, Abbey, in the bunk overhead, is more prone to melodrama, like me. One arm is currently dangling over the side. She favours my side in the looks department too, with her brown eyes and hair, freckles.

John usually wakes me when he gets in from his shift if I've fallen asleep putting the kids down, unless he nods off himself before getting the chance. I squint to make out the bedside clock. It's 20.53. *Christ* – tonight is date night.

Lifting a corner of the duvet cover, I begin to inch out of the bed, patting the floor with my foot. One wrong move and it will all be over. Much as I'd rather a night in front of the box together, John needs a good night out. There's this statistic about how something like 90 percent of couples split up if something happens to one of their children. A lump rises in my throat, and I look around for something wood to touch.

As I inch out, the bedtime storybook slides off my lap and lands on the floor with a thump. *Horrid Henry* – who else? I freeze.

Five seconds pass … nothing.

Ten … all clear.

I move quickly, sweeping the book up, kissing the children lightly on their foreheads and tucking them in gently. If one wakes, they both will, and John will say it's my fault for not putting them in different rooms. I couldn't bear the prospect of the separation anxiety. The separation anxiety *I'd* have to deal with. Maybe down the road sometime, like when they go to college, I think.

'*When* they go to college,' I whisper to myself, blinking away tears. It's a month since we got the news, but I'm still a blubbering wreck.

I tiptoe towards the door.

In the bathroom, I stare at my magnified face in John's shaving mirror. Ironic that being poor in the First World means you buy cheap foods laced with sugar and salt and end up getting fat.

'Still in there, Anna?' I ask the woman in the mirror, and she grins back at me. My mother used to say never judge a book by its cover, like it was the meaning of life.

I brush my teeth, rinse my mouth out, and pat it dry with a towel. Reaching for a hairbrush I reach at my scalp to try and find a parting where the regrowth isn't so obvious. I'm only thirty-nine, but the roots are snow-white. If there's one good thing about the fallout of the recession, though, it's that badger chic is now a trend. That and the fact that nobody talks about going for a back, sack and crack, or vajazzle anymore.

The sound of football chants travel up the stairs from the TV. John must have nodded off on the couch. He arrives home shattered most nights since he started working nights. I'm not even allowed to ring him for a chat. I broke the no-calls rule once – that day a month ago – to tell him Adam was going to be alright. I could tell John had started crying on the other end of the phone because the angry manager with acne on his neck, who's twenty years John's junior, stopped shouting at him to 'turn the phone off' mid-sentence.

I startle at the sound of the doorbell and wish I'd warned Rachel to remember the sleeping children and to use the knocker instead. I hear John's footsteps hurrying down the hall to open it before she rings again. He jangles the chainlock off and works the mortice lock free. It needs a good oil.

I splash my face quickly with freezing water then work some mushed up old ends of bars of soap into a lather too. Smearing the suds over my face, I splash frantically to stop my right eye stinging like mad. I make a blind grab for the towel, but instead of drying my face, I manage to rub a smear of toothpaste into the good eye – so now they're both hopping. I pat around for the make-up bag and rummage out the goop that is several shades too dark for my skin. It's important to make an effort, tonight of all nights. I hurry to the stairs, panting from the exertion.

When I walk into the sitting room John is chatting to Rachel, who's perched on the arm of the couch alongside him with her chin on her knees. I couldn't bend like that even when I was her age, *and* she looks like a young Catherine Zeta Jones – olive skin, chocolate eyes, and a mane of silky black hair.

'Why did you put the locks on the door?' John asks me as soon as he sees me.

'Sorry, old habits,' I say with a shrug.

Rachel twirls a section of long hair that curls at the end like a Grecian goddess, and bites her lower lip as she considers my answer while I glance around frantically for the remote control, locating it under a cushion.

'Hello, Mrs Green,' I say as I lower the volume. I catch her studying me the way she does a lot when she thinks I won't notice, but she looks away quickly. She never holds my stare.

'When are you going to start calling me Rachel?' she asks, feigning horror.

Soon as you stop treating me like I'm your dogsbody, I think, but don't say, obviously. It's humiliating enough having to take orders from someone ten years younger than me. In Budapest, where I'm from, I worked as a toxicologist in the state lab.

'Make-up suits you, Anna,' Rachel tells me, and I'm sorry I ever put it on now. If there's one thing worse than being condescended to, it's being pitied. Au pairs don't get proper pay so it's not like I can even buy any of my own.

'Hard day at the office?' John asks Rachel, touching her back. My stomach clenches.

'I'm just so tired,' she answers, like she'd know the meaning of the word.

'Kids alright?' she asks me.

'They wanted to play Snap before bed, but I was only allowed join in after Adam had put a blindfold on me, and Abbey tied up my hands,' I explain.

John laughs.

Rachel catches my eye and hates me for being more of a mother to the twins than she's ever been. She had to go back to work full time when Adam got ill because they hadn't got medical insurance.

She puts her hand on his face and asks him, 'Are you too tired for a night out, love?'

I cross my fingers behind my back.

'Course not,' John answers, smiling. 'Are you?'

'I'm exhausted,' she whines, then springs up. 'But since when has that ever stopped me?'

I aim the remote at the TV and zap on the nine o'clock news so I won't have to listen to more of her piffle. It's the ninth anniversary of Madeline McCann's disappearance and the reporter's in Praia da Luz.

'Is there anything worse than a missing child?' John wonders aloud.

'A sick, missing child,' Rachel answers with a shudder.

I used to watch Kate McCann's tortured face on the news and think it has to be worse for her to hold out hope that Madeline might still be alive and being tortured by some sicko on a daily basis. But that was before I realised that a mother's default setting is believing you can fix anything as long as your child is alive.

John stands and puts his arms on Rachel's shoulders to turn her towards the door.

'Ring us if there's any problem,' she tells me quickly. 'If either of the twins wake, even if they're not upset.'

'Of course,' I say.

John zips up his leather jacket and gives me one of his looks. A blush rises to my face and I have to put the back of my hand to my face to cool it down.

'You have my number, right?' he asks me, but it's only for Rachel's benefit. He must remember I rang him a month ago to tell him the good news about his son.

'I'll just check the children before I go,' Rachel says.

'They're fine, honestly,' I say, but she ignores me as per usual, not caring if they wake up, because she won't have to get them back to sleep, she's heading out.

I take the chance to sneak a look at John, hoping for one of his smiles, but he keeps his back to me as he heads into the hall.

'See you later,' Rachel says, coming back down.

'What time will you be back?' I ask.

'Eleven,' John says. 'We're only going to the local.'

'I don't want to sound like a hard ass ...' Rachel says. 'But if you could empty the dishwasher and get the children's clothes ironed for the morning, that would be fantastic.'

'No problem,' I say, following them into the hall to close the front door after them. Bitch.

Rachel turns to John as they get in to the car. 'Do you think Anna is weird?'

'I think she looks a bit mad with blue eye-shadow on,' he answers, gunning the engine.

'Not just that,' she says as he reverses out the drive. 'Like, aren't au pairs supposed to sneak their mates in when you're not around, or run up huge bills on the phone, or raid your drink cabinet, or mope, or sulk, or run away – something?'

'She's too old for any of that,' John says, driving out of the estate. 'You picked her on the basis of her looks, don't you remember? So I wouldn't fancy her and have a fling.'

Rachel watches their house gets smaller in the distance from her view of it in the wing mirror. 'She never talks about her family, though. If you ask her about them, she shuts the subject down. I don't know if she has sisters or brothers, or was ever married, or has any children of her own. And she hasn't ever mentioned being homesick, or talked about going home. Then there's the fact that nobody ever rings from Hungary. And she never gets any letters. She never even uses the internet.' Rachel draws a breath. 'She's definitely weird.'

'You're right. Except,' John says glancing at Rachel, 'we'd have been lost without her when Adam got sick.'

Rachel studies her nails.

John reaches for his wife's thigh, gives it a squeeze. 'Are you a bit jealous of her being with the twins all the time, baby?'

Rachel swallows. 'No. I'm just saying she's weird.' She strains her head away from John.

'And it's weird the way Adam and Abbey have started following her around,' she blurts. 'They're like her little lapdogs. Even when we're there, like she's more important than us. And they've got secretive. Do you think she's telling them not to tell us things?'

'No, I do not,' John says. 'It's just a phase.' He pulls in suddenly, puts the hazard lights on, and twists around to face Rachel, waiting until she looks him in the eye. 'You know what the consultant said. If Adam needs more treatment, we're going to have to go to the States to get to the bottom of it. Once we've got a bit of a nest-egg, we can relax. You can pack in working full time, I'll go back to days, and we'll send her home, and good riddance, OK?'

Rachel nods, puts her head on his chest. 'Sorry. I didn't mean for you to think you had to give me a speech. I'll work forever if I have to. I'm not freaking out about me having to work. You know that. I just wish they'd got to the bottom of what made him sick. Then maybe I could breathe again.'

I go back up to the children's bedroom, and climb back into Adam's bed. My box room is as self-sufficient as a prison cell, but the only thing I want is in this room. The house is still, the way I like it. I can only dream what it must be like to own a house and family like this, and with that thought I feel myself start to nod off again.

In the Pig and Heifer, Rachel pats a stool as John arrives over with the drinks.

'Do you think Anna might still be a virgin and that's why she's weird?' she asks as he slides a G&T and a pint of Guinness onto their table.

'What?' he replies, not even trying to hide his irritation now.

'You know? Like that odd little comb-over guy in England that everyone thought had murdered the estate agent. Mr Comb-Over was her landlord but it turned out he was completely innocent. He was only creepy because he was celibate.'

John drinks half his pint back. 'Can we talk about something or someone else? 'Cos I can't remember the last time we had time for an actual adult conversation on our own.'

'A year,' Rachel says. 'Before Adam got sick ... Do you think she'd be pretty? Anna? If she lost the weight, I mean?'

John splutters back his mouthful of drink, then has to go back to the bar asking for serviettes to clean it up.

'Sorry,' Rachel says, when he gets back. 'It's just that celebrities are always having flings with the nanny even though their partners are better looking. What's forbidden is sexy, I suppose.'

John exhales through his nose. 'If you're asking me if I fancy Anna, the answer is no.'

Rachel shoots him a 'seriously?' look.

John rolls his eyes to heaven. 'No. I do not think Anna is pretty. I probably couldn't pick her out of a line-up for the amount of time I've spent looking at her. I've had a lot on my mind.'

'And I haven't?' Rachel asks.

'I'm not rowing. Not tonight.'

'OK, I'm now officially dropping it.'

John sighs heavily. 'I wouldn't mind, but she only bloody well rung me once.'

Anna looks at him. 'She rung you? When? Why?'

John crosses his arms. 'You said you were dropping it.'

'Tell me what she rang you for first?'

'She wanted to tell me about Adam.'

'What about Adam!'

John stares into the middle distance like he's counting to ten in his head. Then he says, 'Anna rang me to give me the good news about what the consultant said. You know, that we were out of the woods. She rang me in work, just before you arrived to tell me yourself. She only rang to let me know he was going to be alright.'

Rachel blinks. 'How would she have known what the consultant said before I'd told you?'

'I thought you'd told her,' John says. 'Was that not it?'

The headlights flashing across the ceiling and down the wall wake me, and I glance at the bedside clock, which reads 21.21. Even I know John and Rachel can only be home this early for one reason. When I hear them shouting outside, I've already guessed what the reason is. I've only myself to blame, I suppose, for growing too attached to these two little mites. I give Adam's head a last loving tousle.

The front door opens with such force it bangs off the wall. The bunk beds even vibrate a little, such is the ferocity.

'She's not down here,' Rachel screams.

I put my hand over Adam's ear so the noise won't wake him, watching the way the springs overhead are already starting to stir. I hope Abbey hasn't just heard her father shout, 'Call the Gardaí again,' before he starts thundering up the stairs.

Adam rubs his eyes. They've done it now. Like I knew they would. The selfishness of adults never ceases to astonish me. Don't they know never to wake a sleeping child?

'Anna,' John says bashing open the door, 'what are you doing?'

Adam puts his arms around me for reassurance. I put one over him, to keep him snug as a bug.

'Babysitting like you asked,' I say, not trying to hide my irritation. I don't appreciate him taking that tone with me just because her ladyship has finally worked things out – that I'm in love with her husband and want her life.

Rachel appears over his shoulder behind him, her knees buckling. For a second I wonder if she'll come into the room on all fours.

'What are you doing, Mummy?' Abbey asks, sitting up. She's got the matter-of-fact tone down to a tee.

'Abbey, darling, are you OK?' Rachel asks, her voice quivering as she stands up slowly.

'What's going on, John?' I ask, using my bulk as a human shield because Adam has started to cry.

John takes a step towards me – arms and fingers spread out – like he's trying to calm a wild animal.

'How did you know Adam was going to be alright the day you rang John?' Rachel asks.

'I didn't,' I think, but the words won't come out. *I just thought it was the thing people say in that situation when trying to reassure someone everything's going to be alright.* I look down and realise what's happened. The air didn't even glint before the knife flashed down into my chest. I only understood when I saw the blood on Rachel's hand – too late to heave myself off Adam.

My last thought is of my mother's old mantra. She told me never to judge a book by its cover the day I told her about the wonderful Irish couple who were giving me a job too.

William Ryan

William Ryan's Captain Korolev novels have been shortlisted for numerous awards, including the Theakstons Crime Novel of the Year, The Kerry Group Irish Fiction Award, the Ellis Peters and John Creasey Daggers, and the Irish Crime Novel of the Year (twice). William teaches on the Crime Writing Masters at City University in London. His next novel, *The Constant Soldier*, has been described by AL Kennedy as 'a nuanced, complex and gripping tale of guilt and love that captures the chaos at the end of World War Two.' It is published in August 2016 by Macmillan.

Murphy Said

Murphy said it was February – a time of the year when the days were over before they really started. Murphy said it was normal that the sun seldom managed to rise above the grassy dunes that ran behind the beach and it was also normal for the light to flow flat across the bay like a long slow wave. It would be different in the summer, Murphy said. Then the days would be long and hot and the sun would hang from the sky like a light bulb and not a cloud would be seen. Murphy didn't know why the summer would be so different. All Murphy knew, he said, was that he wished he'd stop asking stupid fucking questions.

His footsteps cut into the crust of the sand as he walked, from the grass to the water and back again, searching for sea glass. Every few moments he looked up at his surroundings and lifted the cigarette to his mouth. But he didn't stop walking.

Murphy said the sea stretched as far as America. But Murphy wouldn't tell him what America was, only that it was over there, well past the rocks, and too far to swim in case he took the notion.

He rubbed the pieces of glass he'd found against each other and thought of each of them as a memory. Murphy said he'd be able to remember everything soon. Murphy was certain of that. He'd been told so by the doctor – and the doctor knew his stuff.

In the meantime, Murphy would look after him, Murphy said. All they had to do was wait.

In the meantime, he held his memories in his hand.

He was usually alone on the beach. Apart from Murphy watching from the car park – who didn't count. So he was surprised to glance up and see the woman, making the same stitched pattern in the sand as him, walking at the same slow pace. She also stooped to pick from the tide lines of shells and seaweed where the sea glass was most common. As they came closer to each other, she lifted her gaze to meet his.

'Are you after my sea glass?' she asked.

Her blonde hair was pulled back tight against her scalp and her eyes were very blue. A teasing, full-lipped smile softened an angular face. He thought she might be beautiful.

'I didn't mean to.' He opened his hand to show her the glass he'd found. 'You're welcome to them.'

He had a feeling she was from another place – just the way she spoke, as if she were trying out the words for size. He noticed a small tattoo on her neck – a cross pressed onto her pale skin just below her left ear.

'Are you from America?' he asked.

Her mouth tightened, as though she were holding a word inside it. But when it came out, it was laughter.

'No.'

It was hard talking to people sometimes. They were unpredictable. He'd try a different approach.

'Are you from over there?'

He pointed past the rocks – towards America. She took her time answering.

'No,' she said, stretching the word out so that it sounded not very sure of itself. She reached out her hand to take his elbow. Her touch was gentle.

'Are you OK?' she asked. The skin around her eyes was crinkled by fine lines.

'I think so. I had a mishap. So everything's – a bit new. Or at least – nothing's very old.'

He laughed. He knew the laugh sounded nervous but it couldn't be helped. He was nervous.

'I see,' she said. And then she said nothing.

He felt he had to fill the silence.

'I know it sounds strange.'

He was speaking too quickly – so he slowed himself down.

'I meet people, you see, and they say they've known me for years. But I don't know who they are. They know things about me. Strange things. None of it makes sense. I don't think I can ever have been the person they think I was. Murphy says it will all come right. But I don't know if Murphy really knows that.'

'You're making fun of me.'

'I'm not.'

She looked unconvinced. He searched around for something to say.

'I don't know anything about America, you know. Except it's over there, somewhere. And I was over there in America. Before. I only know these things because Murphy tells me them.'

He pointed up towards the car park. He saw Murphy shift his weight and wondered would he come down to them. So what if he did. He was only talking. Murphy was always after him to talk. And here he was – talking. Murphy should be happy.

'I might even know you,' he said, making a joke of it. 'But I wouldn't know if I did.'

He found himself examining her. She smiled.

'Do I? Know you?'

Her answer was careful and it wasn't one he was prepared for.

'Maybe.'

Had her eyes always been grey? She seemed different somehow – her pale skin caught the flat light and seemed to take it in, acquiring a warmer, golden tone.

'Do I know you?'

He looked up towards the car park. Murphy hadn't moved. Shouldn't he be down here by now? Shouldn't he be muttering into his ear as he pushed him up towards the car?

She looped her arm through his, and they began to walk. The only noise was the sound of their footsteps and the slow lapping of the waves.

'So why do you collect the glass?' he asked eventually, worried by the silence – disconcerted by her closeness.

'I make pictures from it. I like the texture, the way the sand has worn each piece smooth.'

He opened his hand once again, looking down at the glass. It was smooth. He stopped. He felt his mouth open and heard the words he spoke.

'Pictures are like memories. That's what I think of the glass as. Memories.'

She didn't agree or disagree but leant over to move the pieces of glass around the palm of his hand with a long finger.

'I see you have only green memories,' she said. 'I'm looking for blue memories.'

He gestured at the whisper-smooth sea and the sand. It was very cold. He wanted to say something but no words came.

'So what happened to you?'

'Somebody died. I remember that.'

He loved remembering things.

'What was her name?' she asked

I don't know if she was a woman.'

'She was.'

She seemed amused he might think differently. They stopped walking once again. A perfect pearl of blue glass lay on the wet sand in front of them. He picked it up and handed it to her. Her expression was difficult to read. She seemed to be searching for the answer to a question she had about him.

'It must be difficult for you. Not remembering anything. Was she close to you?'

'So Murphy says.'

She looked up toward the car park nodded, as if agreeing with Murphy.

'Perhaps it's just as well, then. Perhaps it's better you remember nothing. If she was close.'

'Perhaps. He takes me to places I know, plays me music I used to like. He says the doctor says they're still in there, the memories. It's just my brain can't find them yet. He thinks it will in the end. It just needs a trigger.'

He hummed a bar of a song and then stopped. He wondered where he'd heard it.

'Was this one of the places you went with her?'

She looked around her at the flat sand rising toward the dunes and the car park beyond it, at the crisp blue sea, calm in the cold breeze.

'So Murphy says.'

They were the only people visible. Even they seemed to be fading with the long light. She examined their surroundings.

'Perhaps she's still here too. Like your memories.'

'Perhaps.'

She took his hand and pressed something into it. Then she turned and walked up the beach, towards a break in the dunes – heading towards the trees. The breeze pressed her long grey coat to the shape of her legs. He would have smiled after her but his face was stiff with cold. Instead he made his way back to Murphy's car.

Murphy got out when he saw him coming.

'You must be frozen,' he said, exhaling curls of smoke with each word.

'Cold enough.'

'I've the heater on.'

When they sat into the car's smoky warmth, Murphy reached over, a pack of Marlboros held open in his thick fingers.

'Yeah?'

'Thanks.'

Murphy passed over his own to light it from.

'How did I know her? We were close, you said?'

'Her? That's good. That's progress. Yeah. You were close all right.'

'The woman on the beach reminded me.'

Murphy turned slowly until his whole body faced him. He leaned across to take his cigarette. He stubbed it out in the ashtray, as if he were sticking a knife into someone. Churning it round in their guts.

'What woman?'

'The one collecting glass from the tideline. Sea glass.'

Murphy shook his head, his jaw set.

'There was no woman. I've been watching you walk back and forth for the last hour. No one. I haven't even seen a fucking seagull, let alone a woman.'

'Long, grey coat. Blonde hair pulled back in a ponytail. Attractive. Grey eyes. She had these high cheekbones.'

Murphy said nothing for a moment, but he saw how his hand curled into a fat fist. He wondered if Murphy was going to hit him, and shifted his position slightly so his hands would be free to block the blow. He knew he would be able to block it, somehow. He'd take the fist, pull it towards him and then twist the arm. Push Murphy's head through the window, if he had to.

'Cheekbones?'

He nodded.

'And a tattoo, just under her left ear.'

'A fucking tattoo. A tattoo under her left ear. Let me guess. A tattoo of a cross.'

'How do you know?'

Murphy reached inside the pocket of his coat and pulled out his wallet. He flicked through it till he found a passport-sized photograph.

'This woman?'

'Yes.'

Murphy said nothing for a long time. He just looked at him. Every now and then Murphy opened his mouth to speak but he said nothing. He waited for what Murphy wold say next.

'You are fucking kidding me,' Murphy said.

The days were longer now and sometimes it did feel a little warmer. They'd come to a different beach, in a different place. Each evening Murphy brought him to walk along the strand in the half-hour before the sun set and smoke a cigarette as he watched the seabirds patrol the shore. He walked backward and forwards, towards the cliffs, then back towards the sea wall that guarded the channel to the town's harbour. Murphy leant against the wall, watching him.

This evening the water was out further than he'd ever seen it and he walked where usually the sea rolled. The dark sand it left behind was covered with a thin sheen of water. It was silver in the last of the sun and without a blemish – not even a shell or a footprint could be seen. He dropped the cigarette he'd been smoking but it looked so out of place that he leant down and picked it up again, stubbing it out against his heel and placing the butt in his pocket. His fingers curled around its still warm filter.

He closed his eyes and breathed in the soft sea air.

When he opened them, he saw a guillemot sitting on the sand ahead of him, its black feathers untidy and crooked around its rump. It looked up at him as he approached. He sometimes found dead guillemots stretched out in the seaweed and jetsam at the high-tide mark, their sleek black backs like wetsuits, their long necks pointing inland. This one seemed to be waiting for a similar fate. He knelt on one knee to examine it.

'Look at you,' he said.

He knelt there wondering what to do. He could leave it – it was late, after all. But he imagined waiting all alone on the beach for death. He let his breath out in a whistle. The guillemot flinched at the sound. He supposed he'd have to do something.

He stood up and looked around. A woman of about his own age was walking past and he held his hand up to her, pointing at the bird.

'She must be hurt,' she said, when she reached them. She leaned down to look at the bird more closely. 'Something's not right anyway. She doesn't seem afraid of us, which is good. She must sense we mean her well.'

'You find dead ones along the shore all the time.'

The woman stood and faced him. She smiled.

'Not this one. We'll take it up the beach and give someone a call.'

She smiled down at the bird.

'What do you say to that, little one?'

The guillemot said nothing.

'All right, then,' he said and knelt down beside the bird to take it in his hands. It half-lifted a wing in protest and then was still.

'It's exhausted, poor love. Where do you live?'

The question reminded him that Murphy must be watching them. Sure enough, he was walking towards them. But slowly.

'Outside town. Quite far.'

She laughed.

'Don't worry, I live just over there. I can look after it if needs be.'

He glanced down at the guillemot who returned his gaze, its head arching back so that it could keep him in sight.

'I'm meant to be somewhere,' he said.

'You can walk up to the house, surely?'

Murphy had stopped about fifty yards away, his hand in the pocket of his overcoat. Where he kept the gun. He was smiling. He must have seen the bird.

'I suppose I can.'

'You're not local.'

It wasn't a question. He shrugged.

'I was once. I've been away. I'm just visiting.'

She didn't ask him anything more but he knew she wanted to. She had that look about her. Like he was a lock that needed picking.

'It's good to be home.'

Again, it wasn't a question. He looked up at the town.

'You're from here, are you?'

'Yes. I was away as well. Weren't we all? I came back last year. My sister passed on and it was hard on my parents. Very hard. But time cures all ills.'

'So they say.'

'I haven't seen you around. You must keep to yourself.'

What could he say to that? Not much. They walked in silence. The bird made a gurgling sound but it didn't seem to signify anything.

'She killed herself.'

'I'm sorry.'

'My sister. Out of the blue. She was over to see my parents – she'd moved to America a few years ago – and she hung herself the first night she was back. In the kitchen. They found her when they came down in the morning. No note, no nothing.'

He looked over at Murphy, who was keeping pace with them – his hand still in his pocket. Not looking at them, although there was no question he was aware of them. He wondered why he wasn't coming over. He smoothed the neck feathers of the bird.

'That must have been hard, all right.'

'We thought it must have been something that happened to her. Over there. But we couldn't find anyone who knew her. No one could. There were only the stamps on her passport to prove she'd ever been there. It leaves a hole. Not knowing.'

He said nothing. He saw nothing. In his mind's eye he watched two white feet swing stiff above terracotta tiles.

'We're up here.'

She was pointing towards a line of houses. He wondered what she must see when she looked at him. It was an effort to lift his hand to look at his watch. All he could see was the cord digging into that pale neck, obscuring the tattooed cross. He remembered the warm smell of her – a mixture of sleep and fear.

'I'm sorry.' His voice sounded as though it belonged to someone else. 'I've got to go. I'm meeting a friend.'

'A friend? You mustn't be late. We live at number twenty-two. If you're passing?'

'That would be nice,' he said and did his best to smile.

He started walking along the concrete path that led along the front. Towards the harbour wall, but he couldn't lift his eyes to see where he was going. He heard the woman call after him.

'What about the bird?'

He reached down, his fingers closing around the bird's neck. He squeezed and felt the bones pop. There was no sound. No indication of the change. One moment it was alive. And then it wasn't. The bird hadn't struggled. Nor had she.

'It's dead,' he called back. 'It must have been the shock. I'll bury it.'

He didn't know how long he walked. It could have been miles or it might have only been a few feet but then he was aware of Murphy walking alongside him. The breeze chilled the tears that ran down his face.

'Are you all right, soldier?'

'I'm fine,' he said.

'I'm sorry, if it makes any difference. You know how it was with her.'

'I do.'

'It had to be done. There was no choice. These things happen in our line of work. Loyalties change.'

He looked down at the dead bird, a clump of dead meat and feathers. He handed it across to Murphy.

'Bury this thing for me, would you?'

Murphy shrugged and took it.

'Then we'll get out of here.'

Murphy exhaled.

'At fucking last.'

On the walk to the car he reached inside his pocket and found a piece of smooth glass. It fitted into his palm as though it were meant to be there forever. He savoured the feel of it for a moment.

Then he dropped it on the road.

Louise Phillips

Louise Phillips is an author of four bestselling psychological crime thrillers, each of which was shortlisted for Best Irish Crime Novel of the Year in the Irish Book Awards. Her second novel, *The Doll's House*, won the award. Louise's work has formed part of many anthologies, and she has won both the Jonathan Swift Award and the Irish Writers' Centre Lonely Voice platform. In 2013, she was the recipient of an Arts Bursary for Literature, and in 2015, she was awarded a Writers' Residency at Cill Rialaig Artist retreat. She was also a judge on the Irish panel for the EU Literary Award. This year, she has been longlisted for a CWA Dagger in the Library Award. Her first two novels, *Red Ribbons* and *The Doll's House*, will be published in the US in 2016 and 2017.

Double

Danger often comes without warning, creeping up on you in the same way as ivy grips a wall, slow and unfaltering, and once it takes hold, it can be impossible to pull away, no matter how much you want to.

Meeting him for the first time, I thought it a random encounter, something that could easily have led to nothing. Later, I had the notion it was fated. I don't believe that now. I understand the planning involved.

Leaving the house that morning, the sun shone in a clear blue sky. Pink apple blossoms filled the branches of trees. It was the kind of day that falsely held the promise of new beginnings. Pulling the front door of my detached suburban prison firmly closed, I smelt the hyacinths littering the front lawn. The chill of crisp spring air caused me to absent-mindedly put a hand to my face. I looked around. The road was quiet and empty without the early morning traffic or joggers. The neighbouring children were already deposited at school. I visualised mothers flicking on kettles for cups of tea, making fancy cappuccinos in chrome coffee makers or smoothies to keep their energy levels up.

Earlier, I had scrutinised my image in the full-length hall mirror. I looked attractive within the ornate gold frame. Five decades of rigorously fighting to keep a size ten figure had worked. I wore a simple day dress by Jasmin, navy, fitted and expensive, the hemline resting above the knee, with a white-gold silk scarf casually draped around my neck. The designer sunglasses completed the look. I felt giddy, almost as if I were a young girl again. I hadn't told anyone about my plans, especially not my husband, or our two adult children. If things went well, it might make for an interesting lunch conversation with friends, but that was for later. Perhaps I thought I was making a bold statement, that somehow it was still possible to be wild and free.

The big fiftieth birthday party had been a disaster. I'd never wanted it, but Mark insisted. My husband was like that. He did many things I didn't want him to do. I don't remember when his thoughts and desires began to supersede mine, but since the party I kept getting visions of myself wearing acrylic jumpers, tweed skirts and flat sensible shoes. I saw an older me, sitting in a nursing home the way my mother had done, balancing a spoonful of peas over dinner, most of which never made it to her mouth. By then her lipstick was applied by someone else, with far too much rouge on her cheeks. She looked like a castaway twin of Bette Davis from the movie *Whatever Happened to Baby Jane?* Mark said I was being ridiculous. Perhaps he was right, but a line had been crossed, and like the creeping ivy, the fear of old age gripped tight.

My sense of adventure lasted all the way into town, but once I parked the car I felt consumed by the crowded streets. Dublin had become more cosmopolitan since my heady, carefree younger days. It was faster, tighter, louder. I heard the sound of screeching buses pulling into bus stops and music audible from headsets with the volume set too loud, then the roar of strange voices above the swishing bristles of a road sweeper, constantly turning round and around.

Everyone seemed to know what they were doing, except for me. Most looked in a hurry, as if they too were acutely aware that time was slipping by. On instinct, I sneaked into a coffee shop off Grafton Street. Being early for my appointment, I ordered a large skinny latte and sat with my copy of *Elle* magazine purchased from a nearby shop. I hoped to give the impression I was waiting for someone, rather than waiting for life.

I had been toying with the idea of having an affair for months. Mark had had a few. His female companions were always younger – cliché extraordinaire. Most had a stylish appearance, with a hint of slut on the side. The last one, with white-blonde hair, had amorous lips and a fondness for red high heels. I always followed him as soon as I got suspicious. Traces of his indiscretion were easily found – a stray hair, a whiff of perfume or an unknown number on his mobile phone. The latest model wore a cheap vanilla scent, akin to a vulgar room freshener, and I had wondered if he was letting his standards slip. Mostly, I didn't need to wait for the physical evidence. His behaviour was the trigger – taking the phone into the other room, paying extra attention to his body parts, shaving twice a day, or spending far too long deciding what to wear. The smugness on his face was another tell-tale sign, delighted to be the cat that got the proverbial cream. His sex drive increased too. The illicit behaviour stroked his ego. In the early days, I didn't mind too much. I told myself I had him, his children, money, respectability, all the things I ever wanted, and inevitably I would be the one survivor of his fleeting affairs.

After a while I stopped fooling myself, and soon after that, another kind of stalking began. For a time I felt it put me back in the driving seat. Curious if his affairs were purely sexual or had more depth, it seemed like the next logical step. I wasn't stupid. He likely told his whores how difficult it was to live with someone he didn't love anymore, that I was weak, clinging, and how I'd be crushed if he left. Whatever he told them, a certain pattern emerged.

He liked using his car at night for sex, rather than paying for a hotel room. It wasn't monetary. We had plenty of that. I think it brought him back to his youth, fucking in the dark, all those awkward positions, steamed up windows, along with the aphrodisiac of potentially being caught. He suggested it to me once, shortly after we were married, saying it would spice things up. I told him he was being ridiculous. He didn't refer to it again.

Once Mark left the women home, I then knew where they lived. I began following them instead of him. I liked to play little games, calling to their house or apartment, asking for directions or pretending I'd been given a wrong address. A couple of times I managed to be invited inside. On other occasions I would arrive at coffee shops or bars where they met friends or work colleagues, listening to their conversations, wondering if they'd mention him to others. Unfortunately, it didn't take long for that thrill to fade. Which is why I found myself alone in a café, putting off meeting a man I'd only ever conversed with online. We were due to see each other at Trinity College, no more than a five-minute walk away.

More people bustled into the café. I tasted my latte which was already cold. Most of the tables were now occupied. I closed the magazine, then opened it again, wondering how much longer I could delay the 'date'. After all, being late, I told myself, was a better option than being early. I felt the start of a migraine. The noise in the café seemed louder too – trays clattering, the sharp bang as a new customer slammed their tray down on the long, curved wooden counter, cups and saucers hitting off one another, the metal cutlery crunching, chairs being pulled in and out and the shuffling of feet as the old-fashioned cash register dinged. Everything and everyone was clambering. I had the sense that others were staring at me, as if I was a target. I thought about leaving, not meeting this stranger at Trinity after all, going to an art gallery or a museum instead. It wasn't too late.

A large-framed woman carrying a loaded tray pushed past me. She knocked my shoulder without apologising. I wondered if people thought I was hogging the seat for too long, or if I should order something else to justify my occupation of the space. I was being stupid – nobody cared. I flipped the pages of the magazine again. That was when my eyes looked up, curious as the small brass bell rang above the front door and I saw him. He met my gaze and smiled, as if somehow we already knew each other. My cheeks flushed – embarrassed. I looked away, telling myself not to be ridiculous, he was less than half my age. Still, I eyed him from above the magazine like a silly schoolgirl. I wondered if my original illicit intention for the morning had inadvertently sent out a signal that I was available. I was still staring when he picked up his large Americano and walked in my direction.

'Do you mind if we share?' he asked, putting the cup down on the table.

'No, not at all. It's all yours. I was about to leave.'

'Don't leave on my account.'

I felt his knee below the table touching mine. 'I was planning a visit to an art gallery,' I blurted, and instantly felt foolish.

'What kind of art do you like?'

'All kinds, although my preference is oils, abstract mainly.'

'Why?'

'I like the madness of them.'

He laughed, and I laughed too.

'Your accent isn't Irish,' I quizzed, without thinking – the words coming out too fast.

'Scottish, I'm from Edinburgh.'

'What brings you here?' My throat was dry. I sipped the cold latte. 'Sorry, I'm being too inquisitive.'

'I like inquisitive people.'

I felt a blush come to my cheeks again.

He looked down and stirred his coffee, and I noted a certain shyness within the confidence.

'Circumstances,' he said, almost as an afterthought.

'Sorry?'

'You asked what brought me here.'

'Oh yes, I did.'

He didn't expand his answer any further, and I didn't pursue it. Looking back, perhaps I should have known how dangerous he would be. Anyone who answered a question with one word was already good at hiding things.

I excused myself, going to the ladies. I can't explain how I knew things would happen between us, but I did. A realisation had dawned, one that had been staring me in the face for far too long. My life, all the pointless actions, chores, my husband's affairs, the following of strangers, each of my tedious days floating into the next, was worthless. What I didn't realise back then was how it made the lives of others less important too.

In the ladies, I applied more make-up, face powder to cover my oily T-zone, mascara to add eyelash definition and blusher to make the cheeks glow. I took time applying my lipstick, cognisant of how much age lowers the collagen levels, thinning your lips. I looked well. I saw an expression of liveliness which had been missing for far too long. Part of me wondered if he would still be there when I returned, but another part of me knew he would. Then the reflection in the mirror changed. I saw my mother, stooped, lined and beaten down, and her frantic effort to do the simplest of things – finding money in her purse, putting on her nylons or shoes, chasing apricots in syrup on her plate, and how they all slipped away from her.

Walking back to the table, I couldn't shake my mother's image out of my mind. My new male friend pulled out my chair. The noise level lowered. I smelt the aroma of coffee and wondered how I had missed it before. He told me his name and I told him mine. When his hand slipped down my back, all thoughts of meeting the other man disappeared. The idea of killing my husband hadn't manifested itself by then, but soon it would.

Two weeks into the affair, I began googling effective methods of murder. I did consider if I had gone quite mad, but carried on regardless. I used Mark's old computer in the den, the one he utilised for his secret emails, having cracked his latest password months before. I visualised stabbing a knife into his chest. A century earlier, poisoning would have been the preferred method for female killers, side-tracking the physical disparity between them and their victims. That wouldn't have worked for me, not if I wanted to claim self-defence. Mark had a temper. If I pushed him, he would respond. He had done so before, therefore, he would do so again – his predictability an obvious weakness. If he hit me hard enough, I might get away with it.

It was during an afternoon with my lover, when I was semi-conscious after copious amounts of wine and sniffing far too much cocaine, that I shared my murderous plans. Speaking initially in jest, I was surprised by his response. I attributed his immediate offer of help as mildly hallucinogenic, thinking he was as out of it as me. His plan, not unlike mine, was straightforward in its simplicity – I would get Mark to rough me up, then my lover would make the attack more vicious, describing at length how easily it could be done. Even in my drug- and alcohol-induced state, the idea lingered. After all, Mark had flaunted his affairs in front of me for practically our entire marriage. He didn't care about me; why should I care about him? And the ivy gripped a little tighter.

The conversation of killing my husband manifested itself again a couple of days later. I felt another line was drawn, despite being unsure if I would go ahead with it. Thinking about killing someone is one thing; doing it is very different. I'll admit, even then, the keenness of my lover for the task made me anxious, saying how straightforward it would be, and how we could do whatever we wanted afterward. I visualised my old life whizzing down the sink in gulps of dirty water as the stopper became plucked free. The more times we went over the plan the more it was as if the next step had an air of inevitability about it.

We began planning the best ways to build up the pressure on Mark. How I should keep alluding to how pathetic his life was, making references to the other women and that I had known for years, but had long since gone beyond caring. The word *divorce* would be mentioned too, knowing he would never agree to it. I was his trophy wife, the height of respectability. My family and social connections alone, once rattled, would have a devastating effect on his successful business. He might wonder how many young women would be interested in him when his egotistical empire collapsed around him. Despite his exterior confidence, I knew my husband better than most. Inside, beyond the façade, was a desperate schoolboy, one who still wanted to live up to the expectations of his mother, secretly knowing he was living a lie. It didn't take long before I sensed the deep seething anger bubbling below the surface. He began drinking heavily too. Alcohol fuelled his temper. His cracking point was close.

Perhaps it was gut instinct that initiated the decision to stalk my lover, instead of Mark and his latest concubine. At first I wasn't sure why he was hanging out in the same places as Mark, near his office, in the bar where my husband liked to have a casual drink, or the restaurant he often used for lunch. I thought that he might be studying the target, but that idea evaporated when I found them chatting to one another on a park bench, drinking takeaway coffee.

I had no idea what they were talking about, but the possibility of me being the potential victim instead of Mark hit home fast. An uncontrollable trembling took hold, flashbacks of the intimacy I had shared with both of them, each of their hands on my body; and how now they were mocking me, like I was the butt of a crude, sadistic joke. But it wasn't a joke, and I wasn't laughing. The anger that followed later was preceded by hurt, then revulsion and finally a sense of aloneness unlike anything I had felt before. The noises in the park dispersed, the sounds of idle conversations of passing strangers became faint, traffic sounds from beyond the park gates were no longer possible to hear. My knees began to shake and as I made the decision to flee, a lone robin landed at my feet.

'I adore robins,' my mother used to say, 'they arrive suddenly and quietly, when you least expect them. Such fearless little birds, quite unaware of humanity, except for the close sudden movements initiating their flight.' I realised it was the helplessness of my situation that terrified me most. Like the robin, I could be crushed, unless I too took action.

Once out of the park, my mind went into overdrive, fuelled by the rage that was quickly taking hold. I didn't have a key to my lover's flat, so I made the decision to turn our house upside down instead. Two hours later I still hadn't found anything. I thought about hiring a private detective, but what if time was against me? What if I only had hours and not days? What if they were already on their way to kill me? It might already be too late.

At first I stood in the living room unable to move, hearing the water hiss through the radiators. The heating timer was set for 4 p.m. – Mark would be home in less than an hour. It was then I remembered the loose floorboard upstairs, the one where he kept a small handgun in case someone broke in. He knew I hated guns, that the very look and feel of them sent shudders down my spine.

I took the stairs two at a time, a large kitchen knife in my hand. Pushing over the bed, I used the knife to flip the floorboard. Initially all I saw was the pewter-coloured 9mm handgun, with the small box of ammunition to the side, but then I spotted the folded white pages underneath. Each of the pages had typed notes. The one at the top, which I assumed was the latest, confirmed that contact had already been made with me, giving instructions for another €5,000 in cash to be left at the agreed location point. I searched the other pages to see where that might be, but the page must have been destroyed.

I couldn't go to the police. What if my lover told them about my earlier plan? Hearing Mark's car pull into the drive, I emptied the box of ammunition before putting everything back as I had found it. Mark was already climbing the stairs when I hid the bullets under my pillow. I knew I would have to find another hiding place, but right then the important thing was to act normal. I had lived a lie for a very long time. I could keep living it.

The following day, Mark and my lover saw each other again, only this time they were openly arguing in the street. Was it over more money for sorting me out?

I knew, of the two of them, Mark would be the most suspicious of me. That meant attacking the weakest link. My lover had no reason not to trust me. All I had to do was play the game. I decided his dabbling in drugs was my get-out clause. An accidental overdose wasn't uncommon. It would take some detailed logistics to keep a distance between myself and the supplier, but it wasn't impossible.

Getting the pure heroin was easier than I thought. His drug mule already knew I was the one paying the bills, even if he didn't know who I was. I watched my cash in the plastic bag being picked up by a kid of about fourteen. In case anyone spotted me, I wore boots that made me look taller and clothing non-reflective of my social standing. A dark wig and a cheap set of shades did the rest. I felt quite Machiavellian. I had paid enough money to divide the stash in two. The first would be diluted down by my lover, the same way as he had done in the past. The second I would use for a switch. I visualised him dying in his apartment alone, willing that part to soon be over.

Two days later when the patrol car pulled up outside, I worried I might have been found out. When they asked to speak to Mark, I looked shocked, but not for the reason the police supposed. I realised quickly that they had already connected Mark to my ex-lover, and potentially his death. They told me they would need to take the computer from the den, and I remembered all the site searches on effective killing methods. They would assume it was Mark. I thought about pulling the notes from upstairs, and giving them to the two officers, but that would put me in the frame, giving me a clear motive. As I listened at the door to the police questioning Mark, I decided I would need to destroy the notes. When they asked him if he knew the victim, it surprised me when he answered yes. I thought he would deny it, being a man who rarely admitted any wrong. His next words, said softly, and tinged with such sadness that I wondered if it was my husband speaking at all, shocked me more.

The noises in the house got louder, the sound of the fridge humming from the kitchen, the water gurgling in the radiators, the creaking of the floorboards upstairs, the traffic whizzing past the front door, over and over again. How could he have been Mark's son? It didn't make any sense, except of course, it did, when I put one piece of information in front of the other. He met me to get revenge on Mark. That's why he was so keen on me taking my husband's life. He wanted to punish him for abandoning his own son. All those illicit affairs had to have created at least one offspring, but what about the notes? Who did they belong to?

Mark was still talking, explaining to the police how he believed for a long time that he was being followed, and how once he realised who it was, he understood why. They had talked to each other on a number of occasions, but recently the boy had become increasingly angry and aggressive; how they had argued on the street a few days earlier, and that he never thought it would come to this.

When they walked out of the living room, the two police officers were ahead of Mark, and he asked me how much of it I had I heard. I replied that I'd heard all of it. His meek apology meant nothing. He told me the officers were taking him in for more questions, nothing more. I wasn't to be worried.

I rang our family solicitor, because Mark asked me to. When I hung up the phone, things began to spin around, and again the noises got louder. There was a ringing in my ears. I heard my mother roaring at me, telling me I had been utterly selfish and stupid, and how it was only a matter of time before I would be punished. I had been frightened, I told her, terrified. I was fighting for my life. I thought they wanted to kill me. What else was I to do? But she kept asking, over and over again, what about the notes? What did they mean? Who sent them, if it wasn't Mark's bastard son? It was then that I saw him, the man watching the house. I knew he was watching, because I knew who he was.

My mind drifted back. My mother screaming. My father hitting her, dragging her into the bedroom they shared, and how as a child I closed my eyes tight, putting my hands over my ears, not wanting to hear or see any of it. I found I was doing it again, only this time, no matter how hard I tried, I couldn't shut out the noise, and when I finally opened my eyes, he was beside me, the man I had agreed to meet online.

He took another couple of steps towards me, yanking my hair. I felt something tightening around my neck, the ivy clinging, squeezing and I saw my mother again, the day before she died, when she had gone completely mad in the nursing home, firing plates and cups at the walls, screaming at the top of her voice as the nurses and orderlies tried to restrain her, all in an effort to stop her breaking free. I stood like a stone statue, watching the unravelling of her life, my mother once more reduced to a captive in a pretty prison with grandiose furniture, and in that second, I knew this man would kill me.

I could hardly breathe, but somehow I croaked: 'How much did he pay you?' Ever since childhood, I had allowed others to be in control – not anymore. The ivy loosened. I swallowed hard.

'I can pay you double.'

Sinéad Crowley

Sinéad Crowley has been working as a journalist for over twenty years and is currently arts and media correspondent with RTÉ, Ireland's national broadcaster. She is also the author of the DS Claire Boyle crime series. The first two books, *Can Anybody Help Me?* and *Are You Watching Me?* were shortlisted for Crime Novel of the Year at the Irish Book Awards. The third, *One Bad Turn*, will be published in mid-2017.

Maximum Protection

I knew I was heading in the right direction when I saw the goat. Tethered to a pole and chewing happily on the patch of scrub grass at his feet, he looked so content it was as if the rope around his neck had been placed there at his own request, to save him having to make bothersome decisions about where to wander. As I stared at him, he extended his neck and took a lazy nibble from the handwritten 'HELP WANTED' sign that had been sellotaped to his hitching post. Then he gave me a look that seemed to ask what exactly I was waiting for.

I had visited the Greek islands before, of course. There had been a sodden week in Kos with the lads following our Leaving Cert exams, from which we returned as white as when we left, and, more recently, a fortnight in Rhodes with Darina to celebrate our engagement. The fact she had spent more time worrying about cake-toppers than appreciating the beauty of the Old Town should have been a warning of things to come but still, neither experience had put me off the country itself, and when I found myself suddenly both unemployed and disengaged, I booked a flight to Athens and took a ferry to the prettiest-sounding island I could find.

For the first while I stuck to the tourist areas. My heart was still pretty sore about the whole Darina thing and I needed a decent swimming pool and an air-conditioned bar to help kiss it better. But after a week or so, when I discovered I could prod at my bruises without wincing, I decided to spread my wings and, ignoring the dire warnings of the hotel reps, hired a moped and took to the road.

It was on the third day that I saw the goat and his sign. Curious, I killed the engine and walked over to take a closer look. The midday sun was beating down on me but after a lifetime spent in various degrees of Irish rain I was still finding the Greek climate exotic rather than uncomfortable. If anything, the heat seemed to have a cleansing effect on me and, as I scoured the landscape to see what help was required and where, I could feel the whole damn lot of it, the nastiness at work, the split with Darina, all the shite being sweated out of me, trickling down my back and seeping into the dust below. For the first time in a long time I had nothing to worry about other than what factor sun protection I should be using, and the liberation was intoxicating. The goat snickered and tossed his head upwards and, as I followed his gaze, I noticed that the pole he was tethered to was topped with a wooden sign bearing the legend 'Bill's Bar'. I didn't need to be asked three times.

I pushed the bike down the dusty track, past rows of the ubiquitous and appealingly ugly olive trees. Beyond the horizon the sea sparkled the colour of Paul Newman's eyes, but as I walked closer to the squat grey building at the end of the lane it became obvious why there were no mini-markets lining the path and no brightly coloured signs promising a 'Full English' to go with that night's big game. Bill had chosen a location with spectacular views but, unlike the bars and restaurants along the main strip, his establishment had no direct access to a beach and faced instead onto a cliff, with a sharp drop onto the rocks below. This was not an area to which the tourist hordes would be drawn and for a man like myself who wanted to *control-alt-delete* the events of the previous year, it seemed as close to perfection as I was going to get.

The wooden door to the bar had been wedged open with a wad of yellowed newspaper and I stepped inside, blinking for a moment while my eyes adjusted to the dim interior. All was calm. There was no television regurgitating hourly headlines, no tape recorder feeding out a loop of sanitised bouzouki tunes. Just a stone-flagged floor, wooden tables and a window, its shutters flung open to allow in the salty sea air.

In one corner an elderly, bearded man, cup of ink-black coffee by his elbow, scratched answers in a newspaper crossword. A second chap, in his mid-fifties maybe, stood wiping glasses behind a broad wooden counter. Although his uniform of rolled-up shirt sleeves and black trousers was standard attire for waiters on the island, his caramel-coloured complexion, freckles and reddish, receding hair told me that his first name probably wasn't Dionysus and I wasn't very surprised when he greeted me in an accent that owed more to Athlone than Athens.

'What can I get you?'

I offered him a friendly, if slightly sweaty smile.

'I've come about the job.'

The man grunted, and continued to polish.

'The boss isn't here today. Have you worked behind a bar before?'

I paused for a moment, considering the many ways I could answer the question. I could start with my days spent collecting glasses in the pub down the road, move on to my degree in Hospitality Services that had seen me manage a suburban super-pub by the time I hit thirty-five. It would probably be best, however, to leave out the fact that I'd walked out of that pub a month before without giving notice, frazzled beyond repair by the rocketing staff turnover and the constant questions about cappuccino machines and pre-prepared focaccia that had little to do with the beer I wanted to serve. But all that seemed like too much information so instead I just smiled and extended my hand.

'Yeah. I've a few years put in, all right. Name is Paul, by the way.'

After taking a closer look he returned the handshake.

'Raymond. Nice to meet you. Come around here so and we'll give you a try.'

After two days I stopped asking Raymond when the boss was due back and on the third got him to admit that there was no such person as Bill and that he himself was the owner, manager, keg changer and toilet cleaner of all he surveyed. The deception didn't bother me. Raymond said he'd rather try someone out for a few days than give them the job on the strength of an impressive interview and I, having been duped by many shiny and utterly false CVs in the past, couldn't argue with him. Besides, by then I had fallen in love with the bar and wasn't going to say anything that would risk changing his mind. The place was perfect. It wasn't too quiet, almost every day we were visited by couples or young families anxious to explore a little of the island beyond the central tourist zone. We also hosted quite a few locals, mostly older men who had spent their lifetimes running the bars and restaurants on the main strip and were now content to let their sons prepare vast trays of moussaka instead. But we were never frantically busy and there was time in every day to have a coffee, flick through a newspaper, or simply stand at the door, looking out and wondering why anyone would live anywhere else on earth but here.

The guy in the corner was a permanent fixture and after a few days I knew his routine as well as I knew my own. He came in every day at eleven for a Greek coffee and one of the delicious flaky pastries that were delivered daily, then headed off without a word. He came back in at lunchtime for a beer and a look through the paper, but his main visit was in the evening. Every night at seven o'clock he'd walk in wearing a crisply ironed shirt and take up a position at the centre table, close enough to the window to get the benefit of the air but with his body angled towards the centre of the bar so he could take full part in whatever was going on. He chatted to everyone, tourist and local alike and he could spend an hour or more having the crack with toothless oul lads who didn't speak a word of English. I loved watching them take it in turns to jab at pictures of local football teams in the paper, miming wins and losses with gusto and throwing their heads back in delight at it all.

He was Irish too, the customer, although he never spoke about home. But his presence in the bar intrigued me and I made my mind up that, as soon as I felt my feet were firmly under the table, I'd ask Raymond how the hell yet another Paddy had washed up on such a faraway shore.

My chance came on the Thursday morning of my third week. The bar had been unusually quiet the night before, meaning we had very little prep to do the following morning, and by half-past ten we were open and ready for customers who looked like they were in no rush to drop by. A typical Irishman, Raymond didn't go in for organised conversations, so instead I gave the bar counter a final unnecessary wipe, jerked my head in the direction of the now empty corner table and asked, 'So who's your man, anyway?'

Raymond didn't reply. Instead, he pulled a couple of glasses of the local beer, carried them to a table and set each one down on a fresh beer mat. Realising this was the closest I'd come to an invitation, I grabbed the seat opposite him and took a sip.

'I ran a place back home for nearly twenty years,' he began, then named a pub in inner-city Dublin whose name I immediately recognised. I'd only been there once, years ago on a pub crawl with a mate who was dating a student in the college across the road, and as soon as we'd stuck our heads in the door we'd realised it wouldn't be wise to stick around. This was not a pub for passers-by. Even now, despite the salt air streaming through the window of Bill's, I could still remember the smell of it; a mixture of stale beer and cigarette smoke that remained trapped in the curtains years after the smoking ban had been enforced. That was assuming, of course, that they had implemented the ban in the first place, because this was an establishment where most of the clientele were, in the phrase beloved of journalists, 'known to Gardaí'. Shaven-headed hard chaws sat at the counter sporting tattoos that definitely weren't the Chinese word for 'water' and, on small seats around the edges, grey-haired men sat pouring over betting slips and treacly pints. In fact, the more I thought about it, the easier it was to imagine our customer fitting right in.

Raymond saw my look of comprehension, and nodded.

'Yeah, Eamonn was one of our regulars. Him and his mate Dessie. They came in every night at seven, you could set your watch by them. Dessie used to say it was how the missus kicked him out then so she could watch the soaps in peace and Eamonn – well, Eamonn was a single man, the pub was his whole life. They'd sit there every night, 7 p.m. 'til closing, and I used to think there wasn't a happier pair in the whole world. Like a married couple only better, you know? The picture of contentment. Anyway—'

He took a large slug from his glass and I thought it must have gone down the wrong way because he coughed several times before continuing.

'Where was I? Yeah, Eamonn wasn't married but Dessie's wife was from – how will I put it? – one of the better-known families in the area.'

He tossed out a surname that immediately brought to mind television pictures of Garda checkpoints and stern-faced

334

reporters talking animatedly into cameras about 'an escalation in Gangland activity'.

Raymond was warming to his story now, and continued.

'I never really knew Dessie's missus, she didn't come to the pub very often. But one morning when I opened up there was a couple of Guards at the front door and a clatter of journalists a few steps behind them. Turned out there had been a shooting on the estate the night before, a lad was in hospital and a whole pile of money had gone missing too. You can imagine the type of thing, one gang was dealing and the other lot reckoned they'd gone in on their patch. Nasty stuff. Anyway, it was said around the place that Dessie's wife's family was behind the shooting, and that they had taken the money too.

'The pub wasn't right for the rest of the day, people were jumpy, you know? On edge. Dessie arrived in as usual at seven but he was on his own and then, about an hour later, Eamonn fell in the door, drunk as a lord. In all my years serving him I'd never seen him jarred but he was steaming that night, in a bad way. He started yelling at Dessie, saying he knew he had the money, that it was 'blood money'. He said he should hand himself over to the Guards and be done with it. Called him a scumbag, and all sorts, said he was as bad as the rest of them. I'd forgotten, or maybe I'd never been told, but Eamonn lost two nephews to drugs, years before this happened, and one of them was only fifteen years old.

'Anyway, I let it go for a bit but then Eamonn started to get dangerous, he even picked up a bottle and tried to smash it on the counter, so I had to call the Guards. They took him down to the barracks to sleep it off. The next morning there was even more cops crawling around the place. Dessie's car had been found on Howth Head, and a witness made an anonymous call to say he'd seen him jump into the sea.

'Dessie's missus turned up in the pub that night, crying and roaring and saying he was the love of her life and she'd be lost without him. I don't know about lost but she was in deep shit alright. Turned out Eamonn had been right all along, she had given Dessie the money to hide but he'd gone off with it himself, and ended up in the sea for his troubles.'

'Jesus.'

I drained my glass and looked out the window to where white foam was dancing on top of the greenest of waves. Raymond finished his own drink and shrugged.

'I lost interest in the pub after that, couldn't get out of there quick enough to be honest with you. I sold up, found this place and started again. And then one day Eamonn turned up at the door. Dublin's a small place, someone must have told him I'd opened a bar out here. So here we are! Two oul fellas seeing out our days in the sun. There's no more to it than that, really.'

He pushed his chair back from the table, ready to start work again and for a moment, I was tempted to do the same. It was a beautiful day, I had nothing more stressful ahead of me then a box of paper napkins to fold and an ice machine to clean. But I didn't like being taken for an eejit, even by someone as pleasant as Raymond, so I looked at him, and shook my head.

'And what about the rest?'

Raymond returned my gaze, calmly.

'I don't know what you mean.'

I grinned at him, trying to let on we were all in it together, but I wasn't falling for his story and I couldn't pretend otherwise.

'Come on, man. Eamonn took the money off Dessie, he must have done. It's a great *scéal*, Raymond, and you tell it well, but don't tell me you just *happened* to find a pub with an address that might as well be 'Number One Paradise Lane' and your old *segotia* Eamonn just *happened* to turn up a few months later and ordered a half pint and a whiskey chaser? Come on, pal. I can't buy that, and I don't think you'd expect me to either. Eamonn found out that Dessie had the money and he fecked him off Howth Head, he must have done. Maybe he thought he was doing it for the best, I don't know. But there's more to this than you're telling me.'

Raymond settled back into his seat again, and shrugged.

'You won't find his name on any title deeds. This bar is mine, one hundred percent. And it could be yours if you like.'

I frowned, and then looked at him again and took in what my eyes hadn't initially let me process in the gloom of the bar. The yellowing of the skin that owed more to illness than a lack of sun-cream. The sagging of the flesh around the face, the slight tremor in his hand. I'd seen my own Da go the same way and there wasn't any disguising it once it got to that stage.

'I'm sorry, man. I didn't realise.'

Raymond shrugged again.

'That's how it goes. I've had six great years here, but it's time to go home now. The sister says I can stay with her until – well. For a while anyway. But the bar needs a manager and you're the first chap I've met who I think could be up to the job.'

I turned my head towards the window and inhaled, feeling the salt tickle the back of my nostrils as laughter from a boatload of tourists wafted up to me. Number One Paradise Lane. And then I shook my head.

'I can't do it, man. There's a man dead – Jesus. I couldn't have it on my conscience.'

Raymond gave a broad smile.

'You've forgotten one thing. Eamonn was banged up the night Dessie disappeared. The Guards talked to him, of course they did, but there was no question of him being next nor near Howth that night, he was sleeping it off in a cell with his jacket under his head.'

I shrugged.

'He had him killed then, whatever. Either way, this isn't for me.'

Raymond frowned, suddenly serious.

'You know, Eamonn was right about one thing. That cash that went missing, it was blood money. Earned off the backs of the walking dead, stumbling around Dublin mugging tourists and shooting poison up their arms. You won't find Eamonn's name on any deeds but I'll tell you what you will find in this little village. A new school down the road. A party every year for the locals when the season is over and they've earned a night on the town. A new house for the doctor who suddenly found a reason not to move back to the mainland again. There's been a lot of good done around here, these past few years.'

I could see how sincere he was. And for a moment, I was tempted so hard I could feel my hand tremble, aching to shake his, to seal the deal. This was some life he was offering me. Mornings on the beach, afternoons in the bar, nights spent exploring the island, maybe learning a little Greek, getting to know a few people. No heating bills and no hassle. But Jesus, no. No. A man was dead. That wasn't—

My thoughts were interrupted by the creak of the bar door. It was Eamonn, fifteen minutes late for his breakfast, and he wasn't alone. Raymond jumped up from the table.

'Ah, how's the man? Good to see you up and about anyway.'

The newcomer gave an exaggerated groan.

'The hip is as sore as bejaysus, to be honest with you, but I was doing my nut up there in the house on my own.'

'Sit down there so and I'll get you some breakfast.'

While Eamonn clucked around his friend I followed Raymond back to the bar, mouthing silently.

'Dessie?'

He grinned, then beckoned at me to follow him through to the small kitchen, where a door stood open facing the sea. He lit a cigarette and pointed the jet of smoke towards the cliff edge.

'A witness said he saw him jump, but they never found a body.'

He took another drag before continuing.

'She gave him a hell of a life, you know, Dessie's missus. They married young and he wasn't happy when he found out who her family was, where all their money came from. But sometimes it's hard to get away, unless you make a total break.'

I shook my head, and then another thought occurred to me.

'Are they – are they together?'

'Eamonn and Dessie?'

Raymond didn't laugh at the question but shook his head gently.

'Nah, not like that. But there are many ways to love a person, you know? Many ways to be happy.'

I took a step forwards, looked out into the body of the bar where the two old men were now arguing happily about 14 Across. A bird shrieked, freestyling across the clouds, and I thought about decisions and choices, and how maybe everyone deserves a chance at happiness, no matter how they arrive at it.

I give the goat a bowl of water now, in the mornings before I open up. He never looks at me, but I think he appreciates it.

Liz Nugent

Liz Nugent has worked in Irish film, theatre and television for most of her adult life. She is an award-winning writer of radio and television drama and has written short stories for children and adults. *Unravelling Oliver*, her first novel, won the Ireland AM Crime Novel of the Year in 2014. Her second novel, *Lying in Wait*, was published in 2016.

Cruel and Unusual

I watch a child approach. About three years of age. Her steps are uncertain. She is guided by her mother. The little hand is enclosed in the adult one.

I remember that feeling, the warmth and closeness of a child's hand.

She looks up. Up at me. I see her face, the eyes wide with inexperience, and the wet lips catching the light with their spill of drool. She wants to stop. *Please let her stop.* But no. Her mama is in a hurry. The child is torn from her moment of wonder. Her arm wrenched upwards in an arc of irritation.

How long have I been here? More than four centuries? More than five? I lost count a long time ago. I used to anticipate the changes of climate but now the seasons are like days to me. That is what happens when you live as long as I have.

The singular beauty of a child. It is mostly the little ones who will wonder about me now. It is all part of my penance. I watch them craning to look up at me. I worry that their fragile necks might snap backwards, might kill their beautiful innocence while I observe, helpless to do anything to ease their departure from this tormented life. Occasionally, they will turn to the accompanying guardian and ask 'Who?' and 'Why?' Their companions might cast a glance in my direction and deliver a fairy tale or a guess. The children though, they walk on, looking skywards. They do not know fear. Yet.

The older ones pass me without a glance, their heads about level with the toes of my granite boots. Over the years, a number of people have actually spoken to me. Some were drunk, some were mad. Some were both, but there were some who genuinely wanted to know. Their questions were, of course, rhetorical. Historians, I suppose, who cannot understand why there is no record of my creator or of my identity. Obviously, I remained wordless, although inside I screamed against the injustice of it.

There are moments of delight although they are rare indeed. Parade and protest days are to be enjoyed. Men climb up my back and very occasionally children are settled upon my shoulders to watch the spectacle. I have been draped in flags of several colours, representing clans and counties as brass bands have bragged their way past; missiles have been hurled over my head, dancing girls have kicked their heels, and fights have exploded all within my eyeline. There are times when coloured lights festoon the air around me.

I am kept informed by the conversations that go on around me, the roared headlines of the newspaper vendors. I have seen progress. This scant village green has become the central square of a bustling town. Buildings sprang from a well of sand, lime and water. Carts became cars. The people grew in height and girth. They changed colour. The early silence has given way to noise. Sometimes, it is music.

With every blink of my stone eye, prosperity arrives, chased soon after by poverty. But I have seen destruction too. Beauty replaced by vulgarity. Gentility usurped by incivility. The calm has been replaced by the storm. I am the eye of the storm. I have seen it all. I have seen shame to match my own.

I welcome the prospect of rain (and am seldom disappointed) although the weather has taken its toll on my physique. Storms over the years have amputated first my fingers, then ears, then hands. No *blood*. At first I raged against the pain. Now, I welcome each new wound. At least it is an occurrence. I pray to hell for a tempest that might decapitate me. Finish it.

I hear everything. They do not know that I can hear. I imagine my responses. I curse my sight and my hearing. They are all I have, but I would be truly dead without them, instead of this half-life which I neither need nor want.

When I was a relevant man, one of my obsessions was the need to be clean. In those times, I bathed in the lake each night to rid myself of the stain of the day, raking my skin with branches, crushing petals with which to scent my hair. I took pride in my appearance. But now … layers of grime, oil, soot and dust. The stench of myself. And then the curse of the heavens. The leavings of filthy pigeons decorate my head, my shoulders. Rats scurry up my coattails and urinate in the spaces where my fingers used to be.

You would think that by now I would be used to it. That I would be resigned to the pain, the searing isolation, the yearning anticipation of the end. The Elders must have had evil in their souls to dream up such a punishment for me.

They kept me for ten months in the ice-house while they decided my fate. I railed against it. I now long for its luxury of movement, of life, of communication. Ten months of arraignments, appeals, appearances at the assizes. The excitement. The vilification. Every neighbour denounced my betrayal, even the ones I had saved with my bottles and potions in my role as the apothecary. The villagers were revolted by me. It was not enough for them that I be sentenced to death. They said that death was too easy for me. And though I wished them to hell, I know they did not go there, because that is here, where I am. Still. Alone.

Petrification was my sentence. At least, part of my sentence. At the time I was relieved to have cheated death. I did not know then that immortality was built into the judgement. I did not believe the Elders' condemnatory chants of 'corporal damnation'. To be buried alive in a husk of stone should mean death within days, but the devil must have been consulted for here I am. The process was vicious: starved for one full phase of the moon and then funnelled with concoctions that scorched me from the inside out. Filleted as I was, there would be no more need for food or water. And yet some sorcery keeps me sentient. My heart still beats, a metronome of misery.

In the beginning, I was careful to take orphan girls, or the daughters of pitiful parents. I thought that some may be glad to be relieved of their burden. The defilement and dispatch of their children became an addiction and an obsession; I would not stop myself, needed more and more, and soon there were few girls left. After I had used them for my pleasure, I threw their alabaster corpses into the estuary as the tide receded.

I suppose I grew careless. Bodies washed up on the shore. I did not think my neighbours had the wit to discover me; they were my inferiors. Yet they uncovered my darkness and exposed it, ironically using a simpleton foundling child as bait.

Nine days ago, men arrived with ladders of steel and measuring tools. They surrounded me, critiqued my condition. Dare I hope that I am due for cleaning? A decade ago, something similar happened. Using acids and flame, they left me stainless. It was a very good day. Perhaps the best of them. I thought for a moment that perhaps they might burn all the way through to my soul. That would have been some release. Perhaps tomorrow. Dare I hope?

My wife died of shame, they said. Lucky her. She was a beauty – if you like that sort of thing. Steady, faithful and clean, thank

God, or I could not have endured her presence. The match was arranged by the elders. She smiled all that day. I tolerated the festivities for the sake of decorum. She was very young, though not young enough. She was probably relieved that I left her alone after I was discovered.

And so to yesterday. The men came back with cutting tools. They erected a scaffolding frame around my granite carcass and shouted instructions at each other. One fat fellow wrapped a chain of weighted links around my neck. I could feel the warmth of his putrid breath on my chin. They graded the passing women in numbers from one to ten and spoke of them in terms of such crudity that I should have been revolted, but I did not care. Ecstasy took hold as I anticipated my ending. I could not see behind me but I could hear the tortured grinding screech of machinery. I imagined the wrecking ball poised and ready and anticipated it with an open heart. And then as dusk approached, they left with promises to return in the morning. I spend my last night contemplating the cessation of torment ...

My wife said she loved me once. That was kind of her. I wished I could reciprocate, but maybe even then my heart was encased in stone. I couldn't give her children, *wouldn't* give her children. It would not have been appropriate under the circumstances. She begged me. I sent her to the farrier, who happily obliged. I did not touch that child. They may say I am evil but I have scruples.

Today is a day that will forever stand out. It is hard to conceive that there will be no end for me. There was no wrecking ball. I was wrapped in fabric and tightly bound with rope. And as my head was about to be completely swathed, a final child passed. She looked up and asked the older boy, 'Who's he?' And the boy replied in a mocking voice of menace, 'He's a monster!' And the little girl screeched with laughter and ran a few steps before he caught her with a graceful sweep and landed her over his shoulder. The last thing I saw, before being hooded in hessian.

A crane lifted me from my plinth into this coffin lined with straw. I heard them say that I was going to a warehouse. And here I am. The agony of existence continues, but this time in silence and in darkness. As they sealed this crate and my nightmare entered a new phase of horror, one of them remarked that nobody even knew who I was. And they laughed and left.

My punishment is just beginning. I am sorry. I am sorry. I am sorry. I am not sorry.